# PARLOR GAMES

# PARLOR GAMES

*A Novel*

·

## MARYKA BIAGGIO

**DOUBLEDAY**
NEW YORK  LONDON  TORONTO
SYDNEY AUCKLAND

Bia

This book is a work of fiction. Names, characters, businesses, organizations, places, events, and incidents either are the product of the author's imagination or are used fictitiously. Any resemblance to actual persons, living or dead, events, or locales is entirely coincidental.

All rights reserved. Published in the United States by Doubleday, a division of Random House, Inc., New York, and in Canada by Random House of Canada Limited, Toronto.

www.doubleday.com

DOUBLEDAY and the portrayal of an anchor with a dolphin are registered trademarks of Random House, Inc.

*Jacket design by Emily Mahon*
*Jacket illustration © Horst P. Horst*
*Photo compositing and colorization by SOS Creative LLC.*

LIBRARY OF CONGRESS CATALOGING-IN-PUBLICATION DATA

Biaggio, Maryka
Parlor games : a novel / Maryka Biaggio. — 1st ed.
p. cm.
1. Swindlers and swindling—Fiction. 2. Female offenders—Fiction. 3. Pinkerton's National Detective Agency—Fiction.
I. Title
PS3602.I14P37 2013
813'.6—dc23
2012005514

ISBN 978-0-385-53622-6

MANUFACTURED IN THE UNITED STATES OF AMERICA

1 3 5 7 9 10 8 6 4 2

First Edition

*For my parents, Phyllis and Bill,*

*who made it all possible*

*A single bad act no more constitutes a villain in life than a single bad part on the stage. The passions, like the managers of a playhouse, often force men upon parts without consulting their judgement, and sometimes without any regard to their talents. . . . Upon the whole, then, the man of candour and of true understanding is never hasty to condemn.*

—HENRY FIELDING, *Tom Jones*

# PARLOR GAMES

# THE TRIAL

*I* believe, dear reader—and these words come from the bottom of my heart—that I can truly trust you. Look at yourself. You've sought out my story; you're willing to hear me out through these many pages. Who but a worldly and curious soul would undertake such a journey? Why, already I discern in you the intellect and refinement of a person with an open heart and nimble mind. You and I, my new friend, will become well acquainted over the course of this tale.

But you'll want me to proceed with the telling. That's what you've come for, and I'll not thwart your wishes a moment longer. So choose your favorite spot—a divan in a sumptuous hotel suite, the leather chair in front of your blazing fireplace, or a sun-soaked bench in a sculpture garden—any place, really, where we might enjoy the luxury of uninterrupted time together, and I will tell you the tale of the most dangerous woman in the world—or so the Pinkertons dubbed me.

Today was the first day of my trial in the booming metropolis of Menominee. I narrowed my attire choices down to an indigo dress or a modest black dress with fluted collar. Looking at the black dress, I thought, heavens, it's no funeral, and donned the blue one. It hugged my torso in a becoming manner, but still struck the serious and formal note required of the occasion. I kept my jewelry to a minimum: a simple sapphire necklace and matching earrings; the carved gold bracelet the Baron gave me on our first wedding anniversary; and my three-stone diamond ring with garland filigrees. As much as I love my jewels, this was no time for ostentation.

With the trial slated to open at two in the afternoon, my brothers and I enjoyed a leisurely luncheon at home. Then Paul drove us through swirling snow to the courthouse in his 1916 Apperson Jack Rabbit. He's so proud of that car—with its spruce-green exterior and leather seats as comfortable as a sofa. But, then, his automobile business does stock the latest models in the Upper Peninsula.

"I believe, Paul," I observed from the back seat, "that Mr. Apperson has taught Henry Ford a thing or two with this car."

Gene, who sat beside me, said, "Taught him how to build the most expensive thing on wheels is what he's done."

I chuckled—Gene and I fell easily into the sport of teasing our older sibling—and added, "Now, if only you could find a buyer for it in Menominee."

Paul pivoted his blocky head in my direction. "If I get the chance to sell it."

I resented Paul's insinuation that he stood to lose property in the lawsuit. After Papa's passing, Paul had ordained himself head of the family, even though the best he'd ever managed was a lumber worker's salary—that is, until I financed his automobile business. In truth, the responsibility for substantial support of the family had always fallen to me.

I reached over the front seat and patted Paul's shoulder. "You needn't worry. Have I ever let you down?"

"You're coming damn close," said Paul.

"Oh, don't make it harder than it already is," Gene said. "None of us likes being dragged to court."

I could always count on Gene to take my side whenever Paul goaded me. With a winking nod to Gene, I said, "I'm sure it will all come out fine."

Everyone should have a brother like Gene. He's as loyal as a musketeer, always ready to serve up merriment, and dashing to boot. Today he sported a trim charcoal-gray suit; Paul wore a baggy black jacket and shiny-with-wear wool pants. Gene, at six foot two, surpasses Paul in height and carries himself as erect as a proud stallion. Gene has the sort of looks that beguile women—twinkly blue eyes, a shapely mustache, and tawny-brown hair. Paul, stouter of build and perpetually glum, has only managed to attract a dowdy wife who disdains the revelry Gene and I naturally fall into. How perfectly provident that Gene, and not dull Paul, was named after our charming father.

Paul eased up on the accelerator as we rounded the corner onto Ogden Avenue. Wagon and car wheel ruts grooved the snow-packed streets, and our car jostled over the ridges, bouncing us up and down on our seats. Between buildings and in storefront cul-de-sacs, a gusting wind played the snowdrifts, skimming snow off their thin peaks and carving them into lopsided mounds. The drying cold of winter that hangs in the air even during a snowstorm pricked my bare cheeks and neck; I clutched the folds of my moleskin coat against its bite.

We approached Foster's Dry Goods, and I spied Mr. and Mrs. Foster standing as still as mannequins, gazing out the window. As we drove by, the couple stretched their necks to study us, making no attempt at a greeting.

Gene leaned forward and gripped Paul's seat. "Look at the Fosters admiring your car."

Paul trained his eyes straight ahead. "More likely trying to spot our notorious sister."

"Well, you're wise to drive this car around town," I said, intent on nudging Paul back to some measure of civility. "Surely it's good for business."

Not that Menominee offers much by way of business. I've seen cities all over the world—Chicago, sparkling and booming after the Great Fire; Portland, brash as the Wild West; Shanghai, steeped in trade and mystery; and London, civilized and regal. This town, however, has "bust" written all over it: the sorry storefronts bleached as ashen as driftwood; many of its once-booming lumber mills shuttered; the ice-encrusted shores of Lake Michigan impassable for months on end; and the surrounding forests, once thick with white pine, nearly all logged out. All in all, a rather pitiful place. As for me, I'd rather roast in the Mojave than live in Menominee. The only good thing that comes of being stuck here for this trial is the chance to enjoy my brothers' company.

We parked beside the courthouse, among a hodgepodge of Tin Lizzies and horse-drawn wagons and carriages. The piebald mare only a few feet away drooped her head as snow collected in splotchy blankets on her contoured back. At the slamming of our car doors she neither budged nor blinked. The poor thing—what a shame that this trial forced her to endure such numbing cold.

Positioning myself between Paul and Gene, I hooked a hand under each one's arm, and they escorted me through the front door and up to the second-floor courtroom. Paul opened the door and I stepped forward.

Townspeople had absolutely mobbed the courtroom—to say nothing of the eight to ten newsmen with writing pads at the ready. As we walked in, heads turned and followed us. On the water-stained wood floor, snow melted and puddled around the onlookers' feet. Coats, gloves, and farmers' boots gave off wet-wool, stale-dirt, and manure odors. The pungent brew tickled my nose; I swept my wrist under my nostrils to supplant the stench with my Jasmin perfume.

As we marched along, Gene exchanged soft hellos with several people seated on the aisle. Holding my chin up proudly, I smiled and nodded at those who dared to cast their probing gaze my way.

I wasn't surprised that nearly half the town had shown up for the trial; it's been the talk of the Upper Peninsula for months now. If I had to live here season after season, *I'd* consider it the highlight of the year, too. Imagine how it's been these past months: On afternoons when their husbands toiled at the mill or factory, women gathered over their needlework to speculate and gossip about me. That's not to say the men are uninterested. Oh, no, I can't walk ten feet in this town without a man's eyes trailing me—surreptitiously if his wife is on hand, but even if she isn't, never so boldly as to require a chastening from a sister, the pastor, or whoever might observe him ogling that "swindler May," as the town's women have likely christened me. Why, I wasn't even surprised to hear they'd been rehashing what turned out to be a mistaken pregnancy by hometown boy Robby Jacobsen.

Oh, yes, the womenfolk of Menominee had flocked to the courthouse, and as I stood unfastening my coat at the defendant's table, I noticed *they* weren't too proud to stare. Most of the crowd was older—women without children or chores, I imagine—all gussied up in their Sunday best with their hair neatly combed and hats pinned in place. They packed into the rows and chattered away like youngsters on a sleigh ride. The smattering of husbands accompanying their wives sat hunched over, clutching their hats two-handed, pretending a lack of interest. The fact is, they were all there because this trial is the most exciting thing that's happened around here since the great train heist of '93. Well, who can begrudge them the diversion and entertainment my trial offers?

But such a bleak place the courtroom was, with plain, stiff-backed chairs in the jury box and pew benches for onlookers. Bare light-bulbs hung from twisted brown cords and lit the room as bright as new snow. All the sounds around me—the bailiff's clacking heels, my lawyer and his associate's whispered exchanges, and the buzz of conversation from the crowd—bounced off the high, unadorned white walls like the bleats of animals shut up in a barn.

I took my seat on the hardwood chair next to my attorney, greeted him, and smoothed the folds of my skirt. Through the tall windows lining the room, only bare, spindly treetops could be glimpsed, as if the architect intended to intimidate with narrow, jail-style windows. Radiators pinged, wafting the tinny scent of melting snow on their waves.

The bailiff announced, "All rise," and the assembly shuffled to its feet. Judge Flanagan strutted in, his black gown trailing over the bench steps.

And so began my trial. Now, I've made a bargain with you, gentle reader, and I intend to keep my end of it. I will tell you my story—all of it—and truthfully, as I've never been able to tell anyone before. Then you can decide: Were my actions justified? You, my discerning reader, are the most important juror. You have the advantage of hearing the whole story, straight from the one who lived it. So I say to you now, without hesitation or compunction, hear me out, and then you be the judge.

# MY HUMBLE ORIGINS

•

For the longest time my mother claimed I was born in Eau Claire, Wisconsin. Being French Canadian, she loved all things French. French women, she told me, grasp the importance of appearance and station—they never pass up a chance to impress with looks or feign eminence with the little white lie. And Eau Claire is a lovely name for a town. But I wasn't actually born there. Not that the place of one's birth matters much, but I've promised to tell the whole story.

I was born in 1869 in the village of Fox River Grove, about forty miles northwest of Chicago. My family moved away before I took my first steps, so I never explored the shores of the Fox River myself. But it was an auspicious place for my birth: It's become a lovely resort area, with a gorgeous luxury hotel and famous ski jump.

Back in the 1860s, the Ojibwa Indians gathered in Fox River Grove every winter to sell furs and beadwork. My older brother, Paul, told me Papa used to visit their settlement and trade firewater for beaded necklaces and bracelets, which he sold to laborers in the area for gifts to send their wives. That Papa, he was an enterprising sort.

We came to reside in Fox River Grove because a Mr. Opardy had purchased eighty acres on the Fox River and set out to build a vacation estate there. When Papa heard about the big purchase, he hastened to Illinois and offered his services. He told Mr. Opardy that he'd managed a restaurant in Michigan, and Mr. Opardy hired him on the spot to cook for his building crew.

Papa had never actually managed anything before that job, but he always said you've got to sell what you've got, even if all you've got is salesmanship. By the time the cooking job ended, Papa had accumulated sufficient funds to move our family to Muskegon, Michigan. He secured a contract on a saloon, a simple log-cabin affair on the shores of Muskegon Lake. He named it Dancing Waters, but the locals called it The Watering Hole. Papa loved being by the water and dreamed of sailing up the St. Lawrence and all the way to France to see Paris, which he pronounced "Pa-REE." Someday, he promised, he would take me there, to see the Seine and a ballet.

What can you say about a child's life? My parents were strict about school. Papa lectured me dozens of times about how I'd need an education to land a well-to-do husband; he made me promise I'd never settle for some idler who rented a room over a tavern. After dinner each evening, Maman insisted that Paul and I sit at the table to recite from our *McGuffey Reader* while she stoked the stove and scrubbed the dinner plates and pots. I was always ahead of my classmates because of listening to Paul reel off his verb conjugations and multiplication tables. If you ask me, Maman made us recite our lessons as much for herself as for Paul and me—I believe it counted as entertainment for her, since Papa was away for long hours and she spent her days baking, laundering, cooking lye and potash into soap, and filling seamstress orders.

My fondest memories of childhood are the times I spent with Papa, especially my visits to the saloon. Papa always greeted me the same way, bracing his hands on the bar and announcing, "Gentlemen, *chère* Mimi has come to entertain us. Make way."

The men hugging the bar would take their drinks in hand and ease back. Turning to me, Papa would hold out his arms and say, "Mimi, your admirers await. Come."

I'd run in under the bar gate—I was little enough not to need to duck—and sprint toward him, striding high so as not to slip on the slick floorboards. He'd catch me in full stride, hoist me over his head, and swing me around. As soon as he plopped me onto the bar, I launched into my pirouettes, holding Papa's hand as if we were ballet dancers. How I loved the sound of the men clapping and hooting. I don't believe I've gotten the thrill of it out of my bones, even after all these years.

And to think some people claim I hate men. Such nonsense. Papa was the sweetest person I've ever known. Maybe if I could find a man who's as carefree and cheerful as Papa I'd settle down. But, then,

Papa wasn't much for settling down himself. That's what made life with him so exciting.

Ah, Papa. I miss him still. What a thrill it would be to recount all my adventures to him: I believe he'd be proud. But when I was fifteen, just as I was growing into a young lady, Papa was shot and killed trying to break up a fight at the tavern.

I vividly recall the night he died. I stole off by myself to the shores of Muskegon Lake. There I sat watching day's color drain from the scattered birches and jagged-edged firs. Wind sweeping in off the lake lashed the loose strands of my hair against my bare, chilled neck. I blinked back tears as I recalled him once telling me, "You have more gumption and sense than your mother and Paul put together."

My ears hummed from veiled noises skittering through the forest, as if ghosts stirred among the fallen leaves and floated through the trees. I felt Papa all around me—in the shifting shadows, in the rustle of branches, in the lapping of the lake—and heard his voice: "You have to take care of the family now, Mimi."

I knew that that was what he expected—and that I would have to be cleverer than he was, for the sake of all of us.

We buried Papa the next day, and by then Maman had attained an icy composure. Right after the burial she ordered all of us, "Pack up your clothes. And anything else you want from this miserable place."

Our forlorn family—Maman, Paul, little Gene, and I—took the last ferry of the season across Lake Michigan and boarded a train for Menominee.

# MY PRELIMINARY EDUCATION

·

*B*y the tender age of fifteen, I had set my sights on Chicago: What youngster didn't dream of strolling its modern streets, shopping at the crossroads of America, and gazing upon the sparkling new buildings that had risen after the Great Fire? But Menominee was as good a place as any in 1884 to acquire an introduction to commerce and society. It had over a dozen lumber mills roaring away and possibly the busiest port on all the northern lakes. Maman had a cousin here then, an ox of a man who supervised at Spies Lumber Company. We stayed with his family for a few months, until we took a home of our own on Ludington Avenue.

I finished high school in Menominee and found the teachers much better than the ones I'd had in Muskegon. One of my teachers, Miss Apple, taught me how to manipulate numbers so I could do calculations in my head. I can illustrate. To determine if a number is divisible by 3, add the digits. If the sum is a multiple of 3, then it is divisible. Or, to add 148 and 302, take 2 away from 302, add it to 148 to make 150, and you quickly arrive at 450. I've had innumerable occasions to thank Miss Apple for all those little tricks.

I never did develop any affection for Menominee, though I admit I partook of my share of gaiety in town. Any young girl with a sense of adventure would have found her way into the vaudeville shows and the stores selling fine fabrics, table damask, and hammered-brass lamps. It was in Menominee that I acquired my taste for elegance and lovely things. In fact, before I graduated from high school, Maman had introduced me to the society ladies in town by making certain I was in the parlor whenever they came to order or pick up a dress from her. I reveled in their proper speech, with its oh-so-carefully enunciated words, and their proud, erect carriage, which I practiced in the privacy of my bedroom.

When I started seeing the son of one of the town's lumber barons, Robby Jacobsen, Maman was so pleased: "Oh, May"—as I'd begun insisting everyone call me—"you've landed a real prize in that young man." What she didn't know was that this prize behaved like a gentleman only in the presence of adults.

One spring evening, Robby escorted me to dinner at the Stephenson Hotel and for dancing afterward in their ballroom. I remember the dress I wore that night, though I wouldn't show up at a country fair in it now—a baby-blue cotton thing with puffy sleeves and a high collar. Fit for a child, but not a grown woman, which I'd become as I approached eighteen. Two dances into the evening, Robby walked me back to our table, clapped his hand over mine, and said, "I've got a surprise for you at my house. Do you want to see it?"

Now, I always enjoyed visiting Robby's house. Or should I say "mansion"? It was without a doubt one of the finest homes in all of Menominee—a solid two-story wood building with turrets on the two front corners and a wraparound veranda. Everything about it—the translucent globe lamps, elaborately carved handrails, and Haviland china—declared: We are wealthy and know high style. Still, so as not to show too much eagerness, I said, "After one more dance."

It was early April, and we'd had a long string of nice weather. The snow was nearly all melted, but mud puddles still dotted the streets. Whenever we came upon a mucky stretch, Robby swept me into his arms—he was a strapping five eleven and I a blossoming five six—and gallantly carried me over the puddles. Oh, we did enjoy each other, laughing like youngsters on a lark, both of us playful and without a care in the world. We pulled off some clever high jinks together—once even switching a bottle of cheap champagne for the best in the house at his uncle's hotel.

That night, as we walked up the front steps of his house, Robby looked up and down the dark street, apparently checking for any nosy neighbors, and then lifted me into his arms and carried me over the threshold, as if he were welcoming a bride home.

Setting me down in the entranceway, he hollered, "Hello. Surprise."

His voice echoed into the spacious parlor and down the first-floor hall. No one answered. I was well acquainted with Robby's rapscallion side, so suspicion overtook me. "I see there's no one here."

He dropped to a knee and grasped my hand. "Marry me, May, and together we'll scandalize the town."

"Why, Robert Jacobsen, I had no idea," I exclaimed, for I had no intention of marrying Robby: I wished to try my hand at Chicago's extravagantly wealthy bachelors.

Rising, he scooped me into his arms and bounded up the stairs. Forcing the partly closed door of his bedroom open with his foot, he whisked me into the room and plopped me on his bed, then dropped on top of me and smothered my neck and cheeks with kisses. "Ah, my little bride," he said, massaging my breasts.

"Robby," I cried, bracing my palms against his shoulders and pushing with all my might, "you mustn't."

He budged not one bit. "Please, my beauty."

My breasts tingled, not unpleasantly, beneath his touch, but I persisted in my attempts to push him off me. "I . . . I don't want to get pregnant."

He bounced up on his knees and smiled devilishly at me. "But I've got a sheath."

"A sheath?"

"An English riding coat, a love glove."

"Oh," I said, comprehension dawning on me. It had certainly behooved me, a young woman with men flocking about her, to acquire some understanding about the prevention of pregnancy. So I had educated myself through medical pamphlets.

I don't imagine I need to spell out the rest of the evening. I hadn't planned on entering womanhood that night, but curiosity and the pleasant sensations Robby aroused in me overtook the ill-formed fears conjured by schoolgirl whisperings. For years it'd been clear to me that I had a certain power over the male sex—that is, if Maman's warning to keep my admirers at a distance was any indication. Still, I knew little of the allure of the bedroom. Robby was as good a teacher as any, old enough to have had some experience, not terribly unpleasing in appearance, and a spirited sort. So I allowed the galoot to school me in the ways of love.

By the time I graduated from high school, a few months later, I had completed my preliminary education in the mysteries of the bedroom. But poor Robby, once the deed was done, always fretted about the complications a pregnancy would force upon us.

It wasn't a happy day when I broke the news, over my graduation dinner in the Erdlitz dining room, that his fears had been realized. Once I'd urged him to ingest the only reliable antidote to his unflappable verve—three after-dinner Cognacs—I whispered, "Robby, we have to talk. I'm afraid I'm with child."

Robby scooted his chair toward mine, bumping the table and nearly upending our candle. His broad nose and plump lips, which always gave his face the impression of looming too near, pressed close to mine. "But I thought, that, uh . . ."

"I know, I thought so, too." I glanced around nervously. It was Saturday night, and the town's bankers and lumber barons, accompanied by wives in fresh spring fashions, huddled around dimly lit tables, abuzz with cozy conversation. Blinking my eyes, I said, "I don't know what to do."

"We'll get married right away. I'll tell my parents tomorrow."

I clamped my hands together and widened my eyes. "No, I can't ruin your and my reputation. The baby will be born in under nine months."

"Don't be ridiculous. Who cares what anybody in Menominee thinks?"

"Consider your family, Robby. And my poor mother."

"We can leave, go to Green Bay. You know I'm itching to get out of this place."

"Oh, Robby, you're a real gentleman, that's what you are. But I don't want to start like that—running away like we've got something to hide."

"I don't see what else we *can* do."

Fearing his urgent whisper had carried to the next table, I glanced in that direction to alert him. I tapped a finger to my lips, trying to think of a solution. "What if I went away to have the baby? Found a nice couple to give it to? You could join me later. We could get a proper start."

"I don't want you to go away without me. And I don't want to give up our baby."

"Robby, you can't just think about today, or the next nine months. You have to think about the rest of our lives."

"I am thinking about our future. And your mother, too. When we're married, she won't have to take in boarders and sweat over that sewing machine all day."

"Elsie is not a boarder. She's an employee. And Maman is an excellent dressmaker, which your mother and every other nicely attired lady in town knows only too well."

Robby winced. "Fine, your mother can do whatever she likes. I'm just saying I can provide for you. And your family, too, if you want."

"And if your father disowns you for running off, what will you have then? How will you support me and our children?"

"Damn it, May, I can manage on my own. You think I need my father's money?"

"I only know you'd be a fool to spurn your family and their good fortune."

"You're the last person I'd expect to hear that from. Don't you have any faith in me?"

"Of course I do. I just don't want you to do anything rash."

"I intend to design furniture. You know I've got a knack for it." Robby smoothed his hand over the fine-grained dining table, as if that proved his point. "I want a business of my own. And you alongside me."

"But it takes time to establish a business." I glanced about, at the wall-mounted kerosene lamps flickering over the diners' animated expressions and tingeing the air with smoky scents. I lowered my voice. "And I have to plan for two now."

He glared at me. "I'm trying to plan for three."

"Please, Robby." I cupped my hand over his. "I have to do it my way. Please understand."

"We'll talk about this later," Robby said, extracting his hand and pushing back in his chair.

I slapped my hand on the table. "No, I will not bring scandal on me, you, or some innocent child. I simply won't do it."

Robby flared his nostrils. "I hate it when you dig your heels in, May Dugas. You're worse than an old mule."

I sat up straight and folded my hands on my lap. "That's not a very nice thing to say."

He clamped his lips together and shook his head. "Damn it, sometimes I wish I weren't so taken with you. You're impossible, that's what you are."

In the end, Robby gave me the money to travel to Chicago. A mere four hours into my journey, as the train lurched out of the Manitowoc, Wisconsin, station, I felt the familiar trickle of my monthly visitor. I guess I had jumped the gun—I wasn't pregnant after all. But it was too late to turn back.

# THE TRIAL

*A*s the judge settled into his seat, I gazed across the aisle at Frank and offered a friendly nod and smile. You see, animosity is not my style. But I would have preferred an actual *tête-à-tête* with her: "Frank, dear, I spotted a few strands of gray hair this week—the result, no doubt, of strain from the trial." Then I would tinkle out a laugh and add, "It can't be easy on you, either."

Poor Frank. I should have known she'd take our parting as poorly as any male admirer. Frank is a hardy woman: She freely gives herself over to life's pleasures; she adores fishing and hunting; and she can jest and josh with the best of them. *I* certainly wouldn't have engaged her services if she weren't a first-rate attorney. And I always admired her fresh, self-assured charm, a little like the bluster of a confident young man or a lady testing the lure of her beauty. Not that Frank has anything close to beauty. She's thick of trunk, with matronly bosoms that she secures under double-breasted suits. But when she smiles, her broad cheeks crinkle into plump mounds of delight, and her jolly, deep-from-the-belly laughter never fails to enliven a gathering.

"Please be seated," the judge boomed, drawing his robe aside and planting himself on his high-backed chair. "We are here for the civil case of Miss Frank Gray Shaver versus Baroness May de Vries. Counselor Sawyer, would you like to make your opening statement?"

The sallow-complexioned Alvah Sawyer rose to face the men sitting motionless in the jury box. Clasping his delicate hands together in prayerful pose, he began, "Gentlemen of the jury, I will show you, beyond any kind of doubt, that Baroness de Vries, as she insists on being called, cooked up an elaborate plan to defraud my client of more than a hundred thousand dollars."

As soon as Sawyer rattled off that sentence, my attorney, George Powers, sprang to his feet. "Objection. Her legal name *is* Baroness de Vries." (I had warned him they would try to diminish me and my title. Honestly, it's not as if I manufactured my marriage to the Baron.)

The judge planted a hand on his jaw and shook his head. "Oh, for Pete's sake, Mr. Powers, it's his opening statement. And, Mr. Sawyer, a title is a title. At least grant her that courtesy."

Sawyer tugged at his vest and puffed out his chest. "As I was saying, the Baroness defrauded my client of over a hundred thousand dollars. With her brothers, Paul and Gene Dugas, and assistant, Miss Belle Emmett, she conspired to steal from Miss Frank Shaver all the money and property Miss Shaver inherited from her father.

"How did she manage this? My head spins trying to keep track of her conniving ways. She persuaded Miss Shaver to borrow forty thousand dollars from her family and then ate her way through it like a hungry wolf. She even convinced my client to invest nine thousand dollars in remodeling her mother's home right here in town, over on Stephenson Avenue." Sawyer jerked his head to the side, as if we might actually glimpse my family's house through the brick wall.

"The Baroness's actions were bold as could be. Just three months ago, she tried to cash in one hundred and sixty shares of Westinghouse stock rightfully belonging to Miss Shaver. And in 1913, during the illness of the Baroness's mother, she played on Miss Shaver's kind sympathies and talked her into paying for the medical specialist brought in to tend her own mother, claiming she'd repay the debt. The Baroness even went so far as to trick Miss Shaver into making a will bequeathing the sum of eighty thousand dollars to her, promising she'd do the same."

Sawyer paused and swept his gaze over each juror, as if preparing to serve up some shocking revelation. "Did she repay the forty-thousand-dollar loan? Did she settle up the medical expenses for her mother? Did she write the promised will with Miss Shaver as beneficiary? No, no, and no."

Mutters erupted from the spectators. The judge thumped his

gavel. "This is a court of law, not a playhouse. I will not allow such outbursts."

Sawyer settled back into his tirade, and the onlookers stifled themselves as he harangued on and on. I scanned the faces of my twelve-man jury—twelve Menominee men whose wives have no doubt repeated all manner of titillating rumors about me. Do they think I know nothing of *their* dirty laundry—with my two brothers living in this town for the last three decades and rubbing elbows with the lot of them?

There's jury foreman Arthur Wheaton, a butcher widowed last year, after thirty-some years of marriage to Opal. That Opal could talk circles around an auctioneer. I'll wager Mr. Wheaton is pleased to report for jury duty. The poor man's probably been as bored as a tree stump without Opal's company. Personally, I have no objections to Mr. Wheaton. He's a quiet sort, with doleful eyes, and not much of a backbone. They probably elected him foreman out of deference to his age and state of mourning. Still, he'll just follow the crowd.

Peter Stocklin is the one I worry about. One might think a superintendent at Crawford Manufacturing would beg off jury duty. But not in Menominee, and certainly not for this trial. Such a sight he is—as stiff and proper as a country preacher, with a sinewy ostrich neck. He's prepared to do his duty, by God: I'm sure that's how he sees it. He'll pass judgment just as he pleases, regardless of people's foibles or the mysteries of human intercourse. Mean and ruthless—that's his type. I learned long ago never to trust a man who waxes his mustache into unnatural contortions.

The first day of the trial did not shine a flattering light on me. Mr. Sawyer took plenty of time droning on about my "deliberate scheming," as if I'd planned every single step, right up to this very moment. But if I'm as devious as he implies, why would I behave in such a way as to open myself up to this circus of allegations? These lawyers always try to have it both ways.

Am I surprised that Frank is dragging me to court? Not at all. Frank may be a woman, but she's no different from the many jilted men I've dealt with over the years. She couldn't win my heart with money, so, being a lawyer, she naturally turned to the law.

I can guess what you're thinking, dear reader: What have I gotten myself into? Is my new friend May some unsavory character I'll regret taking up with? I hate to disappoint you, but it's not that simple. I will tell you right now: I never took anything from Frank without giving something in return. I did not set out to ruin her, either in love or in fortune.

But I believe you'll find my story speaks for itself.

# CHICAGO BIG AND BRASH

*I* knew not a soul in Chicago. There I was—eighteen years old, unfamiliar with any city more than two miles square, and marked as an out-of-towner by my battered suitcase and tawdry straw hat. I possessed only a single pair of shoes, the two new dresses Maman had made for me, and a plan that depended wholly on my own wits.

To make matters worse, my brother Paul and I had quarreled before my departure. While I was packing, he'd slipped into my bedroom, quietly closing the door behind him. "Do you know Maman emptied the household savings for your new dresses?"

"I told her not to be extravagant."

"Maman? Not extravagant? With her darling daughter going to the big city?"

Our mother, in fact, was not overly encumbered with common sense, but that was beside the point. "You just don't want me to go."

Paul flashed his open palm toward me, threatening a slap. "Don't you trifle with me."

I gripped the skirt of my faded cotton dress and shook it. "You expect me to help our family by showing up in Chicago in this old rag?"

"You can help by staying right here and keeping this house."

"Stay in Menominee? What future is there in that?"

"Your family's future." He poked his chin at me. "Unless that doesn't matter to you."

"That's precisely what matters." I smoothed out my skirt and returned to my packing, hoping to conclude the conversation. But that only perturbed him all the more.

"You really think some rich man's just waiting for you, like you're Cinderella off to marry her prince?"

I spun around. "I'll wager I can do better than a lumber miller's salary in Chicago. And that's what I intend to do."

That last comment dogged me during the whole train trip. Paul worked hard to support the family, and I ought not to have insulted him. But he'd pushed me to the brink, and I refused to countenance his bullyragging one moment longer.

Still, as I stepped off the train at Chicago's Wells Street Station, I pined for the familiar company of Maman, Paul, and Gene. Row upon row of tracks surrounded me, reaching out behind the station, big as the prongs of a gigantic pitchfork. A putrid odor hung over the expansive train yard—a metallic and sewage-like brew—and I surmised the Chicago River lay nearby.

Along the platform, well-dressed men and women, with the occasional child in tow, ambled past me. Expectant parties milled in chattering clutches under the shadowy sheds, all of them oblivious to the bewilderment of travelers, such as myself, who were strangers to this place. Humidity hung in the late-afternoon air, as thick and suffocating as a wool blanket. As I sauntered along, emulating the nonchalant bustle of the crowd, perspiration prickled my brow. A man in an ill-fitting uniform passed by, leaning nearly horizontal, tugging a flatbed cart overflowing with trunks and suitcases. I ventured a smile, but he only proffered a quizzical, wide-eyed glance, as if he were unaccustomed to simple friendliness.

I marched into the station's cavernous waiting room, where, against one wall, racks of newspapers confronted me. So many newspapers— the *Chicago Banner, Citizen, Chicago Daily Tribune, Knights of Labor, Chicago Times,* among many others—with blaring headlines—"Coffee Prices Tumbling"; "A Senseless Shoemakers' Union Strike"; "Millions Lost in Wheat Panic"; "Jewels Disappear in Mysterious Safe Robbery"; "Protests Against the Return of Captured Confederate Flags"; "Carlisle Graham Survives Barrel Ride in Niagara Waterfall"—that Chicago seemed the very hub of the world, a world so vast I feared it would swallow me up if I did not make something of myself in it.

I parted with a penny for a *Chicago Herald*—it promised the splashiest coverage of Queen Victoria's Jubilee—lifted my suitcase, and prepared to greet my new city. Outside the station, I hired a horsecar, instructing the driver to take me to a modest hotel near the business district, though I had no idea where the business district was, what kind of hotels were nearby, or how much a modest room might cost. Our open, one-horse carriage rattled down Kinzie Street and turned onto State. We crossed over the sluggish, mud-brown Chicago River, which ran under the long bridge, and I wondered whether fish of any sort managed to dwell in its mucky filth.

The carriage wove its way among red-and-bright-yellow trolleys and all manner of fancy carriages and hansoms traveling this way and that. City racket swarmed around me: streetcars dinging as they drifted along; horses' hooves clomping on the brick streets; brougham bells tinkling; and boys in knickers hollering from street corners, hawking newspapers bundled under their arms.

Puffed-up men in derbies and natty frock coats strode, as if they owned the sidewalks, alongside women in dresses with ample bustles, trim waists, and lovely summer colors—peach, sage green, ivory, and baby blue. The women's hats, some decorated with long feathers, others with bows, all broad-brimmed enough to protect the delicate, white-powdered faces beneath them, drifted along the walkways like a sea of fancy bobbers.

As we rumbled down State Street, I tried not to crane my neck, but the gleaming new buildings—so tall they cast long shadows even under June's high sun—filled me with awe. Their wide expanses of glass reflected the passing pedestrians and vehicles, multiplying the busyness of the crowded street scene. I mustn't be daunted, I kept telling myself: I'm equal to this challenge.

><

The next day, after settling into the Howard Hotel, I undertook the task of acquainting myself with the city, its denizens, and the lay of its streets. State Street beckoned me back, and there I wandered into the six-story Boston Store. Up and down the elevator I rode (for the first time in my life), surveying each of the floor's offerings. I stopped on the fourth floor to peruse the bins of silk and spun-cotton chemises and petticoats—so plentiful, and in so many styles and designs, that I would have been hard-pressed to select just one.

The main floor attracted me the most. Close to the front doors, in a cleared area lined with potted petunias, a gentleman of about fifty in a dapper, dove-tan waistcoat sat at a piano playing folk tunes. I lingered nearby, sifting through dresses with elegant bustles, all the time basking in the piano's welcoming melodies and studying women shoppers as they sized up the dresses' lace collars and bead-galloon trimmings. I strolled by the piano player, delighting in his rapt expression. He looked up, nodded at me, and mouthed "Good day"—the first truly warm gesture anyone had offered since my arrival—and I smiled in return.

I circled around to the other side of the first floor, to women's shoes, and admired the selection of Curaçao-kid, pebble-grain, and French-kid styles. But I could afford no purchase, and self-consciousness overtook me, as if I were a maid pretending at her lady's mirror. Reluctantly, I withdrew, promising myself I would return another time.

The next day, I wandered into three small banks to inquire how I might open an account, whether a certain balance would be required, and what benefits each bank could offer. It pleased me to explain that I was exploring several options and would return if I chose to do business with them.

Over the next several days, I visited other places of business, and shops as well, engaging the proprietors in both business exchanges and casual conversations: law firms (in search of a lawyer to advise me on a family matter); architectural offices (in the event I decided to build a home); dry-goods stores; apothecaries; and art galleries. I scrounged rumpled newspapers from hotel lobbies and pored over them by the smoke-stained lamp in my cramped hotel room. An article in the June 22 *Chicago Times* caught my eye:

### *Detective Wooldridge Saves Three from White Slave Trade*
#### CITIZEN TIP LEADS DETECTIVE TO LEVEE ATTIC

Early yesterday morning Detective Clifton Wooldridge, accompanied by a band of three police officers, staked out a house at 404 Dearborn Street. He was said to be acting on a tip from a courageous citizen who picked up a note flung from an upper window of the residence. The detective and his troops stormed the place at dawn, no doubt hoping to take the sleeping occupants-cum-captors by surprise.

An officer on the case reported that Violet Hastings
and her solid man, Bo Cavanaugh, were wakened from a
liquor-laced sleep and proceeded to carry on like stirred-up
hornets, hollering that the police had no cause to be there and
demanding to know whatever happened to their protection,
though not in such genteel words.

Detective Wooldridge and his party made their way to the
attic, where they broke down a bolted door and discovered three
cowering girls, all dressed in flimsy gowns and living in dirty,
cramped conditions. Upon seeing the police they cried out, "We
are saved."

Violet Hastings claimed she had kept the girls there for their
own safety, but Wooldridge told this reporter that the young
ladies had been seized at the train station, imprisoned by Miss
Hastings, and likely slated to be sold to some associate of
Hastings who would force them to work as harlots. Wooldridge
explained, "These places conceal Chicago's most shameful
secret—young women stolen off the streets, locked in rooms
against their will, and desecrated by men who care only about
earning money from their misery."

According to Wooldridge, hundreds of young ladies are
abducted each year by white slave traders and held captive in
one of the many houses that night after night defile women and
the soul of this city. Detective Wooldridge says he will not rest
until he uncovers all the degenerates who trade in white slaves
and that the Levee District ought to know he's not making idle
threats.

Was it true? Hundreds of women forced into prostitution? Perhaps. But I would not be subject to such trickery.

✦✦

By the end of my first week in Chicago, I had greatly deepened the
half-moons worn into my shoe heels, all in the service of elevating
my grasp of the city's sundry businesses and identifying its most
elegant dining rooms. I decided the time had come to try out my
strategy. Donning my lilac dress with French-pleated belt and bow,
I settled in the dining room of the Haverford Hotel and prepared

to attract a gentleman of means. If necessary, I would explain I had traveled to Chicago to tend to some family business.

For six days I dined alone at various hotels and fine restaurants, beating back the fear and desperation that welled up in me as my allowance dwindled. Uncertain as my plan was, I could ill afford to forgo Robby's help, though you, gentle reader, will no doubt grasp how much it pained me to deceive him.

*June 28, 1887*

*My precious Robby,*

*I have found a humble room here in Chicago, in a rooming house run by the kindly Mr. and Mrs. Ellwood. They are very discreet and do not allow mail delivery here so you must write me at general delivery. As fortune would have it, Mrs. Ellwood knows a practiced midwife who lives nearby. Helga is quite solicitous. She is sure the baby will be healthy, and she will gladly help me find just the right family for her. (Both Helga and I believe the baby will be a girl.)*

*This city is so big I am nearly overwhelmed by it. But when I think of you and our future together I manage to summon the courage to carry on.*

*The allowance you so kindly provided is holding up well, as I am being very careful with my expenses. But I would like to take a course in business. It would occupy my time and remind me of you. Just think: We could be a modern couple. I could manage the books for your business, and you could spend your time designing furniture.*

*I think about you every minute of every day, my dearest,*

*All my love,*
*May*

Some might consider books and courses an unwarranted extravagance, especially since I could hardly afford my hotel room. But I had to prepare for my future. In order to pay for an education and stretch my allowance, I moved from the Howard Hotel to a room on South Wabash—a modest room with a narrow bed and mismatched chair and vanity. Thank goodness, Mrs. Farnsworth provided breakfast, a generous fare that included hard-boiled eggs, bacon, and biscuits or bread. Each morning, I slipped an egg into my pocket, and that sufficed for lunch as I explored the city and its neighborhoods.

One afternoon, I ventured outside the downtown district, west along Van Buren, and then wove back and forth among the streets running perpendicular to it. Along one stretch, crowded-in hovels teemed with occupants—ill-dressed women and uncouth children housed in congested quarters. Ropes strung with laundry criss-crossed between the buildings, and weeds sprouted in the alleys on narrow patches of packed earth that had somehow escaped tram-pling by unruly youngsters.

Farther along, I came upon a strip of blocky, unadorned facto-ries with frosted-glass windows and large-lettered signs spanning their entrances—Storm and King Wholesale Dry Goods, McManus Clothiers, and Emery Shoe Company. Alongside the shoe factory, two coal heavers in grimy overalls shoveled coal from a wagon into a chute, and a cloud of coal dust rose up and wafted in my direction. I bustled along, and as I passed in front of the company's entrance, a woman stormed out the door, nearly running into me. Startled, she muttered some strange phrase, trained her eye on the sidewalk, and rushed past me. I'd only had time to observe her unkempt black hair and red-rimmed eyes. Had she lost her job? Did an ailing mother need her at home? I turned to watch her hurry away. She kept her head bent downward, as if ashamed to show her face, and her dress flopped lazily about her legs, revealing the flick and shift of buttocks and bulge of each calf: The poor thing wore no petticoat.

A vexing mix of sympathy and scorn welled up in me—such coarse, bedraggled creatures lodged in this neighborhood, the likes of which never frequented the Boston Store. It seemed Chicago had many sides: the prosperous business-and-shopping district popu-lated by the wealthy and successful; the outlying areas with their factories and poor foreign workers; and the sinful Levee District.

To which did I belong, with my undersized bustle and shoes as wrinkled as an old fisherman's face? A most unsettling notion swept over me: Was it possible the cultured gentlemen I'd been trying to attract took me for a fraud?

I hurried back to my room, brushed off my clothes, and cleansed my face and hands of any coal dust or dirt that might have settled on me. Standing before the flaking mirror over my washing bowl,

I studied myself. Mine was not an unpleasant face, a near-perfect oval, with a dainty set of lips and soft-sloped nose. Perhaps my clothes were not up-to-the-minute, but I had other gifts. I would not succumb to the self-abasement of a haggard factory worker or low-class prostitute. Even if I did not yet measure up to the city's modern styles, I could comport myself with the pride of a patrician, as if I'd chosen to conceal my wealth for reasons of safety and discretion.

Still, I worried I had miscalculated: All the care I took combing and fashioning my thick chestnut hair and the forethought I put into selecting just the right restaurants could not overcome the dated design of my dresses or my lack of acquaintance with Chicago's high society. My future depended on the success of my plan, and it appeared to be failing. Furthermore, I couldn't manage indefinitely on Robby's allowance, especially in view of his first correspondence to me.

*July 8, 1887*

*My dearest May,*

  *I was so relieved to receive your letter. I've been anxious about your condition, and I'm miserable without you. You mustn't ever let so much time pass without writing. You know I worry about you down there in Chicago. And I don't want to hear any of your "I can take care of myself" nonsense. It's a big city, and you've never been to such a place before. You must be careful about who you trust.*

  *I'm sending your allowance and a little extra money for a class. I consider it an investment in our future.*

  *You won't like this, but I've decided we must keep this baby. Look at how my poor Uncle James lost his wife and child to the influenza. A baby is a precious thing, and I simply won't allow you to hand ours over like a sack of potatoes.*

  *I propose that I settle my affairs here, persuade Father to loan me the money to start my furniture business, and then come and fetch you in Chicago. We'll get married right away. We can move to Green Bay. Or Milwaukee if you prefer. I've thought it all through. The baby will be born in our new home. Nobody there or in Menominee will ever know how much time has lapsed between our wedding date and*

*baby's arrival. And we won't be far from Menominee, so you'll be*
*able to visit your mother whenever you wish.*
    *I anxiously await your response,*

*Your loving husband to be,*
*Robby*

Clearly, if I didn't break the engagement off soon, I risked Robby's telling all of Menominee of our betrothal, and I didn't want Paul—or Maman, for that matter—to hear of it. They would only expect me to return to wed one of Menominee's most eligible and wealthy bachelors. Robby's earnestness convinced me all the more of the necessity of forging ahead with the plan I'd already invested many months in.

*July 15, 1887*

*My darling Robby,*
    *You are the most loving man a girl could want. I'm not surprised*
*to hear that you want to keep this baby. But I really must put my*
*foot down when it comes to your plan. I refuse to start our marriage*
*under a cloud of shame. Perhaps you believe the circumstances of our*
*baby's birth can be kept secret, but I must ask you to think about*
*me. The mother always bears the burden of such scandals. I would be*
*forever known as the woman who allowed herself to be sullied before*
*her wedding. I will not marry you while I am with child. I must think*
*about my future, your future, and, yes, what is best for this baby.*
*Imagine what she would have to endure if our families found out*
*about her birth. Please be reasonable.*
    *Thank you so much for the allowance. I have started my class and*
*study every day. I hope to make you proud of me.*
    *Think of me kindly, and with understanding,*

*Your loving wife to be,*
*May*

Dear reader, it vexed me sorely to pretend at this engagement, but my plight was fast becoming desperate. Not only had I not sent any money home, I'd become quite dependent on Robby's allowance. I could not lead him on indefinitely; compassion and fairness dictated that I break off the engagement sooner rather than later. I redoubled my efforts to meet some gentleman who might, at the very least, extricate me from Robby's benefaction.

To my deep chagrin, I only managed to secure dinners with the sort of men who had no intention of anything beyond amusing themselves for an evening. When one man invited me to a dance hall after dinner, I demurred. Despite his immaculate attire, I did not believe his entreaties. He claimed he could find me employment as a secretary (as if that interested me anyway) and assist me in securing a pleasant room at a very good price—just the sort of claims one might expect from a pander.

I needed to meet a respectable man, but I had failed to secure a single introduction to Chicago society. And all this time Robby continued to press me.

*August 2, 1887*

*My dearest May,*

*I know you believe you are doing the right thing, but my plan is quite foolproof, and I refuse to allow you to give up on our baby so easily. I don't give a damn about reputation, and I know you don't either. Have you forgotten how we laughed when Sheriff Hersen bought that gaudy house so he and his wife might host fancy dinners? Or how we zoomed along the lakefront on my bicycle last summer with your skirts flying every which way? You don't fool me one bit when you claim to care about what other people think.*

*Besides, we can start a new life together someplace other than Menominee. I insist you come to your senses. No one's going to know the baby was conceived out of wedlock.*

*Let's get married as soon as possible. With the baby on the way, we mustn't waste time. All is in order on my end. Father has agreed to fund the furniture business. I can be there to pick you up on a day's notice. What is the address of Mr. and Mrs. Ellwood?*

*Your loving husband to be,*
*Robby*

# A START FOR PAULINE DAVIDSON

CHICAGO—AUGUST 1887

*August 10, 1887*

*Robby my dear,*
  *I will not give you the address of Mr. and Mrs. Ellwood. I refuse to take a chance on you doing something foolish. Think about what I have said. Be patient. I promise, my way is better.*
  *I'll write more later.*

*All my love,*
*May*

I had hoped that a few months apart would have diminished Robby's ardor. But now he actually threatened to come to Chicago. Thank goodness, I'd had the foresight to use general delivery for all my Menominee correspondence, which required long walks three or four days a week to the post office at Dearborn and Adams. And from the first moment I set foot in Chicago, I'd shed the name May Dugas.

I was Pauline Davidson now, frequenting Chicago's finest dining rooms and hotel lobbies, praying to attract the attention of a man who could lift me out of my now precarious financial state. But after two months I'd encountered only traveling drummers, a few overeager mashers, some local businessmen, and a simple-witted resort manager. When Mrs. Farnsworth pressed me on my overdue room and board, I knew I needed to change my strategy. If I failed to fend off Robby's impossible plan or somehow establish myself in

Chicago, I would be forced to return to Menominee and, worst of all, admit defeat.

It had become painfully clear that I needed new dresses and a new pair of shoes, which I simply couldn't afford while threatened with removal from my humble room. My funds had run so low that I was reduced to dining out only on the odd occasion that some gentleman invited me, and I did not particularly care for subsisting on boiled eggs and biscuits for days on end.

Perhaps, I thought, employment for a period of time at the Boston Store, or some other such store, would enable me to secure new attire. I had seen shopgirls working on the floor there.

I visited the Boston Store's administrative offices on the sixth floor and asked to see the manager.

The desk clerk looked up from his paper-strewn desk. "May I say what this is regarding?"

I clasped my purse tightly against my abdomen to quiet my rumbling stomach. "I'm inquiring about the possibility of employment."

"Oh, you'll want to see Mr. Jeffries, the assistant manager," he said, rising. "Let me see if he's in."

The clerk returned and escorted me to Mr. Jeffries's office.

A lanky Mr. Jeffries unfolded himself from behind his desk and stood to greet me. "Welcome, Miss Davidson. Please, have a seat."

I walked to the chair beside his desk, sat, and delicately lifted and positioned my skirt to hide my scuffed shoes from his view.

He perched on his chair and folded his hands on the desk. "You're responding to the clerk advertisement?"

"Yes, sir. The position is still open, I trust."

"Well, most likely not for long. What experience do you have?"

"I'm quite familiar with women's wear." I imagined that reporting on Maman's expertise as a dressmaker would not win the day, so I tried my father's favorite gambit—salesmanship. "I worked in a women's clothing shop in Menominee, Michigan."

Mr. Jeffries jerked his head back ever so slightly. "I'm sorry. This position is in draperies and bed sets."

"Oh, I'm sure I could do that as well."

"Of course you could. But we already have several experienced applicants." He rose. "Please don't hesitate to apply in the future, Miss Davidson."

As I closed his office door behind me, the blood emptied from my head. I braced one hand against the wall and clapped the other over my eyes and forehead. Pinpricks of light exploded before my eyes—from hunger, desperation, annoyance, or all these things. Breathe, I told myself, taking several deep breaths. Looking up, I steadied myself and stepped forward on wobbly legs, my stomach rumbling and growling.

I needed a friend.

I took the elevator down to the main floor and, when the piano player finished "Jeanie with the Light Brown Hair," I marched right up to him. "Sir, I have been meaning to tell you for the longest time how very much I enjoy your music."

"And whom do I have the pleasure of thanking?"

"Pauline Davidson." As I spoke these words, dizziness overtook me. I slouched over the piano seat. "Dear me, I'm afraid I might faint."

That is how I made the acquaintance of Mr. Claude Montcrief, who revived me by fanning sheet music and then kindly invited me to join him for his midday dinner at the Windsor Hotel dining room on Dearborn. As we readied to depart, he reached down and took up a walking stick, a smooth-varnished stick with a coiled dragon carved on its ivory top. We strolled out to State Street. He offered me his arm and I took it, though it was I who steadied him, for a shortened leg left him with a lilting gait. The contrast jarred: At the piano, with his fingers flying over the keys and his torso swaying to the music, he was all elegance and poise. But stand him on his feet and he became an oddity—a cripple in a fancy suit. I almost pitied him.

By the time we reached the Windsor, I had quite forgotten his limp, taken as I was with his report that he read five newspapers each morning, loved nothing more than a leisurely fitting session with his tailor, and had an elderly aunt on the North Side whom he visited every Sunday.

After we ordered, Mr. Montcrief flicked his napkin open and dropped it to his lap. He had a round-cheeked, boyish face, with an upper lip that curled when he smiled, and his eyebrows arched high on his brow, as if he were in a state of perpetual observation. He sported a white bib-fronted shirt and powder-gray frock coat and trousers, all nicely set off by a burgundy silk cravat.

"I've noticed you in the store on several occasions," he said. "You shop, but never buy."

"Prudence dictates against extravagance for one such as me. I'm new to town."

"Where do you hail from?"

"A small town in the Upper Peninsula," I told him. I wanted to trust this man with silver-templed black hair and watchful blue eyes. There was something at once both serious and frivolous about him—like a gay entertainer intent on beguiling. Truth is, his manner put me in mind of Papa. "And you," I asked, "are you a Chicago native?"

He flared his hands, as if to invite me into his bemusement. "Hardly anyone here is from Chicago. Perhaps my Michigan town is even smaller than yours. Manistee. Ever heard of it?"

"Why, yes, I have. My family lived not far from there, in Muskegon, for a time."

That led to a round of reminiscence about Michigan summers: lake swimming and his game of gliding under water and snagging his sisters' ankles; my memories of wandering the hills of Menominee with my little brother and foraging wintergreens and strawberries; and our mutual restlessness with small-town life—how he'd left to find someplace more exciting, a place where a piano player might be appreciated, and how I hoped to relieve my poor family's suffering. Lively conversation it was, and all fine accompaniment to my colorful salad of beets and greens and dinner of capon, cranberry relish, and roasted turnips. How easily the food went down, lighting the furnace of my belly and spreading the warmth of contentment to limb and brain. The wine lightened my head, and even after I'd filled my stomach with sufficient food to absorb it, its pleasant glow still tingled my cheeks.

I didn't want dinner to end without learning more about Chicago from him, so over our after-meal coffee I asked, "Do you enjoy your work at the Boston Store?"

"What I enjoy most, after playing the piano, is having money to spend, although the salary at the Boston Store is not overly generous."

"If you don't mind my asking, how do you manage, then? Chicago certainly demands more income than any Michigan village."

He lowered his coffee cup and quietly replaced it on its saucer. "Ah, you've discovered that much during your short stay, I see."

"How could I not?" His company and the dining room's fine décor had put me at ease. This was the kind of life I sought: dining under chandeliers dripping with crystal; folding my hands on lily-white napery; enjoying the delicate touch of thin-edged, blue delft china. And all in the company of a self-assured man-about-town.

"The Boston Store is just something I do for pleasure—and a little extra income. My primary employment is an evening job. At the piano, of course." He twisted his napkin into a tight twirl and nestled it beside his plate. "And you, how do you manage?"

"In truth, not well. My mother is ailing; I should like to send her money to convalesce at a sanitarium." It was a white lie, but I needed more than just a friend: I needed a sympathetic friend. "But it is a struggle simply supporting myself."

"A beautiful young lady such as yourself need not struggle."

"You're too kind."

"On the contrary. I'm only being honest."

"When I first arrived I thought I might easily manage on my own. But my efforts have borne no fruit."

"Perhaps you would be interested in hearing more about my evening employment?"

"If you believe I may benefit from the knowledge."

"I'm the piano player at Miss Carrie Watson's."

"A private residence?"

"Much more than that. A bordello, my dear, of the highest reputation in all of Chicago."

I cast my eyes downward. He had announced it with such bravado, such careless ease, that it took my breath—and words—away. This man needed no pity. He possessed the politician's knack for disarming with brash honesty.

"Forgive me, Miss Davidson, if I have offended you. We need say no more of it."

I lifted my face. "Not at all. I appreciate your candor."

"The city is hard on young ladies. I should hate to see it swallow you up."

"I have no intention of being swallowed up. I need only secure some introductions and I shall do fine." All along it had been my

hope to simply place myself in the path of high-society men in Chicago's finest establishments, but of late I had begun to fear that this
would be neither easy nor straightforward. And now Mr. Montcrief
was confronting me with just the sort of circuitous route I'd begun
to consider, though with the utmost apprehension and ambivalence.

"Yes, that is the dream of many a young lady. Though you, I suspect, have more talents than most."

"Can you advise me, Mr. Montcrief?"

He flattened his right hand over his chest, showing off a thick-
banded gold ring with a square-cut diamond. "That depends on
your aspirations."

"I intend to meet businessmen, society men. And I do not mean
to take up residence in the Levee District."

"In all honesty, Miss Davidson, the surest route to meeting such
men is through Carrie Watson. And her business, I can assure you, is
a far cry from the grog shops, strumpets, and hoodlums of the Levee
District."

"I do take offense now, sir, at what you are proposing."

"Come, now. I mean not to offend, but to flatter. You are the sort
of young lady that a respectable gentleman might exalt in plucking
from Carrie Watson's—shall we say?—influence."

"And how am I to know you speak honestly? Perhaps you stand
to benefit by luring me to this place."

"You are clever, Miss Davidson. So clever I'll not toy with you.
Being the house's piano professor, I, too, have a reputation to
uphold. Each young lady I have introduced to Miss Watson has been
to her liking, as I believe you would be. It would be reward enough
for me to assist you."

Reward enough? I imagined some more venal reward figured in
as well. "How do you know I would meet with her approval? Especially in these old clothes?"

"Because I can see beyond your rumpled dress. You are not just
clever, but shockingly beautiful. You, my dear, are what we Chicago-
ans call a stunner: those eyes as soft and tawny as a fawn's; that sublime hourglass figure; and your lovely, slender hands. All you need
to put the polish on your beauty is some of Miss Watson's primping
and pampering."

He glanced at my crossed hands. I withdrew them, unsure of whether to be offended or flattered, and studied his expression.

He brushed his fingertips together and shot me an impish grin. "Because you possess poise and worldliness beyond your years. Because you could enchant any man." He cocked his head, as attentive as a suitor. "And because I believe we understand each other."

I won't lie—I had considered what it might be like to live the life of a courtesan. But not seriously. Not until now: not until I'd been forced to go without dinner for days at a time; not until I had been threatened with removal from my meager room; not until Robby wrote panicked letters declaring he wanted to fetch me. Still, I did not wish to become ensnared at such a place for any extended period; I had plans for a different kind of life. I braced my spine against the chair. "This is not what I imagined when I set out to make my way in Chicago. I would rather secure some well-paying job."

"The best you'd find is work in a factory at four dollars a week. Or maybe as a clerk at eight or nine—barely enough to subsist on in this city. Miss Watson pays her girls well. She includes generous meals, clean quarters, and a handsome dress-budget."

"And if some gentleman did not rescue me from this place, I'd become a prisoner there."

"Miss Watson does not keep any girl who wishes to leave. She is on the best of terms with the chief of police, for he knows she is respectable and honorable in her dealings." He raised his coffee cup to his lips and gazed at me over the rim. "But you really should have more confidence in yourself."

"You portray it as the most pleasant way to pass the time and earn a living, which I doubt very much it is." Still, part of me wanted to imagine Carrie Watson's as a luxurious abode frequented by Chicago's wealthiest men, wanted to believe I could be schooled there in the art of allurement, wanted to think Miss Watson would outfit me in stylish gowns.

"Miss Watson admits only the most refined clientele and does not overtax her girls. You could do much, much worse than work at a house that gushes each night with laughter and gaiety. It's all in one's attitude, my dear."

"And what, exactly, is the proper attitude?"

"Possessing the secret knowledge that a beautiful young woman is like an exotic fruit—many a respectable man will want to pluck her from the tree."

My mouth had turned cotton-dry. I sipped some water. Was he right? I had bargained on using my charms and wiles to meet Chicago's society men, but the closest I'd come to any man of influence was Mr. Montcrief himself, who had obviously found his own profitable niche at Miss Watson's.

He reached inside his vest, pulled out a black leather billfold, leafed through a dozen-plus bills, and extracted a ten-dollar note, which he slipped onto the tray with our dinner bill. Tucking his billfold away, he said, "And I should hate to worry about you accepting dinners from strange gentlemen."

I could guess his game: showing off his money; pretending it was nothing to him if I declined his offer; and firing off some vaguely frightening insinuation that forced me to act now or forever regret my reticence. Chances were good he stood to gain by introducing me to Miss Watson.

I thoughtfully touched a finger to my lips, studied the table, and turned doleful eyes on him. "If you would be kind enough to buy me a new dress and new shoes, Mr. Montcrief, I believe I would make a more favorable impression on Miss Watson."

# SURPRISING ENCOUNTERS

*T*hree days later, I donned the dress and shoes Mr. Montcrief had purchased for me—a fine enough outfit for meeting Miss Watson, but, alas, unlikely by itself to secure me entry into Chicago's high society. Promptly at one o'clock on a muggy August day, I walked up to a shipshape three-story brick at 441 South Clark Street. I strolled past the building, sized it up, and circled back. White shutters dressed up its windows, with those on the sunny side closed against the day's blazing sun. Gauzy curtains hung inside the visible windows, flowing diagonally to clasps at the corners, as if pairs of ballerinas stood there, posed and inviting. A brass plate with "Miss Carrie Watson" engraved in curled script graced the door, and above it a solid brass knocker stood ready. I gripped its smooth surface and brought it down once on the metal plate.

A Negro maid with a dusting rag in hand answered the door and ushered me through the entranceway, past a covered birdcage, and down a hallway paneled with deep-stained wood. I peeked into the rooms off the hallway and spied parlors with flocked floral wallpaper, French plate mirrors, and Oriental rugs. The day's heat had not yet overtaken the home's dim interior, and the odors of baking bread and stale cigarette smoke mingled in the hallway. We passed by a curved stairwell with a carved wood rail and came up to the doorway of a small room—small compared with the parlors I had glimpsed, but ample enough space for a dainty desk with curvaceous legs, three upholstered chairs, and a bookcase lined with glossy leather-bound volumes.

"Miss Watson will be down directly," said the maid, leading me into the room. She departed, brushing her rag over the top of the wainscoting and leaving the door open behind her. The room, being situated more or less in the center of the house, had no windows, but lamps with incandescent bulbs lit up the desk and room corners. Varnished paneling ran around the bottom half of the room, and celery-green wallpaper decorated with ivory *fleurs-de-lis* covered the walls.

Footsteps tapped down the stairs, beating out deliberate, even steps. I arranged myself into an erect posture and faced the door.

Carrie Watson appeared in the doorway—there was no doubt in my mind it was she—a stately woman of about five eight attired in a white gown with pink lace adorning the arms and bodice front. She wore her chocolate-brown hair swept up and trussed in diamond-studded clips. As her eyes met mine she smiled—a ready, automatic smile that lit up her broad, flat brow, high cheeks, and firm, narrow lips. She was younger than I imagined, probably a bit under forty, and as dignified in her carriage as any high-society dame.

"Ah, Miss Davidson. You are even more beautiful than Mr. Montcrief conveyed. And what a comely dress." She held out her hand.

"Pleased to meet you, Miss Watson." I shook her hand, and just as I noticed the firmness of her grip, its hold evaporated.

"Come, let me show you around. There'll be time to talk later." She led the way down the hallway. "I'm the home's second owner. Fortunately, it was spared in the Great Fire. Here, this is our main parlor."

Miss Watson and the previous owner had obviously spared no expense on design and décor. There were five parlors on the main level, the largest roomy enough to accommodate a piano and a small audience. Oriental rugs of burgundy and rich blues covered the parquet floors, paintings of pastoral scenes and women in flowing gowns decorated the walls, and upholstered chairs and sofas, some with curved wood ribbing, furnished the rooms. A plentitude of brass and glass-dome lamps graced the tables of the parlors and dining room.

The oversized kitchen, at the rear of the main floor, contained two bloated cast-iron stoves, an army of pots and pans hanging from ceiling hooks, and three rows of tables with benches. "This is where the girls take their noon meal," Miss Watson explained.

We descended to the basement, which held a bowling alley and billiards room. In the billiards room we passed the Negro maid bent over one of the room's brass spittoons. She emptied slimy brown globs into a waste bucket and rinsed the spittoon with clean water, all the time ignoring our presence. The scent of cigar smoke hung in the air. "These rooms," I said, "obviously enjoy plenty of company."

"Ah, yes," said Miss Watson with a sweep of her hand, "we offer our guests every opportunity for leisure and recreation."

We ascended the front stairs to the higher levels. No fewer than twenty-two bedrooms, eight water closets, three rooms with four slope-backed bathing tubs each, and Miss Watson's own suite of luxurious rooms occupied the second and third floors. As we wove our way through these living quarters, two girls bounded down the hall toward us, both wearing light, summery dresses and carrying hats that matched the wheat and sky-blue colors of their dresses. Very nice outfits indeed, I mused, imagining what colors I might choose for a few new day dresses.

Miss Watson introduced us.

Rose, a tall, shapely girl, clutched my hand as if we were long-lost friends. "Coming to live with us, Miss Davidson?"

"I may," I replied, glancing at Miss Watson to show proper deference.

"That'd be nice," said Sadie, who had the reddest head of hair I'd ever seen. "It's always fun having a new girl."

"Well, we've got shopping to do," Rose said. "Pleased to meet you."

The twosome trailed off, arm in arm, chattering like sisters on a holiday.

Miss Watson ushered me into the parlor of her suite of rooms. "Please, make yourself comfortable. Nancy will bring the tea directly."

"It's a beautiful home," I said, seating myself on a red-and-gold wing-armed chair opposite the one Miss Watson settled in. Taking in the elaborately carved coffee and side tables, I wondered: Did the girls' rooms also contain such fine furnishings? "And lovingly tended."

Miss Watson's firm lips softened to a smile. "The maids do tend it well. But I'm the one who sees to the girls. And the business." She picked up a bell from the low table between us and rang it.

"Now," she said, "I understand you are new to Chicago."

"Yes, I just arrived in June, from a little town in Upper Michigan." Still, I couldn't help but ask myself: Whatever will I tell Maman if I take up residence here? That I've landed in a respectable boarding-house for ladies employed in downtown department stores?

"And what did you do there?"

"I graduated from high school and left—as quickly as I could."

Miss Watson's face, a soft triangle, was powdered well enough to obscure the shallow wrinkles at the corners of her eyes. "Ah, so small-town life did not agree with you?"

"No, and now that I've seen Chicago, I'm afraid I'm completely spoiled."

Another maid, this one plump and red-complexioned, marched in with a tray and slid it onto the long, narrow table between us.

The maid served our tea, and Miss Watson dismissed her. "Please close the door behind you, Nancy."

Miss Watson picked up her cup and held it poised in midair. "I hope you won't mind if I ask you some personal questions."

"Oh, no, I expected you would want to."

"Are you a virgin?"

"No." I wanted a sip of tea but feared my hands might be trembling. I clasped them tightly together.

"And how many men have you had relations with?"

"Only one, though I chose him because I believed he could teach me well." I surprised even myself with this. It sounded as if I'd planned to seek an interview with the madam of a sporting house all along.

She replaced her teacup. "And do you believe you learned well?"

I held her gaze. "If this man's relish was any indication, I should say I came out top of my class."

She tossed her head back and chortled. "Ah, Miss Davidson, I believe you, I truly do. A few months here and I trust you'll master seduction of all sorts."

I reached for my cup and sipped, smiling at Miss Watson.

"Well, then, I invite you to join our household. Provided you are willing to submit to the house rules."

I didn't yet know if I wanted to join her business, though something urged me on. After all, I had devised no other plan than that which had already failed. So all I could do at this point was keep up the game. "I'd be delighted to join the household. And I would expect you to have rules."

She shifted the cross of her legs and rubbed her palms together. "I bring in a doctor every month to examine all the girls. He checks for health and provides guidance on precautions. You would need to visit his office before you could start work."

"I understand," I said.

"This business is my livelihood, and the girls depend on me for theirs. That means the reputation of the business must be foremost in everyone's mind. I do not tolerate any thieving or trickery. My customers come here for good company and the pleasures of sex, and I want them to trust that that is all they'll get."

I nodded deeply.

"I manage all the customer fees, and I expect you to welcome any gentleman who requests your company. You are not to collect any money, nor should you ever bring it up with a customer, though you may accept tips if they are offered. I am not interested in girls who are looking for a husband. I am not a matchmaker. I only want girls who understand that this is a business and that, as such, it depends on their conducting themselves as professionals. Do we understand each other, Miss Davidson?"

"Very well, Miss Watson," I said, wondering how to reconcile these conditions with Mr. Montcrief's assertion that I could easily find a gentleman to pluck me from the place. "I imagine, then, that you have girls who have been with the business for some time?"

"Oh, yes. Rose, for one, has been with me six years now. You can count on her to help you get settled." She reached for the teapot. "May I pour for you?"

I lifted my cup and saucer, extending it toward her. "Yes, please."

She poured herself a half cup but did not take it up. "As for terms, you will receive twenty dollars a week. No rent is deducted. It and all meals are provided. Each month I will also credit five dollars toward your dress account. You may incur a debt in this account, but it may never exceed your weekly pay. Is this satisfactory?"

"Yes, ma'am." The pay was better than I had imagined it might be. I replaced my teacup and smoothed my hands over my skirt. "I am in need of a few new dresses at present."

She perched on the edge of her seat. "I will give you the address of our dressmaker and send word that you'll be around. You may be fitted for one dress, which can be delivered a week after you take residence."

"That's very kind of you."

She rose. "Now let me show you your room."

→ ←

Dear reader, I did not take lightly the decision to join Carrie Watson's household, but my circumstances afforded little choice. I had depleted my funds, and I sorely wanted to help my family. Maman's dressmaking income was unpredictable, and her unfortunate habit of living beyond her means often taxed the household budget. Although Paul's lumber-mill job was steady, his responsibility to Maman kept him from considering marriage, not that he'd yet found a suitable bride in Menominee. I also worried about my brother Gene, only ten years old and already suffering taunts from the snobbish sons of Menominee's society set. So I naturally wanted to ease the financial strain on my family, and Lord knows I couldn't do that on a factory worker's or clerk's earnings. At the time, Carrie Watson's appeared the only viable option.

As for a reliable paycheck, I wasn't disappointed. I couldn't have imagined a busier residence, nor have I since encountered a more enterprising operation. Miss Watson employed three maids, two cooks, an elderly Negro carriage man, and, of course, Mr. Montcrief, the piano professor. Being new to the household, I was relegated to a small bedroom on the second floor, just up the rear stairs from the kitchen. Try as I might, I rarely managed any sound sleep in the morning hours, what with the clanging of pots and shouts of industry sounding from the kitchen, to say nothing of the heavy-footed delivery men clomping in and out with crates of eggs, gallons of milk, beef and pork cuts, and all manner of vegetables and fruit.

When I finally opened my bedroom door for the day's noon meal, smells of coffee, bacon, pancakes, and fried eggs beckoned me to the kitchen, where we girls gathered for breakfast, visited, and planned our day. Over breakfast and throughout the afternoon, the place teemed with the chatter and rowdiness of a henhouse under rooster raid, banishing the last of my fears that life in such a place was akin to imprisonment. After our bountiful breakfast, we were at our leisure: to read or relax in our rooms or visit in the parlor; to run errands to the dressmaker or apothecary; or to stroll Lake Park. As evening approached, the scents of castile soap permeated the upper floor, where the younger girls giggled away in their baths and the older ones scoffed at their silliness and took advantage of the time to luxuriate and perhaps read in the tub until their time ran out.

Come six o'clock, the maid removed the cover from the birdcage in the entranceway and the resident parrot called out, "Miss Watson's, come in, gentlemen." The parlor slowly filled with our visitors, and the ensemble of piano, violin, and cello performed chamber trios. Dinner was served in the dining room at seven, and we girls dined with the men who came around for an always sumptuous feast. Into the evening, conversation and chuckles enlivened the parlors and bedrooms, and perfume mixed with cigarette and cigar smoke throughout the hallways and up the stairwells.

Many might consider work of this sort demeaning. But I would say it afforded an excellent education. Miss Watson entertained only the most refined clientele, though they sometimes parked their refinement at the bedroom door. House rules precluded me from turning away any guest, but I quickly learned to sort the ill-behaved brutes from the genuine gentlemen and to encourage steady visits from the latter. In two months' time I had cultivated several loyal regulars, including an assistant to the mayor, an artist who only managed sporadic visits, and Mr. Hall, a generous-tipping but cantankerous professor of law who had obviously tired of the company of Rose, quite possibly because she was beginning to show her thirty-two years.

And, after all, men are not terribly difficult to manage. They are rather like puppies: Roll them on their back and convince them you're master and you've tamed them. Of course, there are those who charge ahead, as gluttonous as children gobbling candy. The trick with that sort, if you can first get their attention, is to get the candy in hand and stretch it out like taffy. Ah, yes, aren't a hundred nibbles and groans more pleasurable than one greedy gulp?

Since I no longer needed to worry about shelter and livelihood, I put my energies toward a more traditional education. My own hard-earned money, as well as Robby's allowance, enabled me to enroll in two additional classes. In Business Law I learned about contracts, bailment, promissory notes, negotiable papers, partnerships, and corporations. And I absolutely adored my French class. French is such a beautiful language, the language of my own ancestors.

Early afternoons were my favorite time at Carrie Watson's. With October bringing cooler days to the city, I often strolled along Michigan Avenue or took in the breezy waterfront at Lake Park. But mostly, determined as I was to make myself worthy company for cultured gentlemen, I settled in the parlor with a newspaper, textbook, or novel. (I especially enjoyed Charles Dickens, Wilkie Collins, and William Dean Howells.) And, when he wasn't playing at the Boston Store, I listened to Mr. Montcrief at the piano. I barely knew Beethoven from Baedeker when I first arrived in Chicago, but Claude's music enchanted me. "What was that piece?" I would ask each time he dropped his hands to his lap. Being the solicitous-uncle type and perhaps appreciating my interest in music, Claude took me under his wing, which had the most unexpected outcome. But I will get to that later.

During August and September, Robby had written regularly. But as of mid-October, I hadn't heard from him in nearly two weeks, which I found encouraging. Perhaps he had met some new girl and given up his pursuit of me. And now, having attained a modicum of financial independence, I decided the proper thing to do was break off the engagement.

After composing a note to Robby announcing the sad news, I hastened to the post office to mail it, along with a letter and some money for Maman. A blustery October wind funneled down the streets, buffeting my hat and skirts. I tucked the letters into my purse and gripped my hat brim, steadying it against the chilly gusts. Thank goodness, I'd earned enough money to afford a new wool cloak, which cozily clasped my torso. I burst through the door of the post office, took two steps inside, and spotted Robby, his eyes popped so wide you'd think he'd seen a ghost—when it was merely me, his supposedly large-with-child fiancée, looking about as pregnant as a bean pole.

# A LETTER FROM FRANK

·

MENOMINEE—JANUARY 23, 1917

*U*pon joining the breakfast table before day two of the trial, I found Frank had delivered a letter to the house.

*Dear May,*

*My attorney advises me not to speak to you, and I know I shouldn't even write. If he knew, he'd ask me what in tarnation I'm doing.*

*But damn it, May, you and I both know this trial isn't only about money. I still can't believe it's come to this. Don't all the years we've known each other, the visits with each other's families, and all those highball-charged train rides and transatlantic crossings mean anything to you?*

*I know what you're thinking: You started it. Why'd you have to get up a lawsuit against me?*

*Do you think I wanted to resort to this? That I enjoy sitting across the aisle from you in a courtroom? I detest seeing you under the gun, my own damn attorney smirking every time he calls you Baroness. You think I like old man Sawyer digging through our private affairs and scrounging for dirty linen?*

*But you've backed me into a corner. When you discovered the well was dry, you threw me down it. Oh, no, my dear Baroness, I'm not going to let you get away with it. You and I were in this together until you decided you were only in it for yourself.*

*You know there's a way to stop this confounded trial. My lawyer claims it'd be foolish to negotiate with you at this point. But you and I never played by the rules. Why should we start now?*

*All you have to do is turn over the stocks and the money you owe me. I'd even settle for a promissory note. And then we could get back to enjoying life together. How about celebrating big? We could take the train to Los Angeles and escape this wretched cold weather.*

*Consider my offer, May. You can allow Sawyer to ruin your reputation one day at a time and pretend I never meant anything to you. Or you can open your arms to your Frank again.*

*Here's to good times,*

*Your devoted friend,*
*Frank*

Perhaps Frank believed the first day of the trial had given her an advantage over me, but she had miscalculated. In the spirit of fair play, I didn't even surrender the letter to my attorney. Nor did I respond to it. After all, my attorney hadn't yet delivered our opening statement.

# THE TRIAL

*F*inally, after Alvah Sawyer had taken up hour upon hour with his litany of claims, my counsel took the floor. I must say I very much like my attorney, George Powers from Iron River. He's hardworking and willing to dig for just the right evidence to construct a compelling argument. George is a dapper, fortyish man with high cheeks and a narrow-lipped mouth. And can that mouth talk.

"If it pleases the jury," said Mr. Powers, flaring a palm in my direction, "I invite you to consider my client, the Baroness May de Vries. She is of humble beginnings. You know her family: her dearly departed, widowed mother and her two upstanding brothers. She grew up among you and went on to become a well-educated and well-traveled lady. In 1892, at the young age of twenty-three, she married a wealthy Dutch nobleman, Baron Rudolph de Vries. Although the Baron is now deceased, the Baroness is still welcomed in the courts of Europe. She is, to put it simply, accustomed to the world of wealth and royalty.

"Frank Shaver has had a long association with the Baroness, dating back to 1901. On occasion, Miss Shaver chose to travel with the Baroness, and traveling the world is an expensive undertaking. She spent her money during these trips. From time to time she bought gifts for the Baroness. And now, fifteen years after she met the Baroness, she claims she was cheated. After all these years of knowingly spending her own funds, she says she doesn't know what happened to her money. After keeping close company with the Baroness and her family, even living in their home, she contends she was hoodwinked."

Powers paused and swept his gaze over the jurors. "My client will fight these patently ridiculous charges. They have no basis in reality. They are designed solely to coerce the Baroness into paying out a large sum of money by harassing and distressing her with this lawsuit."

Out of the corner of my eye, I could see Frank shift in her chair. As I turned to look at her, she pursed her lips and shot me one of her you'll-pay-for-this looks. Apparently, she was disappointed I hadn't acceded to the request in her letter.

Powers pulled a sheet of paper from the inside pocket of his pin-striped suit. "Miss Shaver would have you believe that her friendship with the Baroness was a one-way street, that she showered the Baroness with loans, gifts, and living expenses and got little in return. The reality is quite different. In preparing for this trial, the Baroness took great pains to recall the cost of some of the many gifts she gave Miss Shaver over the years—gifts for which *she* never expected compensation."

The insinuation in Mr. Powers's last statement seemed to hit home. Frank's jaw dropped and she swiveled her head about, looking at me, her attorney, and the jurors as if to declare this suggestion of pettiness on her part completely absurd.

"To wit," continued Mr. Powers, reading from the list, "a brooch costing $1,500; a mesh bag valued at $450; a gold ring for $150; a fine evening coat of sealskin valued at $500; a diamond set for $3,000; a bedroom set costing $550; linen for $350; a tea service for $300; a historic prayer book, which Miss Shaver hinted she would like for a gift, purchased for $150; a mantel clock—Miss Shaver has a fancy for historic and artistic objects—valued at $1,700; and a fine marble statue for $2,000."

Mr. Powers folded up his paper, returned it to his suit pocket, and faced the jurors straight on. "Furthermore, while Miss Shaver resided at the Menominee residence owned by the Baroness and her brothers, the Baroness expended $17,500 on the remodel and upkeep of this residence, even though she herself visited Menominee infrequently.

"I ask you, gentlemen of the jury," said Powers, chopping the air with his stiffened hand, "is this the behavior of a person intent on fleecing another?

"Yes, it is true that Miss Shaver gave gifts and money to the Baroness. But the Baroness did the same. Was Miss Shaver only ingratiating herself to the Baroness, a woman of wealth and means, all this time?"

Powers gripped the railing of the jury box and pitched forward. "Is Miss Shaver now trying to take advantage of the Baroness's station because she has spent herself into penury?"

A collective gasp escaped from the onlookers, followed by whispered commotion.

Alvah Sawyer bolted upright. "Objection, Your Honor, these are insinuations with no basis in fact."

Judge Flanagan brought down his gavel. "Order, order."

The courtroom, populated mostly by women, hushed, and the judge directed his attention to Mr. Sawyer. "It's an opening statement, Counsel. You had yours." Looking back and forth between Sawyer and Powers, he added, "I trust both of you will adhere to the rules of evidence when examination of witnesses begins."

Mr. Powers efficiently outlined additional points to shore up our strategy that this suit was a nuisance without basis and thanked the jurors for their time. I breathed a sigh of relief. His argument cut to the core of the matter. He had challenged the very foundation of Frank's claims. I believe he even bested Sawyer's opening statement.

The judge leaned back in his seat. "Mr. Sawyer, you may call your first witness."

Sawyer stood. "Your Honor, I call Miss Frank Shaver to the stand."

# A DELICATE JUNCTURE

·

*I* hadn't bargained on Robby's tracking me down in Chicago, especially at this delicate juncture—so soon after taking up residence at Carrie Watson's, and with my grand plan just beginning to unfold—but love can lead any of us to commit acts we find foolish in retrospect.

Robby, the very picture of puzzlement, rushed up to me and then halted abruptly, perhaps trying to decide whether to embrace me or shake me. He proceeded to unleash a torrent of questions, right there in the expansive post-office lobby: What was going on? Why didn't I look six months pregnant? Why hadn't I written in weeks?

I took his hand. "Please, not here. Come, let's find some nice place to talk."

We went to Robby's hotel, the well-appointed Hotel Davenport, around the corner on Dearborn. (He'd no doubt selected it for its proximity to the post office, which I learned he'd been frequenting for hours on end with the express purpose of intercepting me.) He wanted us to go to his room, but I insisted on the dining room. Hoping to set the tone for a civil conversation, I ordered tea and a plate of cakes, all the time begging Robby to cease his questions until our order arrived.

He pressed his lips together, trying hard to contain what I imagine was months' worth of frustration now laced with confusion and possibly indignation.

"I do owe you an explanation, I certainly do," I began as I poured his tea.

He nodded and moistened his lips, clamping the dainty teacup handle between his chunky fingers and thumb.

I could think of no better explanation than that which I had penned in the letter now stuffed in my purse. "Three weeks ago, I lost the child and became quite ill. Helga attended me. On her orders, I have been confined to bed."

His eyes narrowed. "You look fine to me."

"Yes, I'm much better now, thank you."

"I mean you don't look like someone who's been ill."

"Oh, Robby, I don't know what you expect. I've lost the baby. There's nothing either one of us can do about that."

"That's obvious." He smacked his hands down on the table. "Do you think I'm some numskull?"

I raised my brow and softened my eyes. "No, of course not."

"Why didn't you write earlier? Didn't you think I'd want to know right away?"

"The fact is, I hated the thought of distressing you."

"You think not telling me makes it easier?"

"No, I'm sure it doesn't." I met his gaze straight on. "Robby, there is simply no way to spare your feelings. I'm afraid I must break off our engagement."

"Why, you . . ." His face ignited to bright pink. "After all this. How dare you."

Poor Robby. He took it quite hard, shaming me for subjecting him to months of waiting and torment, for spending his money under the circumstances, and for keeping him in the dark about the baby.

I allowed him his say, and then I told him that he was wrong about being kept in the dark, that I had in my possession the letter which I had intended to mail that very day to prove it.

Unfortunately, that did not placate him. He shoved back from the table, sprang to his feet, and leaned threateningly over me.

"I hope you get what's coming to you, May Dugas," he said, and stormed out of the dining room, leaving me to pay the bill.

And that concluded my affair with Robby. I learned that soon afterward he married the most darling girl in Menominee, and I'm certain he's far happier with her than he ever would have been with me.

→←

Chicago was quite a city in those days—booming, boisterous, and gleaming with newness, as if it'd sprung up overnight on the shores of Lake Michigan. Soaring buildings dominated the streets south of the river, turning Chicago's downtown into the most modern and imposing of any American city. Fashionably attired pedestrians strutted along the sidewalks and wove their way among stylish carriages and streetcars jammed with workers and shoppers. And the Michigan Avenue district—such shops as I had never before set foot in: Marshall Field's, The Fair, and Carson & Pirie; dressmakers and tailors from Europe's capitals; a fur store as big as an auditorium; and apothecaries with every imaginable potion and personal item.

And the jewelry stores! It was in Chicago I first fell in love: with sparkling diamonds; radiant gold; lustrous, graduated pearls; and the pure gleam of platinum. Chicago was where I belonged, with all its commerce, excitement, and entertainment. Why, you could practically see the money changing hands between bankers and builders, shopkeepers and fashionable ladies, and rich men and their consorts. I only wish my memories of it weren't marred by the man who became the burr in my boot. But I'm getting ahead of myself.

My employment at Miss Watson's enabled me to afford new attire, and the gifts of hair combs, bracelets, and necklaces my admirers showered on me lent the finishing touches to my ensembles. Now I found myself prepared to mingle with Chicago society. In my French class I met two delightful sisters, Melody and Melissa, whose father happened to be a well-to-do carriage manufacturer in Detroit. Against their parents' wishes, they had moved to Chicago to enjoy its social set and parties, and within weeks of meeting them I found myself whisked along in their adventures.

On my day off from Miss Watson's, one November evening, I convinced Melody and Melissa to attend a widely publicized lecture on psychophysics by Dr. Joseph Jastrow. We took the roundabout route to Athenaeum Hall, driving down Michigan Avenue at sunset in a handsome carriage. I wore my newest dress, an emerald-colored gown with scalloped patterns on the sleeves, and Melody and Melissa— no strangers to high fashion—complimented me on it and the new citrine and gold brooch I had recently acquired from Mr. Hall, one of my regulars.

Athenaeum Hall held an audience of well over a hundred, but it still felt intimate with its fan-shaped seating arrangement and the delicate swan-necked lamp sconces gracing the walls. Dr. Jastrow, a slim-shouldered man with a coarse gray beard, opened the lecture, which was billed as a demonstration of his new automatic-writing technique, by inviting three people to come up to the stage. (Melody, Melissa, and I raised our hands from the third row, but he passed us over.) "Please take your writing stations," he said, directing the two women and one man to chairs behind desks with pencils and paper.

He instructed them to close their eyes and then intoned, "Pay attention to my voice, only my voice. You are entering a state of calm and relaxation. All your focus is on my voice. Let all other sounds and sensations drop away. Relax; let your shoulders drop. Release any tension in your face. Now find the pencil on the desk. Take it up; lower it to your paper. Turn your thoughts inward. Write, write whatever comes—perhaps words, or pictures, or maybe squiggles. Let your hand take over."

He turned to the audience and, placing a finger to his lips and sweeping an open palm before us, signaled for quiet. For several minutes he stood stock-still before us. Just as I began to wonder if he was hypnotizing us, too, he silently twirled around and said to his volunteers, "You may put your pencils down now."

One by one his volunteers surrendered their writing implements.

"Fine, fine," he said. "Now I will count from five to one, and when I reach one you will open your eyes. Five . . . four . . . three . . . two . . . one."

He snapped his fingers, and his three charges popped their eyes open and gazed at him with the placid, wide-eyed expressions of surprised cows.

"Thank you, you've all done well. Now, if I may see your work." He walked to his first volunteer, a gangly woman of about thirty dressed in a peach-colored gingham dress that served her lean figure as well as could be expected. Picking up her paper, he studied it for a moment, and then, offering his hand, invited her to stand. "And you are?"

"Emily Shapiro." Her complexion colored, and the stiffness of her physique betrayed nervousness.

"Miss Shapiro," he said with the slightest bow of his head. "It is miss, I assume?"

Some in the audience tittered, but I had already observed that she wore no wedding ring. Her nails were trimmed to blunt squares. She was obviously dedicated to pragmatism, to the point where she had subjugated any matrimonial aspirations. Perhaps she lived with a sole surviving parent and worked to help out the household.

"Yes," she said and, apparently mustering her mettle, added, "Did you gather that from my writing, Dr. Jastrow?"

Melody, Melissa, and I chuckled at the prospect of some sport.

Dr. Jastrow grinned. "No, Miss Shapiro, politeness dictated that I ask. But I can see from your writing that you are a competent person. Other people depend on you. You have little time for nonsense. I imagine you hold a position of some importance, though you may not get the recognition you deserve. Does that accord with your circumstances, Miss Shapiro?"

"Yes, I suppose it does. I assist my father in his jewelry business."

It dawned on me at that moment that I could just as easily have accomplished what Dr. Jastrow was doing—reading people's personalities by the way they dress, carry themselves, respond to challenges, and, with some training, perhaps even how they write. It wasn't so much an education I experienced that night as an awakening—an awakening to my own innate talents in the art of influence. Like Dr. Jastrow, I possessed the ability to peer into people's minds and glean their fears and dreams. I'd been selling myself short; truly, I possessed my father's cunning and only needed to apply my talents.

And with problems brewing in my own place of employment, I needed all the cunning I could conjure. Two days earlier, Miss Watson had summoned me to her parlor for a meeting with her and Rose.

"Pauline," Miss Watson began, "Rose has requested that the three of us have a talk, and from what I can gather, such a meeting is long overdue."

Taking my cue from Miss Watson's stern pose, I asked, "Have I offended someone?"

"Yes, I should say quite a few people." Miss Watson leaned over her desk and steepled her fingers. "Rose says you've been standoffish with the other girls. That you put on airs around them."

"I mean no offense." I had kept my distance from the other girls, it was true, but not, as she insinuated, out of a sense of superiority. The fact is, I pitied them—and feared that any tender feelings toward them would lead to attachments and interfere with my plans. "I am new to this way of life. I never had a sister. I guess I don't know how to behave like one."

"Well, you've got a whole houseful of girls to show you." Miss Watson smoothed a hand over her brow, as if to slacken its strain. "Not that I expect you to be a sister to all of them. But I do expect you to treat them with respect."

"Of course," I said, bowing my head.

Miss Watson plunked her hands down on the desk. "Can I count on you, then, to mend your ways?"

"Yes, I will be more attentive to my conduct." All this time I had not ventured a glimpse at Rose, though I discerned her fidgeting in the chair next to me. Poor Rose. I had quickly mastered the art of seeking sponsorship for my departure from Carrie Watson's, but she and most of the other girls were doomed to spend their youthful years there. And Rose had already seen a good number of those pass.

Miss Watson leaned back in her chair.

"Is that all, miss?" I asked.

Rose cleared her throat and said, "There's that other matter."

I shot Rose a glance, raising my eyebrows demurely. She kept her gaze fastened on Miss Watson.

Miss Watson's eyes darted over Rose and settled on me. "I know Mr. Hall has been visiting you regularly. Can you tell me how that started?"

Ah, I understood now what Rose's real concern was. Mr. Hall—who had showered her with the loveliest trinkets—had cast her off, and she wanted to blame me for it. "Mr. Montcrief introduced us over dinner one evening, and the next night Mr. Hall said he wanted to spend the evening with me."

"Did you know he'd been spending time with Rose for some months now?"

"I didn't know for how long, but I had seen him with Rose before."

"And did you do anything to discourage him from seeing Rose?"

"No, miss, I can't see any reason to do such a thing."

Miss Watson shifted from one haunch to the other, turning away from Rose toward me. "Well, our guests are free to choose whomever they want. But I expect you to show some respect for each other's regulars as well."

"Of course," I said.

"Very well, then." Miss Watson braced an arm on her chair and made ready to stand.

Rose blurted out, "But she fixes her hair the way Mr. Hall likes it—just the way I do, swept to the side. She never did that before. And she makes a beeline for him every time he shows up."

"Oh, my." Miss Watson pinched her lips and rolled her head in an arc. "Do you see what this has led to, Pauline? You setting yourself apart from the other girls?"

I folded my hands on my lap and hunched forward. "Yes, miss."

Miss Watson flattened her hands on her desk. "I want both of you to let this matter drop. Mr. Hall will see whomever he wishes to see. It is his choice. And, Pauline, I expect you to take this talk as a warning. I do not want strife in this house. Do you understand?"

"Yes, I do."

"And you, Rose, I expect you to give Pauline a chance to mend her ways. Will you do that?"

I heard the slightest snort escape from Rose's nostrils as she spoke. "Of course I will."

Turning to Rose, I said, "I appreciate that."

Miss Watson concluded the interview then, but I figured life at Miss Watson's would not be as easy for me as it had been. Rose would be on the lookout for anything she could pin on me to cause more trouble. And with Miss Watson insisting I change my ways, it was high time to get serious about leaving, though I had not yet formed any solid plan.

In retrospect, I realize I miscalculated by not cultivating the other girls' society, an error I have taken care never to repeat. In fact, I have since learned that women can be counted on to show great devotion and loyalty when afforded respect and friendship.

# THE TRIAL

*A*s Frank stood and marched to the stand, a buzz shot through the courtroom. Judge Flanagan gripped his gavel. The crowd quieted. I followed her every move: her stocky frame held straight and stalwart; the plump hand placed on the Bible; her usually mischievous expression tempered with solemnity. She skated through the swearing in as if it were a turkey shoot, occasionally glancing in my direction, most likely with the intent of unnerving me. This was her arena. She knew the courtroom, and she probably thought her chances of out-gaming me in it were quite good. I merely held her gaze, my expression abundant with tranquillity.

"Miss Shaver," said Mr. Sawyer, "please tell us the story of your acquaintance with the Baroness, just so we understand the time and events. How did you meet?"

Frank squared her shoulders and looked to the jury. "We met on a train traveling from Chicago to Milwaukee back in 1901. I was in the parlor car, and the Baroness was holding court there, having quite a merry time. I was alone and couldn't help but notice the jolly party at the next table. The Baroness caught my eye at one point and invited me to join them. That's how it all started."

"And what do you mean by 'holding court'?"

Frank tossed her head back and smiled. "Entertaining her entourage—and the whole car, for that matter. May could charm the crown—and bottoms—off a king."

Titters erupted in the courtroom. Once the judge wiped the smile off his face and glared at the onlookers, calm was restored.

"Yes, fine," said Sawyer, "and how did the acquaintanceship get on?"

"We exchanged letters, and six months later, in spring of 1902, when May was on her way back to Menominee, we met in Chicago and spent some time gadding about the city. Her brother Gene joined us, which was the first time I met him. Later, in September of 1902, May visited me at my parents' home in Pittsburgh, and her brother came along and spent a month there."

"And is that when Gene proposed marriage?"

"Yes, and I accepted. Afterward, he invited me for a long visit to Menominee. He had borrowed some money when he visited me in Pittsburgh, which he repaid. But then he started borrowing money again, and it got my hackles up. I told May I was not pleased and asked her to set him straight."

"And did she do that?"

"No. She said I should humor Gene and enjoy his company, which didn't satisfy me. So I told Gene he obviously couldn't support both of us, and I broke the engagement. May came crying that Gene was heartbroken and asked me to reconsider. But I refused."

I glanced at Gene, who merely shrugged. Heartbreak never had been his *métier*.

Sawyer urged Frank on. "And then what happened?"

"We quarreled, and that was the end of our friendship for quite a few years."

"And when did this quarrel occur?"

"In 1903, in Pittsburgh."

"But the friendship recovered?"

"Yes, in 1912, after my father died. I received a letter of condolence from May, and I sent her a thank-you note. She was so anxious to renew our friendship she hotfooted it to Chicago and invited me for a fancy dinner at the Congress Hotel. She told me she'd regretted our falling out and went on and on about how we need never again part."

"And you agreed to resume the friendship on that occasion?"

"In the blink of an eye." Frank bobbed her chin in my direction. "My God, who wouldn't?"

Frank's admission brought a chorus of oohs and aahs from the ladies. My heart thumped. I had to admit I never tired of Frank's artless candor.

"And what happened that first night of your renewed friendship?"

"During dinner, May ordered several highballs for us. I caught her sneaking a few of hers to my side of the table when she thought I wasn't looking. She asked me to go to Menominee with her, but I had business to attend to in Chicago."

Frank leaned to the side so that she had a clear view of me, smiled, and said, "But May could talk a cougar out of a tree, and the next thing I knew, I was on a train headed for Menominee. In November. Without a lick of luggage."

A rustle of amusement sounded around the courtroom. I returned Frank's smile—it had been one of the most memorable train rides I'd ever taken.

Sawyer motioned to Frank with a dip of his head, and she continued. "To head off my worries about not having a warm coat or change of clothes, May ordered the porter to bring us a bottle of Scotch, and the highballs flowed again."

Snickers erupted. The judge cleared his throat.

Sawyer rushed to his next question. "Did you enter into any financial arrangements with the Baroness around that time?"

"While I was in Menominee, she brought up Gene and wondered if I might resume the engagement. I didn't like the idea one bit. She insisted she wanted to somehow join our families together and asked if I'd buy into the Menominee home and take up residence there with her. I agreed and purchased a half interest in the house for six thousand dollars."

"And did you invest any more money in the house?"

"Did I ever. May suggested we increase the value of the house with some improvements, so I plowed another nine thousand dollars into remodeling. After that I took to calling it 'the palace,' because I figured May needed a place fit for royalty, meaning her and her darling Frenchie."

"Her Frenchie?"

"Her French bulldog."

"Did the Baroness ask about the inheritance you received upon your father's death?"

"Not in a direct way. She did go fishing, though. And I don't mean some Sunday-afternoon outing. More like a regular expedition."

The few men in the courtroom took their turn at chortles, causing Judge Flanagan to sit upright. After Frank and her attorney completed this round of questioning, the judge said, "Counsel, it's time for our lunch break."

Judge Flanagan resumed the afternoon session with new instructions: "Mr. Sawyer, I'll ask you to pick up the pace of your questioning. And remember: This is a trial, not storytelling hour."

"Of course, Your Honor," Sawyer said. He turned to Frank in the witness box. "Miss Shaver, you were telling us about events of 1913, after your reconciliation with the Baroness. Was it about that time you met Miss Belle Emmett?"

"Yes, Daisy, as everyone calls her, is May's personal assistant."

"What sort of assistance does she provide?"

"Oh, she sees to correspondence, bills, financial matters."

When Sawyer exhausted his inquiries about the handling of Frank's money, he turned his attention to trips Frank and I had taken.

"Oh, yes," said Frank. "May and I traveled all over Europe—Venice, Paris, the south of France. And there was one long stay in London, and also a trip to Algiers, in 1915. You name it—we were probably there. We gathered towels and linens from so many places that we often jested, while selecting napkins at home, 'Where shall we dine tonight?'"

"I imagine this Algiers trip ran up some costs. Who paid for it?"

"I never knew exactly how much it cost—but Daisy kept asking for more money. First it was for the deposit. Then the balance. Or wine or liquor. At the end of it all, I'd spent about twenty-four hundred dollars."

"And during the London stay, was there talk of a gift of pearls?"

"Yes, May had a collection of pearls from the Baron that she wanted to turn into a necklace. She told me Daisy planned on giving her fifteen more pearls to complete the necklace but said the gift would have more sentiment attached to it if it came from me instead. So I deposited about fourteen thousand dollars' worth of Westinghouse shares in her London bank for the pearls."

"And did that satisfy the Baroness?"

"No, when she found out I had more shares, she said we could use them for our living expenses and asked if I would loan them to her for that purpose. So I deposited another twenty-two thousand dollars' worth of shares, but kept my receipt of debt for them."

Sawyer tugged his vest into place. "Around this time, did the Baroness ask you to write a will out to her?"

"Yes, in late 1914, after France and Germany and all those other European countries started up the war, she told me she might have to travel to Europe at some point and that she was going to make a will out in my favor. She suggested I do the same, so I wrote a will bequeathing eighty thousand dollars to her. But whenever I asked about her will, she told me she hadn't gotten around to it. Now I figure she didn't have that kind of money. But, knowing May, she'll claim she's going to be the first person to live forever."

"Objection," said Mr. Powers. "The witness is not in a position to know how much money the Baroness had or has."

"Sustained," said Judge Flanagan. "And, Miss Shaver, please restrict your answers to the questions before you."

"Yes, Your Honor," said Frank, with the same little smirk I'd seen on those occasions when she resolved to do just as she damn well pleased.

"Gentlemen of the jury," said Mr. Sawyer, quite possibly noticing the droopiness of their eyelids. "I just have a few more questions.

"Miss Shaver, did the Baroness ever request your help with her brother Paul's business?"

"Yes, around 1915. She told me his business was off to a roaring start and if we invested some funds toward the purchase of more automobiles that our loan would pay off handsomely. I lent fifty-five hundred dollars to the business, but never saw any return on it, let alone the original loan."

"Miss Shaver, you have told us of considerable sums of money that you either loaned or turned over to the Baroness after cajoling and manipulation on her part."

"Objection, Your Honor," said Mr. Powers. "'Cajoling and manipulation' implies motive."

"Sustained. Mr. Sawyer, please rephrase your statement."

"Yes. You turned over significant funds in loans or in response to requests, funds totaling a little over one hundred thousand dollars. Correct, Miss Shaver?"

"Yes."

"And you retained receipts for those funds which were loans, shares, or investments, correct?"

"Yes."

"And in 1916 did you show those receipts to the Baroness?"

"Yes, she requested that I turn the receipts over to her. She said she'd repay all of them."

"And did she?"

"Not one cent."

"What happened when you pressed for payment?"

"She said she didn't owe me anything. So I decided the only way I'd ever see any of my money was to take her to court."

Mr. Sawyer slowly pivoted away from the jury, summoning the gravity of an actor, and faced the judge. "Your Honor, that's all I have today."

That concluded day two of the trial. Disheartening, it was. In fact, the whole affair unnerved me. I hated being stuck in Menominee, facing the prospect of being cooped up in a courtroom for days on end. In the middle of winter, no less, with more snow in the forecast. If it weren't for the war raging all over Europe, I'd never have set foot on U.S. soil, and this lawsuit might never have been filed.

My lawyer had gotten off to a good start, but I didn't care for the impression Frank had left with the jury. Thank goodness, we still had an ace in the hole—a document Frank herself had signed.

# PROPOSALS AND PROPOSITIONS

·

*B*eing anxious to leave Carrie Watson's and step out on my own, I hoped my new friends, Melody and Melissa, might afford some such avenue. I had told them I was staying at the Palmer House while I attended to my deceased uncle's will; they believed I seldom saw them in the evenings because I needed to look after my grief-stricken aunt. But this pretense created certain problems: I feared the excuse would sooner or later wear thin, and my engagement at Carrie Watson's prevented me from mingling with their circle of fascinating friends. These cumbersome circumstances, as well as the deteriorating condition of my relations at Miss Watson's, thus forced some action.

After the Jastrow lecture, Melody, Melissa, and I retired to the Palmer House for drinks. We settled on red velvet seats in the lobby and ordered cordials. All around the thick-carpeted lounge, couples and foursomes bent their heads together in hushed conversation. Candle lights flickered across their faces, revealing expressions animated by good humor or, at the least, by wine and spirits.

"Wouldn't you just love one of those new Gramophones so you could listen to music whenever you wanted?" I asked them, taking in the piano player's even-tempered rendition of a Chopin piece.

"Oh, my," said Melody, the elder and more practical of the two, "we just asked Father to buy us a new dining-room set."

Melissa, who was always keen to acquire new playthings or contraptions, rolled her eyes. "You're such a spoilsport."

"Well, I'm thinking of buying one," I said. "But it seems a shame to keep it in a little hotel room that's hardly fit for entertaining."

"You could keep it at our house," said Melissa.

Melody clapped her hands together. "And you could visit and even stay over whenever you wanted."

And that is how I found my way out of Carrie Watson's and into their home. After I gave Melody and Melissa a new Gramophone for Christmas, they made me a bona fide member of their household. Such gay parties and receptions the sisters held in those days. Their lovely home, not far north of the river, on Chestnut Street, attracted socialites, businessmen, and general rounders—a most eclectic mix of Chicago's young people. At the sisters' New Year's Eve reception, I met a promising young man, Charles Dale Andrews, Jr. Dale, as everyone called him, worked as a teller in his father's bank, First Chicago National.

By March, Dale and I had become enamored to the point of serious involvement. One Friday he sent a hansom to bring me to the bank before our planned evening of dinner and a performance of *Richard III* at the Haymarket Theatre.

It was my first visit to his place of employment, and I arrived bearing the mink muff he had purchased for me only two weeks earlier, on the occasion of our still-secret betrothal. My boot heels clicked on the polished marble floor as I made my way toward the stately tellers' booths lining the high-ceilinged room. Dale spotted me before I saw him and hurried out to greet me, his posture more erect than usual, his brilliantined russet hair combed to a tidy swoop.

Dale's appeal lay more in his generous and carefree nature than in his appearance. His arms and legs were too lanky for his compact torso, and his nose was so narrow and delicate it resembled a piece of porcelain. Eyeglasses lent him a studious look and also a certain self-consciousness. You see, he fancied himself the dashing and debonair type: Upon first being introduced to anyone, he would yank off his glasses before offering his customary hail-fellow handshake.

Dale helped me off with my coat and cupped his hand under my elbow. "Darling, I'm so glad you could come around."

Directing me to the bank of tellers' windows, Dale introduced me to the other tellers, who showed the deference due to the bank president's son.

"Come," he said, "we must say hello to Father."

Dale escorted me up the wide spiral staircase to the sanctuary of offices on the second floor. He paused in the hallway and whispered, "Soon, I'll have an office on this floor, too."

I circled my hand around his arm. "I have every confidence in you. Your fellow employees obviously hold you in high esteem."

He smiled and showed me to the solid wooden door with his father's brass nameplate. Rapping gently at the door, he called, "Father, may I come in?"

Dale opened the door and opened his hand, directing me to enter first.

I greeted Dale's father, whom I had met only three weeks earlier, at a reception in their home, with a smile. "Hello, Mr. Andrews. I hope you are well."

The plump Mr. Andrews, who was obviously not only well, but well indulged, rose from behind a six-foot-square desk and lumbered around. His fleshy cheeks congealed into a diffident smile. "Yes, and you, Miss Davidson?"

I offered my hand. "Fine, thank you, sir. Dale has been kind enough to show me around your very impressive establishment."

"Ah, yes, we do our best."

Dale stepped up beside me. "Well, Father, I've closed out my window for the day."

"And where are you two young people off to this evening?" Mr. Andrews directed his gaze at Dale, and I detected the same knotting of his eyebrows I'd observed upon our last encounter. Mr. Andrews either did not approve of me or found his only son disappointing in some way.

A little later that evening, I discovered that both were true. We had just finished our dinners at the Silversmith Restaurant when Dale scratched his forehead and said, "I believe I'll speak with Father about my promotion tomorrow."

"And do you suppose you'll meet with success?"

He shook his head, as if considering a weighty proposition. "I can't hazard a guess. He probably intends to torture me a little longer, even though he's promised me the post."

"Oh, I doubt he means to torture you."

Dale fingered the bowl of his Cognac glass. "You don't know him very well."

I gave him my kindest smile. "Perhaps you should come at it in a roundabout way. Find out his intentions before you ask outright."

"I'm tired of waiting at his pleasure. And keeping quiet about our engagement. Once I get the promotion, we can tell Mother and Father and set the date."

"There's no rush, my dear. They've only just met me."

"I believe they'd like to keep me in the house forever."

"Perhaps it would be best to give them more time to get to know me."

"The thing is, they haven't approved of a single young lady I've introduced them to. I suspect Father wouldn't be happy unless I married the mayor's daughter."

"All the more reason for a long engagement."

Dale raised his eyebrows. "How long?"

I reached out and squeezed his hand. "Perhaps a year. Give me some time to win them over."

"I don't give a deuce about winning them over."

"You don't mean that."

"I do. There's no pleasing them, especially Father. I don't care what he thinks about you. Sooner or later, he needs to understand you're the one I'm marrying."

"Let's at least wait until you've received your promotion."

Dale swooped his cigarette close to his mouth and held it there. "I won't wait forever." He inhaled deeply and forced out a narrow draft of smoke.

>‹

A few weeks later, in mid-April, Dale invited me for Saturday dinner at his family's home. He said he intended to announce our engagement that evening. I urged restraint and patience, but Dale insisted he'd burst if he tried to keep our secret one day longer. I had little choice but to acquiesce and brought out my most modest dress for the occasion, a turquoise-blue gown with a high-necked lace collar.

The Andrewses lived on the Near North Side of Chicago, a short carriage ride from Melody and Melissa's, in a handsome two-story brick house large enough to entertain a crowd of forty. The home had a distinctively unpleasant odor, like a combination of mothballs, mold, and overused perfume.

Mrs. Andrews welcomed me in the entranceway with kisses directed at the air around my cheeks and escorted me to the parlor to join the menfolk for "a spot of sherry before dinner." What a profile the woman made—her hefty bosoms might have toppled her, save for the solid hips that counterbalanced them. Mr. Andrews was also portly, carrying perhaps forty pounds around his midriff. I wondered if Dale would balloon to similar proportions in his advanced years, a prospect that did not please me.

"Darling, hello," said Dale, coming up to me and kissing my forehead.

As Dale came around to my side, I turned to Mr. Andrews. "Hello, sir. Thank you for having me to your lovely home."

The maid served our sherry, and we seated ourselves, by couples, on two separate sofas.

Mrs. Andrews addressed me. "Pauline, we've never had a chance for a proper visit. Tell me, where is it you're from?"

"A small town in Michigan's Upper Peninsula, Menominee. It's on Lake Michigan and well known for its shipping."

"And what is your family's business there?"

I had told Dale all this, though I hadn't been able to bring myself to admit that my brother worked at a lumber mill. Still, it appeared Dale hadn't told his parents. Or perhaps they wanted to hear it directly from me. "My father is deceased, but my brother is in the mining business."

"Oh," said Mrs. Andrews, flattening a hand over her heart. "I didn't know about your father."

"It's been quite a few years now. Though I still miss him."

Mr. Andrews pulled his vest down over his belly. "Yes, well, it seems everyone from the U.P. is either in mining or lumber. Do you know that it was lumber from the U.P. that rebuilt this city after the Great Fire?"

"Oh, yes, it's quite a booming industry there. I have some relatives in lumber, too," I said. After all, Maman's cousin did supervise at Spies Lumber.

We soon retired to the dining room and took our places around a well-appointed oak table with carved claw feet. Imagining the three of them seated around that vast table for breakfasts, luncheons, and suppers, I sympathized with Dale's desire to make a separate life for himself as soon as possible. Everything about this room—its fat-legged furniture, the burgundy velvet wallpaper, the sour odor of old carpets—set my teeth to aching.

The maid served a spring-vegetable soup from a tureen on the sideboard and exited through the swinging door off the dining room. The door had barely ceased its whooshing when Dale picked up his spoon and said, "Mother, Father, Pauline and I are to be married."

Mrs. Andrews cocked her head at Dale. "Really? Well, this is a pleasant surprise." But of course what she meant was that it was an unpleasant surprise. She turned and stretched her hand across the center of the table toward me, though we could never have touched across the expanse. "I'm so pleased, Pauline. We really must become better acquainted."

Which meant that she didn't like me one bit and didn't judge the prospects for liking me in the future to be very good. I put my spoon down and imitated the stretch of her hand. "I shall look forward to that."

Mr. Andrews's face had lost a few shades of pink, but he managed to suck his belly in enough to reach his wineglass and raise it toward Dale and then me. "Congratulations, son. May you two be very happy."

I believe Dale was the only happy member of our foursome that evening. The prospect of relinquishing their only child to me obviously did not thrill Mr. and Mrs. Andrews. And, to my chagrin, Dale had not yet secured his promotion. The only blemish on Dale's happiness that evening was my announcement that we'd decided on an engagement of at least a year.

⇥⇤

Two months later, with summer's warmth settling on Chicago, Claude Montcrief, the piano player from Carrie Watson's house, contacted me out of the blue with a business proposition. It seemed Claude had been approached by a mining engineer with a plan for making thousands in copper-mine stocks. Claude explained that they needed someone who was familiar with the Upper Peninsula and he'd thought of me. I will admit I was skeptical about the prospect of a lucrative business deal involving Upper Michigan's mines, but out of loyalty to Claude I agreed to explore the matter with him and the engineer.

We arranged to gather on a Tuesday evening at Fitzgerald and Moy's, one of Chicago's most opulent saloons. Claude met me at the door and escorted me across the tavern's multicolored tile floor to a back room that was no doubt typically occupied by poker players. The translucent plates of leaded glass lining the upper panels of the fifteen-square-foot room were interrupted only by the door we had entered and another door on the opposite wall. The tinkle of cutlery and glassware and the din of conversation sounded from the main room, and the closed-in space smelled of tobacco and cigar smoke.

"Pauline," Claude said after closing the door, "allow me to introduce Mr. Reed Dougherty."

Dougherty rose from his seat and bowed. "Miss Davidson, a pleasure to meet you."

"Likewise, Mr. Dougherty," I said.

Dougherty, a man of thirty to thirty-five with an angular frame, spoke in a silky baritone. He looked familiar, and it occurred to me I might have seen him at Carrie Watson's.

As I seated myself opposite him at the round, felt-covered table, Dougherty locked his penetrating dark-brown eyes on me—in the manner of an admirer first taking in my God-given beauty. He wore a navy-blue suit, an unadorned white shirt, and a slightly askew blue cravat, the sort of plain but respectable attire one might find on a country storekeeper. His large hands, as well groomed as a surgeon's but as muscular as those of a farmer, were quite at odds with his fine-featured cheekbones and straight-lined nose—all in all, a handsome face in a not-quite-classic but understated way. In fact, I found him an odd jumble of traits: savvy but not terribly refined in manner, as if he had accustomed himself to relying solely on intellect and grit; and light-handed in gesture but melancholy of expression, with his blade of a mustache waxed to a forlorn downturn.

"May I offer you a glass of port?" Dougherty asked, lifting a bottle and tipping it over a glass.

Claude and I joined Dougherty in his toast: "To our business. May it be profitable."

Dougherty eased his glass down and turned to Claude. "I trust we can speak confidentially?"

"As we agreed," said Claude.

Dougherty smiled at me. "All three of us?"

"Certainly," I said, studying Dougherty's shadowy, deep-set eyes.

Claude leaned toward me, reached under the table, and patted my hand. I knew my assistance in this matter meant a great deal to him. Upon greeting me at the door, he'd whispered confidentially: "Thank you for coming, Pauline. I sorely hope this deal works. I could do with a little extra cash just now."

Dougherty reached into a large envelope and pulled out a parchment of thick stock. He eased it across the table. "A sample certificate. For your inspection."

Claude slid the sheet toward me and brushed his fingertips over the embossed emblem at its top.

"*Certificate of Purchase, 100 shares of Hull Copper Company*," the title read. Below that a paragraph began with "*The bearer of these shares . . .*" I took in the paragraph about share ownership and surveyed the bottom of the page, which contained two signature lines, a blank one for the bearer and another signed with flourish by a Theodore X. Hull and dated that very day, June 16, 1888.

Dougherty leaned back in his chair. "All very legitimate in appearance, as you can see."

Claude nodded. "Yes, and will we be meeting the illustrious Mr. Hull?"

"There is no Mr. Hull. Nor is there a Hull Copper Company." Dougherty folded his hands on the table and pitched forward. His gaze slid over Claude before coming to rest on me. "It's just the three of us."

"Can you tell us a bit more, Mr. Dougherty," I asked, meeting his steadfast eye, "about how you propose we proceed?" Experience had taught me that his looks demonstrated more than a mere interest in my potential as a business partner.

"First I want to know that you are both with me on this. That I can count on your discretion and cooperation."

Claude shot me a what-do-you-say glance. I signaled him with the slightest of nods. He turned back to Dougherty. "Yes."

Dougherty looked to me, angling his eyebrows questioningly.

"You can count on my discretion," I said.

Dougherty drummed his fingers on the table. "You understand that what I propose is not exactly legal? But that it stands to yield handsomely?"

Claude brushed his palms together. "And can you assure us we won't be apprehended, Mr. Dougherty?"

Dougherty concentrated his brow. "I have thought this through down to the minutest detail. If you are willing to act quickly and decisively, we will all come out the richer. I propose a three-way split, after expenses."

Claude dipped his head and slapped his hand on the table, as heady as a poker player showing a royal flush. "Very well, then."

Dougherty drew his torso up stiff and straight, like a cat considering a pounce. "Are you both still with me?"

I took his exacting requests for confirmation as evidence of the gravity and also the momentous opportunity of his proposal. Not wanting to tarry or disappoint Claude, I said, "Yes, Mr. Dougherty, we have both said we are with you."

"Fine, fine. Then let me introduce our assistants." Dougherty rose, marched to the door behind him, and opened it slightly. "Ladies, would you kindly join us?"

In waltzed Rose and Sadie from Carrie Watson's house.

Dougherty said, "Miss Davidson, I believe you are acquainted with Miss Thomas and Miss Chesnick."

"How nice to see you," I said, nodding to each of them, "Rose, Sadie." The sight of these two did not please me. After leaving Carrie Watson's, I'd avoided any contact with the girls. Why Dougherty should bring them into this matter was beyond me.

Dougherty kept his eyes trained on me. "You know them from your employment at Carrie Watson's, correct? You once resided there, didn't you?"

"Mr. Dougherty," I said, summoning my firmest voice. "Are we here to do business with you, or do you have something else in mind?"

"I only wish to understand the nature of your acquaintance with Miss Thomas and Miss Chesnick."

"I don't see what that has to do with the matter before us."

Dougherty turned to Rose and Sadie. "Miss Davidson was at one time a resident of Carrie Watson's, was she not?"

Rose glanced at me and crossed her arms. "Most certainly. And the favorite of quite a few gentlemen."

At that, Dougherty called over his shoulder, "Mr. Andrews, you may come in now."

The rear door to the room swung open, and Dale and his father burst into the room, whereupon all hell broke loose.

*P*inkerton detective Reed Dougherty had a roomful of people to answer to that night at Fitzgerald and Moy's: my loving fiancé, Dale, trying to get close enough to punch him; Dale's father, staving him off; Rose and Sadie, beholding the scene with devilish amusement; and a puzzled Claude, shooting questioning looks at everyone.

Dale leaned toward Dougherty, stiffened his arms, and knotted his hands into tight fists. "What's the meaning of this? How dare you treat a lady so rudely."

Dougherty stood and faced Dale, cocking his head attentively. "I beg your pardon, sir. But it's better the truth comes out before rather than after you've been hornswoggled."

Dale flared his nostrils. "What truth? How do I know you haven't paid these ladies?"

"She greeted them by name," said Dougherty. "She betrayed herself."

Claude, slapping his palms on the table, asked Dougherty, "What's going on here?"

Dougherty held a palm up toward Claude. "Patience, please, Mr. Montcrief."

Dale's father tightened his grip on Dale's arm and tugged him away from Dougherty. "Son, calm yourself."

Dougherty turned to Rose and Sadie, who stood in the corner giggling and flouncing their skirts like tattling schoolgirls. "We don't need to detain you ladies any longer."

Although I suspect they would have been thrilled to stay and observe the hoopla, they shuffled up to Dougherty. Rose offered him her hand. "I trust we'll see you soon, Mr. Dougherty."

"Yes, of course, Miss Thomas. Good evening, ladies."

Rose and Sadie sauntered toward the door, and as they exited Rose tossed me a smug leer.

Dale maneuvered close to Dougherty again, sloughing off his father's grip. "You'll see them soon? Are you in cahoots with them?"

Dale's father put his hand on his son's shoulder. "Son, it's not just that."

"What is it, then, Father?"

"She agreed to sell fake stock certificates. You heard her."

Claude jumped up out of his chair and shook a finger at Dougherty. "You sneaking bastard, you tricked me. You used me."

Dougherty jiggled his head, as if to chastise. "Please, Mr. Montcrief, there's no call for that."

Claude pounded a fist on the table. "If you dare to arrest me, you'll have Miss Watson to answer to."

"Don't worry," said Dougherty, "I intend you no harm. You are free to leave."

"Completely free?" Claude asked, his face etched in disbelief.

"Nothing more need be said of your involvement in this matter."

Claude leaned over and said to me, "I'm sorry, Pauline," and hurried out of the room.

Dale yanked away from his father's hold and said, "Can't you stay out of my affairs?"

All this time I'd been observing the commotion and sizing up the situation. Dale's father had obviously hired Dougherty to upend our engagement. But, worst of all, I faced the threat of being charged with selling fake certificates. I deduced that extricating myself from this predicament required that I first concede the engagement. Taking in a deep breath to still my pounding heart, I rose and directed my remarks to Dougherty and the elder Mr. Andrews. "Gentlemen, I understand you wish Dale to break off our engagement. Out of respect and consideration for him, I will allow him to do so."

Dale rushed to my side and clutched my hand. "No, Pauline."

"Dale, this pains me, too. I'm truly sorry." I turned to go, but Dale only gripped my hand tighter.

Mr. Andrews stepped toward Dale. "Let her go, son."

Dale glared at his father.

"Dale," I said, "you must release me."

He let go of my hand. I kissed him on the cheek, nodded to Dougherty and Mr. Andrews, and departed, holding my head high and concentrating on taking smooth, even steps.

＊

The next morning, I sent a message to Mr. Andrews at the bank, requesting a two o'clock meeting with him to discuss the urgent matter of his son's reputation.

Right on schedule, Mr. Andrews appeared at the Palmer House meeting room I had reserved—a green-and-gold-wallpapered room with no windows, a twenty-foot-long conference table, and plush swiveling chairs.

The coffee service I'd ordered awaited us in a silver pot. I poured two cups and invited him to join me at the table.

He took a seat across the corner of the table from me and pushed his chair back, as if to keep a safe distance. "Miss Davidson, I am a busy man. I trust this won't take long."

"I assure you, sir, I, too, would rather be elsewhere."

He took a sip of coffee, replaced the cup in its saucer, and shoved his coffee away. "What is this about my son's reputation?"

I stirred my coffee, studying how the rich cream swirled into the brew and turned it a caramel color. "Did it ever occur to you that in ruining my reputation you have jeopardized his as well?"

"Marrying you wouldn't exactly enhance his position."

"Doesn't honor make any provision for a young lady trying to turn honest and respectable?"

"It certainly makes no provision for dealing in fake stocks."

"That is not the question." I brought the coffee cup to my lips and tipped some of the warm liquid into my mouth.

"Then what is?" He leaned forward. I detected a quiver in his jowls. "I'll not be threatened by you."

"Naturally, there will be questions about why Dale and I have broken off."

"So you *are* threatening me."

I cupped my hands together over my breastbone. "I am merely asking you to consider this: You have caused your son to breach his promise of marriage. One moment I am happily engaged, and the next . . ."

Mr. Andrews's cheeks reddened. "Tell me what you want and let's get this over with."

"I would like twenty thousand dollars and assurances that you and your detective will say nothing of what happened last night."

"Or what, Miss Davidson?" He scrunched his thick eyebrows together.

"Or I will let it be known exactly why the engagement broke off. And where your son met his fiancée." Of course Dale and I had actually met at Melody and Melissa's, but I divined that intimating we had met at Carrie Watson's would compel him to quickly accede to my request.

He looked down his nose at me and tightened his expression into a glare. Did he fail to grasp the seriousness of his circumstances?

Lowering my voice to a discreet murmur, I said, "I should prefer to spare all of us the publicity of a breach-of-promise lawsuit."

He squinted his eyes at me like a judge considering a plea. "And if I give you twenty thousand dollars, will you assure me that'll be the end of the matter?"

"Yes."

He stared at me as if he wished I would disappear. Abruptly he grabbed his hat off the table. "Very well, come by my office tomorrow afternoon, at one-fifteen. No earlier and no later. I will arrange for Dale to be out then."

"Fine, at one-fifteen."

He rose, headed for the door, and swung his girth around. "And you will agree to have no further contact with Dale."

"That is understood, sir."

He shook his hat at me. "If you fail to keep any part of this agreement, you'll very much regret it."

"I have every intention of honoring our agreement, Mr. Andrews."

>＜

But it wasn't Mr. Andrews I found in his office the next day. Detective Reed Dougherty sat at his desk, looking for all the world as if he owned it—his slender frame sunken into Mr. Andrews's oversized leather chair and a leg splayed over his knee. Like a chameleon, he'd switched his attire to that of a businessman: He sported a steel-gray suit, matching vest with mother-of-pearl buttons, and a black necktie with a perfectly symmetrical knot. His presence made me wonder: Could Mr. Andrews be balking at our deal? Surely he wouldn't risk a lawsuit, to say nothing of a scandal, merely to see me charged with some trumped-up crime.

"Miss Davidson, we meet again," Dougherty said, not even rising to greet me. "Please, have a seat."

"Mr. Dougherty," I said, "a pleasure, I'm sure."

Once I'd seated myself, Dougherty rolled his chair up close to the desk and snapped to alert. He opened a drawer, extracted a bulky envelope, and handed it to me. "My client asked me to convey this to you."

The envelope bore my name, but no other markings.

"Please, open it," he said. "Be sure you're satisfied with the contents."

I lifted the envelope's unsealed flap and pulled out two stacks of crisp bills secured with paper bands. Dougherty likely wanted to see me drool and count, but I merely thumbed the bills of one stack, assuring myself they were all hundreds and sufficient in number to sum to twenty thousand dollars. "Yes, this is as agreed."

"Mr. Andrews asked me to arrange one more detail." He tilted his head back and studied me through the bottoms of his shifty eyes.

How, I mused, could I have ever found this man the least bit appealing? I slipped the bills back into the envelope and met his gaze.

"I'm to escort you directly to the train station."

"You expect me to leave town?"

"That's the general idea."

"Without my belongings?"

"With whatever you have on your person. And the money, of course."

"And what am I to tell my friends?"

"Tell them whatever you like. It's your choice: Take the money and leave town, or don't take the money and leave town."

Mr. Dougherty, who is not lacking in confidence, had a barouche waiting outside the bank for us. He escorted me to it, opened the door, and held out his oafish hand. I placed my hand lightly atop his and, holding myself erect and balanced, stepped up into the carriage.

Dougherty settled opposite me in the roomy compartment. I leaned back against the black leather seat, withdrawing from the window's view, and said, "This was your idea, wasn't it?"

Dougherty curled his fingers and studied his nails. "Only advising my client on what's in his best interest."

"And do you think it's a crime for a girl to try to lift herself out of poverty?"

Dougherty checked the nails on his other hand, as if trying to annoy me with his blasé manner. "How you got to Carrie Watson's is no concern of mine."

"You're no stranger to the place, either. I knew the minute I laid eyes on you I'd seen you there."

Dougherty swung one of his long legs over the other. "Mr. Pinkerton understands it's all in the line of work. I specialize in lady criminals."

"Your association with Miss Watson compromises your own legitimacy."

"I, unlike you, have nothing to hide."

"Do you think I'm ashamed of trying to help my poor widowed mother?"

"One would hope you'd stay within the bounds of the law in doing so."

"And printing up fake stock certificates—is that within the law?"

"I do what is required to meet my clients' needs."

"You may be a Pinkerton, but you're not above the law. One of these days, some judge will instruct you accordingly."

"So far, every judge I've crossed paths with has been more interested in apprehending the criminals than the crime-stoppers."

"And the engagement of a girl trying to better herself is a grievous crime, indeed."

"Come, come, Miss Davidson, I suspect you never intended to marry Mr. Andrews."

"That, Mr. Dougherty, is a matter of the heart beyond even your fine investigative powers."

He threw his head back and chuckled. "You've got about as much heart as any other whore."

"I suspect the size of my heart far exceeds yours." His oily voice and manner of superiority rankled to the bone. "And I suppose you're proud of yourself. Proud of making a career of outmaneuvering women who are disadvantaged by their gentle sex."

"Gentleness is not something I'd accuse you of."

"And you are certainly no gentleman. Does your mother have any idea of your despicable line of work?"

"I also have a poor and widowed mother. I'm confident she approves of my profession, which is something we can't say about your mother."

"You have no idea whatsoever of my mother's circumstances."

This invigorating exchange ended at the train station, where I boarded the Chicago & Northwestern for points north, hoping to never again set eyes on Reed Dougherty. But that was not to be.

# MY FIRST DIAMONDS

·

MILWAUKEE AND MENOMINEE—

JUNE–NOVEMBER 1888

By the time the train pulled into Milwaukee, I had devised a plan for reassembling my belongings, as well as my composure. I posted a letter to Melissa and Melody, with a hundred-dollar bill inserted, explaining that an urgent family matter had necessitated travel to Milwaukee: Would they please purchase a portmanteau and pack and ship my personal effects to the Plankinton Hotel on Grand Avenue?

To assuage the sting of a broken engagement and my untimely dislodgment from Chicago, I purchased a few essentials: undergarments and a petticoat; two new day dresses and an evening gown; an ivory hairbrush set; some tortoise-shell hair combs; and a pair of French-kid shoes. Yes, Milwaukee's merchants separated quite a few of my hundred-dollar bills from me. Then again, I couldn't stroll the halls and lobby of Milwaukee's finest hotel, the Plankinton, day after day in the same dress, even if I did possess an envelope fat with cash.

I found Milwaukee a poor sister to Chicago, its lakefront mired with ships of trade and transport, the June weather just as muggy as Chicago's but without the cooling avenue breezes, and its shops second-rate by comparison. Wandering its downtown streets, I did discover five jewelers with fine enough wares, I hoped, to satisfy my yen for some special purchase. Though they were not as rich as Chicago's jewelry stores, choices still abounded, requiring multiple visits to three select shops. Should I settle for a jewel-studded brooch in the shape of a fan with matching earrings? Would a ruby-and-platinum filigree ring suffice to impress dinner companions? Did I require more instruction on the qualities of pearls before venturing the purchase of a pearl necklace? All my doubts and questions vanished one late-June morning upon a third visit to Ernst and Son Jewelers.

"Miss Davidson, we have a new item which may soon be released for sale. Come, let me show it to you." The elderly Mr. Ernst led me behind the counter, and as we passed the well-stocked glass cases he steadied his hunched torso by sliding a hand along the cases' oak frames. We were the only two in the store, save for the younger Mr. Ernst, who busied himself arranging the display in the front window. A bouquet of pastel-pink lilies graced a glass center table, permeating the store with sharply sweet aromas.

"Yes, yes," he muttered upon opening the door to his small office, "I daresay you'll find this of interest. Please, have a seat."

"How kind of you to think of me," I said, settling onto a simple wooden chair. Neat stacks of papers covered one side of his desk. He closed the door, and the room's mustiness overcame the showroom's lingering floral scent.

Mr. Ernst flicked the switch of his lamp, and its incandescent bulb lit up a fuzzy circle on the desktop. He eased down into his desk chair and tugged at a side drawer, opening it wide enough to pull out a flat case. Gripping the case with both hands, he set it down, then opened the cover and swiveled the case around and under the lamp's glow to reveal its contents.

I restrained a gasp. Against the case's black velvet interior, secured around a raised ridge, lay a gold necklace of seven yellow diamonds. The center diamond, a beveled rectangle, glistened in its thin-edged gold casing, and the three diamonds branching from each side of it decreased in size, but not luster, showing off the middle diamond like bridesmaids attending a bride. I had never before seen yellow diamonds, and the artful setting of these seven gems electrified me. Fingering the delicate gold chain, I said, "Yes, it's lovely. Quite unique."

"The middle diamond is ten carats, and the diamonds on each side sum to ten also. Thirty carats in perfect balance."

I pulled my head back to evaluate the effect. "Why, yes, I see what you mean."

"And yellow diamonds are, as I'm sure you know, much sought after. These are from South Africa."

"And what is the cost of this necklace?"

"If it should be released for sale, it will be thirty-eight hundred dollars."

"Oh, I'm afraid that's out of my range."

"I can't say for sure it will be put on the floor anyway."

"It is a private sale, then?"

"In a manner of speaking." He brushed his palms together. "I must work out some details with the former owner."

"Then I imagine some sadness attends this piece."

"Yes, Miss Davidson, you are so right."

"Well, I thank you for showing me. And if you should release it for sale, perhaps we can speak again."

I returned to the Plankinton for luncheon. There, seated in a plush, high-backed chair, under glistening crystal chandeliers, I imagined that necklace gracing my throat, playing off my emerald-green gown, and garnering admiring looks from the gentlemen and ladies strolling among the magnificent furnishings of the Plankinton's lobby and corridors.

Three days later, I returned to Ernst and Son. "Mr. Ernst, I happened to be in the neighborhood and thought I'd inquire about that lovely necklace."

Once we had settled comfortably in his back office, he said, "Your timing is superb, Miss Davidson. I have this very morning worked out the details of the sale."

"So it is for sale?"

"Yes, under one condition."

"I'm willing to entertain your condition, though I must say the price is still something of an impediment."

He pulled the necklace case out of his drawer and flipped it open toward me. "You will never find another necklace like this, I can assure you."

I resisted the urge to glance at the piece and instead studied him. "And the condition?"

"The buyer must agree not to wear it in Milwaukee."

I brushed a hand over the middle diamond. The piece was as beautiful as I remembered. "Really? How unusual."

"Yes, I'm inclined to agree with you." Mr. Ernst braced an arm on his chair and shifted his weight.

"May I ask the reason for this condition?"

"It's a sad story, I'm afraid." He scratched at his fuzzy gray sideburn. "A personal tragedy."

I leaned back and gazed at him, but he offered no elaboration. "I don't mean to pry, sir, but if I am to seriously consider such a significant purchase, I should like to understand the grounds for the condition."

"A reasonable request," he nodded. "But I must ask for your discretion in this matter."

"Of course, I would hate to deepen the sadness surrounding it."

He braced his elbows on the desk and leaned over them. "The owner, whose name I cannot reveal, recently lost his wife. She died quite unexpectedly, of the galloping pneumonia, after a trip abroad on which he had surprised her with this very piece. Now the poor gentleman can't look at the necklace without the most painful of memories. He wishes to sell it and never again lay eyes on it. And he demands that the sale be conducted privately."

Mr. Ernst had held his story back so long, and then told it so earnestly, that I questioned its veracity. I was willing to wager the piece was stolen. "The poor gentleman," I said. "I can altogether understand the sentiment behind his wishes."

"I don't believe he would have wanted me to say as much as I have. I trust you will not repeat his sad story, or the circumstances under which you learned of it."

"No, I wouldn't dream of it," I said, determined to test my theory. "But I honestly can't afford to pay more than twenty-eight hundred dollars for this piece."

Mr. Ernst stroked the loose flap of skin sagging from his neck. "I'm afraid I cannot sell it for such a low price."

"What a shame. I might perhaps be the perfect buyer. As you know, I'm only stopping briefly in Milwaukee. And am unlikely to ever spend much time in Wisconsin."

"Yes, well, there's something to be said for that." He wove his fingers together. "Would you consider bringing your price up a bit. Perhaps to thirty-two hundred?"

I pinched my mouth into a thoughtful pucker and studied the piece. "If you will meet me halfway, at three thousand, I can assure the utmost secrecy in this matter."

And so I turned someone else's sorrow—or knavery—into my own immeasurable delight. Despite the expense, I have never regretted the purchase. That necklace returned every cent invested in it, and more.

After eleven leisurely days in Milwaukee I received my portmanteau from Chicago, checked out of the Plankinton Hotel, and continued the train journey to my dear family in Menominee.

> <

In the ensuing months, the compensation I'd received from Mr. Andrews slipped through my fingers as freely as fine grains of Lake Michigan sand. What reason did I have to squirrel away the money? After all, life is a carnival, and I could well afford the price of admission.

My most satisfying purchase was the Menominee home I bought for Maman, Paul, and Gene. Maman's gratitude was well worth the fifty-eight hundred dollars it cost. When I brought her around to see it before closing the sale, she exclaimed, "Oh, May, it's a dream come true," and threw her arms around me. Paul, of course, inquired about how I could afford the purchase of such a fine house, and I had to explain my heartbreak over Dale's breach of our engagement and how his father, the cause of the breach, had at least had the decency to recognize the damage he'd done to my reputation. The whole family rallied around me that summer of 1888, and I in turn took delight in procuring Queen Anne furnishings and some lovely oil paintings for their new home.

Five months after I left Chicago, my funds had dwindled to a dangerously low level, and Menominee presented no means of fattening my purse, let alone affording a modicum of entertainment. How tedious the ticking of the great mantel clock became, how wearisome Paul's constant prodding about how I should be managing my funds, how musty the house's shut-in air. I craved new adventure.

Our family had finished Thanksgiving dinner and retired to the parlor when I announced, "It's time for me to move on. I believe I'll go west, to Portland."

"Whatever for?" Maman asked, as if I'd proposed joining the circus.

"To replenish my funds."

Paul huffed, "Don't know why you piddled away what you had."

"How I spend my money is my own affair. I have been generous with this family." What Paul didn't know or wished not to acknowledge was that his job at the lumber mill couldn't last forever. Sooner or later, he and the whole family would be dependent on me, though I knew better than to hurt his pride by laying that reality before him. The kindest course was to let him consider himself the family's mainstay as long as possible.

True to form, he said, "Don't count on me sending you any money."

"I wouldn't dream of it."

"Like that fool Rob Jacobsen did."

Maman's eyes darted from me to Paul. "Robby Jacobsen? What's he got to do with this?"

"Maybe May will explain that for you," said Paul.

I cleared my throat. "Robby was under the mistaken impression that we were to be engaged, and that if he kept me in an allowance I would become his wife."

"That's not how I heard it," said Paul.

"You can listen to rumors from people who don't know my personal affairs, or you can believe me."

"Oh, don't go, May," Maman said. "You belong here, with your family."

"I don't want you going, either," said Gene. "It's boring when you're not here."

I wasn't surprised to hear this from an eleven-year-old whose older brother harangued him endlessly about his lessons and chores, though I wished he hadn't said it in front of Paul, who crossed his legs, leaned back in his chair, and said to Gene, "It's probably just as well. Give you more time to do your lessons."

Maman said, "But Portland is so far away."

I reached for her hand. "But how can I help you in Menominee? It simply doesn't afford the opportunities of a larger city."

Maman pulled her hand away. "I'd rather have stayed in the old house with you than in this new house without you."

"Oh, Maman, I'll visit. I promise."

"How can you visit from way out there?"

"Just let her go," said Paul. "She'll do whatever she damn well pleases anyway."

I assured all of them, even Paul, that I would hold them close to my heart, write often, and always consider their well-being.

Before I left, I took Maman aside and showed her my new diamond necklace. "You mustn't tell anyone about it. It's one of the secret spoils of my broken engagement."

She couldn't resist trying it on. And then she hugged me. "My goodness, May, I guess you *do* know how to take care of yourself."

# THE TRIAL

## THE VALUE OF A DOLLAR

·

### MENOMINEE—JANUARY 24, 1917

When Alvah Sawyer called Frank back to the stand on day three of the trial, I prepared myself for more shilly-shallying.

"Miss Shaver, we haven't talked much about you."

Frank folded her hands in her lap, pretending at a humility we both knew was altogether alien to her. "No, sir."

"Can you tell us about your parents and your upbringing?"

"I was born in Pittsburgh and am an only child. My father was in property development, and my mother's father was a banker. They ran in circles that hosted dinners for well-off families and served lovely feasts and French wines. You could say I grew up surrounded by generous and wealthy families."

I noticed Frank was taking pains to put on the proper parlance of her upbringing, which she rarely used in the parlors or dining halls, to say nothing of the streets, of Menominee.

"And did you have to worry about money when you were growing up?"

"Oh, no, I had everything I could want. My parents didn't show off their wealth, but I knew there was plenty of money and that someday I'd inherit it."

"So you believed money would never be a problem for you?"

"That's correct."

"You thought it was a bottomless pit, right?"

"Yes, I always thought there'd be money whenever I needed it."

"Did your family pay for your education?"

"Yes, after I graduated from the University of Pennsylvania they paid for my law schooling at the University of Michigan."

"And they helped you set up your practice in the Chicago area?"

"They helped me buy a home in Highland Park and sent me a three-thousand-dollar allowance until I started making a respectable income from my practice."

Where, I wondered, was she going with this—besides showing she could play Little Miss Proper and Innocent? Perhaps Sawyer had encouraged her to strike a virtuous demeanor.

"So there was never any question that money was there for you if you needed it?"

"No question whatsoever."

"Would it be correct to say that until the events of the last few years you didn't understand the value of a dollar and thought there was no limit to your family's resources?"

"Yes, that would be accurate."

I couldn't keep my jaw from dropping. This was her strategy? To claim that she didn't know the value of a dollar? That she believed her supply of money was unlimited? I stared at Frank; when she glanced my way, I rolled my eyes.

><

At the judge's urging, the pace picked up in the afternoon. Still, Frank's attorney explained that he was unlikely to complete his direct examination of her by the end of the day.

"Miss Shaver," began Sawyer, "you traveled with the Baroness to Hot Springs, Arkansas, early in 1913, correct?"

"Yes."

"And this was soon after your reconciliation with her?"

"Yes."

"And how did the Baroness impress you on this trip?"

"She was decked out in jewelry and a dress fit for a queen."

"Can you describe all this for us?"

"She wore a yellow-diamond necklace that she said was worth a hundred thousand dollars and a ring with two pear-shaped diamonds worth eight thousand. Her dress was royal blue with fancy gold filament woven into the front piece. And Tokyo's collar was made of platinum and lined with an ungodly number of diamonds."

"Who's Tokyo?"

"Her French bulldog."

The onlookers chuckled in amusement at Tokyo's introduction into the proceedings. Even I was grateful for the touch of levity.

"How many diamonds were in the collar?"

"More than I could count—six hundred and eighty-eight, according to May. She said she'd been offered twelve thousand dollars for the largest one."

"Did she make a point of telling you the value of these things?"

"She played coy at first, but, once I commented, she rattled off a string of high numbers that would've made anybody's head spin."

"And what conclusions did you draw about the Baroness's financial status at the time?"

"What she probably wanted me to conclude—that she was as wealthy as King Midas."

"And did this impression have any bearing on how you conducted your financial affairs with the Baroness?"

"It sure did. I assumed she didn't need my money, except for short-term use, and that she'd return everything she borrowed and be as generous with me as I'd been with her."

"She led you to believe your friendship was a permanent and secure one, didn't she?"

"Yes."

I couldn't see what in the world Frank's wishes for a permanent friendship had to do with her financial claims, but since the judge called for a brief recess at that point, Sawyer had little opportunity to pursue the matter.

# THE WILDS OF PORTLAND

·

*I*n December of 1888, I took the train to Portland and arrived to find a city redolent of mud, fresh mist, and the tang of fresh-sawed timber. During my stay at Carrie Watson's, one of the girls had mentioned she'd spent a year at a reputable establishment in Portland run by Emma Black. So upon my arrival I presented myself to Miss Black, who kindly offered me a position, thus assuring me of a healthy income and a comfortable vantage point for learning the lay of the land in my new city.

Having no idea how long I might reside at Emma Black's, I set about cultivating my relations with the other girls. One shapely twenty-eight-year-old, Sue Marie Littleton, appeared especially receptive to my sisterly overtures. She was uncommonly tall, a commanding five nine, with almond-shaped eyes, a wide, expressive mouth, and a statuesque neck. She barely bothered to tame her fox-red hair, securing the mass of it at the back of her head and leaving stray strands dangling deliciously about her temples, ears, and neck. Whenever I spied her entertaining in the parlor, be it with other girls or some of the gentlemen, she gamely invited me to join the group, smiling and regaling all of us with the self-assured presence of the actress she had formerly been.

One April day, when the sun had consented to show its bright face in Portland, I invited her for a walk. As we strolled down Broadway, Sue Marie tilted her hat to shade her face from the sun's rays. Looking to me, she said, "Such a dainty parasol."

"I purchased it in Chicago."

"Your wardrobe could turn a princess green," she said, lacing the words with her homey Kentucky curl. "Chicago must have gone down easy with you."

"It's a fine city. I hated leaving it."

"Why did you leave?"

"Why else? Heartbreak."

Sue Marie cackled. "Not *your* heart?"

"A young man broke off an engagement with me. I couldn't bear the city after that."

"Oh, do tell the story."

I liked Sue Marie, I truly did, and I sensed that we had much in common, but I wasn't ready to bare my soul. "It's not terribly interesting. And what about you? I've often wondered why you gave up the stage."

"That was ages ago."

"I don't doubt you have great talent."

"Ah," she said, tossing her head to the side, "you'd be right at home on the stage yourself."

I twirled my parasol. "I prefer to act on the stage of life."

"Well, tickle me, aren't we two peas in a pod," said Sue Marie, taking my arm. "As for the theater, top billing and good pay only go to the cream of the crop, and, believe me, they have to scrape their way up. Besides, I'm after more money than that."

It was my turn to laugh. "I understand altogether."

We approached the corner of Broadway and Salmon, and she steered us onto Salmon, under the shade of the trees' limey-green leaves. "How'd you like to be my partner?"

"Partner in what?"

"In finding a pot of gold."

"How do you propose we do that?"

"First by saving enough money to dress like royalty." Sue Marie flicked her hand, as if to say, the rest is obvious.

"Ah, my father always said: 'It takes money to impress money.'"

She tipped her face toward mine. "We'd make a good team."

"You're serious, aren't you?"

"As a preacher in the pulpit."

"Then," said I, "two peas in a pod we shall be." And so began my saga with Sue Marie.

The clientele at Emma Black's wasn't as uniformly distinguished as that of Carrie Watson's in Chicago, but Sue Marie and I hoped that patience with what Portland had to offer would reward us in the long run. There was one particular fellow at Emma Black's, however, whom I wish I'd never met, a physician by the name of Dr. Willard Farnhardt. Willard had a clear white complexion such as any woman would envy, but on him it looked sallow and ghostly. His eyes were sunk deep into his sharp-boned face and darted about like bats in flight. Lanky he was, nearly to the point of emaciation. The first evening I ever dined by his side, over the house's home-cooked dinner, I observed him picking at his beef roast, drawing a few sinews to his mouth, and chewing laboriously. I came to suspect that his preferred nourishment was not meat, nor even liquor, but cocaine.

By November of 1889, Willard's attentions had not only turned from amorous to matrimonial but taken on frightening proportions. He had issued an ultimatum: If I did not agree to leave Emma Black's and become his bride, his life would be unbearable, his actions unaccountable. He expected an answer once and for all on the third Saturday in November. All day I dreaded his visit, and, as if in sympathy, the weather took a turn for the worse. The temperature plummeted to freezing, and arrows of icy sleet buffeted the house's windows.

Willard greeted me in the main parlor, his gaunt physique clad in a black suit, scoop-front waistcoat, and stiff white shirt with sharp, winged openings at the collar. During dinner with all the other girls and gentleman guests, his mood remained decidedly dour, despite my efforts to cheer him or, at the least, entice him to join the conversation.

An *Oregonian* reporter launched our dinnertime discussion with news of the Nickel-in-a-Slot, a music machine that had just been unveiled in San Francisco; Willard scoffed at everyone's enthusiasm for the new invention. When talk turned to Jack the Ripper's depravity, I asked him to venture an opinion on the ripper's psychical state. He merely snorted. While several of the other gentlemen speculated about whether Nellie Bly—who had just interrupted her journey to visit Jules Verne—really could make it around the world in less than eighty days, I jested he should join their wager. And when Miss Black recommended a book she'd just read—*A Study in Scarlet*, with the brilliant detective Sherlock Holmes—I inquired as to his reading preferences.

He took none of this bait and offered only whispered asides to me—about how fetching I looked in my midnight-blue gown, how much he looked forward to our private time together, and how he intended to shower his new bride with gems of all shapes and sizes. After dinner, he declined to join the other gentlemen for cigars over a few rounds of poker and instead approached the maid who collected the evening's fees and escorted me up the stairs to my bedroom.

He retracted the wick on my lantern until it dimmed to a dull flicker, removed a flask from his vest pocket, and gulped greedily from it. With a haughty laugh, he said, "That, I assure you, is the last time I will hand money over for the pleasure of your company."

In the darkened room I could not read his expression, but my heart galloped at the foreboding in his words. "Please, Willard, let's enjoy each other's company and not worry about the future."

"But the future is exactly what this is about, my dear. Have you forgotten I asked for your answer tonight?"

"No, not forgotten. Only hoped that you would understand the impossibility of what you propose."

"Impossible? Why ever is my proposal impossible?"

"Because you're a gentleman, and it wouldn't be right for us to consider any other arrangement."

"That, my dear, is not your concern. What you consider impossible is within your reach. How can you refuse the life I offer?"

"I'm not meant for such a life."

"Do you dare to refuse me?" He backed up against my window. "Will you cast me out into the cold world by denying my heart's only desire?"

"No, I will happily see you every night. But I do not wish to marry."

He unlatched the window and flung it open. Cold wind and sleet blasted into the room and whipped the sheer, lacy curtains into contorted whorls. My dresser lamp flared and died. His spindly torso twisted and turned, silhouetted in the window against the street lamps' hazy glow.

Chilled, I hugged myself. "Willard, what are you doing?"

He climbed onto the windowsill. "You mean everything to me. Do you see that now?"

"Please, this is foolish. Come down." I hastened toward the door, fear shooting through my veins like a lightning charge.

"Do you still refuse me?"

"Not you, I don't refuse you. Only your offer of marriage."

A wild-eyed grimace flitted across his face as he turned from me and—I could hardly believe my eyes—leapt from the window. A dull thud and bleating wail sounded from the street below.

"No," I screamed. I flung my door open and ran down the stairs. "Miss Black, Miss Black," I called, desperate to find her and only vaguely aware that I might be upsetting everyone who saw me rush through the central parlor, the sitting room, and finally the kitchen, where I found her. "Miss Black, there's been a terrible accident. Dr. Farnhardt jumped from my window."

The rest of that night was a blear of panic and disorder. Miss Black took command of the situation, ordering one of the maids to run for a doctor and another to contact the police commissioner. The doctor reported Willard had broken both his legs in the fall and summoned an ambulance to transport him to the hospital. Commissioner Eagleton interviewed me in Miss Black's presence, assuring her that he considered the incident a curious mishap and nothing more. Then he left to check on Dr. Farnhardt's condition—"both of body and mind," he said, winking at Miss Black.

After the commissioner departed, Miss Black and I were left alone in her parlor office. "Pauline, this is a most upsetting state of affairs. Everyone is shaken up—all the girls, our clients, and me, too. I do not need this kind of attention."

"I'm terribly sorry, I truly am. I did everything I could to reason with him."

"You should have come to me earlier, as soon as he announced he intended to marry you at any cost. I do have some experience in these matters."

"Yes, miss." I cast my gaze downward. "I've learned a lesson."

"I should hope so. This is a business, a business that requires tact and discretion, and you have failed me on both counts."

"I understand. It will never happen again, I promise."

"You will keep me informed of any such problems in the future."

"Yes, miss."

"And one more thing. Your dressmaking debt is unacceptably large. You are to place no new orders, and I will hold back five dollars a week until your debt is settled. Is that understood?"

I nodded, though I knew my sojourn at Miss Black's was fast coming to an end.

It was after midnight when I retreated to my room. Sue Marie brought up a steaming pitcher of water and helped me out of my gown, petticoat, and undergarments and into bed. She cleansed my face, neck, and arms with a warm cloth, soothing me all the time. "There, there, your Sue Marie'll take care of you."

"I've annoyed Miss Black," I said, looking up at her.

Sue Marie held up the covers and nestled in bed alongside me. "Don't worry. Anybody could see Farnhardt's scales are tipped."

I closed my eyes. "I keep seeing him flying out of my window."

"What a fool. You should have seen him lying on the ground, bellowing like a calving cow."

"He jumped because of me."

"It wasn't your fault," Sue Marie said, nuzzling my head into the crook of her neck.

I brushed my mouth over her neck. Pulling herself up on an elbow, she lowered her face to mine and kissed my cheeks, eyelids, and lips. She slipped her hand down over my breasts and abdomen to between my thighs. Her fingers stroked and tingled me until, becalmed by the tenderest caresses I had ever known, I fell asleep in her embrace.

# SAN FRANCISCO'S CHARMS

·

*T*hree days later, Sue Marie and I departed Portland—ahead of schedule and behind on savings.

As our train chugged into San Francisco on a dull gray November afternoon, it dawned on me that I'd arrived at yet another outpost of our vast country. I had assumed I'd find a metropolis greatly enriched by the gold in California's hills, but this was a city still seeking its way into the future. Compared with Chicago's glimmering buildings of fresh brick, clean-cut stone, and wide windows, San Francisco's hodgepodge of wooden storefronts and blocky one-, two-, and three-story structures appeared as tattered and ready to ignite as parched tinder. And whereas the signs on Chicago's buildings exemplified simplicity, San Francisco's stores fairly chattered with slogans and advertisements.

But what struck me most was the city dwellers: workers in thick pants that bunched about their knees and ankles; businessmen in well-worn suits and derby hats, only a few with the formal frock coats or stylish straw boaters that were common in Chicago; and men fresh from the countryside, tanned and unshaven, with scruffy coils of hair running down the backs of their necks. In short, all manner of men, but sparser numbers of women. I began to comprehend Sue Marie's claim that a young lady might easily strike gold in San Francisco.

Sue Marie insisted we take up residence at San Francisco's finest hotel, the Palace, if for no other reason than to be seen there—and not at some less desirable accommodation. But our funds could only keep us in this style for little more than a week, which meant we would need to work fast. After transporting our trunks to the hotel in a horsecar, we hiked up and down San Francisco's hilly streets, exploring the city.

Settled in the hotel room our first evening in the city, Sue Marie stretched out on the bed, massaging one bare foot against the other. "We need to find a jeweler tomorrow. One who deals in used pieces."

I hung the last of my gowns in the closet and sank into an over-stuffed chair beside the bed. "What for?"

Sue Marie reached down her dress bodice, flipped out a pocket compartment, and extracted a gold ring with a single raised diamond. She twisted the ring between thumb and finger, showing off the sparkle of its diamond. "To sell this."

I reached out my palm. As she plunked the ring into my hand I asked, "Where'd you get this?"

Sue Marie chuckled. "From Farnhardt's jacket. That night."

"So that's why the police searched the rooms. Where did you hide it?"

"In the attic, over my room."

"And you never told anyone?"

Sue Marie flipped on her side and tossed her head with the nonchalance of a bored youngster. "In that place? Full of wagging mouths?"

"And if they'd found it, you'd have ended in jail."

"You should be thanking me for quick thinking."

"But we're partners."

"So?"

"We shouldn't take foolish risks." Sue Marie and I had argued two days earlier over her proclivity for snatching jewelry. She'd filched a pair of earrings from a woman who'd fainted at the train station in Portland, and we were fortunate to have boarded the train before the theft came to light.

"This one paid off, didn't it?"

I unlaced my shoes and propped my sore feet on an ottoman. "It was harebrained—risking arrest over a ring that won't bring in more than forty or fifty dollars."

"You can go back to the bordello business or stick with me."

"You sure about this plan? I tried dining by myself in Chicago's finest hotels, and it didn't work."

"What about your banker fiancé? How'd you meet him?"

"By way of introduction. After I'd landed in society circles."

Sue Marie plumped up a pillow under her head. "But this is San Francisco. And we're going to knock 'em out with our gowns."

I knew Sue Marie expected me to play second fiddle, but in hopes of turning the tables, I remarked, "Yes, I do look forward to stepping out as an heiress."

"You're not playing that part."

"Aren't I?"

"No, you're playing my companion."

I got up and sat down beside her on the bed, twisting around to face her. "I wouldn't be any good at that."

"You're putting on a regular Sarah Bernhardt right now."

"Playing the companion requires better acting skills."

"Oh, piffle," said Sue Marie. "Think I can't see through your flattery?"

"We need to work together, don't we?"

"We sure do."

"Then let's settle this fairly." I drew my legs up on the bed. "With a contest."

She narrowed her eyes at me. "What kind of contest?"

"To see who makes the better lure."

With a disdainful shake of her head she said, "No. I'm the one who came up with the plan."

I reached out and fingered the strands of hair falling about her temples. "Think about it. Don't we want the best lure playing the role?"

Sue Marie pushed my hand away. "I don't give a pollywog's legs."

"Aw, Sue Marie, please?"

"Please what?"

"Please, let's have a contest." I patted my prayer-poised hands together and raised my eyebrows pleadingly.

"And if I win, you'll quit your bellyaching?"

"Promise."

She put on one of her roguish sneers. "Then in the lobby. Tomorrow."

I rearranged myself on folded knees and leaned toward her. "We'll sit at opposite ends. And count the men we meet over an hour."

"No starting up conversations. We just wait for takers."

"Agreed," I said, falling on her and tickling her sides until she dissolved into a wriggling mass of squeals and yelps.

＊

The next afternoon, I allowed Sue Marie to dress first. Then I refreshed my moss-green gown with a moist towel, fluffed it up, and took out my prize possession: the yellow-diamond necklace I'd acquired in Milwaukee. Never before had I worn it in public: There'd been no occasion. In fact, no one but Maman even knew of it.

I carmined my lips, powdered my cheeks, darkened my eyelashes with dabs of castor oil, and—*voilà*. Promptly at five, I stepped out of our room, gripped the polished golden railing, and descended the stairs, relishing the plush carpet absorbing my mincing steps. I trained my eyes on the lobby opening up before me. Sue Marie sat in a wingback chair, upright with expectation. I took a few steps in her direction and came close enough—within thirty feet—to allow her a good look at me. Her gaze traveled up from the fullness of my skirt, over my bodice of corded braids, and landed on my necklace. Her eyes widened. What is it they say in lawn tennis? Advantage—yes, that's it. I believe I scored a point for my own confidence, and possibly one against Sue Marie's, just by sporting that dazzling piece.

At the end of the appointed hour, the score was five gentlemen for me, three for Sue Marie. When the lobby clock struck six, I reached into my purse and extracted the room key.

"Excuse me, gentlemen," I said to the pair of brothers sitting beside me. Rising, I dangled the key in Sue Marie's direction and mounted the stairs to our third-floor room.

Sue Marie let herself in a few minutes later. "You're a sly one, aren't you?"

"And you, my dear, are a delightful companion. I shall look forward to your assistance with every detail of my itinerary."

Sue Marie smirked. "Don't let it go to your head, Princess Bordello."

I palmed my pinned-up hair. "I believe I'll leave Miss Davidson behind. Henceforth, I shall be Pauline Townsend."

＊

My dear Sue Marie made dinner reservations for me that evening, taking care to select a table that would prominently display my attire and jewels. While I dined in the Palace's Grand Court, she took her own dinner in the privacy of our room. Over the next five days, I had many offers for table mates and dined with several promising prospects, but on the sixth evening, a most unusual man came to my attention.

I was seated at a table with two middle-aged gentlemen, businessmen of obvious good fortune—if only middling physical constitution—when the conversation turned to living arrangements.

"And do you enjoy this hotel, Miss Townsend?" the lanky Mr. Amperson asked, nervously fingering his glass of whiskey.

"Yes, though spending day after day in the same hotel room can get wearisome."

"I find that on my business travels as well. For a few days it's a novelty, but it does get old."

Mr. Zimmer, whose Adam's apple bounced when he spoke, cleared his throat. "That's why I keep an apartment at the Shoreside, a suite with a balcony looking out on the Bay."

I could have sworn he told me he resided elsewhere. "But I thought you lived on Nob Hill?"

"Yes, I do. But it's boring living in the same house day after day," he said, chuckling at his own cleverness.

"When I've settled my business affairs, I believe I'll consider a house or apartment myself," I said, though in truth the notion of settling down in some conventional neighborhood, even in San Francisco, bored me.

Mr. Amperson caught the waiter's eye and then looked to me. "As it happens, I own an apartment building on Powell Street. Each time a room opens, I redecorate. Always a fine room to be had there, should you ever be interested."

How delightful—two gentlemen vying for me. I reasoned that Mr. Amperson would be the more pliable of the two. Sue Marie could investigate his holdings and reputation, but with the Palace taking a toll on our finances, we couldn't afford to tarry. I turned to Mr. Amperson. "And is this a good time to be in real estate?"

"Quite good, actually. The city is booming; newcomers are pouring in every day."

Not to be outdone, Mr. Zimmer added, "And they're buying. The furniture business has never been better."

The waiter arrived, and I ordered and leaned back in my chair. Overhead, the hue of the Grand Court's stained-glass dome deepened. Dusk had settled. The table and wall lamps now outshone the outdoors' ambient light, and the stained glass reflected its golden glow on the diners' faces, the clean tablecloths, and my periwinkle-blue gown.

Out of the corner of my eye, I noticed a gentleman standing twenty feet to my side, studying me in the most unabashed manner. I turned and met his gaze. He had the darkness of a foreigner, a broad, pronounced jaw, and cocoa-brown eyes. A shock of wavy black hair swept back from his square forehead, and a trim mustache gracefully outlined the shapely curve of his lip. His compact yet proud bearing showed off a barrel-thick chest clad in a tailored dinner jacket. In a word, the man was dashing—and much younger than my dinner companions. He placed a hand over his abdomen, bowed to me, then strode off, unhurried but purposeful.

When I bade good night to my dinner companions and started for the stairs, this same man reappeared from the corner of the lobby, as if he'd been waiting for me. He approached, bowed again, and said, "May I introduce myself, *señorita*? I am Juan Ramón."

"Mr. Ramón," I said, dipping my head. "I am Pauline Townsend."

"Yes, I know." Though accented, his English was quite clear.

"Oh? How is that?"

"I asked the maître d'." Opening his hand toward the hotel's bar, he asked, "Would you permit me to buy you a drink?"

He escorted me to the bar, where he ordered brandy for us.

"I take it, Mr. Ramón, that you do not reside in San Francisco?"

"No, I am from Guatemala. But I travel much. And you—is California your home?"

"No, no. I'm from Chicago."

Our waiter delivered our drinks, and Mr. Ramón lifted his glass. "To the most beautiful woman in the world."

"How you flatter, sir."

"It is true. Never in all my journeys have I encountered such beauty."

"Then your compliment means all the more, coming from a man who has seen much of the world."

"How can I tell you?" He spread a hand over his heart. "You are lovelier than the most delicate orchid bloom."

"Ah, Mr. Ramón, that is quite enough about me," I said, though my heart fluttered under his moony gaze. "What is it that brings you to San Francisco?"

"I am an importer of coffee." His held his head high. "Do you like coffee?"

"Yes, I do, though I'm woefully uneducated on the subject."

"You must permit me to teach you. Perhaps tomorrow I can take you for breakfast?"

→ ←

And after breakfast Mr. Ramón insisted we dine that evening at the Palace. By then I'd learned he was a man accustomed to having his way. "Waiter," he snapped when we'd been sitting for only a few minutes, "the lady would like . . ." He turned to me.

"I'll have a glass of champagne."

"And Pisco punch for me."

As the waiter trailed off, I said, "You are an adventurous man, Mr. Ramón. I've heard many stories about the famous Pisco punch."

"And all true." He flapped his hands in a grand but-of-course gesture. "But you must call me Juan. That is how my family and friends call me."

"Very well, then: Juan it shall be."

"And may I have the honor of calling you Pauline?"

"I should think that first names are quite in order, under the circumstances."

When his flaming drink of Pisco punch arrived, my handsome Mr. Ramón toasted to "life's pleasures," swirled the flaming drink in its glass, and, as the blue flames flickered out, brought the drink to his lips and gulped it down all at once.

I laughed. "You do embrace life, don't you?"

"Yes, and for dinner, I insist on the house specialty—roasted squab. And then I will hire a carriage, and we will go to the Cliff House."

"Ah, you will spoil me, Juan."

He leaned over the corner of the table and circled his hand around my fingertips. Fastening his glistening eyes on mine, he said, "That is exactly what I intend to do, *mi florecita*. You will not object, will you?"

# SPOILED SPOILS

·

*S*ue Marie didn't object to Juan's spoiling me—that is, not once she'd verified his status as a successful importer. By playing the part of an assistant to a coffee dealer and exploring possibilities for bringing more coffee business to San Francisco, she discovered that Mr. Ramón had made his mark on the city. And a few weeks later, after I stole a peek into his wallet and spied a picture of him with a woman and two little boys, Sue Marie's enthusiasm for our liaison was sealed.

"You have to get him into a compromising position," Sue Marie said, pacing our hotel room. "Ask for an apartment. And an allowance."

I relaxed in our room's overstuffed chair. "At the right moment."

Sue Marie stopped in her tracks in front of me. "The right moment, my fanny. We're almost broke."

"Where'd all the money go?"

The look she gave me could've scared a bear. "I need to eat, too."

Snuggling the folds of my robe over my legs, I said, "Some things take time."

"Listen," she said, looming over me. "While you're being wined and dined, I'm climbing streets steep as mountains and wringing every last drop out of our pennies."

"Fine, fine. I know what I'm doing. Let me play it my way."

"Yeah, you won the lead role—you'd better play it."

⇢ ⇠

That evening, Juan and I stepped into a cabriolet outside the Palace, and Juan ordered the driver to the Poodle Dog. As we trundled through the city's misty rain, we passed by department-store windows decorated with nativity scenes, and a caroling party strolling arm in arm. Still, save for the clomp of our horse's hooves, a glum quiet pervaded our carriage compartment.

I nestled up alongside Juan, who had been morose from the minute we'd stepped into the carriage. "Don't you love this time of year?"

I surmised he had not embraced the spirit of Christmas, for he clenched his hands on the tops of his knees and asked, "Why were you talking to Mr. Schmidt in the lobby?"

"Oh, him," I said, circling my hand around his arm. "He insists on exchanging pleasantries every time he sees me."

"You do not encourage him?"

"Goodness, no." I kissed his cheek, resolved to shower him with affection the rest of the evening. As my acquaintance with Juan deepened, the veneer of his charm had thinned, and the surliness of a wronged husband occasionally surfaced. "I haven't the slightest interest in any other man."

"I will take you away for Christmas, to San Diego."

Much as the prospect of escaping San Francisco's damp chill appealed to me, I couldn't abandon Sue Marie. Besides, our money was dwindling fast. "Travel again? I've barely gotten settled here."

"We would only stay long enough to warm up in the sunshine."

"What I'd really like is a home for you and me right here in San Francisco." I nestled my chin on his shoulder and looked up at him. "If I had an apartment with a kitchen, I could prepare coffee exactly as you like it. I could be waiting for you each day."

"No, we have my suite at the Palace."

"A hotel room," I said with a heaving sigh. "Please don't take offense, but it seems tawdry."

"An apartment is not practical."

"But you're away on business so much."

Juan stiffened beside me. "It makes no sense to pay for an apartment and my hotel when I travel."

I pressed one hand over my bosom. "Are you saying you don't want to spend the money on me? That I'm not worth it?"

"Don't be foolish."

"I hate having all those men ogle me in the lobby."

"And if you had an apartment, how do I know you would not see other men there?"

I let go of his arm and pulled away from him. "I would never do that. How could you think such a thing?"

I pouted all the way to the Poodle Dog. Finally, once we were seated, Juan apologized. To keep his spirits up, I fawned over him while we dined and pointedly ignored the glances of passing men.

When we took up our carriage again, on our way to the Tivoli Opera House, I entwined my fingers in his and cast my eyes downward, studying the walnut-colored skin of his broad hand. "Juan, I can hardly believe you accused me of considering another man."

He cupped his other hand over mine and twisted around. "Forgive me, *mi florecita.*"

The trace of a whimper escaped from my throat. I closed my eyes and clamped my lips tight together, trying to suppress the tears pressing at my eyelids.

"Do not cry. You shall have your apartment," said Juan, kissing my forehead.

I blinked my eyes open. "On Powell Street?"

"*Sí,* wherever you like. A place for just the two of us."

> <

In January, Juan secured and furnished an apartment on Powell Street—a lovely one-bedroom affair with a living-and-dining area, a serviceable kitchen, a bathroom with modern plumbing, and wallpaper so freshly applied I could still smell the pasty glue. Although Juan had acceded to my request for a weekly allowance, which Sue Marie insisted on budgeting, the amount was insufficient for the apartment expenses, my dress budget, and her room at the Palace—or any other hotel, for that matter. She was forced to take employment at Lillie Winters's brothel on Columbus Avenue, though she registered quite a protest: "This is not what we planned. I won't put up with this for long."

"Don't be so impatient. I've only just settled into the apartment."

"He hasn't even bought you one trinket. You better figure out how you're going to cash in on your Mr. Ramón."

Then my Mr. Ramón upset the whole apple cart. One afternoon

in February, he arrived home with two carved-wood puppets. "Look what I found for my little ones."

"Little ones?" I asked, closing my Sherlock Holmes story and rising from the couch. "You have children?"

Juan stood before me, holding one of the puppets in each hand and grinning mischievously. "*Sí,* two boys."

"Where are they?"

"With their grandmother, in Guatemala."

"You never told me."

"It is not your business." He arranged the puppets in seated positions on the couch.

I felt small, deceived, unimportant. I studied the floor.

Juan came up close to me and grasped my shoulders. "Why would you care about another woman's children?"

"You mean their mother." I looked at him with soft eyes. "Where is their mother?"

"My wife died three years ago. Her and the new baby."

I flattened a hand over my heart. "Oh, Juan, I'm so sorry."

"It does not matter now." He drew me into his arms. "I have you, *mi amorcita.*"

&rarr;&larr;

I told Sue Marie the next day, during her afternoon visit to the apartment.

"So much for a tidy job of blackmail," she said, throwing up her arms as she leaned against the kitchen counter. "After all the trouble to get you set up here."

I cast my glance around the room—at the heart-pine flooring I'd recently polished, the fickle potted plants I tended, and the window's lace curtains, which had taken up an afternoon of shopping. "Believe me, the last thing I wanted was to play wife."

"You've got it better than me, sister."

"I should leave him," I said, retrieving the coffeepot from the stove and signaling her to follow me to the dining table. "We could move on."

"And give up after all the time we've put in?"

"He's getting terribly possessive."

Sue Marie plopped down at her place setting. "We don't have enough money for moving on."

I poured coffee for us, sat, and stirred some cream into my cup. "Then I'll ask for more allowance."

"We can do better than allowance money. His coffee business rakes in plenty."

"So? You expect me to sell the company out from under him?"

"No, just find the money."

What could I do but forge ahead? Sue Marie and I had an agreement, and I could hardly complain while she slaved away at a bordello.

As of early March 1890, Juan was not only jealously guarding me from other men's eyes, but working long hours, which left me cooped up in the apartment for days on end. I had come to dread his mocking inquiries about my activities. They verged on meanness and forced me to determine his state of mind by reading the compression of his brow and the twitch of his mustache.

I wanted to leave him, but his zealous watchfulness, as well as my partnership with Sue Marie, left me little choice. After sitting down to dinner in our apartment one evening, I said, "Juan, you're neglecting me. I hardly see you in the evenings."

"I am with you every night, except when I do my business travel." He chomped down on a morsel of steak, as if to close the subject.

I placed my fork down beside my plate and studied my lap. "You come home and shut yourself away at your desk for hours."

He dabbed at the corner of his mouth with his napkin. "That is how it is. I must see to my business."

"I miss you. All day I wait for you, and then you work for hours."

"We will go away this weekend." He reached out and cupped his hand over mine. "Every weekend, if you want."

"But it will be the same when we come home. Let me help you with the business."

"No." He braced his knife upright in his fisted hand. "It is not work for a woman."

"I can help. I studied business and business law in Chicago."

"It is my job."

"But I want to. I could keep the ledger. I could manage your correspondence."

"No, it is not right," he said, cutting a chunk of steak and waving it at me. "Now eat."

Over the coming month, I carried out a campaign of careful timing and expert complaisance. A wild-horse trainer could not have coaxed more gently or patiently. It took weeks of seduction—"See how well I know you and what you like?"—tear-shedding—"You don't trust me"—and cajoling—"Many important American businessmen have their wives and lady friends assist them"—before Juan relented. At first he merely allowed me to sit with him and update orders in his ledger. But before March ran out, I was writing orders and occasionally accompanying him on calls to his businesses. By early April, I had proven myself a competent and efficient bookkeeper and assistant.

"Juan, shall I collect on the orders while you're in Seattle?"

"It would do no good. Payments can only be released to me."

"But I could deposit them, couldn't I? The funds would be in the account, should you need to wire for them."

"I have already covered the week's orders."

I stomped a foot down and eyed him pleadingly. "And how will we take our long holiday if you try to do all the collections on Friday?"

He shook his head. "Then go ahead. But deposit the checks right after you collect. I don't want them kept here."

"Of course, Juan. I know that's how you run your business."

I did collect that week. I took the smallest check, eighty-eight dollars from Goodson's Wholesale Coffee, to a bank in Oakland. "I'd like to open an account in the name of Juan's Coffee Imports, please."

"And who will be the signers on this account?"

"Until further notice, only myself."

I rushed home and sent a message to Sue Marie to come around right away with eighty-eight dollars from our funds, which I intended to deposit in Juan's San Francisco bank. Then, so as to reconcile the accounting, I recorded that Goodson's had paid their week's bill.

"Aren't you a clever one," Sue Marie cooed when I informed her I'd opened an account.

I grabbed her hands. "He'll be in Los Angeles for a full week at the end of the month."

"How much do you think you can collect?"

"A few thousand."

She pulled back from my grasp. "Is that all?"

"Don't get greedy," I said, hoping she wouldn't fight me. "Soon enough we'll be able to move on."

She studied me for a few moments. A smile drifted across her face. "I can say good-bye to the whorehouse."

My eyes circled around the kitchen, taking in the beastly cookstove and the cups and plates I'd neatly arranged in their glass-fronted cupboards. "And I to the shut-in life of a wife."

>‹

The day before Juan was scheduled to return from Los Angeles, I collected on the outstanding accounts and cashed the checks at my Oakland bank. Sue Marie visited in the late afternoon so we could put the finishing touches on our plan to steal away in the morning. I counted out the money for her on the bed, beside my open, packed suitcase.

"That's it—$2,216?"

"I told you not to expect much." I tucked the money alongside my jewels in the false bottom of my suitcase.

"Doesn't he have any money around here?"

"No, he doesn't keep money here."

"What about those diamond cuff links?"

A key wiggled in the entrance door.

"My God, it can't be." I slammed my suitcase shut and shoved it under the bed.

"Hello," Juan's voice called.

Turning to Sue Marie, I whispered, "Pretend we're on our way to the market."

"I'm in here, Juan," I answered, emerging from the bedroom with Sue Marie trailing behind.

"Ah, *mi florecita*," Juan said. As he caught sight of Sue Marie, a puzzled expression rippled his features.

I rushed up to him and kissed him. "What a surprise."

"I thought we could start early on our holiday," he said, looking over my shoulder at Sue Marie.

"Hello, Mr. Ramón," said Sue Marie.

"Miss Littleton, nice to see you again."

Clapping my hand over his arm, I said, "Why don't you relax, and I'll have Sue Marie help me at the market."

"May I take you two to dinner?" Juan asked.

"No, no. You rest up."

Sue Marie and I bounded down the stairs and out into the late afternoon's overcast skies. As we turned onto the street, I took her arm and said, "Act casual, he might be watching us."

"Your packed suitcase is under the bed."

"I can say I was packing for our holiday."

"How will you get it out of there?"

"I'll have to send him on an errand in the morning."

"Damn," Sue Marie said. "Why'd he have to show up and upset our plan?"

"It's not ruined. We just have to think."

"There's nothing to make him suspicious, is there?"

We turned off Powell, out of sight of the apartment window. I stopped and grabbed her arm. "I didn't update the ledger."

"Will he check?"

"He might. Unless I can distract him." How could I do that, I wondered, as we neared the neighborhood market. I turned to Sue Marie. "Can you cook?"

"One thing. Pork chops and greens."

"Then I'll tell him you insisted on cooking for us, so that he and I can plan our holiday. After you leave, I'll get him right to bed and insist he not bother with the ledger."

"We better be sharp," said Sue Marie, picking up the pace, "and not give him time to suspect anything."

I nodded. "It'll take some fancy footwork."

"Fancy footwork?" Sue Marie flapped her hands. "Leave the kitchen to me, and I'll get us out of here faster than a fox after a rabbit."

→ ←

Juan lit up a cigar as he leaned back from the dinner table. "Your friend, she is a very talented cook."

A cool spring rain pattered on our windows, but the kitchen stove had blazed for nearly an hour, rendering the apartment overheated and claustrophobic. I pushed my picked-at dinner to the side. "She is a treasure, isn't she?"

Sue Marie glided in with a tray and placed it on the sideboard. "Let me clear the table."

Juan looked up at her as she reached for his plate. "Very nice, Miss Littleton. The pork was as tender as butter."

Sue Marie plucked our plates from the table. "The greens are a Kentucky specialty. Were they to your liking?"

"*Sí,* very tasty."

Sue Marie disappeared into the kitchen with the tray.

"Pity it's so rainy tonight," I said. "I hope it'll clear by morning."

"How is Sue Marie getting home?"

"She can get a carriage on Powell. And we can have the rest of the evening to ourselves. Just you and me."

Sue Marie returned with three drinks on a tray. "May I join you for after-dinner drinks?"

Juan rose to pull out a chair for Sue Marie. "Please, Miss Littleton."

"This is my own creation," Sue Marie said, placing the drinks before us and taking her seat. "It's slightly bitter, but excellent for digestion."

Bitter? She wouldn't dare resort to that back-alley ploy of knock-out drops, would she? And put our plan at risk?

Juan reached for his drink. "To my lovely ladies."

"Juan," I said, "did you finish unpacking?"

Juan scooped up his glass. "No, I'll finish later. To your health, my dears."

I tasted the drink. It was sweet and strong, like rum laced with sugar, but not bitter.

Juan sipped a bit and puckered. "Most unusual. Bitter under the sweet."

I reached out to restrain Juan. "I really don't care for it. I'm sure Sue Marie won't be insulted if you don't finish it."

Sue Marie shot me a shut-your-mouth look.

Juan clapped his free hand over mine, lifted the cordial glass to his lips, gulped down the rest of the drink, and exhaled. "Ahhh."

"I'll clean up and get dessert ready," said Sue Marie, leaving us at the table.

The sounds of colliding metal and china clanged from the kitchen as Sue Marie cleaned the pots, plates, and utensils she'd dirtied during her culinary escapade. I kept a close eye on Juan, trying to figure out if his drink had been fixed. The kitchen noise subsided and Sue Marie peeked out, craning her neck to see over Juan's shoulder. I truly hoped she hadn't slipped him knockout drops. I had enough to worry about: making it through the night without questions about the ledger; retrieving my suitcase; and getting us out of town before Juan visited his bank in the morning.

"Tell me, Mr. Ramón," she said, striding toward us, "have you tried apple pie? It's an American specialty, you know."

Juan, who had grown taciturn, twisted around toward her and, like a pendulum unable to stop its momentum, pitched off his chair and onto the floor.

I bolted to his side and crouched over him. "Juan, Juan."

His eyes rolled back. He lolled his head toward me and spoke with a thick tongue. "My heart . . . bad. Please, a doctor."

Sue Marie looked down on him, a hand worrying her brow. "Mr. Ramón, oh, Mr. Ramón."

I shot her an accusing glance. Just as I thought—she'd plied him with knockout drops.

Juan's eyes closed and his limbs flopped at his sides, strewn at odd angles.

I bent over his face and held my hand under his nostrils. His breaths came in ragged pulls. "Juan, can you hear me?"

He budged not one bit.

I looked up at Sue Marie. "Look what you've done."

"It won't kill him. Let's get out of here."

I stood, grabbed her by the sleeve, and dragged her into the bedroom, shutting the door. "He has a weak heart. He needs a doctor."

"We can't risk it."

"Are you crazy? If he dies, we'll be charged with murder."

"He's just knocked out, you fool."

"He could be dying. We have to do something."

"All right, fine. Get your coat." Sue Marie bustled out of the room.

I ran to the closet and grabbed my coat and a broad-brimmed hat.

As I fastened my hat, Sue Marie rushed back into the bedroom, waving Juan's opened wallet. "I can't believe it. All he has is a measly hundred fifty-seven dollars."

"Never mind. Let's get him to a doctor."

"No," she said, stuffing Juan's wallet into her purse. She reached for my arm. "We have to get out of here."

I backed away from her grasp. "I'm not taking a chance on a murder charge—for you or me."

"Don't be stupid. We'll catch a train and get out of town."

"I won't do it. Not until I know he's safe."

She grabbed me by the hand. "Let's go."

I hitched my free arm around the bedpost and braced myself against her tug. "I'm not budging."

She tried to unhook my arm from the post.

I wrapped both my arms tight around the bedpost. "I don't want you charged with murder."

"You're in on it, too," she said, grabbing me around the waist and yanking me so hard my corset pinched.

"I've got the money." I released the bedpost and stood blocking her way to my suitcase.

She dropped on her stomach and lunged under the bed for my suitcase.

I dropped down on top of her and straddled her back, grabbing her legs so she couldn't kick her way free. She tried to push back from under the bed, but I kept all my weight on her.

"Let me go," she hollered.

Then I thought of her employer. Bordellos always have a doctor to call on. "Miss Winters can find a doctor. Let's get him there, and then we can leave."

"All right, all right," she said.

"Promise?"

"Yes, let me go."

"Can I trust you this time?"

"Yes, now get off me."

I stood and released her.

She wriggled out from under the bed, rose, and shot me a look of disgust. "I'll get a carriage."

It took both of us and the driver to drag Juan down the stairs and into the carriage. The driver hurried his horses through pouring rain and pulled up to a three-story cream-and-green Italianate house. Sue Marie ran in and returned with a short, burly man. He and the carriage driver hauled Juan around to the back door, and Sue Marie and I trailed along at the tail end of the sorry entourage. The two men laid Juan out on a sofa in the parlor, his hair dripping wet, face glistening with moisture, and clothes soaked.

We found ourselves in a compact room named "the Forty-Niner's Parlor," which was decorated with red wallpaper, gold pans, and a red velvet sofa and sitting chairs. I pulled the carriage driver aside and asked him to wait for Sue Marie and me by the rear door, hoping we could fetch our suitcases and leave as soon as possible. I knelt over Juan. His breathing was slow but steady.

The back door slammed. I pivoted around to check it; the carriage driver had slunk off. Sue Marie and I were stuck without a carriage—while a heavy rain poured down outside. I wondered if the man who'd helped carry Juan in was the house driver, and if he might be compelled to drive us to Juan's apartment. I looked around the room and caught the man's eye. He wiped his face dry with his sleeve, all the time glaring at Sue Marie and me as if he'd rather spit on us than say, "How do you do."

The white-haired Lillie Winters stormed into the room and closed the door. "What's the meaning of this?"

I stood and walked to Sue Marie's side, keeping my eyes downcast.

All meekness, Sue Marie said, "We were having dinner with Miss Townsend's gentleman and he passed out. He needs a doctor."

Realizing introductions would not be forthcoming, I said, "He has a bad heart."

"And what business is it of mine?" Miss Winters's big-boned frame towered over Juan's prostrate body. She stared at Sue Marie. "Well?"

"I would have brought him to a doctor but I thought it might look bad, especially if anybody found out where I worked."

Miss Winters cast a doubting scowl at Sue Marie and turned to the man who'd helped carry Juan in. "Angelo. Go get Dr. Ford."

Angelo dashed off, and Miss Winters faced Sue Marie again. "The doctor will want to know if anything contributed to his state."

"He'd just had dinner, that's all."

Miss Winters planted a hand on her hip. "Did you give him knockout drops?"

Sue Marie clapped her fingertips to her cheek. "Why would I do that?"

Miss Winters let out a snorting humph and said, "You know very well."

Over the next hour, Sue Marie, Miss Winters, and I kept watch over Juan while a stream of perhaps a dozen girls passed by the doorway, peering at the scene and whispering among themselves.

When the doctor arrived, he pulled a stethoscope out of his bag, leaned over Juan, and checked his chest and pulse.

Sue Marie brushed her palms together and turned to Miss Winters. "Pauline and I should really get back to Mr. Ramón's apartment."

"Oh, no, you won't," she said, glaring at Sue Marie. "You brought him here, and you'll see this through."

While I tried to cook up a reason for us to leave, heavy footsteps pounded down the hallway, approaching the parlor.

A thickset, veiny-nosed police officer elbowed his way through the girls jamming the doorway. "What's going on here?"

Damnation, I thought, the carriage driver must have squealed.

The doctor said, "This man was brought here unconscious."

Juan, who had been roused with some smelling salts, moaned with grogginess.

The police officer pulled a chair up alongside Juan. "Can you tell me what happened, sir?"

Juan shook his head. He managed only halting words. "Passed . . . out."

The officer nodded.

Juan tried to sit up but only managed to scoot himself closer to the arm of the sofa, which he flopped against. He reached inside his jacket pocket. "My . . . wallet."

The police officer looked around at me, Sue Marie, and Miss Winters. "Who brought him here?"

Miss Winters poked her chin at Sue Marie and me. "The two of them."

The officer stood. "And where did you bring him from?"

"His apartment," I offered, frantically trying to devise some escape from the officer's scrutiny. But running was impossible—there were too many people blocking the doors. Besides, bolting would have only confirmed our guilt.

"Was he conscious then?"

"Barely," I said, fearing Sue Marie and I were cooked. "But he keeps his wallet on his dresser at home."

The officer bent over Juan. "Did you have your wallet on you at your home, sir?"

Juan nodded.

The doctor gathered up his instruments and turned to the officer. "I'd like to get him to the hospital."

"Of course, in a minute," the police officer replied. He stepped toward Sue Marie and me. "I'm afraid I'm going to have to search you two ladies."

"Oh, I remember now," said Sue Marie, reaching into her purse and offering up the wallet. "I took it out of his vest when he passed out. I thought it might have his doctor's name in it."

The officer snatched the wallet from her hand.

Juan held his hands up and studied his wrists. "Where are . . . my cuff links?"

Miss Winters rolled her eyes and shook a finger at Sue Marie. "I will not put up with thieving by any of my girls."

My God, she'd snitched his cuff links, too. Her thieving ways had finally caught up with her—and me.

The officer wagged his head. "You won't have to, Miss Winters. Young ladies, I'm arresting you on the charge of larceny."

# OUT OF THE FRYING PAN

.

*I* have never been so mortified in all my life. Dear Lord, I prayed, may Maman never learn of this. The police officer searched us—right in front of Juan, the doctor, Miss Winters, and four gaping girls—and discovered Juan's diamond cuff links in Sue Marie's not-so-secret dress pocket. Then he carted Sue Marie and me off to the Tenderloin precinct jail and photographed each of us in front of a white wall. By the time we were marched into a ten-by-ten cell with only a sink, toilet, and two bunks, I was so angry I could have boxed Sue Marie's ears. Her shenanigans had led to nothing but complications for me. The last thing I needed was that scoundrel Reed Dougherty getting wind of this arrest and using my past to seal a conviction against me here.

We were the only prisoners on our side of the cell block, though I presumed that men inhabited the block beyond ours. Looping one of my arms around a cell bar, I watched the lone guard on duty retreat through the door at the front of our corridor. I scowled at Sue Marie. "They've got a photograph of me."

"Don't worry," she said, eyeing the keyhole and removing a pin from her hair. "They don't have your real name."

"Pictures don't lie, you fool."

"They took my picture, too." She wriggled her tortoise-shell hairpin around in the lock, but with no results. "You see me squawking about it?"

I took my metal hairpin out, bent one of its prongs to a ninety-degree angle, and handed it to her. "You and your stupid schemes. Why couldn't you leave well enough alone?"

Sue Marie stuck her hairpin onto the top of her messed-up hair and poked the one I'd rigged into the lock. "Because he was nothing but a skinflint."

"We never talked about fixing his drink."

Sue Marie smirked. "Did you think I was planning a church picnic?"

"If I'd known, I wouldn't have gone along with it."

"Oh, quit playing holier-than-thou. You've been complaining about him for months."

"That was no call for knocking him out. Or stealing his cuff links."

Sue Marie extracted the hairpin from the lock and spun around toward me. "At least you're done with the piker."

I gasped. "And jail is better?"

"Maybe better than a whorehouse," she said, plunking herself down on the bottom bed.

"Sometimes I wish I'd never met you," I said, glaring at her. My affection for Sue Marie was quickly being supplanted by annoyance with her exceedingly poor judgment. "And don't think you're getting the bottom bunk, either."

The next hour, between the guard's occasional comings and goings, we bickered like a couple of old maids. But picking the lock was getting us nowhere. So we wised up and figured we were in this together and had better find a way out of it together. Besides, putting up with the stench of urine and clammy concrete walls for even that long was enough to turn us as agreeable as honeymooners.

When the guard, a young, pink-complexioned fellow with sandy hair and freckles, swung around again to check on us, Sue Marie played as if she were passing out, and I asked if he could please bring us a moist cloth. The guard returned and poked a soggy rag between the bars. Once I'd revived Sue Marie, I asked his name.

"Warren, Benjamin Warren," he said.

"Thank you for helping us, Benjamin." I reasoned I could get away with calling him by his first name, given the barely discernible blond whiskers poking out on his boyish face.

"Think nothing of it, miss." He shuffled his feet, as if uncertain whether to leave or stay.

I faced him square-on. "I suppose you've seen all kinds of outlaws."

"I could tell stories like you've never heard," he said, nervously fingering his buttons.

"Oh, tell us a story," Sue Marie said, coming to life on the lower bunk.

He leaned his shoulder against our cell. "Hmm. Well, last year we had a fellow in here who kidnapped a baby girl and tried to get the father to hand over a sack of gold for her."

I widened my eyes and gripped the bars. "What happened? Did you save the baby girl?"

"It took some smart police work, but they got the little girl back. The crook's over in Alcatraz now."

"Alcatraz?" I poked my face against the bars. "They don't put girls in Alcatraz, do they?"

"Nah, just men."

"What's going to happen to us, Benjamin?" Sue Marie asked.

I glanced over my shoulder, took in the dreamy-eyed look she was giving Benjamin, and frowned with disapproval. I didn't trust her to handle this. She must have gotten the message, because she slumped back against her pillow.

"Can't tell," said Benjamin. "Don't get many girls charged with theft."

"And it was all a big misunderstanding," I said. "It's not right we're here."

"Then what were you doing with his wallet and cuff links?"

I looked steadily into his face. "He planted those things on us."

His eyes got as big as silver dollars. "Why would he do that?"

"Think about it," I said. "If we had robbed him, why would we fetch a doctor when he passed out?"

He shook his head. "Well, I sure am sorry. I suppose the judge'll get it all sorted out."

I latched woeful eyes on him. "That Guatemalan has money coming out of his ears, and he wants us locked up."

Benjamin screwed up his face. "No foreigner's going to get away with that."

"But he is, Benjamin," I said, remembering my father telling me that a man's name is the sweetest sound to his ears. "We're being railroaded."

"Why would a coffee seller want you in jail?"

I looked down at my feet and shuffled them on the cement floor. Raising my head, I motioned Benjamin closer and said in a soft voice, "You can't tell anybody, Benjamin."

"Tell what?"

"The reason."

"Why not?"

I reached my right hand between the bars and clutched the folds of his coat arm. "Because my life—and my friend's—would be in danger."

He cocked his head. "Well . . . all right, then."

Standing statue still and pleading with my eyes, I let the words break out in a fury, as if they'd been sealed up against their will. "He and I were engaged. When I found out he has a wife in Guatemala, and one in New York, too, I called it off."

"Really?"

I pursed my lips and nodded.

He swallowed, as if trying to get the truth down, and then said, "You have to tell the judge."

"No." I reached my other hand through the bars so I could grip both his arms. "He told me if I ruin his reputation I'll pay with my life."

Benjamin looked down at my hands.

I clenched him tighter.

He cupped one of his hands over mine. "You really think he'd kill you?"

Sue Marie started crying. Finally, she remembered how to act.

"I know he would. Benjamin, you have to help us."

"I can't do that."

"Please, you've got to let us out. If we don't get out of San Francisco, we'll never be safe."

"I don't want you to get killed, but I've got a job to do."

I sank to my knees and ran my hands over his hips and down his legs. Circling my arms around his calves, I looked up at him through the bars. "Our life is in your hands."

He crouched down and took my hands in his. "I got it. I can tear up the booking sheet."

"Oh, God bless you, Benjamin," I said, standing and reaching out to stroke his cheek.

He smiled, undid the keys from his belt, and opened the cell door, mumbling, "A bigamist. If that don't take the cake."

"Thank you, thank you," I said, throwing my arms around him and then stepping back and looking up into his eyes. "Benjamin, could you destroy our photographs?"

Sue Marie grabbed my arm. "Come on, let's get out of here."

"Oh, no," he said, swinging the cell door closed. "That'd be impossible."

"Never mind that," said Sue Marie, yanking me forward.

A door banged from the front of the precinct. Benjamin stiffened and perked up his ears. "Somebody stopping on his beat. Quick, this way."

Benjamin motioned us to follow him, and we headed down the corridor toward the back of the cell block. "Here. The transport door."

When we reached the door, he gripped the knob and hesitated. "Say, you weren't pulling my leg, were you?"

I flattened my back against the wall beside the door, ready to spring out. "No. And I'll tell you one more thing: Juan Ramón doesn't even run a legitimate coffee business. He's a spy for Spain."

Sue Marie and I vamoosed out of the Tenderloin precinct station, out into the wee, dark hours of morning. The city's lumpy landscape lay before us, spotted with the blinking lights of gas lamps. We made a beeline for Lillie Winters's house, our feet pattering over the damp brick streets and echoing against eerily quiet buildings.

We fetched a ladder from the carriage house, and Sue Marie climbed it and let herself into her bedroom. From the top step of the ladder she dropped her suitcase to me. We put the ladder away and hurried over to Juan's apartment to retrieve my suitcase. Then we hustled down to the docks, keeping to side streets all the way. We walked the length of the docks, nosing around for a quiet corner, and settled behind a row of empty shipping bins. With suitcases for pillows and coats for blankets, we slept until wakened by cawing seagulls.

Business hours could hardly come soon enough. Once the port offices opened, we booked passage on the only ship sailing that day, the *Emperor of Peking.* I can't say as I relished the prospect of journeying to China, but with larceny charges hanging over our heads and the police likely keeping an eye out for us, we had no alternative. At least we had enough money for the crossing and, I hoped, a new start in Shanghai.

# THE TRIAL

*W*hen court resumed, Sawyer began by querying Frank about communications between herself and me.

"The Baroness wrote you many letters and telegrams from 1913 to 1916, correct?"

"Yes."

Sawyer walked back to the plaintiff's table, retrieved a paper, and strode up to Frank with it. "Is this a letter she wrote to you in December 1913?"

"Yes."

"Your Honor, may I read this?"

The judge nodded.

The slightly stooped Sawyer positioned himself before the jury box, his bow legs spread like those of a broken-down cowboy. "The letter, gentlemen, reads: 'My dear Frank, I cannot tell you how pleased I am at the renewal of our friendship. All these long years I have missed your entertaining ways and delightful companionship. We do have great fun together, don't we? I never again want to lose that. I'm so glad you agree that we need never again part. Now, I intend to sail to London for the New Year and want you to join me. We can take the train to New York together and celebrate New Year's Eve there first. Say you will, please. Daisy can take care of the particulars. Your loving friend, May.'"

Sawyer deposited the letter at his table, and walked back to Frank. "And did you celebrate New Year's Eve in New York with the Baroness?"

"Like it was the end of time."

"Was liquor served at this party?"

"Liquor is served at all May's parties."

"And did you indulge?"

"Yes, against my better judgment. I'd sworn off liquor altogether after May and I quarreled in 1903."

"And what was the result of your drinking?"

"I was sick as a dog the first part of the crossing. Needed the doctor on board to attend to me."

"How did the Baroness take this?"

"She came around to my room often and took some meals with me. She offered to be our purse holder and suggested we pool our funds. So I gave her my six hundred dollars in cash and a check for fifteen hundred dollars in stock dividends. Soon after we landed, she said the money was gone, so I had to wire home for more."

"Miss Shaver, yesterday you mentioned a gift of pearls. When and exactly how did this come about?"

"It was 1913, while we were in London. I remember this clearly because it was shortly after the Baron's death. Even though he and May had been apart many years, she was suddenly shot through with sentiment, which made no sense, because she'd told me years before that she never loved the Baron. Anyway, she claimed he had given her thirty-five prize pearls that she'd always wanted to make into a necklace. Daisy intended to give her fifteen more pearls, but May told me that, due to the significance she attached to the pearls, such a gift would mean more coming from me. So I gave her fourteen thousand dollars in stock shares, and she selected fifteen pearls, which cost ten thousand dollars."

"And did you ever see the leftover four thousand dollars?"

"No," said Frank, pointedly fixing her gaze on me.

Alvah Sawyer changed his line of questioning at this point, shifting the focus to Daisy Emmett, which prompted Judge Flanagan to empty the courtroom of the jury and spectators for the rest of the day. The lawyers and judge proceeded to argue the legal ins and outs of including Daisy and my two brothers in the lawsuit. Sawyer claimed they were all accomplices in a conspiracy. But my attorney argued, first, that there was insufficient evidence of any conspiracy, and, second, that bringing them into this case would confuse the jury as to who was on trial and whose conduct was at issue. In the end, the judge ruled that they could be tried separately if, depending on the outcome of this case, a grand jury determined that their involvement warranted it.

We recessed around 4:30 p.m., leaving me time to mail out the new baby gift for my dear friends Helen and David O'Neill, a young Chicago couple whom I had introduced. The darlings had just had their first baby, and I'd ordered an engraved sterling-silver rattle to commemorate the joyous occasion.

>\<

The next morning, Frank ascended to the witness stand for a third round of testimony. She was not only getting her day in court—she was getting several long and drawn-out days. I hoped she found all the attention edifying. The townspeople certainly enjoyed the show. Each day the crowds hoping for seats grew larger, and this morning many had to be turned away, which no doubt upset them after they'd trekked to the courthouse in such frigid weather as had blown in overnight: It was minus four degrees at eight this morning.

But the crowd of sixty who did get seats probably regretted wasting their time, for Sawyer and Frank spent the morning wading through envelopes of bills and papers—bills for hotel expenses in Menominee; bills for my mother's illness and burial; expenses for Daisy's room in a Paris hotel; drayage and freight bills; tailors' bills; and papers recording all manner of such petty Menominee household expenses as milk and bakery items. Every chance he got, Sawyer worked in questions like "So the funds to pay for this were obtained by fraudulent representation?" or "Were you led to believe you would be paid back?"

My attorney objected quite often. Judge Flanagan finally agreed that this exercise had run its course and directed Sawyer to compile the items under consideration. Sawyer proposed to break the list into three categories, which he claimed would account for every penny of the $106,252 requested in the suit.

Goodness gracious, I almost felt I should apologize to the poor spectators who had given up a warm hearth to listen to all this tripe. But, then, this pesky trial is dragging out much longer than necessary, even with the judge urging Sawyer to condense his examination at every turn.

I believe, however, that the spectators who chose to remain for the afternoon enjoyed themselves.

"Miss Shaver," said Sawyer after the lunch break, "the Baroness sought your help with a wide array of living expenses, correct?"

"Oh, yes, even when we weren't together, I heard about her finances."

"Would you please read these two letters from the defendant, starting with the one on top." Sawyer handed Frank two sheets of paper.

"The first one's dated November 18, 1914," said Frank. "'Dear Frank, I hope you are well and that your work on that real estate matter is progressing. It is unbelievably cold in Menominee of late. I dearly hope that Chicago is not suffering the same blistering winds and drifting snows. Although I miss you very much, I cannot blame you for staying away just now. Only one thing worries me. I want Tokyo to have a coat, because the weather is so cold up here and he really must get out for exercise. You know how dear he is to me, and I should be very unhappy if he is not fit and healthy. Please see what you can do. Love, May.'"

Frank grinned at me and I returned the gesture, knowing the affection we shared for Tokyo. She shuffled the letter to the bottom and took up the next sheet. "This one's from December 2, 1914. 'Dearest Frank, we had a lovely Thanksgiving together, though your absence was noted and you were missed by all. When will you finish with that beastly real estate business? You really ought not deprive us of your company for so long. I for one won't stand for it. The world is in such shambles, with Germany running amuck and now France and England declaring war on Turkey. Who knows what's to come of it all? I detest being so far away from you. If you cannot come home for Christmas I have decided to spend it with you in Highland Park. Let's talk about taking a trip to some sunny and warm place, perhaps Algiers. The war hasn't touched it at all, and I understand it's quite lovely in the spring. Love, May. P.S. Tokyo adores his new red coat and warm fur collar.'"

Laughter welled up from the bottom of my belly. Frank tossed her head back and guffawed. The whole courtroom laughed. Even the judge allowed himself a chuckle.

Then the questioning turned to another coat.

"Miss Shaver," said Sawyer, bracing an arm on the witness box and angling for a view of me. "The Baroness, through her lawyer, reported that she made you a gift of a sealskin coat. Is this true?"

"No, she only said she would."

"Please tell us about this."

"We were shopping in New York—in 1913, I believe—when we came across a moleskin coat that caught May's eye. When I bought it for her, she said she'd pay me back and also have her sealskin altered to fit me. But then she never gave me the sealskin. And I never got my money for the moleskin, either."

I could hardly believe Frank included gifts given and promised as part of a lawsuit. I always thought a gift was a gift. When someone presents me with a gift, I do not expect to sign an IOU for it. And when I present a gift, I intend it just as that—a gift, for heaven's sake. Given that, it simply makes no sense to recount the rest of the afternoon's testimony.

# THE FORBIDDING ORIENT

*I*n late April of 1890 Sue Marie and I established residence at the Queen's Hotel in Shanghai, a British-style hotel brimming with portraits of the royal family and inhabited by English businessmen and the odd family on tour. We set about regaining our footing by mingling with guests, sometimes as a pair and other times on our own, in the lobby and over dinners in the Kensington Room. Some evenings we ventured out to the Shanghai Gin Club, where we danced with Englishmen and the occasional American.

But all was not well between Sue Marie and me. Barely a month after we'd arrived, we quarreled over how to manage our modest funds. I preferred to open a bank account and require both of us to sign on withdrawals; she wished to keep all the money on hand—under her management, of course. We'd been unable to agree, so she counted out half the money and slapped it into my palm.

The next morning, I surmised the storm had blown over when she asked me to go to the Londoners' Gift Shop and buy us some rosewater. The errand took nearly an hour in Shanghai's pedestrian-clotted streets, which required me to navigate among Chinese obviously quite at home with the bump and brush of crowded-in shoulders.

Upon my return, I noticed Sue Marie, outfitted in her deliciously yellow day dress, conducting business at the registration desk. When she spotted me approaching, she turned her back on the desk and worried her hands about her purse.

"Sue Marie," I asked, "are you going out?"

She stepped away from the desk. "Yes, well, I left a note in the room, but I might as well tell you. I'm leaving."

"What do you mean, leaving?"

"Leaving, striking out on my own," she said, perturbation creeping into her voice.

It took me a moment to comprehend. "But we're partners."

"I'm tired of you telling me what to do. And San Francisco sure didn't make us rich."

"Is that all I am to you—somebody to help you get rich?"

Sue Marie smirked. "We were after the same thing. Don't play innocent with me."

"But we're more than that to each other."

"Did you think I was looking for a wife?"

The breath escaped my lungs. I felt I might faint. "But you can't just walk away. Not in a strange place."

"Can and will. My luggage is already in a cart."

My mind buzzed with questions. I rubbed my fingers over my temple. "But what will you do?"

She drummed her fingers against her purse and looked around me, toward the door.

I maneuvered between her and the door. "And what am I supposed to do?"

"Do as you please. Find somebody else to play maid for you."

I knew people in the lobby might be watching, but I couldn't help myself. I grabbed her arm. "No, Sue Marie, don't leave like this."

"Oh, quit making such a scene," she said, lifting my hand off her arm and nudging her chin toward the door. "Mr. Brosney is waiting for me."

I turned around. A big-eared young man stood by the door, watching us with wide eyes. I looked at Sue Marie, pulled in my lower lip, and pleaded with my expression. She merely tossed her head. A shiver shot out from my core, convulsing my arms, neck, and head. I could hardly bear the thought of Sue Marie's abandoning me. "Please, don't leave me."

"Good-bye, Pauline." She walked around me to Mr. Brosney, took his arm, and, without looking back, strolled off.

I stood reeling at the edge of the lobby, as wobbly as an old Chinese woman on tiny pegged feet, dejected and discombobulated, a veritable stranger in a foreign land. How could my own dear Sue

Marie cast me off like chattel? I wanted to be alone with the surge of distress welling up in me, with the tears threatening to break. As I turned to retreat to my room, a hefty man in a summery off-white suit swept up to me.

"Excuse me, miss," he said, his flat-featured face exuding calm and concern. "I couldn't help noticing. Are you in need of some assistance?"

His British accent struck me as civilized and genuine all at once, and his button nose and pink complexion gave him the appearance of kindliness. He had a soapy, well-scrubbed scent about him, and I guessed from the hints of creases around his eyes that he might be in his mid- to late thirties. Struggling to regain my composure, I folded my hands over my chest. "It was nothing, only a disagreement."

He cocked his head in a consoling pose. "Are you quite all right?"

I heaved out a deep breath. "I've just had a shock."

"Come, let's sit in the lounge. At least let me get you some water." He escorted me to a table in the hotel lounge and ordered a glass of water. After Mr. Hugh Carlyle introduced himself, he turned his most earnest attention to my distress.

"Can I provide any assistance, Miss Townsend?"

"No, no. She was my traveling companion."

"Forgive me if I seem to pry, but has she caused you a problem?"

"She's decided to go off on her own, which was totally unexpected."

"Ah, she's abandoned you. I say, even at twenty paces, her heartlessness chilled me to the bone."

"Yes, I thought we were dear friends."

"No true friend would behave in such a manner. She's proved her brutishness, and I daresay you deserve better."

"I thought I could count on her."

"And now you're left by yourself?"

"Completely."

"You know no one else in Shanghai?"

The way he put it quite upset me, bringing the cold reality down on me as it did. Why, I was barely acquainted with the hotel neighborhood, to say nothing of the city of Shanghai. I patted a hand over my heart to calm myself. "Not a soul. And it seems such a forbidding place."

"I can remedy that," he said, with a decisive dip of his head. "Will you permit me to show you around? Shanghai has such sights to see."

I swallowed some of the cool water the waiter had placed in front of me. The flush of my skin and quivering of my nervous limbs subsided. I summoned my most grateful smile. "I feel better already."

Three days later, on a sunny June Saturday, Mr. Carlyle hired a mule-drawn carriage and toured me around Shanghai. First we wove our way through the shopping district and took in the wares displayed in their wide windows—intricate ivory carvings, elegant water paintings, fine cloisonné, and lovely silk carpets. Well-dressed foreigners strolled the streets, mingling with Chinese women in colorful silk robes and men in muted and flowing wide-sleeved garb. The sight of all these exotic scenes and goods and the singsong cacophony of Chinese voices filled me with childlike wonderment.

"Can we stop, please?" I asked Mr. Carlyle. "So I can explore that shop?"

"Of course," he said, grinning so broadly I wondered if the delight he took in my enthusiasm exceeded even my own pleasure.

We sauntered through the aisles of a curio shop filled with jade and ivory carvings and stone chops of milky gray, burnt orange, and endless other variations on earthy tones. When a miniature horse statue—a proud, muscular stallion with a mane of thick, swirling coils—caught my eye, Mr. Carlyle indulged me with its purchase.

Next we traveled to the Jing'an Temple and strolled the perimeter of its interior court. Before the steps to one of the temple buildings, a Chinese man paused and crouched. An old stooped woman—his mother, I surmised—leaned over his backside; he circled his arms around her legs, lifted her onto his back, and carried her up the stairs.

"Why, I've never seen anything like that," I remarked, taking Mr. Carlyle's arm. How amazing it all was. Here I was in China, worlds away from my own family. I imagined recounting this scene to Maman and Gene and watching their eyes sparkle with awe. My older brother, Paul, with his misguided notions of familial duty, would probably have scoffed at this, or, for that matter, any of my stories.

"Yes," said Mr. Carlyle. "The Chinese are quite devoted to their elders. They're a very honorable people."

"They are, aren't they? I've never felt a bit afraid among them. Not even in large crowds."

After we'd covered the temple grounds and buildings, Mr. Carlyle asked, "Shall we tour the business district?"

On the drive through Shanghai's busy streets, I could think of little other than the harmony and closeness among these people and my devotion to my own family. And whenever my thoughts turned to family, I remembered my dear papa. How intrigued he would have been by China. Papa, who had dreamed of sailing all the way up the St. Lawrence Seaway and across the ocean to France, would have relished tales of my Shanghai adventure.

"Look here," said Mr. Carlyle from the open-air seat of our carriage. "We're coming into the International Settlement. You'll find some American interests here."

"But mostly British, of course," I said, nodding in the direction of the Royal Bank of London.

"The French keep to themselves in a concession just south of here. You know those French—haughty to the end."

"The trade must be lucrative for everybody involved."

"Oh, yes. Someday this business district will rival even London's." Turning to me, he asked, "Have you ever been to London?"

"No, though I should love to see it."

He patted my hand. "Then you must let me take you someday."

My friendship with Mr. Carlyle was obviously blossoming, and I truly appreciated his taking me under his wing. He was a delightful and considerate companion, and I was beginning to think I might entrust myself to his care, at least for the time being. After all, he navigated Shanghai with great ease and demonstrated agility managing the Chinese.

We returned to the hotel, and he invited me, as he had done the previous two evenings, to join him for dinner. It was over our dessert of hasty pudding that he announced, "I've business in Hong Kong next week."

I truly regretted the prospect of parting with Mr. Carlyle, but I had no claim on him. I'd assumed that the owner of a British mining interest would be bound to move on sooner or later. "Oh, and will you be gone long?"

"It's hard to say. Several executives from other businesses are gathering, and I'm required to be at their disposal."

"I shall miss your company."

Mr. Carlyle massaged his chin with his fingertips. "The thing is, I hate to leave you here on your own."

I bowed my head. Though I had met other men in my few weeks in Shanghai, I felt safest with Mr. Carlyle. When I looked up, he was studying me.

Steepling his fingers, he asked, "Would you care to join me?"

In truth, from my first sight of the Shanghai Harbor bustling with rickshaws, dockworkers, and hunched-over Chinamen speeding along on errands, I'd fallen in love with the Orient. Having heard that Hong Kong also offered wonderful shopping and that its port was among the most beautiful in the world, I beamed at Mr. Carlyle. "I should like that very much."

> <

Just as I began to put my faith in Mr. Carlyle, I made a most disconcerting discovery—and quite by happenstance. Upon our arrival in Hong Kong, he installed us in the Lu-Chou Hotel, which he explained was sufficiently removed from the one at which his fellow business executives had gathered to spare me "boorish blokes spouting about metals and mining morning, noon, and night."

The day after our arrival, Mr. Carlyle begged my indulgence. "I've an important meeting today, and it's quite possible I'll need to spend a few days away on business. I'll send word later."

Of course I was disappointed. He'd dragged me all the way to a strange city and then abandoned me. To amuse and occupy myself, I strolled the area surrounding our hotel. June is quite hot and humid in Hong Kong, worse even than Chicago at its muggiest, so I stopped for a respite at a nearby hotel, the grand-looking Olympia, which obviously catered to an English-speaking clientele. Although Mr. Carlyle hadn't named the hotel of his business compatriots, I wondered if this might be it. The ample ceiling fans cooling its lobby, as well as curiosity, drove me to explore the hotel shop, corridors, and dining room.

To my great surprise and consternation, there, in the open-air dining room at the heart of the hotel, I spotted Mr. Carlyle lunching with a woman and three children. They sat near the middle of the room, on tightly woven rattan chairs, partially shielded by one of the room's many potted palms. A few minutes of observation revealed that Mr. Carlyle was on quite familiar terms with the foursome, for the two girls and one boy dangled their legs impatiently, and both Mr. Carlyle and the woman I presumed to be his missus alternately chided the youngsters and exchanged the most casual of conversation.

I'd had a late breakfast, but, overcome with befuddlement, I decided to calm myself with a spot of lunch and requested a table on the other side of the dining area. As I strolled past the little family, I offered Mr. Carlyle the slightest dip of my head. His eyes blinked rapidly and he shifted in his chair, as if to warn me against engaging him, which I had not the least intention of doing.

Witnessing Mr. Carlyle with his family distressed me a great deal, and after lunch I hired a sedan to take me to the harbor. There, from the shelter of my covered chair, I spent a long hour watching junks and sampans crisscross the choppy waters while I contemplated my plight. The scents of onion cakes and boiling oil wafted my way from a nearby lane thick with open-air food shops, but they only stirred nausea in me. I could not have felt more alone and dejected, on my own now a world away from all that was familiar to me. First Sue Marie had deserted me, and now it appeared that Mr. Carlyle, whom I had grown quite fond of, had deceived me.

⇢⇠

When I returned to the Lu-Chou Hotel late that afternoon, I found Mr. Carlyle nursing a drink in our suite. He'd drawn the curtains on the room's southern windows, leaving the room darkened but unavoidably overheated.

He jumped to his feet. "Where have you been?"

I opened my eyes wide and blinked to adjust to the room's darkness. "I've been wandering aimlessly, worrying about what's to become of me."

Despite the room's warmth I noticed his collar remained buttoned to the top. He plopped his drink down on the side table. "Did you enjoy your lunch at the Olympia?"

I untied my hat ribbon and cast the hat on the sandalwood dresser. "How could I, distressed as I was?"

"It was altogether annoying, you sitting there, spying on me across the room."

Ripping my gloves off, I gripped them taut in my hands. "I in no way disturbed you or your lunch companions."

He leaned back on his heels and softened his tone. "Yes, well, my sister and her children surprised me with a visit."

"Your sister?" I asked. "Where is she visiting from?"

"Liverpool."

"Then she's very far from home herself." Did he truly expect me to believe he was this upset about being discovered with his *sister*? "Perhaps I can keep her and the youngsters company while you attend to your business."

"I would rather you not."

"You'll at least introduce me, won't you?"

Mr. Carlyle's usually placid face flushed to radiant pink. "I'll do no such thing."

"And why not?"

"It wouldn't be proper."

I flopped my gloves on the easy chair and planted a hand on the chair back to steady myself. "If she's your sister, and I'm your companion, what's not proper?"

"I don't want you upsetting my family."

"And what about me? You never told me you had family here."

"They're only visiting briefly. I didn't know they were coming."

"And do you intend to strand me in a strange city?"

Mr. Carlyle's arms stiffened at his sides. "No, of course not."

"You've put me in terrible straits."

"I'll pay for your return to Shanghai."

"You led me to believe I was more than a dalliance."

The sinews of his neck tightened. "I did not."

"How dare you? You invite me to travel with you, and you don't mention any family. What do you take me for?"

"I regret the circumstances."

"You deceive me, and regret is the best you can muster?"

He threw his hands up in resignation. "I'll pay you. I'll write a check right now."

"And how much do you believe my inconvenience is worth?"

"A thousand pounds."

I gasped. Having acquainted myself with the British currency, I understood this to be a sizable amount. Mr. Carlyle's wealth obviously exceeded his capacity for honesty. "A thousand pounds?"

He must have thought I judged the sum to be inadequate, for he rushed to defend it. "It's plenty. You can live in style for a year on that."

Mr. Carlyle appeared altogether willing to part with his money, and I had Maman and my family's sorry finances to consider. I glared at him, holding my head high. "And you can go back to your wife and pretend nothing happened."

"Leave my family out of this."

"I believe my troubles are worth a good three thousand pounds."

After I impressed upon him the dismal state of my—and his—plight, Mr. Carlyle agreed he'd done me wrong. He wrote a check for the amount I requested and packed up the remainder of his belongings.

I was alone again, though with sufficient funds to make a fresh start and wire a goodly sum to Maman. For why, fair reader, had I ventured to strange lands if not for my dear family's sake? But Hong Kong had left a bad taste in my mouth; I wished only to leave the city and the vexation it had visited on me far behind.

# AMERICANS IN TOKYO

•

TOKYO—1890–1891

ow could I resist Japan, where women are appreciated as cultured companions and schooled in how
to make careers of this fine art? I reasoned I could
fare far better in Japan than the only place in the United States with
female suffrage, Wyoming. Here I could apprentice under Tokyo's
revered geishas and mingle with the most distinguished men in all
of Japan—businessmen selling exotic goods all over the world, owners of the fishing fleets that plied the sea's bounties, even officials of
the royal court.

Upon arriving in Tokyo, I secured a suite at the gleaming, brand-
new Imperial Hotel, a stately and imposing facility that afforded
plentiful opportunities to meet wealthy Japanese as well as foreign
businessmen and dignitaries. I acquired a closetful of fine silk kimo-
nos and learned how to make my face up in the Japanese style, first
by applying white powder and then the lip and eye ornamentation
that stood out so vibrantly against it.

Soon I found myself mixing with men of all nationalities. I was,
however, the companion of no one man, for I was perfectly content
to keep company with a variety of influential men, among them a
French count and a member of the Argentine legation. My unfortunate relationships with Juan Ramón and Hugh Carlyle had taught
me to exercise care in choosing a gentleman friend, and I resolved
to bide my time and enjoy the freedom afforded by my unexpected
wealth as long as possible.

One festive evening claimed a regrettable place in my memories
of Japan. A diplomat from the Japanese Embassy in Canada, Mr.

Ishiguro, requested I accompany him to a gathering at the most exotic geisha house in Tokyo, the Yoshiwara. That evening, the house had been reserved for a gathering of Japanese businessmen from Narita. The party, apparently much impressed by having been invited to this renowned house, hired a photographer to memorialize the occasion. Before dinner the photographer summoned all of us to the main hall and arranged us, in two rows, before an expansive screen of tiny farmers plowing fields with yaks at the base of an imposing mountain.

Now, I am not particularly keen on photography—perhaps because my first picture was taken by the police in San Francisco—but I did not wish to upset Mr. Ishiguro or the guests, and I imagined this portrait would be the private property of only the visitors. So I took my position in the front row and smiled demurely for the photographer, keeping my face cast downward in the manner of my Japanese sisters. The rest of the evening went off quite nicely, and I forgot all about the photograph until some time later.

Each month, the Imperial Hotel hosted a reception for their honored guests in a high-ceilinged room of beige walls painted with towering bamboos and peacocks resplendent in fanned tails. It was at one of these events, in February of 1891, that I met Johnny Graham, a young New Yorker with a tall, trim silhouette and eyebrows so flaxen they blended with his fair complexion and lent his sky-blue eyes the appearance of perpetual wonderment.

While we stood apart from the groups of conversing notables, clutching our flutes of champagne, I asked, "What brings you to Tokyo, Mr. Graham?"

"I'm on my *Wanderjahr*. I've visited Paris, Calcutta, Peking, and gads of points in between."

"How exciting. I love to travel."

"You must. Not many American women would venture all the way to Japan."

"It's the most exotic place I've ever seen, though I must say I'm glad for the company of an American."

Mr. Graham looked around the dimly lit room at the attendees settled into small clutches—European, American, and Japanese men, a few with wives or lady guests—and lowered his voice. "Don't you find the Japanese a bit stiff?"

After a glance this way and that, I said, "Not compared with the British."

Mr. Graham tossed his head back and unleashed a burst of carefree laughter. I was beginning to like Johnny Graham—his casual frankness, immaculate teeth, and hands as delicate as a piano player's.

Composing himself, he bent his head to me. "Are you here by yourself?"

"Completely."

"Did you arrive on your own?"

"Yes."

"What courage. It's not easy to navigate these foreign countries."

"Given enough money, one can navigate any place." That night, I certainly looked as if I had "enough" money. I wore teardrop diamond earrings and a floor-length apricot kimono embroidered in pale-yellow and white peonies.

"Where in the States are you from?"

"Chicago." I sipped my champagne. "My father was in the restaurant business."

He tucked a hand in his pocket and studied me. "Forgive me, but I can't get over my amazement. You're traveling Japan completely on your own?"

"Yes. But why should you be amazed?" I assumed Mr. Graham was unattached. But, wary of repeating my unfortunate experience with Mr. Carlyle, I asked, "You're doing the same, aren't you?"

"Yes, but it's nothing for a man," he said, rocking on his heels. "Do you have plans to see any other places?"

"Not at the moment."

"This is my last stop before the States."

"And what happens after your world tour?"

"I take over my father's business." Mr. Graham's eyes twinkled with the unpretentious bonhomie of one who is confident fortune will favor him. "Tokyo is my last hurrah before settling down in New York."

"What business are you in?"

"Imports. Art, antiquities, furniture—that sort of thing."

"How impressive. That must require specialized knowledge."

He shrugged and said, with an utterly charming lack of pretense, "I majored in art history at Harvard."

Mr. Graham's obvious good breeding blessed him with an honest cordiality, sportive cheeriness, and a dash of naïveté, all of which I found pinch-me beguiling. We fell into each other's company that evening with the ease of long-separated friends renewing their affinity. As the reception broke up, Johnny said, "I'm not the least bit tired, and it's a crystal-clear evening. Let's take a rickshaw to Ueno Park."

The sun sets early in Tokyo in February, before six. But we'd had a string of sunny days with temperatures approaching sixty degrees, and as we traveled the city's streets that evening, the cool air did not chill so much as invigorate.

"I've a special spot to show you," said Johnny after paying our driver. He trotted ahead, pointing to a row of bare cherry trees. "Come, it's beyond those trees."

I lifted my kimono and broke into a shuffling run. "Wait for me."

"No, *you* catch *me*," called Johnny, not slowing at all.

We ran, laughing at our childishness, along a gravel path. We passed through a row of trees, and the landscape opened onto a rectangular pond rimmed by a grassy expanse. Johnny halted and stretched out his arms, as if embracing the world. "Look up. Look at the stars."

I ran to his side; he scooped me into his arms and twirled us around. Both of us cast our gaze upward, and I nearly lost my balance, save for his sure grip. We stopped, winded, our giddiness turning to wonder at the sparkling sky. Johnny let me go, shucked off his jacket, and said, "Here, lie down so you can see the whole sky."

He reclined beside me, his shoulder brushing mine.

Stars scattered across the moonless sky, as bright and twinkly as those of a deep Michigan night. Only here, half a world away, I felt I was seeing them anew. Then I remembered an evening I hadn't thought of in years. "Once, when I was a little girl, my father took my two brothers and me to a meadow filled with fireflies."

"I love fireflies," Johnny said.

"I dodged and darted from one firefly to another, until I'd caught three all at once. Papa was sitting on the edge of the meadow, watching us. I scampered up to him with my treasure. 'Look, Papa, fireflies for you,' I said and opened my hands. As they flitted away I squealed, 'Come back, Papa's fireflies.' He gathered me in his arms so that we were both looking in the same direction, and pointed at the North Star. 'See that bright star? I'll catch it for you.' Then he reached his hand out and clenched it closed. Now, whenever I look at the North Star, I think of Papa."

Johnny reached his arms to the sky and cupped his hands together again and again. "Here's another and another and another for you."

Then I did something I'd never done before—or since. Because I saw no reason to wait, because I did not wish to wait, *I* kissed *him*. His lips melted into mine, his delicious warm lips, in a kiss I shall never forget as long as I live.

→ ←

In the weeks that followed, Johnny and I became nearly inseparable: strolling through Tokyo's Yanesen neighborhood, admiring its cute, compact wooden houses; bowing to women sweeping their doorsteps; and giggling at children running gleefully through narrow corridors. We marveled at the city's temples with their stacked layers and swooping roofs; filled our evenings with sake and laughter; and bounded back and forth between his first-level room and my second-floor suite, as carefree and playful as youngsters on their first resort holiday.

One evening, I picked him up for dinner in his room and spied a small photograph on his dresser. "That's your mother and father with you?"

"Yes, Mother insisted on a photo session before I left last year. And I liked that one well enough to bring it with me."

Johnny sat between his parents, his father's square face yielding to a soft grin and his mother beaming proudly.

"Your mother's beautiful. You get your good looks from her."

"Mother is wonderful. We've always understood each other. Of course, Father loves me, and I him, but more from a distance."

I picked up the portrait. How handsome Johnny looked, with his blond hair neat and shiny, his expression radiating contentedness. As I regarded him at that moment, at a time before we'd even met, sentimentality washed over me—sentimentality I hadn't known I was capable of. "Can I keep it in my room? So I can always have you near?"

Johnny wrapped his arms around me and kissed my forehead. "Yes, but you'll never find me far away."

> <

One early March evening, after dining in my suite, Johnny reached under the pillow beside his seat and pulled out a slender box. Handing it to me, he said, "For you, Pauline. The most fascinating and clever girl in the world."

"Oh, Johnny, what have you done?"

"Open it."

I slid the cover off the ebony box. Nestled against a bed of rippled black silk lay a dazzling string of pearls. I flattened a hand over my heart. "They're beautiful. As round and shimmery as tiny moons."

"Yes, well, they're Japanese." Johnny reached out and brushed his fingers lightly over my neck. "Only the finest pearls in the world would do for you."

"Oh, Johnny, you make me feel like a princess." I took the pearls from the box and walked to the mirror over my dresser. "Help me put them on."

Johnny came up behind me, fastened the clasp, and turned me around toward him.

I gripped his shoulder and hand in a dancer's pose and swung us about in a waltz step. We laughed and dipped as I hummed "The Blue Danube," dancing in a tight circle in the space between my bed and dresser. Oh, Papa, I thought, can you see me now? I've found that man you told me to look for: someone with an ocean of money who makes my heart dance with delight. Except money and pearls don't matter, Papa—for with Johnny I've recaptured the joy and abandon of that little girl who used to twirl pirouettes for you.

> <

One afternoon two months later, while I tended to some correspondence in my room at the Imperial Hotel, my maid Kotone informed me that a gentleman wished to see me.

"Did he present a calling card?"

Kotone, a slight sixteen-year-old with a dainty nose and sharp chin, stood before me, clasping her hands over the broad waistband of her kimono. "No, he said he is Mr. Graham's friend and wishes to surprise you."

That's odd, I thought. Johnny hadn't mentioned any visitors. Nevertheless, I sent Kotone to show him in.

I rose from my desk. Kotone minced through the door, her floor-length kimono tight around her ankles, with my visitor trailing behind.

I could hardly believe my eyes. Was it really Detective Reed Dougherty? All the way from Chicago? He was as lanky and lean-faced as I remembered and, unlike at our first meeting, wore fashionable attire—a pebble-gray jacket with matching waistcoat and, in the newest style, a floppy bow tie. My mind whirred with questions. Who had hired him? Could it be about the larceny charge? Might Juan have sent him to track me down?

I signaled Kotone to my side and whispered, "Get Security."

As she slipped out of the suite, I turned to the Pinkerton and knit my hands together, budging not one inch from where I stood beside my desk. I had no intention of offering the cad a seat. "Mr. Dougherty, you were not expected."

"I'm delighted to see you as well."

"I can't imagine we have any business."

He set his frame in a sturdy pose, five feet from me, his chin upturned like that of a pompous judge. "But we do. It appears you're engaged in yet another of your adventures."

"I'm on no adventure. This is where I live now—quite far from the place you once asked me to leave."

"But not far from your old tricks."

"You've no cause to threaten me."

He fingered the felt derby which he held over his abdomen. "I'm hoping it won't come to that."

I pulled myself up straight to expand my diaphragm and inhaled. "You should know I have friends with influence in this city."

"And I must ask you to part with one particular friend."

This was my suite, paid for with my own money, and here was the person I most detested in the world invading it. Had I been a man,

I would have hoisted him by the scruff of his starched collar and booted him out. "Who my friends are is none of your business."

"John Graham does happen to be my business."

Oh, no, I thought. Not my Johnny. I fixed a steely gaze on Dougherty. "Then you should be having this conversation with him."

"As it happens, I have talked to him."

"You have no influence over me here. But, more to the point, I am doing nothing illegal."

"Mr. Graham's return to New York is long overdue."

"Mr. Graham is free to do as he pleases."

"Not when it goes against his father's wishes."

"Then his father should take the matter up with him."

"In fact, he's taken it up with me." He clutched his lapel and assumed a jaunty pose. "And I suspect you would prefer not to have a certain photograph brought to his or John's attention."

"You must be mistaken." Was it possible he'd acquired the photo taken by the San Francisco police? I had no choice but to call his bluff. "I do not pose for photographs."

"But I do have a photograph."

"I don't believe you."

"You can believe me and leave Mr. Graham, or you can take a chance on me revealing your past."

My throat constricted, but I pressed on. "There is no photograph for me to be concerned about."

"What a pity. You seemed so at home playing the geisha."

I laughed, more relieved than humored. I brushed my hand over the desk, buying a moment to shift strategy, all the time aware of Dougherty's eyes probing me. "You think a photograph of me with a party of Japanese dignitaries will matter to Johnny?"

"A whorehouse is the same the world over."

"I was merely a guest of the house. That photo means nothing."

Dougherty paused a moment, as if to weigh his options. "No, but the other picture probably will."

The door opened, and my maid hurried in with two uniformed men scurrying behind her. I called out, "Take this man away. He has stolen property from me."

The security guards seized him, and one commanded, "You come."

Dougherty flailed his arms and tried to shake free of the men. "I've stolen nothing. I'm here on official business."

"He's taken two photographs from me," I said. "Tell them, Kotone."

Kotone translated for the security guards, who nodded to me and ordered Dougherty in their stilted English, "You come with us."

The guards turned Dougherty toward the door.

"Fine," he said over his shoulder, "we'll straighten this out later."

"Good day, Mr. Dougherty," I said, as the security men hauled him off. "You can answer to the authorities now."

I threw open the sashes of my suite's front window. Along the avenue neatly pruned trees displayed shimmering lime-green leaves, but I took no delight in them, nor in early May's perfumed floral airs. My hands shook, and I clucked my cottony mouth to moisten it. Dougherty was not only the last person I'd expected to see in Tokyo, but the last person I ever wanted to see.

Now Dougherty's client, Johnny's father, wished to come between Johnny and me. I didn't believe for one minute that Johnny had deceived me: He had no wife or fiancée; he was on his world tour; and though his father had badgered him about returning to New York, Johnny had explained there was no urgent need for him to take up the business. That left only one reason for his father's concern. Money.

I needed to buy us some time—out of the reach of Dougherty's scrutiny and threats.

"Kotone," I called out, "go downstairs and see what they're doing with that man."

I kept watch at the window. Minutes later, the green-garbed security men emerged from the hotel. As they escorted Dougherty down the street, he jabbered, no doubt making a last-ditch effort to escape their clutches.

Kotone returned and joined me at the window. "They take him to police."

"As they should." I drummed my fingers on the windowsill. "When the security men return, please ask if the police will be holding him."

Kotone nodded. "Yes, miss."

"But first let's have some of that nice chrysanthemum tea. Both of us."

When Kotone brought the tea tray, I said, "You must tell me about the Japanese countryside. Come." I led the way to the couch. "Please sit with me."

Stiff-backed, she eased down on the couch, her hands planted at her sides.

I patted her hand. "What are the nicest places to visit in summer?"

"Kyoto is very pretty, very old. Beautiful temples and Kamo festival soon."

I poured tea for both of us and handed her a cup. "Yes, and where else?"

"You could go to Fujiyama. Very big mountain. Very pretty from train."

"I'll have to talk it over with Johnny." I held the teacup under my nostrils, breathing in its sweet floral scent and relishing the soothing steam.

Kotone sat beside me, her frame quite still as she tilted her teacup to her lips.

I sipped my tea. Its delicate taste stimulated my own glands, assuaging the dryness of my mouth and calming my rattled nerves. Placing my teacup on the tray, I faced Kotone. "Please see to my laundry this afternoon. I'll want to pack in the next day or two."

# MY OWN DEAR JOHNNY

·

*J*ohnny had gone out to his bank that day to conduct some business, so I left a message at the desk asking him to join me for a late-afternoon stroll. When he returned, we took a rickshaw to Ueno Park and set out under its canopy of broad-branching cherry trees.

I took Johnny's arm as we stepped onto a wide walkway at the park's center. "How was your day?"

"Not very agreeable, really."

The finely graveled path crunched beneath our feet. "I'm sorry. What made it disagreeable?"

"Nothing I need to bother you about."

I suspected Johnny had received yet another missive from his father, perhaps via his bank, asking him to quit Tokyo. Or perhaps Dougherty had upset him. I nestled my hand into the crook of his arm. "You never told me about your dinner with that associate of your father's."

"Oh, yes, Mr. Dougherty. Quite a nice fellow."

The late-afternoon sun broke through the tunnel of trees here and there, warming my back, and I steered us toward a stone bench in some deep shade. "Did your father send him here on business?"

"No, Father only asked him to stop and see how I was doing. And pass along the news from home."

Apparently, Johnny's father preferred to handle this matter discreetly. Or maybe Dougherty realized he needed to tread delicately, in view of Johnny's attachment to me.

"Nothing's wrong, I hope."

"Not at all; we're meeting again tomorrow."

Just as I feared. Dougherty was sinking his claws into Johnny, and I couldn't risk any more meetings between them. I could only hope the police would hold Dougherty long enough to keep him away from Johnny. I paused at the stone bench, inviting Johnny to sit beside me. "And is Mr. Dougherty staying in Tokyo long?"

"I'm not sure." Johnny leaned back and braced his hand on the bench. "He seemed to know about you."

The coolness of the stone seat seeped into my legs. I forced calm onto my expression, suppressing the fury seething in my veins. "Really? What?"

"Just that I was seeing someone. Father must have passed it along. Anyway, I told him we're having a marvelous time."

"Oh, Johnny, I don't want it ever to end." I rested my head on his shoulder. Should I just tell him everything? No, I couldn't stomach the thought of dashing Johnny's trust in me.

I felt Johnny tense up. Pulling my head off his shoulder, I looked him full in the face. "What's wrong?"

He smoothed a hand over his forehead. "Father's put a limit on my withdrawals."

"Why would he do that?"

"To force me to come home."

"Oh, Johnny, I don't want to lose you."

"Soon I'll have to go home."

"Let's go away first. Just you and me. Take me to Mount Fuji for my birthday."

Johnny leaned over his knees and studied his feet. "I'm running low on funds."

"Don't worry about money. I have money."

He nodded, letting the idea sink in. "Yes, I could stand a break from Father's constant letters."

"Can we leave tomorrow?"

"Well, I'm dining with Mr. Dougherty tomorrow night. How about Friday?"

If the police released Dougherty before Thursday evening, I would have to keep them apart, but without making a fuss. First I needed to find out how long Dougherty would be jailed. I clapped a hand on Johnny's thigh. "You promise? Friday morning?"

He nodded, concentrating his lips in his own endearing way of showing resolve.

I wrapped my arm in his and nestled close to him.

He kissed my forehead and asked, "Can you have Kotone make the arrangements?"

"Of course," I said.

As we rose to leave the park, I nudged Johnny. "Look at the young couple over there. Don't they look happy?"

→ ←

By the time Johnny called on me the next afternoon, Kotone had ascertained that the police were still holding Dougherty. Although they had questioned him about the whereabouts of the stolen photos, Dougherty had revealed nothing. Since time was of the essence, I asked Johnny if he'd begun packing for our trip to Fujiyama.

He relaxed into the pillows on my suite's low-slung sofa. "I had some other business to attend to. I can pack in the morning."

"Why not tonight?" The golden crane-patterned wallpaper of my suite reflected the afternoon sun piercing the windows. Suddenly it struck me as monotonous. How many months had I sat in this room surrounded by the same walls, the same simple furniture?

"I'm dining with Mr. Dougherty this evening."

I hurried to the sofa and sat beside Johnny. "He hasn't sent you word?"

"Of what?"

"That he's indisposed."

"No, why should he?"

I crossed my legs at the ankles and swiveled toward Johnny. "Mr. Dougherty is not who you think he is."

Johnny leaned forward, bracing his hands on his knee tops. "What do you mean?"

"It would be best if you didn't see him again."

"But that would be an insult. What's this about?"

"I'd rather not embarrass your father. Please don't ask any more questions."

"But my father sent him here. If he's sponsored Dougherty's trip, he has a right to know."

I swallowed and moistened my lips. "Dougherty is being questioned by the police for theft."

"Theft?"

"And I guarantee he'll lie to your father about it."

"You're sure?"

"I saw Security escort him out of our hotel. You can ask the authorities."

"How do you know he's in jail?"

"I have connections with city officials. Why wouldn't I know what happens to Americans in Tokyo?"

"Are you sure it's Dougherty?"

"Mr. Reed Dougherty, a lanky fellow with a horsy face. Staying at the Seiyoken Hotel. Isn't that him?"

Johnny frowned. "Yes, yes, it is."

"Well, I'm afraid you won't find him at dinner tonight."

⇒⇐

Johnny and I left Tokyo the next morning, while Dougherty languished in jail. But I knew Dougherty would be released sooner or later, so to throw him off our trail I changed plans.

Once Johnny and I reached the outskirts of Tokyo, I told him, "We're going to Kyoto instead of Mount Fuji. I wanted to surprise you."

We checked into the Hotel Okura in Kyoto a few days before the Kamo festival. On festival day, we secured seats with a commanding view of the parade: ox carriages overflowing with geranium leaves and an envoy of people dressed in colorful, flowing silk garb.

"Incredible," Johnny said, as awed by the display as I was. "And it's such a sublime city. Let's stay for your birthday."

We spent the next week touring Kyoto's beautiful temples: Kiyomizu temple, situated on a steep hill and offering a commanding view of Kyoto; the shimmering Temple of the Golden Pavilion, a three-story temple topped with a bronze phoenix that sparkled under the clear May skies; and Fushimi Inari Taisha, a shrine at the top of a pathway lined with thousands of thick, bright red posts.

I turned twenty-two on May 23, and that evening Johnny escorted me to a small restaurant in the heart of Kyoto. He had obviously taken great care in selecting and arranging the dinner. Once we finished dining, the whole staff—two male cooks and three waitresses—presented themselves in the doorway of our private chamber to wish me a happy birthday.

Johnny folded his hands and dipped his head, Japanese-style, to show his gratitude. "*Arigato*. We're ready for our dessert now."

When the staff retreated, I reached for Johnny's hand. "Life with you is the sweetest adventure."

Johnny raised my chin with his fingertips, leaned close, and kissed me. "I forget the rest of the world when I'm with you."

"You are my joy, my peace."

"My dear, dear Pauline. I could never have dreamed you up."

The curtain to our room parted and our waitress shuffled out of her shoes. She entered and placed a bowl of colorful round delicacies in front of each of us.

"Oh, cream *anmitsu*," I said, "my favorite Japanese dessert."

The waitress's mouth betrayed the slightest smile as she plucked a little pitcher of dark liquid from her tray and placed it in the middle of our table. She looked at Johnny. He nodded, and she took a tiny box off the tray and put it beside my bowl. Bowing, she retreated, and the curtains to our room rippled closed behind her.

I stared at the box, so small it made me wonder: Could it be a ring? My heart pounded. My cheeks and ears flushed with excitement.

Johnny took up the pitcher and poured sweet black syrup over our dessert bowls. "Would you like to open your gift?"

Taking in a deep breath to calm myself, I lifted the box, gripped the bottom with my quivering fingertips, and pulled the top off. A ring. A diamond ring. I looked up at Johnny.

"Will you marry me, Pauline?"

I clapped a hand over my heart. "Oh, Johnny, I can hardly believe it."

"You'll be my fiancée. We can travel to New York together."

I wanted nothing more than to say yes, to guarantee a life of happiness with Johnny. But I had thought of just one way to foil the obstacles Dougherty had thrown in our path.

"I can't tell you how happy you've made me." I reached for his hand. "Only can't we stay in Japan? Can't we get married here?"

"Darling, my family will love you. I wouldn't dream of depriving them of a wedding in New York."

"Can't we just live here? I'm so happy here with you."

"And I with you. We can be happy anywhere, dear girl, as long as we're together."

"I have plenty of money to get us started. Together we could buy antiquities and export them to the States."

Confusion crept over Johnny's features. "But I can't let my family down. Everything's been planned, from my schooling at Harvard to an office designed just for me. With a desk my grandfather brought over from Scotland."

I gulped. I could never explain why I wanted to stay in Japan.

Johnny patted my hand. "Don't worry, darling. It'll be perfect—you and me in a home of our own in New York."

I wanted to tell him everything, right then and there: I'm not Pauline. I'm not the daughter of a well-to-do restaurant owner. I've made mistakes. Dougherty is trying to separate us. He thinks I'm after your money. It's not true. You're my own dear Johnny. I love you. As I've never loved anyone before.

Johnny cupped his hand over mine. "Please say yes, my darling."

I couldn't bear to crush Johnny's spirit. My trusting Johnny believed everything I had ever told him. Never had he doubted me. To him I was a sweet girl with an innocent past. His Pauline.

I gazed into his beckoning eyes. "Yes."

He reached out for my hand and slipped the ring on my finger.

My throat nearly burst from the lump of sadness massing in it. I looked at him, my eyes misting over. "I love you, Johnny. I love everything about you."

"My dear, wonderful Pauline."

Pauline—how the name grated at my ears, signifying, as it did, nothing but pretense.

I clasped his hands. I wanted to never let go.

Johnny squeezed my hands. "Everything will be perfect. Leave it all to me."

→←

Johnny's happiness that evening only intensified my agony: I desperately feared losing him. Once Dougherty reported back to Johnny's father, his family might well refuse to meet me—or spurn Johnny if we married. I had to somehow spare Johnny the heartache of family abandonment. I had to outwit Dougherty.

Just as Johnny and I prepared to depart Kyoto and hasten back to the States, I received a message from Reed Dougherty: "I think we should take up that business we failed to resolve in Tokyo."

Dougherty had managed to track us down despite my efforts to evade him. I had little choice but to meet the roving detective, so I sent word that I would call on him late that afternoon at his out-of-the-way hotel. (He obviously hadn't had sufficient influence to secure any of the finer hotels in town.)

He welcomed me to a shadowy private room in his hotel's dining area and poured cups of sake for us.

I knew my options were diminishing, but my love for Johnny drove me to try my hand. "Mr. Dougherty, you seem terribly determined to make an issue of something that is none of your business."

He sat on a pillow with his gangly legs crossed at the ankles. "It became my business once John started draining his bank account for you."

Out of habit, I picked up my sake cup. But the thought of taking sake with Dougherty repelled me, and I quickly replaced it. "Johnny is free to spend his money as he wishes."

"It's not exactly his money. It's family money, and his father asks that the spending stop."

"You can't separate us. What do I care about a couple of photos?"

"Obviously enough to ransack my room."

"You made such a fuss about them. My curiosity was aroused."

With all the leisure of a lord out for a Sunday stroll, Dougherty sipped his sake and placed his cup back on the table. "I'm sure Johnny and his family would also find them fascinating."

If only I could get the photographs. Perhaps it would rob him of the proof he needed to turn Johnny's family against me. "If you'll turn over the photographs, I'll leave Johnny."

"And if you'd found them in my hotel room, I suppose we wouldn't be having this conversation."

"I told you, I'll quit seeing Johnny if you hand them over."

"That wouldn't help you."

"Why not?"

"One set is in government custody."

"And what do you propose to do with them?"

"Nothing if you leave Johnny."

"That would make Johnny very unhappy."

"According to you."

"I know how Johnny feels."

He eyed my engagement ring. "I see you've extracted a promise of marriage from him."

"Extracted? How dare you insult Mr. Graham with such a cheap insinuation."

"I can tell you with the utmost confidence that his family will not countenance the likes of you."

"You can't keep us apart."

Dougherty tapped his fingers on the table. "If he stays with you, his family will cut him off. But, more to the point, you're wanted for larceny. And if you dare to set foot on U.S. soil with John Graham, I'll have you arrested."

# THE TRIAL

*O*ver the course of the Friday-morning session, Sawyer finally wrapped up his overly solicitous questioning of Frank.

"Miss Shaver, when did your friendship with the Baroness end for a second time?"

"In July of last year, after she learned my inheritance was drained and that I was up to my neck in the Highland Park mortgage."

"How did she respond to this news?"

"She dropped me like a hot penny."

The women onlookers (excepting the reporters, there were only women in the courtroom today) muttered to each other, as if this were the damning news they'd been waiting for all along. But they hadn't bargained on the evidence my attorney was about to introduce.

After Sawyer yielded the floor, Judge Flanagan turned to my lawyer. "Mr. Powers, I assume you would like to cross-examine?"

"Yes, thank you, Your Honor." Powers rose and marched to the witness box. His pomaded gray hair glistened under the glare of the courtroom's bare lightbulbs. "Miss Shaver, you graduated from high school in Pittsburgh and attended the University of Pennsylvania, didn't you?"

"Yes."

"And did you have occasion to learn arithmetic along the way?"

"Of course."

Powers took a few steps to the right, toward the jurors. "So you do know how to add and subtract?"

"Yes."

"And you graduated from the University of Michigan Law School?"

"I did."

Mr. Powers paced back to the witness box. "Started a law practice in Chicago and Menominee after that?"

"Yes."

"Did you have to manage or oversee the finances of those practices?"

"I had an assistant tend the books."

"Did you ever check the books?"

"Monthly."

"Did that involve counting dollars?"

"Not exactly. It involved checking the expenses and collections."

Powers stroked his hand over his chin, as if contemplating some weighty matter, and then, releasing his hand, asked, "Then how can you claim not to know the value of a dollar?"

Frank paused. Several of the jurors leaned forward. The court-house mice likely pricked up their ears at the sudden silence.

I recited a prayer of quiet gratitude for my attorney. My side had taken quite a bruising during Frank's direct examination. And with over a hundred thousand dollars at stake, I needed a strong defense. The fact is, I didn't have that kind of money.

Frank held her head up high. "I meant exactly what I said. I grew up with plenty of money; my parents never flaunted the family wealth; and I expected my inheritance to last a long time."

"Are you saying that, when you inherited two hundred thousand dollars from your father's estate, you considered that an unlimited amount?"

"I'm saying two hundred thousand would have lasted a lifetime if May hadn't come along."

"That's not what I asked. Did you think that sum was unlimited?"

"More or less."

"Even when you withdrew tens of thousands at a time?"

"That's how I grew up, believing that there was always more."

"How can a lawyer not understand the simple matter of subtraction?"

Sawyer shoved his chair back and stood. "Objection, counsel is badgering."

"Sustained," said Judge Flanagan.

Mr. Powers walked to the defendant's table and selected a paper from the lineup of pages he had spread out there. Approaching Frank, he said, "Miss Shaver, I'll ask you to examine the signature on this sheet."

Frank took the sheet from Powers and examined it. "Yes, that looks like my signature."

"Does it look like it, or is it your signature?"

"I guess it's my signature."

"And do you recall signing this on December 11, 1915?"

"Vaguely."

"Will you read it, please?"

In an uncharacteristically subdued manner, Frank read, "By this document I, Frank Shaver, hereby release the Baroness May de Vries from all debts and loans, and everything else that may be construed as such."

Powers had been studying the floor, as if to absorb every word of the reading. "Now, Miss Shaver, you are an attorney, correct?"

"Yes, but there were extenuating circumstances."

Powers rushed in. "You signed this contract, did you not?"

"Yes, but I didn't understand it."

"Do you deny this is a simple contract, understandable to a layman?"

Sawyer rose. "Objection, argumentative."

"Sustained," said Flanagan.

Powers forged ahead. "What didn't you understand, Miss Shaver?"

"I was very ill at the time; I couldn't take it all in."

"Did you know the word 'everything' was in it?"

"No, I didn't know what was in it."

"You signed without carefully reading it, without noticing the word 'everything'?"

"I was ill."

"If you were ill, why did you entertain signing a contract?"

"Even when I'm ill, I can always write. And talk." Frank gripped the sides of the witness box and pitched forward. "The fact is, I trusted May and she tricked me."

With a sigh, I relaxed in my chair. We had a signed release. No amount of squirming or wheedling on Frank's part could undo that.

# A JOURNEY OF SOUL SEARCHING

·

*A*s the crew pulled up ropes and the ship drifted away from Tokyo's harbor, I sought a perch at the rear starboard. The lumbering *Maiden of the Seas* turned and headed for open water, destined for Vancouver, Canada. I leaned over the ship's rail to study Tokyo's bustling shoreline and the buildings rising beyond its piers. Johnny was back there, at the Imperial Hotel. And I, standing apart from my fellow travelers in mourner's black, already grieved our loss.

By now he'd probably awakened and discovered my note and the engagement ring (for I could not keep sweet, innocent Johnny's ring under the circumstances): "Forgive me, Johnny. I love you, but we cannot be together. I am not who you think I am. Though I will treasure your memory always, I beg you, for your sake and mine, to forget me. I am leaving Tokyo—and you—today, because I am not good enough for you. Yours, Pauline."

All I could think of was Johnny reading my words, crying out in anguish, and racing out of the hotel in search of me. Even now he might be standing at water's edge, watching my ship dwindle on the horizon.

Tears, unbidden, streamed down my cheeks. I hated writing that farewell note, wrenching myself away from Johnny. Only the necessity of my sacrifice spurred me on. My poor, dear Johnny. He wouldn't understand, couldn't understand. Even if Dougherty broke his promise and told Johnny everything he knew about me, it wouldn't have mattered to him. Sweet, naïve Johnny would have told me he loved me just the same. But I knew his family would never accept me, and I refused to condemn Johnny to a life apart from them. My love for him compelled me to save him from my mistakes. If I'd allowed my selfishness to prevail, I would have ruined the man I loved—my trusting, loyal Johnny.

The ship picked up speed, its propellers churning the waters in its wake and heaving it over the waves. The chill, damp air misting my face and neck sent shivers through me. With each lurch of the ship, my stomach writhed. I believed I had found my one true love in Johnny. But now the cold, hard metal of the ship parted the waters, speeding me out onto the deep sea, dispatching me to an uncertain future. A future without Johnny.

Dirty smoke belched from the ship's two stacks, roiling into a murky trail pointing back to Tokyo's harbor. Might Johnny check the boat departures and discover I'd taken this ship to Vancouver? Would he board the next ship, the one sailing for America, and try to track me down?

Much as I hoped he would find me, I knew I couldn't allow it. I would spend only one day in Vancouver, long enough to purchase a train ticket and continue my eastward journey. Even if Johnny took the next ship out of Tokyo, he'd never make it from San Francisco to Vancouver in time to stop me. Nevertheless, fantasies filled my mind: I imagined Johnny finding me, swooping me into his arms, insisting we need never, ever part.

Still, in numb conviction, here I was, rushing away from him. How it stung my heart to know that each day at sea and each mile of rail would take me farther and farther from Johnny.

All I had ever wanted was a respectable and happy life. Yes, I admit, I desired the ease that wealth brings, but not money simply for money's sake: money so that I might enjoy travel, fine dining, and exotic sights in the company of someone I loved.

Had I ruined my chances for such a life? Were my prospects doomed ever since hunger and destitution drove me to Carrie Watson's in Chicago? After all, my association with Miss Watson had given Reed Dougherty the ammunition he needed to break up my engagement to Dale, my hopes for a life with Johnny. Had I erred in joining forces with Sue Marie? If I'd never met her, I wouldn't have been seduced into the plot that landed us in jail. Could I ever live these things down?

How different my life would be if I'd never crossed paths with the

Pinkertons. I could hardly believe Dougherty had tracked me down in Tokyo. How incredible that he'd managed to foil me with the only two mistakes I had ever made in my life—being desperate enough to enter Miss Watson's employ, and being foolish enough to allow Sue Marie to use me for her schemes.

I couldn't undo my past, but I could learn from it. I would go someplace where no one knew of my mistakes, find the dignified and cultivated life I longed for, and live it honorably, albeit without Johnny.

I'm sorry, Johnny. So sorry my mistakes cost us a future of bliss. May you find happiness with someone more worthy than I.

*I* spent the rest of the summer in Menominee, basking in the acceptance and easy amiability one can find only with family. Young Gene had sprouted into a lean fourteen-year-old, rambunctious as a colt raring to run the range. Maman still took in sewing orders, but only for people she was "partial to." As for Paul, he rose with the roosters six days a week to slave away at the lumber mill.

Over those late summer months, thoughts of Johnny rushed into any empty space in my mind, every idle moment of my time. I hashed and rehashed the events leading to our forced parting—the incredible happenstance of it all, how Reed Dougherty had robbed me of the love of my life. Could I have done anything differently? Should I have called Dougherty's bluff? No, no, I always answered the same way: I'd done the right thing for Johnny. Young and well educated, he had the assurance of a position in an established business and the welcoming society of his well-to-do family. How could I have allowed him to turn his back on this bright future? No, if I had stayed and permitted Dougherty to tell Johnny of my past, Johnny would have clung to me all the same. But the cost to him would have been more than he could or should have borne.

⤳ ⤶

As the leaves in Menominee took on red and pumpkin hues and fall's chill tinged the air, my thoughts turned to travel. Before the funds I'd acquired from Mr. Carlyle in Hong Kong ran out, I resolved to explore London. And to get to London, I would have to journey through New York. Johnny was most certainly settled there by now.

Perhaps I could catch a glimpse of him—undetected, of course—just to assure myself that he had adjusted to his new life. Still, I knew I'd need to stay on alert for Dougherty, in case he expected me to resurface there.

I would require a companion for my travels. Upon arriving in New York, I placed an advertisement in the "Women Wanted" employment section of the *New York Herald*. I knew exactly what I wanted in an assistant: She must be competent, worldly, well versed in fashion, and not overly serious. In my room at the Gilsey House, I interviewed the candidates, dismissing one after another of the dreary lot. Late in day two of my search, yet another applicant knocked at my door.

"Yes, come in," I called, too disheartened to rise and open the door after hours of wearying exchanges with the most humdrum creatures.

The door opened to reveal a young woman dressed in a rather daring outfit for an October day, albeit an unseasonably sunny one: a cream-colored blouse and matching skirt, tawny lace-up shoes, and a toque decorated with a few slips of purple aster. Her broad mouth, close-set eyes, and longish face suggested an alert pensiveness. The whole effect—her fashionable but out-of-season dress, the self-assured look on her plain face, and a hint of expensive gardenia perfume about her well-proportioned figure—was as incongruous as a rose blooming in snow.

I rose to greet her. "Hello, I'm May Dugas." I had chosen to use my real name again, since I had nothing to hide from anybody in New York. Besides, if Johnny—or Dougherty—hoped to find me here, they would not be searching for May Dugas. And, after all, I had resolved to make a fresh start.

"Pleased to meet you, miss." Her torso dipped in the slightest approximation of a curtsy. "Belle Emmett at your service."

"Please, have a seat." I directed her to the overstuffed chair I'd had installed for the interviews and took my seat opposite her. "Tell me, have you had any experience as a lady's assistant?"

"Yes, I have." She sat upright, with hands folded on her lap, and her expression danced with lively intelligence, as if she were on the verge of delivering some brilliant nugget. "Here in New York. For the past three years."

"And what were your duties?"

She unclasped her hands and patted her fingertips together.

From the pink flush of her smooth complexion, I estimated her age to be eighteen or nineteen. "Anything and everything. I was maid to Mrs. Edmund Swinburne."

"Was? Are you no longer in her employ?"

"No, Mrs. Swinburne will be leaving the city."

"And you'll not accompany her?"

Miss Emmett cast her eyes to the side a moment and tilted her head back in a prideful pose. "Mrs. Swinburne is going to live with her sister and brother-in-law. Mr. Swinburne was just sent to prison for insurance fraud."

I nodded. "And you are all honesty, I should say."

"I hope my employer's ill-chosen deeds won't disqualify me."

Who was I to hold such a thing against her? Besides, the girl had spunk. I smiled at her. "I should think a weeklong trial is in order. Would that be satisfactory?"

Miss Emmett accepted the terms of my offer, and I asked her to begin the very next day by taking me on a tour of New York. As she gripped the doorknob to let herself out, she turned and asked, "What of New York have you already seen?"

"I've walked Central Park and the Brooklyn Bridge. Seen the shops on Fifth Avenue. And dined at Delmonico's."

"Hmm," she said. "Would you like to see the other New York, then? Its people and merchants?"

"I should like that very much."

> <

Miss Emmett, in a sturdy blue day dress quite appropriate to the season and nature of our outing, met me in the Gilsey lobby promptly at 10 a.m. We boarded a carriage she had arranged for our tour, a dull red brougham with fraying seams and a musty interior.

"Carry on, Dicky," she called to a boy of no more than fifteen sitting in the driver's seat. With a jiggle of the reins and a heigh-ho, we were on our way, traveling at a trot over the city's cobblestone streets.

"You know the driver?" I asked.

"He's my brother. He's been working for the Swinburnes, too."

"And this brougham?"

She hesitated a moment, and I wondered if a long story might be in the offing. But if that was the case, she opted for the short one. "He's borrowed it for the day."

Miss Emmett and I sat side by side in the compact brougham, with me taking in as much scenery as the two-by-two side windows allowed. The day had turned chill, with thick clouds blocking out the sun. As the carriage turned, I spied a church with a tall, knob-decorated spire rising above all the neighboring buildings. "What a beautiful church. How it reaches to the heavens."

"Oh, that's Trinity Church," Miss Emmett said. "One of the oldest buildings in Manhattan."

The carriage trundled over several narrow streets, and the harbor came into view.

"And that round building," said Miss Emmett, pointing out her side of the carriage, "is Castle Garden. Where they process the immigrants."

We passed by the building's domed rotunda. Two flags as wide as small houses—Old Glory and the New York State flag—graced the poles on opposite sides of the building's dome, their rippled weight snapping under the harbor's steady wind. In front of the building, wagons packed with people, trunks, and lumpy sacks wove among a horde of pedestrians—men in rumpled pants and jackets, women in droopy dresses, and wide-eyed children muddling along beside their parents. Our carriage slowed as we merged with the clutter of wagons and walkers weaving about in front of Castle Garden.

I couldn't take my eyes off the multitude of people in all their slatternly garb.

"It's like this nearly every day," Miss Emmett said.

Our carriage cleared the clot of wagons, and Dicky turned onto a street bordering the harbor.

"Would you care to stroll the piers?" Miss Emmett asked.

"Yes, let's do."

She rapped on the front of the compartment, and Dicky pulled the carriage to the street side. Before we could let ourselves out, he had jumped down and opened the door for us. Dicky, whose neat jacket could not hide the ill-fitting pants roped around his skinny waist, offered his hand and stole a glance at me as he helped me out.

We walked along the pier, passing an array of ships in the harbor: the ocean liner *La Gascogne*; sailboats of forty- to fifty-foot lengths;

and tugboats coming and going. Fall's cold air wafted in from the river, carrying scents of fishy seawater and the ships' dusty coal smoke. As we approached one of the jutting piers, the sounds of splashing and children yelping increased, arousing my curiosity as to the cause of the commotion. We strolled to the other side of the pier. There the shore sloped into the water, and young boys and girls in nothing but undergarments ran about in the shallows while a loose gathering of women in scarves and shabby dresses watched. Given the chill of the day, the youngsters' squeals did not surprise me.

"Swimming?" I said to Miss Emmett. "At this time of year?"

"No, no," she said, chuckling. "They're bathing."

Behind me a burst of laughter sounded. I spun around to discover Dicky doubled over and clapping a hand over his mouth. When he saw me, he straightened up and said, "Not swimming, miss."

I turned to find Miss Emmett hunched over in a feeble attempt at restraining her amusement, whereupon I, too, burst into laughter; it was a good while before the three of us regained our composure.

"Oh, dear me," said Miss Emmett. "I've worked up an appetite. Do you like oysters, Miss Dugas?"

"I love them."

We returned to the carriage, and Miss Emmett instructed Dicky to drive us to City Oysters and Seafood, a raucous restaurant overlooking the Hudson River.

As Miss Emmett and I settled at a table by the expansive front window, I asked, "Won't Dicky want lunch?"

"Dicky can take care of himself. He's been working on his own for two years now."

"Driving a carriage?"

"Yes. He learned about horses and driving by frequenting Central Park. Did chores for lessons."

We ordered our oysters, and I asked Miss Emmett, "Do you have any other brothers or sisters?"

"Had a little sister. Died when she was six."

"Are you from New York?"

"New Jersey, right across the river from here." Miss Emmett poked her chin, and I followed her gaze to the jagged string of buildings on the opposite shore.

"Do your parents still live there?"

"Mother does. We don't know where Father is."

"What was his work?"

"He used to own a grocery store."

The clang of plates and utensils rang out around us, and the buzz of chatter pulsed over the jam-packed booths and stools. I leaned across the table to better hear and be heard. "What happened to his grocery business?"

"He sold it. Or lost it gambling." Miss Emmett shrugged. "Took up professional card playing."

"So he travels around doing that?"

"He's made a life of train and boat travel. Playing cards with strangers."

"You mean with people who don't know he's a card sharp?"

Miss Emmett nodded, her lips clamped in glum resignation.

"And your mother. How does she manage?"

"She takes in laundry. And Dicky and I help as much as we can."

I reached out and patted her hand. "We have a few things in common, I'd say."

She studied me with unblinking eyes. "How's that?"

"Having mothers who are on their own. Who need our help."

A smile of knowing recognition flitted over her face. "Most people call me Daisy. I'd be pleased if you would, too."

> <

It appeared that Daisy Emmett was someone I could trust. She was not afraid to tell the truth, but she showed good judgment, too. After we agreed on her salary, I apprised her of my intent to journey to London, which pleased her greatly. But first, I explained, I wished her to make discreet inquiries about an old friend, a young man now in the arts-and-antiquities business in New York.

Two days later, she strode up to me in the lobby of the Gilsey. "Miss Dugas," she said, "I've news of John Graham."

I slipped a marker into the page of my *Baedeker's London and Its Environs*. "Yes—what did you learn?"

"I think we should go to your room."

I closed the book on my lap. "Why?"

She stood as erect as a pine tree, her five-foot-six frame looming over me. "You said you wanted to be discreet, didn't you?"

I rose and headed for the stairs, all impatience. "Must you be so awfully good at following instructions?"

Once in my fifth-floor room, Daisy led me to my easy chair and commanded, "Sit."

I eased down and looked up at her.

She unfurled a *New York Sun* and pointed to a column. "It's old news now. Happened two weeks ago."

My eyes latched on the column headline: "John D. Graham Found Dead in Apartment."

I stared at the words "John D. Graham." "No, no, it can't be," I said. "It can't be my Johnny."

Daisy cocked her head to meet my gaze. "Your Johnny?"

"We were engaged."

"Did you meet him in Tokyo?"

"Yes."

"Oh, my."

"Please," I said, more as a desperate prayer than anything else, "don't let it be him." I pictured Johnny: bounding up our hotel stairs and turning to scoop me into his arms; glowing with awe at Japan's intricate, soaring temples; laughing so hard at my imitations of Kotone that he rolled off his chair. Johnny, so spirited, so full of life, couldn't be gone.

"I'm sorry, then, for it *is* your Johnny." Daisy ran her hand down the column. "It says here he killed himself for love of a woman he met in Tokyo."

I crumpled over my knees. "Oh, no. Oh, Johnny, please forgive me."

Daisy brushed her hand over my back. "You loved him."

I buried my face in my hands. The headline's words imprinted on the dark screen of my tight-closed eyelids, glaring at me like an indictment. "I killed him. I killed him."

Daisy gripped my shoulder. "Don't say that."

"It's true." My insides sloshed. Nauseous, I crumpled over. "I didn't have the courage to stand by his side."

"How could you have known?"

"What does that matter?" I dug my fingernails into my forehead. Their sharpness cut into my flesh. I wanted to feel pain. "Johnny's dead. And it's because of me."

# LONDON AIRS

*I* refused to leave New York without first paying tribute to Johnny. I enlisted Daisy's brother to transport me and my miniature memorial to Trinity Church Cemetery on Riverside Drive. I obtained directions to Johnny's grave from the groundskeeper and set out down the designated row of gravestones in my simple black dress and wide-brimmed hat and veil. As I caught sight of Johnny's fresh grave, I clutched my belly—it chilled me to imagine his once-vital body lying there, inert in its coffin. The earth mounding before his marble headstone glistened under October's misty sky, its newness a personal rebuke: You might have saved him.

Closing my eyes, I silently recited my last words to him: "My dear Johnny, forgive me for not honoring our love. You will always be my Romeo." I opened my eyes to the quiet midday, to the place that would be Johnny's home forever. A morning rain had moistened the tree trunks and fallen leaves, deepening their hues to burnt brown and rust. A piquant mushroom odor—of grass and loam and dying leaves—chafed at my nostrils.

"Dicky," I said, calling the reluctant youngster to join me at the graveside. "You can unwrap the stone now."

Dicky unfolded the burlap covering to reveal the simple memorial, a slender, foot-wide stone plaque on a solid base, and handed it to me. I placed it at the foot of Johnny's grave, so that he might gaze down upon it, and walked to the head of the grave, where I could view its inscription:

TO MY JOHNNY, FOR WE WERE ONCE
A PAIR OF STAR-CROSS'D LOVERS.

Once I had completed my private remembrance ceremony, I couldn't quit New York fast enough. It pained me to look at the tall buildings, walk through Central Park, or dine in any of its fine restaurants. All I could think was, Johnny might have eaten in this very place, Johnny must have gazed on these buildings, Johnny probably trod this street. I wanted to blame someone: Reed Dougherty for his unscrupulous, coldhearted pursuit of Johnny and me; Johnny's father for hiring a Pinkerton to do what a family member could and should have done; and Johnny's family for not giving us a chance. But what good did that do? Johnny was gone, and I'd had a hand, unknowing as it was, in his tragic end.

Never again, I vowed. Never would I permit myself to mix with a young man under the thumb of a reproving family. Never again would I risk wounding someone as decent and innocent as Johnny.

The path to my new life materialized quite clearly: I would slip into the respectable and cultured life I'd sought all along, and in doing so I would avoid giving Dougherty, or any of his ilk, leverage over me. Such was my frame of mind upon setting foot in London in November of 1891.

→ ←

I wished for two things from London: to distract myself from the pain and sorrow of Johnny's tragic death, and to insert myself into London's high society. I hoped to satisfy both in the West End theater district, where I took a suite at the Shaftesbury Hotel for Daisy and myself. Soon enough, Daisy had researched the London theaters and discovered that the Royal English Opera House, which had closed after one run of *Ivanhoe*, was struggling to reopen. Convinced the venerably named establishment warranted my support, I offered modest sponsorship for its new production of André Messager's opera *La Basoche*. After a run of the opera, the theater planned a grand party on closing night in January 1892. I was to attend with another donor, Alfred Cooper, the brother of the conductor, and his bachelor son.

"I suspect," I told Daisy as I seated myself at my maple vanity and opened my jewelry case, "that Mr. Cooper is anxious to introduce me to his son."

"Why shouldn't he be?" asked Daisy, pulling out the necklace compartment. "Everyone wonders why you've not stepped out with any gentleman."

The yellow-diamond necklace, I thought, would look lovely against my jade-green gown. I pointed to it. "By rights I should be wearing black. Except then I'd have to explain to everyone who I'm mourning."

Daisy picked up the necklace, lowered it around my throat, and latched it. She folded her palms over my shoulders. "You can't do anything about Johnny. You have to live your life."

"If only I could convince my heart of that."

Daisy closed the jewelry box. "You shouldn't put off insuring your jewelry any longer."

I centered the necklace's middle diamond against my gown's tufted bodice. "Why don't you go to Lloyd's tomorrow and look into that."

→ ←

When the lobby bell at the Royal English Opera House rang, Mr. Cooper and his son escorted me to our second-level box. The elder Mr. Cooper offered me the prize seat, the one with the best angle on the stage. I chatted with the younger Mr. Cooper and gazed out on the masses settling in the house's layers of plum-colored chairs and gilded black boxes. The clattery fits and starts of the orchestra's tuning wafted from the pit. The conductor took up his baton. As the audience hushed, I turned my attention to the stage, and my gaze passed over a box on the opposite side of the theater. A red-complexioned man—of middle age, I guessed—stared at me. Even as my glance met his, he continued in his steadfast enterprise. I shifted in my chair to optimize my view of the stage and waited for the curtain to rise, all the time noticing out of the corner of my eye that this man gazed steadily at me.

It was not unusual for me to be acquainted with the box holders, but I'd never seen this gentleman before. His perfectly knotted silk tie, satin-collared frock coat, and cross-over vest suggested either great wealth or dignitary status, even if his behavior indicated otherwise.

At intermission, the Misters Cooper and I made our way to the Stalls Bar. As I sipped champagne with my companions, a bald gentleman approached our party and addressed me. "Pardon me, Miss Dugas," he said in an accent as thick as the Black Forest, "I am the secretary to Baron de Vries, and he wishes to make your acquaintance."

I studied him. Yes, just as I thought. He'd been sitting next to the man whose eyes had bored through me all of Act One. I glanced at the elder Mr. Cooper, whose expression had turned quizzical, and then back at this man. "Please tell the Baron that I am occupied with my own acquaintances at present."

That should have put an end to the Baron's rude comportment, but the next morning a message arrived at my hotel room: "Dear Miss Dugas, As we have not been introduced, I hope you will forgive the presumption, but I humbly request your company for dinner tonight, or any other evening this week. You may send word to me at Claridge's. Yours, Baron Rudolph de Vries."

"This man is exasperating," I told Daisy over breakfast.

"He's a baron. And probably altogether respectable."

"He's impudent."

"He's taken with you. At least let me find out more about him."

Over the next month, the Baron persisted in sending two or three messages a week, sometimes including flowers, which likely commanded dear prices during London's dreary February. Would I, he begged, accompany him to the opening of Oscar Wilde's play *Lady Windermere's Fan*? Might I like to attend a lecture on Egyptian antiquities at the British Museum? All the while, Daisy continued to press me to accept his invitation.

"He's criminally wealthy," she said, arranging the fresh bouquet of tulips he'd had delivered. "He's a medaled sportsman. Why not give him a chance?"

"I don't care for him."

"Because he's not Johnny?"

"He does suffer by comparison."

"You can't replace Johnny."

"Then because he's arrogant and insolent."

"You've never exchanged a word with him. How can you know that?"

I scampered to her side and shook his note under her eyes. "'Miss Dugas, I am determined to meet you.' Who is he to impose himself like this?"

"He's his own man. You said you wanted an independent man."

"Independent, yes. A fool, no."

"You're the one being foolish." Daisy threw her hand out in an arc, directing my attention around the suite. "How are you going to pay for this when your bank account runs dry?"

"Something will come up. It always has before."

Daisy slapped a hand to her hip. "You're testing my loyalty. I have a mother depending on me. I can't manage without pay."

Never before had Daisy sounded such a note of alarm. Although I had grown accustomed to trusting that each day would take care of itself, Daisy's life had not been so blessed. And I had brought her here all the way from New York. I looked into her teary eyes. "Very well, inform him that he may pick me up for dinner this Thursday at seven."

> <

As I descended the stairs at the Shaftesbury Hotel, I spotted the Baron in the lobby, standing erect beside a carved wood chair and dressed in a black Prince Albert coat and a black bow tie. With clipped step he marched up to me, reached for my hand, and bowed. "Miss Dugas, I cannot say what a great pleasure it is to meet you."

As he rose from his bow, he raised my gloved hand to his lips and kissed it. Though he sported a thick, dun-brown mustache, a spot of thinning hair on top of his head revealed shiny pink skin. He held his long-waisted torso bent slightly forward, as if to make it easier for our eyes to meet, and he appeared taller—close to six feet—than I had guessed he was, with a trim figure not at all compromised by his middle-aged years. His olive-flecked hazel eyes played brightly against his reddish complexion, and a broad forehead dented and gave way to a nose that sloped sharply from a bump at its midpoint. We stood suspended for a moment on the hotel's expansive burgundy-and-navy Persian carpet, beneath leaded-glass gasoliers, while he held my hand and gazed into my eyes.

"Yes, Baron," said I. "We meet at last."

"Please, do call me Rudolph."

I nodded.

In a long step and swivel reminiscent of a military move, he came to my side and offered his arm. "Shall we go to dinner?"

With a graceful lift of his other arm, he put on his top hat. I pulled the folds of my pelisse together, and the Baron escorted me out of the hotel to a glass-windowed landaulet.

We seated ourselves side by side on plush velvet seats, and he offered and arranged a wool warming blanket over my lap. "You must forgive me for burdening you with my insistence all these weeks."

"You are a man who is not easily deterred."

"You are a woman who is not easily forgotten," he said, his words thick with a Dutch accent. He lifted a corner of his mustache into a half smile. "I only hope you will let me prove that I can be a pleasing companion."

We drove along Shaftesbury Street, beneath ornate green lamp-post spires and past theatergoers in their formal wear. I snuggled my hands together under the blanket. "I would love to hear about your family."

"My father is deceased. Mother lives at our property in Dalfsen, with my two sisters."

"Your sisters aren't married?"

"The elder, Miriam, is widowed. She lost her husband in a terrible boating accident."

I tilted my head. "How tragic."

The Baron leaned back and crossed one leg over the other. "She is managing. Mother keeps her busy assisting with the property."

Wondering if a man of his age still answered to his mother, I inquired, "Your mother's property?"

"The family's actually, though it is in my name."

"And the other sister?"

"Cornelia is only twenty. A very lively girl. She loves to ride horses."

The Baron asked after my family as well, and I told him about Papa's success in the restaurant business and how, after his untimely death, our family had retreated to northern Michigan's bountiful forests and sandy lakeshores. As our carriage horse trudged through London's streets, past countless chimneys puffing smoke into the dusky night sky, we settled into a lively exchange about the contrasts between life in America, London, and Holland. I might have said that London's fogginess reminded me of San Francisco, or that Japan's sublime temples outshone England's blocky churches, but I had resolved to make no allusions to the unfortunate chapters of my earlier life.

Dinner was pleasant enough, and though my appraisal of the Baron softened after our evening together, my initial reservations stood. He put great stock in himself, his property, and his sport as a shooter, all of which did nothing to disabuse me of my first impression about his abiding self-importance. Still, I consented to dine with him again, though I begged a busy schedule and pushed the date out two weeks hence. Meantime, to assuage Daisy's concerns about our finances and to stretch my bank account until fortunes changed, I moved us out of our suite into a cozy but tastefully furnished flat on Piccadilly.

Over the spring and early summer months, the Baron persevered in his attentions, insisting each time we parted that I consent to another meeting. Though he took me to the finest restaurants, toured me through the British Museum and Kew Gardens, and proved generous in his gifts not only to me but to Daisy as well, I did not find my heart moved by him.

Then, one July morning, while Daisy and I prepared to go marketing, we were surprised by an urgent rapping. Daisy hastened to the door, and when she opened it I heard the Baron's voice.

"Miss Emmett," he asked, "is Miss Dugas in?"

After twisting around to question me with her eyes, Daisy said, "Yes, she is."

The Baron stood in the doorway, leaning first to one side and then the other, trying to see around Daisy. Upon catching my eye, he said, "May, I must speak with you. Will you invite me in?"

I'd been sitting on the sofa, composing a shopping list. I hated that he was seeing me in a simple yellow day dress, but he seemed to take no note of it. I put down my pen and paper. "Yes, of course."

Daisy stepped aside, allowing him to enter, and said, "I'll just excuse myself."

Daisy shut the door behind her, and a flush-faced Rudolph hurried in and sat down beside me on the sofa. "I am sorry to barge in on you. Please forgive me."

By this time alarm was rising in me. Might Dougherty have tracked me down? Would he dare to sully my reputation yet again? "What is it, Rudolph?"

Rudolph bent forward, bracing his elbows on his knees and nesting his face in his hands. "My baby sister, Cornelia. She has been killed in a riding accident."

I reached out and cupped my hand over his trembling shoulder. The depth of his sorrow washed over me, like the sun's rays on springtime ice. I tightened my grip, hoping the tenderness enlivening me might soothe him. "Oh, Rudolph, I'm so sorry."

He crumpled onto my lap and sobbed.

⇥⇤

Less than a month later, Rudolph invited me to dinner at the first restaurant we had dined at in London—Wiltons. This time, however, the dining room was empty, except for one table in the middle of the room. A host of tall-stemmed candelabras graced the perimeter of the stucco-walled room, bathing it in a golden light. I hardly noticed our waiter, so unobtrusive was he. Over the next two hours, our glasses brimmed with claret, a squash soup prompted reminiscences of our first dinner in this very room, and plates of pheasant, Brussels sprouts, and slivered carrots appeared as if by magic.

After dinner, as I sipped my cream-laden coffee, Rudolph rose from his chair and stood by my side. He reached for my hands, brought them to his lips for a kiss, and formed them into a bowl. Dropping to a knee, he reached into his vest pocket and extracted a velvet pouch. He untied its drawstring and tugged it open.

Spilling pearls—thirty-five, I later counted—into my cupped palms, he said, "You are to me the most precious pearl. Never will I find one more perfect than you."

The pearls, warm to the touch, shimmered in the candles' halcyon glow. I lifted my eyes to Rudolph's. They, too, sparkled, but with the dew of ardor.

He placed his hands around mine. "Marry me, my darling."

*M*y attorney began his afternoon examination of Frank by hammering away at her credibility on the matter of loans.

As Powers strolled casually toward the witness box, he asked, "Miss Shaver, did you ever try to borrow money from the Baroness?"

Frank frowned. "No, I did not."

"Did you, on the occasion of boarding a train to Chicago in December of 1913, ask the Baroness for money in the presence of her assistant, Miss Daisy Emmett?"

"No, that can't be."

"Why not?"

"Whenever we got on the train, Daisy headed straight for the dining car."

At this, the ladies in the courtroom found cause for merriment. I turned and sought out Daisy, who was sitting among the onlookers. She shot me a look of consternation, which faded when I myself smiled in amusement.

Mr. Powers swished a hand over his jaw. "Miss Shaver, do you recall celebrating your birthday with the Baroness on Valentine's Day of 1915 at the Windsor Hotel in Montreal?"

"That I do recall."

"Did you invite Miss Emmett to this party?"

"Yes, at May's request."

"Did you, at one point, open your purse and exclaim that you had no money?"

"No."

"Did you try to borrow money from Miss Emmett to pay for the party?"

"No."

"You deny trying to borrow money from Miss Emmett in Montreal?"

"Objection," said Sawyer. "My client answered his question."

"Sustained," said Flanagan.

Powers smoothed his palms together. "Did you ask the Baroness to give you the money to cover the hotel costs for the party?"

"Absolutely not."

Such bold, outright denials! I glanced at Daisy. She looked the way I felt—as if a horse had kicked me in the belly. Both of us, with dropped jaws, shook our heads to signal to anybody who might look our way how outraged we were by Frank's lies.

"Let me be clear, Miss Shaver. You never borrowed or attempted to borrow money from the Baroness?"

With a firm dip of her head, Frank said, "That's correct."

Powers again returned to the defendant's table, grabbed an envelope, pulled several papers from it, and advanced on the witness box. "Can you identify these items, Miss Shaver?"

Frank shuffled through a half dozen or so sheets. "They're checks made out to me from May's account."

"And did you endorse these checks?"

Frank flipped the checks over and examined each one. "Yes."

"And do they total roughly three thousand dollars?"

"Are you asking me to perform arithmetic?"

The sarcasm did not escape me, or the rest of the courtroom, though my tolerance for Frank's witticisms was wearing thin.

"Yes, Miss Shaver," said Powers, "if you would please."

Frank took her time thumbing through the checks. "Yes, about that."

"Do you still contend you never borrowed money from the Baroness?"

"Yes."

"Objection," said Sawyer. "Counsel is badgering."

Judge Flanagan knotted the lapel of his robe in his hand. "Mr. Powers, I will instruct you again to conduct your questioning without being argumentative or repetitious. I will release you from your duties if you do not obey this court."

"Yes, Your Honor." Powers took a deep breath and turned to Frank. "Miss Shaver, can you explain the meaning of these checks?"

"They're for expenses."

"If they're for expenses, why are they made out to you?"

"Because I generally paid our expenses."

"What expenses were they for?"

"Could be for almost anything."

"You can remember every dollar the Baroness borrowed from you, every dollar you spent on her, but you cannot remember what these checks were for?"

"No."

"If you don't know what expenses these checks were intended to cover, how can you say they were not loans?"

"Because I did not borrow money from May. She borrowed money from me."

"You have not answered my question, Miss Shaver. Can you prove these were not loans—yes or no?"

"No, I just know they're not."

After a brief recess—and before Sawyer could attempt to repair Frank's tarnished credibility during his redirect examination—my attorney dished out another unpleasant surprise.

"Miss Shaver, do you know a Mr. Wayne Schroeder of Chicago?"

"Yes, he's an electrician who worked on my office."

"Did you discuss this lawsuit with him?"

"He asked about it after he read something in the newspaper."

"Do you recall the conversation?"

"Generally."

"Can you recount it for us?"

"He said something to the effect 'I see you're trying to get some money back from the Baroness,' and I said something like 'We'll see how it goes; these things take time,' and he said, 'I hope it works out for you,' and I thanked him for his concern."

"Did you not tell him you could blackmail her and get certain sums of money?"

"No, that word is not in my vocabulary."

I, for one, thought that she answered awfully fast. Despite her denial, the seed had been sown. All in all, Powers scored some damning points during his cross-examination of Frank. How could she account for all the checks written to her from my account?

Try as he might to undermine our case, Sawyer could not make the checks disappear, to say nothing of the release signed by Frank.

# THE SACRIFICES OF MARRIAGE

*T*he Baron and I wedded in a private ceremony at his Dalfsen family property on November 20, 1892, with Rudolph in a regal, trim black suit and me, the shy bride, in a flowing white gown with layered sleeves. All his family attended—his mother and sister, as well as three sets of aunts and uncles and a smattering of cousins—as did the Duke and Duchess of Norfolk and nearly a dozen members of the Dutch royalty. As for my family, I had to content myself with sending them photographs—one of me and Rudolph, another of the complete wedding party in the airy front parlor of the estate. Daisy, who had accompanied me to Holland, spent the wedding day unpacking and arranging our personal effects. ("A maid at a wedding? It wouldn't be fitting," Rudolph had said. "And it would upset Mother.")

As I accustomed myself to the company of the Baron and his mother and sister, Daisy took up a modest third-floor garret. In her position as my personal assistant, she spent many hours with me in my boudoir on the second floor, during which time she often complained about her circumstances: "It takes forever for news from Mother to reach me, and I miss New York's newspapers," or "I know I should be grateful for the steady pay, but, my goodness, this is a dull place."

I could hardly argue with her about the boredom of the routine or the seclusion of the estate, but my marriage to Rudolph offered many benefits: I was a baroness, a married woman of twenty-three making a fresh start. The mistakes of my past faded into the background, eclipsed by my new status and of no consequence to those who might have wished to use them against me. Nor did my memories of those slips any longer beget solitary moments of self-recrimination. Of course I saved a corner of my heart for Johnny, though I could do naught now but accept that terrible tragedy.

Surprisingly, Rudolph had become dear to me, and his attentiveness pleased me. Once he'd won me over, he spouted less about himself, and I realized that all the trumpeting that had annoyed me during our courtship had merely been an attempt to impress. Before we married, he consented to set me up with a sizable bank account so that I needn't pester him about every button or bauble I desired. He loved me passionately and indulged my every whim—in mail-order books, jewels, and champagne. He came to my bed nearly every night, as eager as a youngster half his age, but as considerate and gentle as the seasoned man he was.

The family lived in a stately four-story brick home, which was rightly called De Vries Castle. Its lowest level, which housed the kitchen, storage, and work quarters, let in feeble light through narrow windows high on the walls at the ground level. The spacious entry hall on the main level led to the dining room, two parlors, a smoking room, and the library. Six roomy bedrooms, two adjoined and all with sitting areas, graced the second floor. A third level, the servants' rooms, nestled under the roof. Daisy, plus the three lady servants and two butlers who'd served the family for many years, inhabited these steep-ceilinged rooms, all of which offered lovely views of the estate through squat dormer windows.

Before long, the Baron and I settled into a routine of strolling the grounds, weather permitting, afternoons at four. The castle sat in the middle of a grassy five-acre parcel surrounded by a majestic forest. I enjoyed the privacy and time away from the house that our survey of the grounds afforded: Although Rudolph's mother and sister were kind enough to me, the stiff formality of our interactions—including the burden of having communications between his mother and me translated—wore on me. One early-March day, nearly four months after our wedding, Rudolph and I met in the entryway for our daily walk.

"Your mother tells me the daffodils and tulips will soon bloom," I said, my mood brightened by the clear blue skies and sprays of wild hyacinths sprouting at the lawn's edges.

Rudolph squinted as we turned onto the graveled lane marking the estate's west side. "Do you remember the flowers I had delivered to you in London? They were all from hothouses in this area."

"I can't wait to have fresh flowers in the house," I said, "to cheer us all up."

"I shall pick some for you myself." Rudolph cupped his hand under my elbow. "My dear, I leave next week for that shooting tournament."

"What shooting tournament?"

"Did I not tell you? It happens every year. In Gotha, Germany."

"Is that far from here?"

"A three-day journey."

"Can I come along?"

He chuckled. "No, it is all men. Nothing really for the ladies to do."

"Can I take a trip, too?"

"Not now. Mother's elderly aunt is arriving Saturday, and she will want to see you."

What I didn't say was that I had not the least interest in seeing her, though I had little choice but to endure this wifely burden. Over the coming years I came to dread these all-too-regular visits from relatives. There I sat, at the dinner table or in the parlor, listening to them carry on about Earl So-and-so or Uncle Such-and-such, trying my best to appear fascinated with the goings-on of people I cared not a whit about. On those rare occasions when talk turned to worldly events—why ever America should meddle with Hawaii when it already possessed nearly a whole continent, the treachery of that Jew Alfred Dreyfus, or New Zealand's "lamentable" enactment of women's suffrage—I enthusiastically offered my views, only to find them knocked down by their provincial proclamations. Often, especially when older guests came around, they dispensed with translating their exchanges for me and simply lapsed to Dutch. Try as I might to learn the language, Dutch proved exceedingly difficult to master. So I sat dumbly looking on, pretending amusement when they chuckled over who-knows-what. I counted the minutes until I might politely retreat to my room and the company of Jane Austen or Rudyard Kipling. By the time I managed to gracefully excuse myself, my cheek muscles had invariably seized up from the smile I'd dutifully plastered on for endless hours.

Rudolph's excursions became more and more frequent over the years, and he only occasionally took me on a holiday—once to Paris and twice to Amsterdam. To pass my time at the estate, I learned to ride, though Rudolph prohibited me from jumping. I devoured every book I could get my hands on. I took up light gardening, not because I enjoyed the labor, but because it afforded solitary time in the open air. Still, far too often I found myself relegated to the company of his mother, Lady de Vries (who spoke not a speck of English), and his sister, Miriam (our faithful translator). Eventually, the courteous coexistence that had first characterized our exchanges gave way to intrusive prying.

One week in the high summer of 1895, a second cousin of Rudolph's visited with her husband and children. The two boys and one girl spanned ages four to eight—the most unruly years of childhood, if their behavior was any indication. Every day they ran about, bounding across the grass and rolling down slopes, all the time unleashing monstrous squeals of delight. I prayed they would take up a quiet game of hide-and-seek in the woods, but their doting parents forbade them to venture out of sight of the castle.

A few days after they departed, Rudolph also left for one of his competitions, and that evening Miriam said to me over dinner, "Wasn't it wonderful having children around?"

She muttered a translation of her question to her mother.

I speared and sliced an asparagus. "They certainly were a happy bunch."

Miriam conveyed my remark to her mother in Dutch.

"I should have liked nothing more than a child with my husband," said Miriam, "but we were not so fortunate." Again she rattled off her meaning to her mother.

I tried to steer the conversation to a more pleasant topic. "I've often meant to tell you how handsome your husband looks in that photograph on the mantel."

Miriam followed that with a brisk sentence to her mother. Then, surprisingly, she passed over the chance to talk about her husband, which she usually did with the least provocation, and said to me, as casually as a cat contemplating a swim, "I know Rudolph would love a son, or even a daughter."

Again she intoned her remark to Lady de Vries.

During the pause that ensued, I restrained myself from quipping: "How strange that Rudolph would confide such an intimacy to you when he has not spoken to me of it."

Meantime, Lady de Vries eased her fork and knife onto her plate. She spoke a few words to Miriam and, as she turned expectant eyes on me, Miriam translated: "Mother asks if you wish to have a child."

"I would like nothing more," I said. But in truth I wished no such thing and was taking measures to assure that our conjugal relations did not leave me with child. Still, I did not appreciate the insinuation afoot that evening. I was certain both Miriam and her mother had taken note, perhaps by gathering intelligence from the maid, about how often Rudolph's bed went undisturbed. I could only surmise they blamed me for some condition that precluded motherhood.

Having surrendered my adventurous spirit for the settled respectability of marriage, I bore the unpleasantries Rudolph's family hoisted on me with a fair degree of tolerance. But I missed my mother and brothers and had no idea when I might see them again. They had not fared well after the Panic of '93. Even out-of-the-way Menominee had been hard hit, and the belt-tightening among the city's wealthiest severely curtailed my mother's dressmaking business. But, worse yet, Paul's employment at the lumber mill had become sporadic. Thus, in 1896, a year after my younger brother, Gene, graduated from high school, I sent him money from my account—with Rudolph's knowledge and consent—so that he might attend dental school. He had mentioned such an interest, and I hoped that taking up a profession would not only help the family's finances, but also position him to marry well.

Around this time, Daisy's simmering discontent boiled over: "I didn't exactly hire on to be relegated to a cramped room in some country estate"; "None of the maids speak a word of English, not that I wish to mix with them"; and "You'd best not spend from your account too freely; you never know when you might need the funds."

Soon enough, I, too, yearned to escape the shackles of tight-sheeted domesticity. Come January of 1897, I had embarked on a campaign to convince Rudolph to move us to London. Finally, in the spring of 1898, Rudolph and his butler, as well as Daisy and I, took up residence in a splendid house on Cork Street in Mayfair. Our central location afforded easy access to all of London, and, after almost six years of "the peaceful country life," I delighted in outings to plays, fine restaurants, and musical entertainment. Daisy, too, was much happier, especially after she convinced Rudolph, via my importuning, to bring her brother Dicky over from America to serve as coachman for the household.

But barely one year into our London sojourn, when I informed Rudolph I'd exhausted the account he'd set up for me upon our marriage, tensions flared between us.

"Good heavens," he said, sitting upright in his desk chair and brandishing his pen, "where did all the money go?"

I stood before his desk, attired in the day dress I knew to be his favorite. "You've seen the gowns I've had made. You know I sent money to my family. And Daisy needed some gowns for London, too."

"Gowns? Why, you could have bought several thousand with all that money."

"I made the money last nearly six years. Surely that's not unreasonable."

"How did you ever manage that antiquities business in Japan when you can't even keep track of your own money?"

"I did keep track of it. I know exactly how I spent it."

"And what do you expect me to do?"

"I'd be grateful if you would replenish the account." I folded my hands and bowed my head. "Please spare me the indignity of bothering you every time I need a farthing."

He leaned back in his chair and glared at me. "I shall set you up with half the original amount, and I expect it to last four years. I'll not give you another pound before then."

Of course I accepted his somewhat generous offer, but Daisy took umbrage at this treatment, especially when I informed her I would no longer be able to afford her bonuses.

As she arranged logs in my bedroom fireplace for the evening warming, she complained, "It'll be a hardship on Mother, me not sending her that money."

"I've no choice. Unless I come into more funds or turn a profit by investment."

She knelt on the hearthrug, her back to me, and scraped a match against the brick, releasing a whiff of sulphur. When the match flared, she jerked back, then leaned over and lit the kindling. She fanned the fledgling fire with the bellows until it erupted into robust flames, then stood and faced me. "If I help you, will you pay my bonuses?"

"Help me how?"

"With coming into more money."

"If it's enough to cover what you wish to send to your mother, then yes." I drummed my fingers on the arm of my chair. "But how do you intend to do that?"

She sighed and swung her head from side to side. "I'm not sure."

That was the last I heard from her on the matter for some time.

>‹

In June of 1899 a committee of London theater supporters organized a Shakespeare Ball, and Rudolph and I received an invitation. The charity ball, with a steep admission of two hundred guineas, attracted droves of costumed revelers to the Albert Hall. Once I'd convinced Rudolph to attend as Mark Antony, Daisy and I set about shopping for my Cleopatra costume and accessories. We designed a white gossamer gown and adorned it with a long golden sash. The sash, secured low on my waist with a golden fan scarab, flowed down to the hem of my gown. I draped a royal-blue scarf around my shoulders and tucked a conical crown—like one I'd seen in a National Theatre poster board—over my swooped-up hair. Daisy selected my jewelry: "Gold and more gold, you must drip with gold," she said. On went all my gold bracelets, my finest gold-and-diamond earrings, and my prized yellow-diamond necklace.

Daisy also insisted on Egyptian garb for Dicky, who had grown into a strapping, if somewhat sullen, twenty-one-year-old with jet-black hair and deep-set brown eyes. "Dicky will escort you in separately, with the Baron entering first and exiting last," she said. "That will make for a grand show, don't you agree?"

How right she was. When I entered, Rudolph stood on the long carpet awaiting me, with photographers clustered along the entrance walkway. As I strolled in on Dicky's arm, oohs and aahs escaped from the guests. The photographers readied themselves for my entrance with Mark Antony. I found I didn't mind the flashes of their cameras in the least, especially when my picture appeared in that week's *Illustrated London News*.

Rudolph, casting his eyes upon his laced sandals, lent me his arm as we stepped onto the carpet. "Ravishing, my dear. Could there be a more beautiful Cleopatra?"

I looked into his flushed face. "As I am Egypt's queen, thou blushest, Antony."

"Ah, my queen," said he, not to be outdone in quoting, "how I love your infinite variety."

I had a wonderful time that evening, meeting up with some of my old friends from the Royal English Opera House and mixing with Rudolph's London crowd. Rudolph and I danced as we'd never danced before. I believe I quite wore him out, for we stayed until nearly all the partygoers had left.

But the evening ended on a dreadful note. Once ensconced in our carriage, I yawned, covered my mouth, and let my hand drop to my chest. "My necklace," I exclaimed, "it's gone."

Rudolph felt his way around the carriage seat. "It's got to be here. Didn't you have it on all evening?"

I raised myself up from my seat. "Is it there?"

Rudolph checked the area I'd occupied. "No. Could it be back at the hall? Did you take it off anywhere?"

"No, and it has a solid clasp."

Rudolph thumped the front of the carriage and opened his door wide enough to call out, "Dicky, stop under that lamppost ahead."

Dicky pulled the carriage over.

"Bring the lantern," ordered Rudolph.

Dicky hopped down from his seat, the carriage lantern swinging in his hand. While he and Rudolph searched every inch of the carriage's interior, I stood loitering on Kensington Road, a chilled and panicked Cleopatra.

Rudolph threw up his hands. "No sign of it."

"We have to get back to the hall," I said.

We climbed back into the carriage, and Rudolph ordered Dicky, "Stop if you see a bobby."

As we approached the Albert Hall, we did pick up an officer, but by the time we arrived, all the guests had departed. Only three workers remained, two gathering glasses on trays and another slouching along over a sweep broom. The bobby questioned them and asked them to empty their pockets, and then Rudolph, Dicky, the officer, and I searched every area I'd traversed in the course of the ball. But we found no necklace.

Rudolph told the bobby, "It must have been stolen, though I can't imagine how."

The pasty-faced bobby looked to Rudolph and then me. "You're sure you had it on when you arrived?"

"Oh, yes," I said.

Rudolph said, "I saw it on her."

"I did, too," said Dicky.

The officer wrote up a theft report and asked each of us when we had last seen the necklace.

"I remember seeing it when I visited the ladies' room," I said, "a good hour before we left."

Rudolph spoke up. "I noticed it when she made her entrance, but I failed to pay close attention after that."

The officer looked to Dicky. "She had it on when she arrived, but after that I can't say. I was waiting in the carriage."

I'd lost my precious yellow-diamond necklace, the one I'd had since 1888, my first substantial jewelry purchase. Although I should have been pleased that it was insured by Lloyd's of London, the piece was irreplaceable, truly a one-of-a-kind work of art. At first Lloyd's balked at honoring the claim, threatening to turn the case over to Scotland Yard. But the newspaper photos proved I'd worn it that night, and the bobby's report was unassailable. Finally, after Rudolph expressed his indignation to the Lloyd's agent handling the claim, they relented. The payout was substantial, for I'd insured it for its full value, which had increased quite handsomely over the ten years I'd owned it. Still, I cried over the loss of that dazzling piece.

→←

Over the next two years, I found myself more and more discontented with Rudolph, who had become quite contrary: "Use your own money if you must go to plays every Saturday," or "Mother and Miriam will not be happy that we are staying only two weeks at Christmas," and "No, I refuse to mingle with the masses at Queen Victoria's funeral. They can bury her well enough without me—or you, for that matter."

In truth, he'd grown tiresome, and I missed my family. Then I received a letter from Maman informing me that Paul had lost his lumber-mill job and Gene, two years post-dental training, still hadn't secured a dentist position or managed to set up a practice in Menominee.

I reported the news to Rudolph at luncheon and said, "My family needs me. I must go back to the States."

"Would you like me to go with you?"

I'd anticipated such an offer from him, reluctant as he was to let me out of his sight for a single evening. "I think it's best if I go on my own. I'll try to make it a quick trip."

Upon Daisy's urging, I withdrew all the money from my London account: "You said you might want to invest it, and America is the place for that."

In September of 1901, Daisy, Dicky, and I journeyed to Liverpool and boarded the SS *Majestic* for New York. Oh, how I looked forward to reclaiming the spirit of adventure I'd bottled up during almost nine years with Rudolph and his family.

# ACQUISITIONS OLD AND NEW

·

*I* so loved my well-appointed first-class cabin on the SS *Majestic*, the leisure of afternoons lolling in a deck chair, the beauty of sunsets at sea. In fact, I enjoyed everything about that crossing: my newfound sense of freedom; the utter relaxation of life without appointments; the companionable dinners. And after sacrificing so many youthful years to country life and reaching the age of thirty-two, I was pleased to find that men still flocked to me.

I never imagined, however, that my convivial chats with one particular American businessman would pay high dividends. Near journey's end, Mr. Harry Drummer, an athletic but balding widower on holiday with his son, began to seek me out for late-afternoon cocktails. He jested he was "not only vice president, but finances pooh-bah" at Churchill Downs.

"Ah, Mrs. de Vries, there you are," he said upon finding me chatting in the saloon with Daisy and Dicky. The aura of cigar smoke floated about him. "May I join you?"

Mr. Drummer hailed from Kentucky, just like my old friend Sue Marie, and I took some comfort in his long-voweled Kentucky drawl. I introduced him to Daisy and her brother, who drifted off to freshen up before dinner.

Mr. Drummer guided me to a seat by a porthole and ordered drinks for us. "What'll you do when we land?"

I twisted my wedding ring to center its diamond on my finger. "My family is expecting me in Michigan. But I might stop a night in New York."

"Well, I guess Robert and I'll do about the same. Duty calls in Louisville."

I gazed out the porthole. The seas surged with choppiness, the worst of our ten days at sea. Although I'd escaped a bad case of seasickness, the ship's pitching did gurgle my stomach. "Goodness," I said, "this roughness is a bit unnerving."

"Swivel around here," he said, rising to help me rearrange my chair and, in the process, suggestively clasping my shoulder. "It'll help if you look at the horizon."

I allowed—but did not yield to—his touch. "I wonder how long these unruly seas will last."

He settled in his seat again. "The captain says just another day."

I took a few deep breaths. "Yes, that's better."

Mr. Drummer braced his forearms on the table and leaned toward me. "Say, weren't you talking about making an investment?"

"Yes, if I can find a worthy speculation."

He lowered his voice. "Churchill Downs is planning to build a racetrack outside Hot Springs."

"How far along are you with the plans?"

"Oh, it's all on paper now, but we're about to buy some property near Lawrence station. Place should be booming once we break ground."

I grinned. "To say nothing of when you open the track."

"Horse racing *is* lucrative." Mr. Drummer swung his head in a loop. "Yes, it is."

"Have you broken the news yet?"

"No, it's strictly on the hush. If you'd care to join me for dinner, I can fill you in on the details."

Our drinks arrived, and I swooped mine up and tipped it against his. "To shrewd investing."

>←

In early October, our ship steamed into New York, where I found the newspapers plastered with reports of McKinley's assassination and Czolgosz's trial and impending execution. The mood in the city was so somber I was loath to loiter even a day. I packed a suitcase and sent my wardrobe trunk ahead to Menominee with word that I would soon follow. Daisy, Dicky, and I took the train to Hot Springs and checked into the Arlington Hotel. That day and evening, we saw the sights in downtown Hot Springs, which was booming with rowdy visitors and gambling games—not that I had any interest in gambling myself. Before Dicky could search out the local ruffians, as was his wont, I sent him off to track down a horse and carriage for us to rent, and on the second day he drove the three of us to Lawrence station.

We arrived in the afternoon, parched from the journey, and toured all the dusty roads around the train station looking for a place to stay. But we found little by way of accommodations: a hotel with a sagging porch and a boardinghouse. So I ordered Dicky to drive us back to the station.

I thumped on the carriage compartment to signal Dicky to pull over.

When he jumped down, I opened the door and said, "Go in that tavern and ask if there are any nice hotels in the area. And please bring us some water."

After a few minutes, Dicky emerged with glasses of water for Daisy and me, which we straightaway gulped down. He leaned against the carriage door, his hand braced on the door and a foot propped on the step.

"There's a place several miles down the road," he said. "Potash Sulphur Hotel."

Dicky used the tavern keeper's directions to drive us there. The eighty-four-room resort featured grounds with an archery range, badminton nets, and two bathhouses for taking the waters. The property sat atop a knoll, and behind it golden grasses rippled down to a river. Trees nestled along the river's curves; their leaves had changed to oranges and browns but still clung to the boughs. The picturesque scene nearly tempted me to take off my shoes, skip down the hill, and dabble in the cool river waters.

We checked in, intending to relax for a few days before continuing our journey. I carried my suitcase down the long second-floor hall to my room. The construction seemed solid enough; I discerned only minimal creaking of the floorboards. But the paint on the hallway walls peeled away at the seams, and the doorknob to my room jiggled in its socket before catching. Blue-and-green floral wallpaper decorated the walls of the thirty-square-foot room, though the sun had faded the parts washed by window light. Acrid scents of perspiration and stale kerosene hung in the air. I brushed my hand over the liquid-and-cigarette-stained veneer on the bird's-eye–maple dresser and inspected a lantern of about 1870s vintage stowed on a corner shelf. The bed, though covered with a clean, hoop-patterned quilt, squeaked when I sat on it. Upon turning in for the night, I couldn't help but roll into the bed's slumping middle; many bodies had obviously occupied its recess. I cracked my window to freshen the room, and the babbling river and rustling leaves lulled me into a dreamy slumber.

Daisy, Dicky, and I met in the breakfast room the next morning and seated ourselves on chairs smoothed down in their leg channels. I asked Daisy and Dicky to report on their rooms, which sounded as sorry as mine.

Studying the frayed edges of our beige tablecloth, I said, "This place could use a serious sprucing up."

We sat near a wide window at the rear of the dining area. Dicky eyed the weathered window casing. "Maybe a good gutting."

"At the least, new wallpaper and furniture," said Daisy.

As we finished our flat cakes and ham, the owner's wife, white-haired Mrs. Honeyman, came around to greet us.

"I just want to welcome you folks to our little piece of paradise." Her cheeks plumped into cheery mounds as she spoke, and she clasped her hands over her round, aproned belly.

I reached out to shake her hand. "I'm Mrs. May de Vries. These are my traveling companions, Belle and Richard Emmett."

Daisy and Dicky greeted her with nods and smiles.

"Pleased to meet you," she said.

I looked into her baby-blue eyes. "You have a lovely property here."

"Well, thank you. We've been cherishin' it for thirty-eight years now."

"I'm surprised to see so few guests."

"Oh, in its heyday people came from all over. But now it's mostly regulars."

"Is that likely to change in the near future?"

"No reason it should."

"That adds to its appeal," I said, glancing out the wide window overlooking the resort's rolling property. "It's very peaceful."

With a "You folks enjoy your stay, now," she sauntered off, swaying back and forth on her bowed legs.

I sipped my coffee and meditated on the view of rusty leaves glistening in the sun.

As Mrs. Honeyman sidled up to a table a few down from ours, Daisy whispered, "They don't know about the racetrack."

I replaced my coffee cup. "That appears to be the case."

"How do you want to handle it?"

"You and Dicky go into Hot Springs and track down some information about property sales, especially places comparable to this one. That'll help me determine a fair offering price."

Dicky pulled up out of his slump. "Might take some time to find some sales."

"Stay overnight in Hot Springs if you'd like." I calculated—two rooms and four meals for two, but not enough to tempt Dicky to drink intemperately—reached into my coin purse, and handed Daisy a twenty-dollar bill. "For your expenses."

Daisy tucked the money into her skirt pocket. "We'd better get going."

Daisy and Dicky dropped their napkins on the table and rose.

I caught Daisy's eye. "And for goodness' sake, be discreet."

"You might have noticed: I'm actually quite good at that," said Daisy, scraping her chair back into place and marching out with Dicky.

→←

After Daisy and Dicky returned, I pored over the newspaper listings and property-sale records they'd retrieved, calculating what I considered a more-than-reasonable offer for the hotel.

I'd not yet met Mr. Honeyman, though I'd observed him speaking with his wife earlier in the day. His body type contrasted so sharply with his wife's that they looked quite comical together. She was about five four, roly-poly, and stood at a backward slant, with her weight centered on her heels. But he reached a good five ten, with twiggy arms, lanky legs, and a stooped torso. Perhaps they'd made a more handsome couple in their younger years.

I strolled to the lobby that evening and found the owner working at his desk behind the counter. "Good evening, Mr. Honeyman. I'm one of your guests, May de Vries."

His putty-gray mustache wriggled about his lean face as he settled a chew into his cheek. "Yes, the wife tells me she met you at breakfast. What can I do for you?"

"I'd like to buy you and Mrs. Honeyman coffee tomorrow. Might you have time to discuss a business matter with me?"

He scrunched up one side of his face. "You mean your bill?"

"Heavens, no. My and my companions' rooms are all paid up."

He frowned as if he couldn't imagine what other business there might be.

I looked around the lobby. "You have a lovely hotel here. I must say, we are very much enjoying our stay."

He nodded and ventured a smile. "Well, I suppose we can meet you around ten."

The next morning, I showed up in the breakfast room a bit before the appointed hour, dressed in my most conservative day outfit, a pastel-peach dress with a white lace collar. Mr. and Mrs. Honeyman emerged from the kitchen promptly at ten and sauntered over to the corner table I'd selected. Mrs. Honeyman carried a tray with silver coffee service and fine china cups, which was probably a personal set. I'd not seen anything like it at the breakfast offering.

I rose to greet them. "Mr. and Mrs. Honeyman, I'm so pleased you could join me."

"Why, sure, honey," said the missus as she placed the tray on a nearby table and set out our coffee service.

I insisted on pouring the coffee, and we chatted for a bit about how they kept up the hotel and its grounds. Mr. Honeyman explained that they themselves took on kitchen duty, but they hired two groundskeepers and two maids to do the heavy work. "The wife and I are getting on in years. Can't do as much as we used to."

I lifted the pot and freshened our coffee. "Have you ever thought about selling?"

Mr. Honeyman cocked his head. "I don't reckon we could afford to do that."

"Are you carrying a contract?"

"No, we paid that off years ago."

"What if I offered you fifty-two thousand dollars?" I knew this to be a generous offer, considering that the hotel hardly ever filled up and sorely needed repair and renovation.

Mrs. Honeyman's eyes popped to alert, and Mr. Honeyman glanced at her and lifted his palm, obviously warning her to keep quiet. He planted his other hand on the table edge and straightened his arm, pulling his torso upright. "Now, we'll have to think on this, Mrs. de Vries. Not something we really planned on doing."

"Of course, by all means. And please don't forget to put this coffee on my bill."

The Honeymans did think on it. They proposed a price of fifty-six thousand, and we met in the middle, at fifty-four thousand, which I believe satisfied all three of us.

>←

Mr. Honeyman and I recorded the sale the next day in Hot Springs, and I arranged to transfer funds for the first installment from my New York bank. We agreed that the remainder would be disbursed upon the closing of the sale. When I informed Daisy that we could be on our way, she invited me to her room "to discuss a private matter" with her and Dicky.

They offered me the wooden chair in Daisy's room, and I sat and braced myself against its back. "Now, what's this all about?"

Daisy, who sat beside Dicky on the bed, glanced at him and gave me one of her I'm-perfectly-serious looks. "You're going to Menominee next, aren't you?"

"Yes. You know you're welcome to come along."

"Dicky and I want to visit our mother. Didn't really have time to do that on the way in."

Was this what they were fussing about? I flapped my hand at them. "Oh, heavens. Of course you can do that. I'd never stop you from seeing your mother."

"Dicky and I will require sixty dollars for our fare and expenses."

"That's reasonable."

"That's not all," said Daisy. She crossed her legs and straightened her spine. "I stopped sending money to Mother after you emptied that first fund from Rudolph."

"Yes, I'm sorry. You know that forced me to stretch the new account."

"If I'd kept sending her money all this time, it'd amount to one thousand fifty dollars."

"That sounds about right."

"You said you'd make up the money for Mother if I helped you come into some funds."

"And I will keep my word. I couldn't ask for a better assistant than you, Daisy."

Daisy nodded to Dicky and turned to me. "Dicky has something to show you."

Dicky levered himself up off the bed and pulled out the bottom drawer of Daisy's dresser. He extracted a soft cloth pouch and handed it to me.

The black pouch weighed heavily in my hand, as if the contents were concentrated—like gold or lead.

Daisy grinned at me. "Go ahead, open it."

I loosened the slip string on the pouch and poured the contents into my palm.

"My yellow-diamond necklace. Dear God, I've got my necklace back." I bounded to my feet and hugged Daisy, Dicky, and Daisy again, all the time shedding tears of joy.

# THE BONDS OF FAMILY AND FRIENDS

·

*T*he next day, I bade Daisy and Dicky good-bye. They caught the morning train to the East Coast, and I left in the late afternoon, bound for Michigan.

As my train chugged out of Lawrence station, I squeezed by the other passengers navigating the car's narrow corridor. My sleep compartment, which was barely wide enough to turn around in, featured a neatly made-up bed, an overhead storage rack, and, on the opposite side, a counter with an inset wash basin and two wide but shallow drawers. I deposited my suitcase on the bed, unlatched it, and dug out my yellow-diamond necklace. Bracing myself against the counter, I stood before the mirror and fastened it on. Such a beautiful piece, I thought; I'll never tire of gazing at it.

I'd shaken a finger at Dicky during our private meeting, "So you're the one who nabbed my necklace."

His expression brightened with one of his rare smiles.

"As I was leaving the ball?" I asked.

He nodded. "A little trick I learned on the streets of New York."

And then Daisy took my hand. "So you mustn't ever show it in public, either in England or anywhere else."

But I could wear it in the privacy of my own quarters and, in some distant future (after everyone had forgotten it was a stolen item, with the insurance money already disbursed), once again dazzle admirers with it.

→←

I was traveling on my own for the first time in nearly a decade, with nary a soul to answer to. It was exhilarating. My first full afternoon on the train, I circulated about the lounge car, where I met several august gentlemen. No sooner had I accepted Mr. Ramsey's invitation to dinner than Mr. Weber joined us and asked if we had dinner plans. Turning to Mr. Ramsey, I said, "Why not make it a party?" Mr. McFarland came along soon thereafter, and the three gentlemen escorted me to dinner. I asked to be seated at a table that could accommodate one more person, just in case someone else happened along. Mr. Ramsey ordered a bottle of claret and told the waiter not to rush us.

Mr. McFarland, a wiry young man with a red beard that tangled at its fringes, said, "Mrs. de Vries, I understand I should be addressing you as Baroness."

"Technically, yes," I said. "But we're not at a royal ceremony, are we?"

The hollow-cheeked Mr. Ramsey sat up straight, adjusting the collar of his starched white shirt. "At least tell us how you came to marry a baron."

"It's a long story. We married at his home in Holland. My goodness, it'll be nine years next month."

"If you don't mind my asking," said the solid Mr. Weber, "how did you meet a baron?"

"Gentlemen, I'm just a simple girl from Michigan—a modern Cinderella, you might say."

Mr. Weber thumped one of his sausage-fingered hands on the table. "Ach, I don't believe it."

"Honestly, I grew up in a log cabin in Muskegon. I can tell you all about it."

"Please do," said Mr. McFarland, with a sweep of his arm.

"My father owned a tavern. I had an older brother, Paul, who walked me to and from school every day. One day, when Paul took sick, I stopped at my father's tavern instead of going straight home. A fiddler stood on a table in the corner, sawing away at that fiddle and making everyone merry. When I walked in, the men lined up to dance with me. Mind you, I was only seven, but my father had taught me how to dance. I reeled from one man to the next and had such a wonderful time I arrived home very late for dinner."

"What a naughty Cinderella," said Mr. Weber.

"My mother was furious, hollering at me for worrying her to

death. 'But, Maman,' I said, 'I had to help Louise with school lessons.' 'I don't care what Louise wanted,' she said. 'Please,' I begged, 'please forgive me.' She said, 'When flowers turn blue. Now off to bed. There'll be no dinner for you tonight, or tomorrow, either.' Once the house quieted, I scrambled out my bedroom window with a candle lantern. I found a thicket of wintergreens and feasted on their tender new leaves. Then I picked some tiny forest-floor blossoms, arranged the miniature bouquet in an inkwell, and left it on the kitchen table with a note apologizing to Maman. By morning, the blooms had turned indigo blue."

"And did you have dinner the next night?"

"My favorite—perch and potatoes."

The men lit into laughter, and the woman at the next table—a solid-framed woman in a stylish wool suit—guffawed.

Once her laughter subsided, I turned to her. "Would you care to join us?"

"You bet I would," she said, striding over to our table and sticking out her hand. "I'm Frank Shaver. From Chicago."

It turned out that Frank, who I guessed to be roughly my age, was quite a storyteller herself. The men she'd attended law school with had dished out a lot of guff, and she regaled us with some of her comebacks: "Better watch out, buster, we might meet across the aisle in some big case"; "Is that the best insult you can muster?"; and "You think a woman'll be out of place in a courtroom? Well, at least my voice carries, which is more than I can say for that banjo twang of yours."

Frank and I took to each other like old school chums. When she announced she needed to retrieve her bag for the next stop, I said, "Gentlemen, if you'll excuse me, I'll see Frank off."

As Frank and I sidled along through the cars, I asked where she was from.

"Grew up in Pittsburgh. My parents still live there. But the place is too stodgy for me."

"But Chicago, you couldn't call it stodgy."

"Oh, no. Sometimes the excitement's not the right kind, but it keeps the law and lawyers busy." Frank opened the door to the next car and guided me through, as amiable as a gentleman showing a friend around. "How long are you in the States for?"

"I hope to stay awhile," I said. "Catch up with my family in Menominee and see to some business."

"I love the U.P. Get up there every summer to fish."

"Really? Well, you'll have to stop in Menominee and visit."

"I'll take that as an invitation."

"What kind of law do you practice?"

"Wills, contracts for small businesses, property sales. Just two of us in the office, so we end up doing a little of everything."

We flattened against the windows to let a party of four pass.

"Really? I just bought a resort hotel in Arkansas. I could use some legal advice."

"I can help with property contract matters, as long as they're not particular to Arkansas law." Frank yanked her suitcase off the storage rack.

I asked, "Do you know Michigan law?"

"I sure do. Went to law school at University of Michigan."

"I may need your counsel in the future."

"I'd be glad to be of service."

By the time the train pulled into Milwaukee, we had exchanged addresses and promised to write each other.

><

With my train scheduled to arrive in Menominee early in the morning, I rose at five to dress and pack. I'd set aside one special outfit for my arrival: a maroon dress with a multilayered skirt, puffed sleeves, lapels brocaded with black braids, and a narrow embroidered strip of white fabric binding the lapels—an altogether regal look.

The train pulled into a dark and drizzly Menominee shortly after six. I stepped down my compartment steps onto the familiar platform and took in the red station—more shrunken and dull-colored than my memory had painted it. A pine-scented breeze carried hints of burning wood. Plopping my traveling case on the platform, I hugged myself for warmth. I'd neglected to pack my pelisse, and fall had not lingered here: It was nearly cold enough for sleet. I lifted my face into the bracing mist and surveyed the jagged treetops silhouetted against dawn's milky sky. A rush of memories—of rambling through Michigan's pine-needled forests, running barefoot along its sparkling shores, and warming up on chill mornings before a blazing woodstove—flooded me with nostalgia.

"You there, May."

I followed the voice—Maman's—and she, Paul, and Gene hurried up to me, shuffling flat-footed on the platform's rain-slicked slats.

I flung my arms around Maman. "It's been too long."

"By ten years," she said, nearly hugging the breath out of me.

"And, Paul"—I turned to him—"missed you, big brother."

He embraced me. "You, too, little sister."

"And who do we have here?" Little Gene was not so little anymore. At twenty-four, he'd matured into a handsome young man, with a comely, chiseled face and lively ocean-blue eyes. I reached up to hug him. "My goodness, you must be six feet tall."

"Six two, sister." He lifted me up in his arms, swung me a quarter turn, and eased me down. Chuckling, he asked, "Or should I call you Baroness?"

I patted his cheek. " 'M'lady' will do."

Paul reached for my suitcase, and Gene, who was dressed quite fashionably in a wool jacket and plaid vest, offered his arm. I nestled my arm in his and squeezed up close to him.

Maman walked to my other side, took my hand, and led me down the platform. "You wouldn't believe all the talk around town. Our very own baroness coming to visit."

I believed it when we walked through the double-boxcar-sized train station, which was unaccountably crowded for such an early hour. All eyes turned on us. Some of the smattering of gentlemen fingered their hat brims as I passed, and the ladies either nodded or attempted modest curtsies. To be honest, although I knew Menominee had never before laid eyes on a baroness, all the attention surprised me.

Another surprise awaited me when we reached the house. The furniture did gleam from a fresh polishing, the carpets smelled fresh, and the kitchen counters sparkled, but the pantry contained fewer than twenty jars of put-up vegetables, mostly tomatoes, green beans, and beets.

While Maman prepared a breakfast of egg-battered bread, I asked, "Didn't you do your usual canning this year?"

She kept her back to me. "Sure I did. We've just been eating more from the pantry this fall."

"You been buying much from the butcher?"

"Not much. Hunting season opens week after next. Paul'll get a deer."

It pained me to think of it: While I had been living the rich life in London, Maman had been struggling to get by with her garden, a few laying hens, and paltry supplies of flour and sugar. Still, I didn't want to fuss about it. I poured myself another cup of coffee. "Meantime, let's go shopping and buy some fancy canned food. And stop by Daltry's and get a roast for dinner."

"That'd be nice," said Maman, flipping the bread onto a platter and pretending at nonchalance.

Paul stomped into the kitchen. He'd changed out of his cotton shirt and black dress jacket into a dull-green flannel shirt. "You'll do no such thing," he said. "I'll be going out on the lake after breakfast. We'll have trout for dinner."

"Mmm, fresh-caught fish," I said, twisting around to smile at him. "I won't turn that down."

I could have predicted Paul's resistance to my offer, stubborn and proud as he was. But fishing and hunting couldn't stock the pantry or buy coal for the furnace.

→ ←

It took me only one day to determine how to help my family—and at the same time handle the remodeling and management of the Potash Sulphur Hotel.

I found Gene lounging over the *Menominee Herald* in the parlor my second morning at home. "Gene, I need you to help me with an errand. Will you get the carriage ready?"

He flipped the newspaper to the next page. "I was going to meet some fellows this afternoon."

I gripped the center of the paper and lowered it to catch his eye. "I have something to discuss with you."

He uncrossed his legs and set the paper aside. "If you say so, m'lady."

When we got to Shimek's Furniture Store, I asked him, "If you were furnishing a hotel from scratch, what sort of things would you buy for it?"

Gene stroked his chin. "Aren't you mysterious?"

Mr. Shimek swaggered up to us and asked if we needed help.

"Oh, no. This is just a scouting visit," I said. As he rambled off, I turned to Gene. "Come, now, tell me how you'd go about it."

"Do I have unlimited money?"

"No one has unlimited money."

He headed down the store aisle, passing by the couches. "I'd do the rooms first. Figure out some kind of coordinating theme. Stylish but not too expensive."

We stopped at the beds and dressers. Gene pointed to a bed with square, four-foot-high posts and a headboard edged with scrollwork. "Like that, tasteful but not too ornate. And that matching dresser over there."

I nodded. "What else would you put in the rooms?"

"In the suites, a couch and maybe a secretary. In the regular rooms, a stuffed armchair, maybe two if there was room. And curtains and bedspreads to match the upholstery."

"And the lobby?"

"I'd splurge there. Sprinkle it with a few comfortable sofas and lots of stuffed armchairs. And coffee tables and side tables for drinks and newspapers."

"What about decorations—paintings, rugs, and such?"

"I'd put up paintings of the lakeshore and area lighthouses. Maybe a few deer racks. And acquire some quality carpets. Should plan on a lot of feet passing over those carpets."

"Hmm," I said, turning toward the door, "shall we discuss it over luncheon?"

Once on the sidewalk, Gene offered his arm, twisted his head toward my ear, and whispered, "But first I'd check the Sears and Roebuck Catalog. Likely to find better prices there than at Shimek's."

After we'd been seated at a corner table in the Erdlitz Hotel's dining room, Gene flattened his forearms on the table. "Are you going to tell me what this is all about?"

I revealed my recent Arkansas purchase and asked, "Can I hire you to remodel and manage the place?"

"Why, you little fox," Gene said, leaning back and appraising me with crossed arms. "Why not ask Paul? He's handier with tools."

"Because I need someone who gets along well with people. Workers can always be hired."

Gene chuckled. "I don't know. Don't think I'm cut out for that kind of work."

"What kind of work are you cut out for?"

"Haven't figured that out yet."

A waiter headed in our direction. I put a hand up to warn him off a moment. "What about dentistry?"

"Who wants to muck about in people's mouths all day?"

I drew my spine up straight and glared at him. I'd paid for his dentistry schooling and this was how he thanked me? "What have you done lately to help Maman put food on the table?"

"Now, that's not fair."

"Do you expect to live off my contributions all your life?"

"Of course not."

"I'll pay you well. And deposit a portion of your pay with Maman. You won't even have to think about it."

He nodded, knowing full well he had no choice. "All right, then."

"Good, you'll leave next week. The remodeling will take at least six months."

><

Two weeks later, I received my first letter from Rudolph. While I'd been traveling, he'd had no mailing address for me, but I'd written him three times, informing him of my movements and the resort business.

*November 8, 1901*

*My darling May,*

*How lonely the house is without you. I even miss Daisy's cheerful face and Dicky's way with the horse and carriage. That nice elderly couple who live next door have had me to dinner once or twice a week. (Remember the Allens? They helped us find the nearest grocer and the shortest route to the train station.)*

*Miriam is well, but Mother took a spill and broke her ankle. Of* course, she is terribly aggravated over being in a wheeling chair. She cannot get around without Miriam or her maid, and you know how she hates depending on others. I will leave London sometime this month and spend Christmas and January with them, unless you can hurry back for Christmas. If so, I can wait for you and we can travel together.

It sounds like the hotel purchase was wise, that is, if it turns out as you hope. But do be careful about taking advice from strangers. From what little I know of America, not all its businessmen are above reproach. In any event, I expect you to not become encumbered with the hotel. If it truly is a good speculation you should be able to take your profit once word gets out about that racetrack.

Darling, I think of you constantly and miss you more than words can say. Please come home soon. I promise I'll take you to the theater and opera, just as we did those summer months after we first met. We'll have a grand time.

Write soon, and tell me of your plans, my dearest.

All my love,
Rudolph

# GENE AND FRANK

·

*I* begged my husband's indulgence—I couldn't possibly be home for Christmas—and informed him I'd embarked on a thoroughgoing remodeling of the Arkansas resort, a project that sorely required my supervision. And since Rudolph was incapable of understanding the sort of financial woes burdening my family, I explained that the situation required delicate handling to avoid wounding anyone's pride, at least not Maman's and Paul's.

As for Gene, it wasn't his pride that concerned me but, rather, his ability to oversee the remodeling and effectively manage the business. Thus, I provided detailed instructions, required frequent reports from him, and meted out funds for the expenses in small lots.

Five months after Gene traveled to Arkansas and undertook the remodeling, a number of important decisions had cropped up, and I suggested we meet in person to discuss them. I chose Chicago, because Frank and I had been corresponding regularly and she'd invited me to visit. When I mentioned having my brother join us, she said she'd love to meet him.

Such delight I took in my return to Chicago, relishing the carriage ride from the train station through Chicago's gleaming downtown: its upright citizens bustling about their business in springtime attire; buds plumping out on the trees; avenues lined with potted pansies and violets; and here and there a shiny new automobile zipping around the horse-drawn carriages. Not even the knowledge that Dougherty resided here dampened my spirits—after all, I was now a baroness living a respectable life.

Inviting though the evening's sun-warmed streets and brick buildings were, Gene and I found ourselves exhausted from our travels and business discussions, so, our first night in town, we asked Frank to meet us for dinner in the hotel's dining room.

"You couldn't have picked a more modern hotel," Frank said as the maître d' escorted us to our table. (I'd insisted Frank take a room—at my expense, of course—at our hotel, the Auditorium Annex, so that we'd have more time to visit.) "It was built for the Columbian Exposition."

Gene pushed Frank's chair in for her and circled his glance around the high, gilded ceiling. "And to think May wants me to turn a broken-down Arkansas firetrap into this."

Frank and Gene had a giggle at my expense.

"Only an approximation," I said. "It's a rather different clientele."

Frank, who wore a long-sleeved, burgundy dress that showed off her buxom build, turned to Gene. "How do you find Arkansas?"

"Scorching hot already," Gene said. He caught the eye of a nearby waiter before continuing. "Would you believe it?"

"I found it quite pleasant into fall," I said.

Frank smiled at me. "I suppose it's all part of the bargain—heat half the year and temperate weather the rest."

"I'm sure Gene is grateful to be employed," I said, mostly for his benefit. "After all, he could be fighting in the Philippines."

Frank shook her head. "Roosevelt's winding it down. Public's turned sour on this war."

"You know," said Gene, "you can actually build down there in the winter. Can't do that in Michigan. Or Illinois."

Frank leaned toward me. "I've never been that far south."

Just as I said, "You must visit," Gene rushed in with, "Then come on down."

Frank threw her head back and laughed. "Two invitations! How can I resist?"

"Sir?" said the waiter who glided up to our table.

"A bottle of your best champagne, please," said Gene, once again proving his aptitude for spending my money.

"Now, tell me about this Arkansas purchase," Frank said, putting on her business demeanor. "Everything in good legal order?"

Even though Frank had put the question to me, Gene responded, wagging his head in my direction: "Better ask the mastermind. And moneybags."

"Yes," I said, "I've got the title. And Gene's managed to keep some rooms open. So the cash is flowing."

"That must be demanding," Frank said to Gene. "Tending to guests while you're remodeling."

Frank, who'd blustered about keeping men in their place at our first meeting, surprised me by fawning over Gene as she did.

Like a playful pup, Gene slapped his hands to the table. "How else can I find poker companions?"

We all had a wonderful time getting acquainted that evening. When talk turned to the hotel business, Frank freely shared her expertise in real estate, including sales strategies. But I hadn't expected Gene to pour on the charm as if he were a gentleman gone courting. He'd turned into a real ladies' man. And I had to admit: He was passably managing the hotel remodeling.

After dinner, we dropped Frank off at her room, and Gene walked me to mine.

"My, my," I said, "aren't you and Frank thick?"

"She's one of a kind, that Frank. A woman you could take to the ballroom *and* gambling hall."

"You're not serious? She's a good five years older than you."

"What's wrong with that?" Gene winked at me. "I like older women."

"Oh, fiddlesticks," I said, borrowing one of Maman's favorite expressions, "though it might take an older woman to keep *you* in line."

Regardless of what I thought, Gene and Frank obviously enjoyed each other's company, bantering and baiting each other like brother and sister. But it was Frank and I who formed the strongest link of our triangle. We had a ripping good time: sharing *tête-à-têtes* on morning walks while Gene slept in; and shopping at The Fair and Carson & Pirie, where I found a silk nightgown, French-made shoes, and the most irresistible three-stone diamond ring.

At the end of our four-day visit, Frank told me: "By God, I can't believe I allowed you to host me in the city I live in. There's only one answer to that. You have to come to Pittsburgh and stay with my family. Absolutely no later than my next visit there."

I reported to Rudolph that I'd befriended a capable woman attorney who advised me to complete the remodeling before putting it up for sale. Yes, I told him in response to his most recent letter, the racetrack was under construction, its site was near the hotel, and the track would open sometime in 1904 or 1905. But his impatience would not be assuaged.

*August 2, 1902*

*My dear May,*

*Do you know that as of next month you will have been away a full year? I understand that your family needs you, but we can easily provide any assistance they need from a distance. You have installed your brother Gene at the hotel. I trust Paul, who is obviously more industrious, will soon find employment in Menominee. You have them on the right track now.*

*I must remind you that you have another family—me, Mother, and Miriam. You belong with your husband. I need you here to help me. Mother has recovered from her broken ankle, but she gets out very little now. I think she is afraid of another accident. That means her world is limited to visitors, and I fear that pettiness is taking over her outlook. You and your cheery disposition are exactly what this household needs. Not that I require you to stay here year-round. We still have the London home, and I know how you love it. I would never dream of depriving you of the joy that London society and its distractions provide.*

*Only I must insist that you make plans to return soon. A full year apart is intolerable. We are husband and wife. Please write soon, and tell me when you will return.*

*All my love,*
*Rudolph*

I informed Rudolph that the remodeling was nearing completion and that I wouldn't linger in the States any longer than necessary. However, I didn't want to leave any loose ends. To nurture my blossoming friendship with Frank, I accepted her invitation to visit Pittsburgh in September. When Gene found out, he begged me to finagle an invitation for him as well. I objected on the grounds that he had work to do, but he promised that his assistant manager could handle the few remaining projects.

I broached the topic with Frank during a phone call to arrange the details. "Gene says he's jealous of me getting to visit you."

Without missing a beat, Frank replied, "Well, hell's bells, tell him to come, too. There's plenty of room at the house."

"Plenty of room" proved to be an understatement. Frank's parents lived in a spacious three-story stone home with the most lovely touches: stone columns supporting an iron fence that skirted the cobblestone street; a four-story turret with a tile dome and gargoyles circling its spiraling levels; and, behind the house, a cutting garden with the cutest stone cottage for potting and storage. A copper weathervane of Mercury topped the turret, and a trellis of jasmine lined the entry walk, with just enough bloom to sweetly scent the entranceway.

Gene and I arrived on the same train, and Frank toured us around the home and property, showing off a wood-framed sun porch decorated with wicker furnishings and African violets. We ended up in a large sitting room on the main floor, admiring a river-rock fireplace and the collection of Egyptian amulets and tomb figurines displayed on its mantel.

"You'll meet the lord and lady at dinner," said Frank. "Come, I'll show you your bedrooms."

We climbed a curving staircase to the second level, passing a sitting bench nestled into a window alcove. Frank motioned us to follow her down the second-floor hallway. She swung the second-to-the-last door open. "Here's your room, Gene."

I peeked in. Gene's room sported masculine décor—solid burgundy wallpaper, paintings of fox hunts, and a tall case holding old rifles.

"Why, Frank," said Gene, sidling up to her, "you know me too well."

I had to chuckle. Gene was no sportsman. He only hunted when Paul insisted on it, and all he knew about guns was that the barrel required pointing.

We left Gene, and Frank showed me to the room at the end of the hall, which was decorated in the style of an English country estate, with an antique wall clock, a poster bed covered with embroidered pillows, and paintings of an English-style garden and outdoor tea service. "It's a lovely room," I said, kissing Frank on the cheek. "So welcoming and comfortable."

Over dinner, we had the pleasure of meeting Mr. and Mrs. Shaver.

"I've heard so much about you from Frank." Mrs. Shaver looked to me, then Gene, her sky-blue eyes sparkling against her delicate complexion and the snow-white hair she'd swooped into a chignon.

"And I must thank you," said Gene, between spoonfuls of clam chowder, "for welcoming us to your lovely home."

Mr. Shaver, from whom Frank had apparently inherited her sturdy frame, turned to me. "I understand you and the Baron are in property investment."

"I wouldn't consider it an ongoing venture. We own residences in Holland and London. I'll soon be selling the Arkansas hotel."

"Yes, well, that sounds like a worthwhile investment."

"And I understand that you, sir, helped design the Westinghouse air brake?"

"Yes, Mr. Westinghouse is a wonderful man to work for. He's built a sound company."

Gene pitched his frame toward Mr. Shaver. "Do you still have occasion to work with Mr. Westinghouse, sir?"

"Oh, yes, the man works longer hours than most anybody else. That's why I have such confidence in the company's stock."

The maid swept in and scooped up our soup bowls.

"Some say Roosevelt's overreaching on the Panama Canal rights." The way Gene hunched over and gazed at Mr. Shaver, one might have thought him a petitioner for a post. "What do you think, sir?"

"Oh, without question, moving forward on the canal will be a boon to U.S. business."

→←

As we neared the end of our scheduled one-week visit with Frank and her family, I overheard Gene remark to Frank, "Perhaps next week we can tour Fort Pitt." As soon as Gene retreated to his bedroom to dress for dinner, I knocked on his door.

"Yes, come in," said Gene, as casual and relaxed as a seaside vacationer.

I let myself in and closed and leaned against the door. "What's this I hear about you and Frank going on an outing next week?"

Gene undid the top button of his shirt and circled a finger around the collar to loosen it. "I'm thinking of staying on a little longer."

"And why haven't you mentioned this to me?"

"Frank's my friend, too."

"You've got work to do in Arkansas."

"Another week or two won't matter," said Gene, sitting down on his bed and crossing one leg over the other.

"We need to finish the remodeling. Rudolph expects me home as soon as possible."

"It's practically done. William's got it all in hand."

"Still, I'd prefer that you return with me. We have matters to wrap up."

"Such as?"

"The installation of those lamps for the lobby, and the last of the bills for the workers and materials."

"William can handle all that."

"And the general management? I don't expect the property to sell tomorrow."

"All right, all right. If you let me have one more week of vacation, I'll work every day until it's sold."

&gt;&lt;

I returned to Arkansas by myself and spent the next three weeks overseeing the completion of the remodeling in anticipation of putting the hotel up for sale. Thank goodness, William proved to be a competent assistant, for Gene's stay in Pittsburgh stretched on and on—to a full month. But I could hardly be annoyed with him when he wrote to tell me he'd asked Frank to marry him and she'd accepted. In fact, I was overjoyed: I heartily congratulated him and told Frank it pleased me in the utmost to welcome her to the family. Perhaps their marriage would provide the security Gene—and the whole family—so sorely needed.

# FOR RUDOLPH'S FAMILY

·

*I*t had been over a year since I'd absented myself from my husband's side, so I wasn't surprised when Rudolph insisted I return to Holland by Christmas. I left Arkansas in October and relegated oversight of the hotel sale to Gene. For safe measure, I asked Frank to review any documents related to sale offers. She was altogether amenable: "You can count on me; it's all in the family now," to which I'd responded, "I can hardly believe we'll soon be sisters-in-law."

Before sailing for Liverpool, I decided to stop a few days at the home of Rudolph's uncle and his wife, who lived in New York City. I'd had occasion to get acquainted with Philip and Saskia during their visits to Dalfsen in the early years of my marriage. Six years ago, they had relocated to New York and taken a home on West Fifty-eighth Street.

Philip and Saskia had decorated their brownstone in the latest style, Art Nouveau, with elegant swan-neck lamps gracing side tables and finely crafted furniture of curvaceous design in every room. My first evening in New York, we dined in their cozy dining room and afterward retreated to the parlor for Cognac. As I relaxed in an armchair with legs as arced and branching as deer antlers, I asked, "Are you settling permanently in New York?"

Saskia, a large-proportioned woman with the grace of a ballerina, smiled at this. "We rather enjoy the city's offerings. Especially the Metropolitan Opera. It's surprisingly good."

"I've never been." Knowing that Saskia had performed some mezzo opera roles in Holland, I said, "But your appraisal makes me want to go."

Saskia's wide-set green eyes brightened. "Really? I could get orchestra seats for us. Why don't you stay on for a while?"

"I shouldn't. I've finally put the hotel up for sale, and Rudolph is expecting me."

But within two days I had relented. The truth is, I'd fallen a little in love with the couple: with Saskia's flair for Art Nouveau décor, infectious love of opera, and generous, unpretentious manner; as well as with Philip's sad-looking face, unfailing chivalry, and charming habit of chastely kissing Saskia's cheek at the slightest excuse.

Then, the day I planned to secure my ticket for the crossing, Saskia insisted we have a serious chat and asked the maid to prepare tea service for the three of us.

We sat in our customary places in the parlor. The usually suave Philip cleared his throat, as if to summon courage. He set his high brow and narrow jaw into solemn thoughtfulness. "There's something we'd like to discuss with you, May. A rather sensitive matter."

"We're family," I said, inching to the edge of my seat and perching there. "You can speak openly with me."

"I've bid on an iron-mining interest in Mexico. A very large contract."

"Has the bidding closed?"

"It should have, but I've learned the time's been extended. We don't really know how these things work over here."

"You're worried about how it's being handled?"

"Yes. I submitted a rather handsome bid, thinking that would settle the matter."

"And the contract is obviously important to you."

He clamped his hands together. "My business may not survive without it."

I knew Philip's business manufactured cast metal items—cooking vessels mostly. "Your business is struggling?"

"It's hard to compete with all the new U.S. companies."

"I see." I eased my cup and saucer onto the side table. All this time, Saskia had held herself statue-still, shifting her gaze only enough to track the measured volley of our exchange.

Philip gripped the arm of the settee, leaned to the side, and crossed one leg over the other. The corner of his mouth twitched. "I need this contract to sell in the American market. And I know you've managed business deals in Japan and the U.S."

They needed—and trusted—me. How could I not help such darlings? Turning to Philip, I said, "If there's anything at all I can do, I will be glad to help."

The next morning, Philip arranged our travel to Mexico City and wrote Rudolph a long letter explaining the circumstances. I spent the day bustling about: purchasing clothes suitable for the conduct of business, as well as books on Mexico and the Spanish language; requesting that Frank submit a bid to the Mexican government on behalf of Iron Mountain Mining (a company I invented to serve the purpose of the trip); and unpacking my steamer trunk and packing two suitcases for what could be a stay of a few weeks in Mexico. Still, I managed to dash a cablegram off to Rudolph: DARLING MUST ASSIST PHILIP ON BUSINESS IN MEXICO STOP MORE TO FOLLOW FROM HIM STOP LOVE MAY STOP.

One of Philip's business associates had wisely cultivated a contact in the Mexican government. During the train journey, Philip briefed me on his findings: the names of parties submitting competitive bids; transaction dates; and offices and entities involved. I made a record of the information for future reference and secreted it away in the bottom compartment of my traveling case. Philip wired for a reservation for himself and Saskia at the Gran Hotel Ciudad de México, a luxurious establishment near the National Palace. I later made my own reservation at the same hotel.

When our train arrived in Mexico City, we took separate carriages to the hotel. As much as I enjoyed their company, I had a job to do, and it required the utmost discretion. I used my rudimentary Spanish to request transport to the Gran Hotel, and my driver embarked on a winding journey through a maze of streets: past a mix of buildings, some in smooth adobe, others with Spanish-style towers and arches; among donkeys and the occasional horse, their heads dipping and rising as they pulled their carts and wagons; and along a broad avenue with a line of electric cars. Mexico City was unlike any other city I'd ever visited: set in a bowl-shaped valley and surrounded by mountains; its streets teeming with men in broad-brimmed hats and women in bright-colored dresses; the air thin and dusty; but everywhere people, great hordes of people, as if they'd decided en masse to throng the late-afternoon streets.

When I walked into the lobby of the Gran Hotel, wonder tinged with disappointment washed over me. If only I could have shared the moment with Philip and Saskia. Standing in the middle of the Art Nouveau lobby, I hardly knew where to look first: at the canopy of turquoise, yellow, and red-orange stained glass arching high above; at the open-cage elevator of coal-dark metal flourished with golden knobs; or at the curving layers of wrought-iron rails lining the upper floors opening onto the lobby. Perhaps later, once we had managed the business deal, the three of us could enjoy it together. But for now our communications would be restricted to behind-closed-door meetings in our hotel rooms.

The next morning, I set out on my mission. I ordered a carriage and asked to be driven to the Palacio Nacional. The ride took me only three blocks from the hotel. If I had known the way well enough, I would have simply strolled the distance. November's weather, crisp but dry and sunny, certainly presented no impediment. Henceforth, I resolved, I would walk and enjoy the avenue's tall, open-branched trees and gardens of exotic plants, some with leaves as large as fans and others with thick, pointed shoots.

The National Palace's fortress-strong front stretched the length of a New York City block. Atop the tower at the building's midpoint, the Mexican flag's green, white, and red bands sagged in uneven parallels. In order to open the palace's bulky doors of carved concentric geometries, I had to grip the handle firmly and shift the whole of my weight backward. Along the first level's wide corridor, people stood in lines before service counters staffed by men in olive-green shirts. I walked to the end of this corridor and found another of the same length, this one with closed doors that probably housed workaday administrators.

The palace's air smelled of grimy chalk, as if its surfaces had absorbed the oils and perspiration of thousands. On the walls, rich-colored paintings depicted Mexican history: warriors of an ancient civilization gathering beneath a stone temple; a landscape of the fledgling Mexico City against a background of misty mountain peaks;

a military battle against Spaniards in the city streets; and Mayans harvesting corn and honoring the sun. I strolled the whole rectangle of the building, acclimating myself to the business-like clip of men in light-colored suits, their furtive glances, and the droop of their swarthy mustaches.

The high-level officials, I reasoned, must occupy the second floor. Mounting the stairs, I reached a hallway of inlaid marble floors with high ceilings supported by arched buttresses. Reddish-brown wood doors separated broad expanses of the halls, suggesting that large or multichambered offices lay behind them. At the end of one of the corridors, four guards stood at attention in front of an unmarked door, perhaps that of President Porfirio Díaz himself. I surveyed the complete rectangle of this floor. Fewer persons walked these halls, and those I did pass studied me with open curiosity. I saw not a single woman on this level. Maybe that would work in my favor—if I could convey the authoritative tone of one who grasped government business dealings, as well as the diplomacy and tact they required.

I closed the loop of my walk before the door labeled "Secretaría de Recursos José Elvira Pérez." Spreading my shoulders square and high, I opened the door. A young man in a suit too wide for his sloping shoulders looked up at me, raising his caterpillar-thick eyebrows. The nameplate on his desk read "César López Álvarez." He leaned forward in his seat, his left hand spread over a document, his right hand gripping a pen. Open wood boxes on the side of his desk brimmed with papers. I assumed the closed door at the rear of the twenty-by-thirty-foot waiting area led to the inner sanctum of the Secretary of Resources.

"*Buenos días, señor,*" I said, striding to his desk.

Mr. López Álvarez smiled and nodded. "*Buenos días, señorita.*"

"*¿Usted habla inglés?*"

"Yes, a little."

Ah, I thought, one tiny problem solved. "I would like to make an appointment to see Secretary Elvira Pérez."

"What is your business, *señorita*?"

"The iron-mining contract. I'm Florence Walker, from the United States. A representative of Iron Mountain Mining." I'd removed my wedding ring and donned a business-style suit for my new identity.

He reached for a worn notebook and flipped it open. "He is very busy until next week."

It was only Tuesday. I doubted I could afford to put this off until the following week. "Not even ten minutes someday this week?"

"No, *señorita*." He hunched a shoulder as if to ease the bad news and tapped the page of the notebook. "He can see you next Tuesday. At noon."

"Please do schedule me." I touched my fingertips to the edge of his desk. "And can you tell me, *señor*, the best museums to visit in Mexico City?"

After a perfunctory exchange of pleasantries with Mr. López Álvarez, I hiked back to the hotel. But the altitude left me winded, and I was unable to strike a fast pace or take much delight in the brisk air or cloudless azure sky.

Once the hallway outside Philip and Saskia's room emptied, I knocked on their door. No answer. I scribbled a note and pushed it under the door. They can't have gone far, I thought: They know I was to visit the National Palace this morning. For over an hour, I waited in my room. Although hunger gnawed at me, I dared not leave for fear of missing them. Finally, they rapped on my door.

I ushered them in, and we settled around the coffee table.

Saskia, uncharacteristically subdued, patted Philip's thigh.

"Is everything all right?" I asked.

Philip moistened his lips, and his mouth clucked with dryness. "The winner will be made public this Friday. I've been outbid."

# ONE LAST BID

·

MEXICO CITY—NOVEMBER 1902

*S*o much for our plan." I walked to my hotel-room window and gazed absently down on the avenue. Spare-branched treetops stood inert in the breezeless sky. Beneath their boughs, suited men, perhaps officials from nearby offices, and the occasional woman sauntered along, all of them probably making their way to a midday meal. My stomach rumbled; I smoothed a hand over it. Hungry as I was, I had to think.

I glanced over my shoulder at Philip and Saskia. They sat side by side on the couch, hunkered over their knees and staring at the floor.

"All this way," said Philip. "And for what?"

Saskia draped her hand over Philip's shoulder and muttered something in Dutch.

I strode before them and stood akimbo. "From what little I understand, the Díaz government isn't above striking back-door deals."

Philip looked up at me. Early afternoon's bright light deepened the creases between his eyebrows and the wrinkles tugging at his mouth. He shook his head. "True, but it is not easy to penetrate their circle."

"We mustn't give up yet." I'd set out to help Philip with this business matter, and I was determined to succeed.

Philip leaned back on the couch and looked up at me. "The announcement won't be made until Friday," he said, a hint of hopefulness lifting the end of his sentence.

Saskia allowed herself the glimmer of a smile. "If anyone can solve this problem, it's May."

"I must manage an audience with Secretary Elvira Pérez," I said. Grabbing my hat from the dresser, I rushed to the door. "If you'll excuse me, Florence Walker has business to conduct."

When I got to the National Palace, I found the door to the Secretary's office locked. I walked around the second-floor rectangle twice, trying the door each pass. When, on my third go-round, I spotted Mr. López Álvarez unlocking the door, I hurried to let myself in.

"Señor, do you mind if I wait and see if the Secretary can spare a few minutes?"

"I doubt he will be available, *señorita,* but you may stay."

I sank onto the red sofa against the wall perpendicular to his desk. Although I wished to strike a friendly note with Mr. López Álvarez, I simply couldn't summon the energy for conversation. Arranging my skirt comfortably over my knees and legs, my hands on my lap, and my spine flat against the sofa, I endeavored to rest my body and compose my thoughts. Once Mr. López Álvarez's absorption in his work exceeded his interest in my presence, I even closed my eyes.

Not an hour later, a man in a sand-beige suit rushed in. He glanced at me as he passed and then greeted Mr. López Álvarez by his first name. After that, they spoke rapidly in Spanish. Although I could not comprehend the content of their brief discussion, I discerned that the visitor, who threw up his hands as he hustled off, left disappointed.

I looked inquiringly at César.

"You see," he said, "not even his son can get in."

"His son." I slanted my head in thoughtfulness. "I believe my associate met him last year. I've forgotten his name."

"It is Alonso Elvira Alamo."

I rose. "Yes, that's it. I really should convey my regards. If you'll excuse me."

I bolted out of the office and headed down the hall to the stairway, lifting my skirt enough so I could lengthen my stride to a trot. There he was, rounding the corner at the bottom of the stairs.

I bounded down the steps on the balls of my feet—to keep my heels from clacking on the marble stairs. As he opened the main door, I called out, "Señor Elvira Alamo."

He pivoted around. "*¿Sí?*"

He stood stock-still, his compact five-seven-ish frame centered in the doorway. Bright light glowed around his head, sun-blinding me to his expression. Had I surprised him? Was he annoyed?

A million tiny sunbursts sparked before my eyes. My legs wobbled like rubber. Then I fainted.

⇥⇤

Moist fingertips dabbed my cheeks. I fluttered my eyes open to find myself lying on the red couch in the Secretary's office. Mr. Elvira Alamo knelt beside me, spritzing my face with water, and César stood beside him, gazing down on me.

"*Señorita,*" said César, "you are well?"

Mr. Elvira Alamo swiftly withdrew his hand, as if he'd been caught at an uninvited intimacy, and asked, "Shall I get a doctor?"

His voice, as fluid and sonorous as a cello, calmed me. He fixed his chocolate-brown eyes on me in an expression concentrated with concern. He had an oval face, with a refined brow and gently sloping nose, and his black hair coiled against his skull in a mass of curls—reminiscent of a bust of Apollo. I flushed at the realization that he had carried me here. Lifting myself up on my elbows, I said, "No, no, it's the altitude, that's all."

Mr. Elvira Alamo rattled some command to César, who rushed out. He offered his hand. "Are you able to sit up?"

I gripped his smooth, dry palm and righted myself. "Forgive me for inconveniencing you. I'll be fine."

Mr. Elvira Alamo rose from his knees and seated himself beside me. "You have just arrived here?"

"Yes, late yesterday." I blinked from dizziness and slouched forward. My limbs tingled with weakness. The spasm in my hollow stomach reminded me: I was voraciously hungry.

"Where are you from?"

"Michigan. I've come to see your father on business."

Mr. Elvira Alamo chuckled. "First you must rest. I will take you to your hotel."

César returned with a glass of water. I gulped every drop, relishing its coolness coating my tongue, coursing down my throat, and pooling in the pit of my stomach.

"Thank you. I needed that."

Mr. Elvira Alamo escorted me down the stairs to the street and signaled for a carriage.

He helped me into the compartment and sat across from me. "Are you feeling any better?"

"Yes, a little. I've overexerted myself."

"Do you have any traveling companions?"

I smoothed my thumb over the inside of my bare ring finger, assured by the absence of my wedding ring. And I knew no one could have seen me with Philip and Saskia. "No, I'm here alone."

"Then you must allow me to stay with you. Until you are sure you do not need a doctor."

"No, really. I don't want to bother you."

"I insist," he said. "You are a guest in my country."

At the moment, I could think of little other than food. "Then, if you would allow me to buy you a meal, I would be grateful for the company."

But Mr. Elvira Alamo objected when I requested the bill for our afternoon luncheon, which turned into a relaxed, indulgent affair. "You are in Mexico, *señorita*. The man pays here. And we are not finished. You must try our special coffee drink, with chocolate."

"What a lovely meal," I said, waving my hand over the table. "The ceviche, the pambazos. Everything."

The sun slanted under the eave of our west-facing window, intensifying the ocher reds and yellows of our scraped-clean plates. The satisfaction of a meal much needed and agreeable company to pass it with suffused me.

Mr. Elvira Alamo looped his arm over the back of his chair. "You were hungry, *sí*?"

I nodded. "I couldn't have asked for a better introduction to Mexican cuisine, Mr. Elvira Alamo."

"*Por favor*, you will call me Alonso."

"Then I am Florence."

"And how long are you visiting, Florence?"

"At least as long as my business takes. I must meet with your father."

"He is not an easy man to see."

"I have an appointment next week, but I'd hoped to see him sooner."

Alonso planted a finger on his cheek, as if he were concocting a plan. "He will attend a state reception Thursday evening. Would you like to join me?"

"That would be lovely."

Alonso's complexion glowed with an umber burnish, and he smiled with the abandon of a guileless youngster. "Perhaps tomorrow you will permit me to show you around the city? To the places I have told you about?"

→ ←

I spent all of Wednesday afternoon sightseeing with Alonso, touring the expansive Zócalo, the Metropolitan Cathedral, and Alameda Park. When he dropped me off at the Gran Hotel in the early-evening hours, I took the elevator to the third floor and waited for an opportunity to knock undetected on Philip and Saskia's door. This time they were waiting for me.

Saskia took my hand and whisked me in. "I can't wait to hear about your day."

"Florence, darling." Philip stood by the couch in a black velvet smoking jacket, a thumb tucked into his red sash belt. He chuckled—I imagined over using my assumed name—and pointed at a bottle of brandy on the coffee table. "Come, have a drink."

Saskia and I joined Philip around the coffee table. He poured for us, and I lifted my glass in a toast: "To the next step."

Without taking a sip, Saskia lowered her glass to the table. "You've had some success?"

"It's too soon to use that word. But Alonso has promised to introduce me to his father tomorrow evening."

"Does Alonso hold a government post?" Philip asked.

"He's a lawyer. And, from what I can gather, an unofficial assistant to his father."

Philip rolled his glass between his palms. "Then we should discuss strategy."

"I have an idea," I said.

By the time we'd reviewed my plan twice, the bottle's contents had dropped a few inches and I was ready to declare, "Enough, for goodness' sake. Isn't there a Dutch version of that expression about beating a dead horse? Or don't you trust me to think on my feet?" Instead, I said, "I have to tell you about the most thrilling experience I had today."

Philip blinked his eyes into focus.

I set my glass on the table. "Alonso knows the curator of the University of Mexico's rare-book collection."

Saskia, as alert as daybreak, folded her hands on her lap and tilted her head.

"He showed us a fourteenth-century copy of Dante's *Divine Comedy*."

"How extraordinary," said Saskia.

I held my right hand up, contemplating my fingertips. "I touched a page of the *Inferno*."

>←

"I must keep you by my side," Alonso said as we walked arm in arm into the National Palace. "All the men here will want to steal you from me."

"They wouldn't dare," I said, pleased I'd packed my maroon gown. It was perfect for the occasion.

He raised his eyebrows in an is-that-so question.

I squeezed his arm. "Not that I would want to be stolen from you."

The palace's interior courtyard flickered with fist-thick candles planted on iron pedestals. At the court's center, blazing firepots arranged beneath canopies provided sanctuary from the chill night air. Waiters in white jackets carried trays of refreshments, handing them off and then glancing away, like shuttlecocks batted from one racket to another. As we waded into the thick of the gathering, Alonso signaled a passing waiter and whisked two drinks off his tray.

He offered me a glass. "Wine for you?"

"Please," I said, accepting the glass and tilting it toward the crowd. "Are these all government officials?"

"*Sí*. And their guests."

"What's the occasion?"

"A Belgian delegation is visiting."

I sipped my wine and surveyed the guests. "On any particular business?"

"They want to sell steel rails for our National Railroad."

"They're not bidding on the iron mining?"

"No, they want the rails business." Alonso steered us toward a table overflowing with hors d'oeuvres.

I tucked my hand under his arm. "I imagine the bidding is all very confidential."

"It depends on who you are."

Squeezing his arm, I said, "You're obviously a man of many hats."

Alonso glanced sidelong at me, arching an eyebrow. "Spoken by a woman of mystery."

"For the moment," I said, hunching a shoulder, "I'm a businesswoman."

"And you are worried about your company's bid."

"Of course, but I also have other business with your father."

Alonso reached for an empanada. "Tomorrow they will announce the winner."

"And you say you don't know much about it."

"He *is* my father."

I swung around in front of him and brought my face close to his. "I have some information that may be of interest to him—about the bidding. Do you think you could arrange a private meeting tonight?"

"For you, I will try," he said.

→←

The meeting arranged and the reception winding down, Alonso and I scurried to the Secretary's office and settled on the couch in the waiting room. The tap, tap, tap of a man's compact heels sounded in the hallway, the volume of their beat ever increasing until they stopped abruptly. Secretary Elvira Pérez entered. He was short and thickset, with shiny black hair and eyes like those of a lynx—quick and concentrated.

I stood and extended my hand. "Señor Elvira Pérez. It is an honor to meet you."

"Señorita Walker," he said, giving my hand a delicate squeeze and motioning toward his office. "My pleasure. Please, come in."

He opened the door to a spacious office—of perhaps seven hundred square feet—with a rectangular red carpet emblazoned with the government seal, a desk situated two-thirds of the way from the entrance, and oil portraits of distinguished-looking men lining the walls. Secretary Elvira Pérez motioned for Alonso and me to seat ourselves in the thick-armed wooden chairs in front of his desk.

He eased into the carved high-back chair behind his desk. "You are from Iron Mountain Mining, Señorita Walker?"

"Yes, sir. As you know, we submitted a bid on the iron contract."

"We had many bids. I regret to inform you that yours was not the highest."

"Yes, I know."

Mr. Elvira Pérez tucked his steepled fingers under his chin. "May I ask how you learned this?"

"Not from Alonso, I can assure you."

He and his son exchanged amused glances. The Secretary looked to me. "I assume that means you will not tell me how you learned."

"I'm sorry, *señor*. I can't."

"Do you also know that we will announce the winning bid tomorrow?"

"That is why I wished to speak with you this evening."

Mr. Elvira Pérez interwove his fingers and rested his hands on his desk. "Yes?"

I looked down at my lap and demurely raised my eyes. "I believe I can bring in a better bid."

"From your company?"

"No, sir. My company has made its best offer."

"Then from whom?"

"A Dutch company."

The Secretary tilted his head questioningly. "If it is not your company, why involve yourself?"

"I have several reasons. Most would not interest you. Except perhaps one: your son." I smiled at Alonso, who sat back in his chair, his eyes bright with mirth. I looked back to Secretary Elvira Pérez. "I am here alone, and he helped me when I needed assistance. I should like to repay the kindness."

Mr. Elvira Pérez spread his interlocked hands, flipping his thumbs up. "Is it truly as simple as that?"

"I have no financial connection to this Dutch company, sir, if that is what you're asking."

"And what can you tell me of it?"

"It is based in Holland but also has a U.S. office. By happenstance, a contact of mine learned they have great interest."

"This all sounds very vague." Mr. Elvira Pérez tossed his head in a show of impatience or perhaps exasperation.

"I know your time is valuable, *señor.*" I leaned forward on my chair. "I offer you the same discretion I am affording the source of my information."

"I would have to reopen the bidding to even consider this."

I knew from Philip's report that his department had manipulated the bidding period to allow a Mexican company to win the contract. "Yes, I understand you may not wish to open the bidding a second time."

Even if Mr. Elvira Pérez wondered how I had gathered this intelligence, he showed not the least discomfort at my insinuation that the bidding had been fixed. Or perhaps he cared little about that. Still, I was an American, and he probably preferred not to alienate American business interests. He shifted in his chair and drummed his fingertips on his desk. "And you think this would be worth my trouble?"

Secretary Elvira Pérez appeared anxious to be done with me. I could think of only one way to convince him that what I desired most was to serve his interests. "You could name the figure that would make it worth your trouble, sir."

The Secretary massaged the tuft of beard below the center of his bottom lip and regarded me with somber, inquiring eyes.

I returned his gaze, softening the lines around my eyes and mouth into respectful complaisance.

He reached for his pen and a slip of paper and dashed out a line. Holding the paper before me, he said, "Can your party have its bid on my desk by ten tomorrow morning?"

Studying the number, I said, "I can convey the message that they must if they wish to be considered."

He crumpled the paper in his fist, pocketed it, and stood. "Now, what you have come for, *señorita.* The view from my office is lovely this time of night."

Mr. Elvira Pérez was obviously signaling that our meeting was over—and that I should pretend it had never even happened. But this only confirmed my hunch that he considered it a fruitful exchange and that my mission had been accomplished.

# LOVE, SO HARD TO RESIST

•

hree days later, on the last day of November, I hurried to Philip and Saskia's room at the arranged hour.

Saskia let me in, and we traded kisses on the cheeks. Philip turned from the window and strode to me, hands extended. "My dear May."

"I shall miss both of you terribly," I said, clutching Philip's hands.

Philip lifted my hands and kissed both of them. "I will never be able to thank you enough."

"I'm delighted I could be of assistance," I said, my cheeks warming with the pride and contentedness of having handily delivered a favor.

Saskia hugged me. "I hope your dear husband won't be dismayed by your delay."

"I'm sure Rudolph will understand."

They turned to leave.

"Oh, one more thing," I said. "Philip, did I give you the notes I took on the train?"

He paused and looked at me, his hand on the doorknob. "No. Why?"

"I can't seem to find them."

"Well, they're of no consequence now."

And then they left me standing alone in their room. Save for the rumpled bedcovers and the lingering scent of Saskia's peppery carnation perfume, no sign of their presence remained. I looked around—at the dresser and coffee table devoid of any personal effects, at the curtains billowing over the windows from which Philip had so often gazed at the city. I missed them already.

My goodness, I thought, I nearly forgot: I wanted to admire the lobby's Art Nouveau design with them. I dashed out the door and trotted down the stairs, reaching them just as they neared the lobby exit.

"Philip, Saskia," I called out.

As they turned toward me I saw, through the lobby doors, Secretary Elvira Pérez. Had he come to see them off?

Philip frowned at me. Saskia's eyes widened with alarm.

"Oh, excuse me," I said, feigning surprise in hopes of creating the impression I'd mistaken them for someone else. That, however, seemed implausible in view of their singularity—not just one, but two distinctively large-sized and well-dressed foreigners. I spun around and retreated, praying that the reflection on the outside glass had prevented Mr. Elvira Pérez from recognizing me.

I could have kicked myself for the stupidity of it all. After pulling off such a coup, I'd allowed myself to slip at the last possible moment. Still, the winner of the bid had been publicly announced, and the Mexican government was unlikely to pass up such good money. No, I calculated, Philip's contract was safe, despite my lapse.

→ ←

Although Philip and Saskia had offered to stay on (for we feared that leaving at the same time would arouse suspicion), I had insisted on their departing first. Why not avail myself of the opportunity to see more of Mexico and enjoy Alonso's company? So, with Alonso as my guide and companion, I proceeded on a whirlwind tour of Mexico City's many offerings: the remains of a once-exalted Aztec temple; the city's European-style plazas brimming with life; such beautiful churches as the Basilica de Santa Maria de Guadalupe; and restaurants—every day a charming new restaurant. We dined with government officials at arranged dinners; with Alonso's associates at casual, spontaneous gatherings; and twice alone, all the while conversing in the pressed manner of suddenly intimate travelers sharing borrowed time. Night after night, we breezed up and down Avenida Dieciséis de Septiembre, dining, dancing, and stealing kisses in dim doorways.

I was scheduled to board the train for New York one week after Philip and Saskia had departed. But a complication had arisen.

Against my better judgment, contrary even to my will, and despite my married status, I was falling in love with Alonso. And he with me.

"Don't leave yet." He leaned across the space between our carriage seats and enfolded my hands in his. "We have just begun to see into each other's depths."

"You're making it hard for me. I must travel to London as soon as possible."

"Those people in London can wait." He stroked his thumbs over my fingers. "Stay with me."

My heart thumped. I could picture my dear Rudolph's pleading eyes. How anxiously he waited for me, even as I'd repeatedly postponed my return to him. It was just that he'd bored me so the last few years, carping about ridiculous matters: the prudence of my hiring such an "outrageously expensive" dressmaker; why ever I needed to see Sarah Bernhardt play Lady Macbeth a second time; and my "lax management" of the cook's schedule. Still, I'd pledged myself to him, remade my life around him. He was my Baron, I his Baroness. "No, Alonso, I must leave."

He clutched my hands tight in his and locked his eyes on mine. "You know I adore you. Tell me you don't love me."

My throat constricted against the lump expanding in it. Ah, love—it is so hard to resist: the electricity of the lover's fingertip touch; the ecstatic embrace that melts one to the core; the utter exhilaration of two-become-one. Under the gaze of his soft, pool-deep eyes, my heart fluttered with joyful anticipation. Alonso—as sure-footed and self-assured as a mountaineer—had braved his way into my heart. I felt at home beside him; he'd freed my soul. I wondered: With him might I regain a glimmer of the happiness I'd known with Johnny? Through my watery eyes, his face blurred to shimmering bronze. "My life is elsewhere, but my heart is here with you."

He leapt up and came to sit at my side, putting one arm around my shoulder, the other on my thigh. "Then stay. Make a new life here, *mi amor*."

I leaned on his shoulder and tangled my arm in his. "You're not going to let me go, are you?"

He nuzzled his face to mine and brushed his lips over my cheek, around my earlobe, down my neck. "Come away on a holiday with me. Let me drink you in some more. And then, if you still wish, I will let you go."

> <

I dared not tell Philip and Saskia that I planned to spend two weeks in Cuernavaca with Alonso. Instead, I sent them a telegram: CIRCUMSTANCES REQUIRE ME TO STAY AND KEEP UP APPEARANCES STOP PLEASE ALERT RUDOLPH TO DELAY STOP.

Both Alonso and I preferred a private and leisurely holiday after our hectic sightseeing and the many hours spent with his associates and companions in Mexico City. Fortunately, his family's vacation home in central Cuernavaca afforded ample opportunities for relaxed meals for two and romantic strolls around the picturesque city.

A day before the end of our two-week stay, we sat breakfasting on his east-facing veranda. The sun coaxed gold-orange hues from the surrounding adobe walls and warmed the metal of my chair and the iron rail I draped my arm over. As the cathedral bells finished tolling ten o'clock, I reached across the table and cupped my hand over his. "Being here—with you—is like dancing on clouds. I could stay forever."

Alonso looked down at my hand. "I am supposed to return for work on Monday and be home with my family for Christmas."

"You see," I said, wondering if I could ever tear myself away from him, "we can't hide from the world forever."

He turned my hand palm-up and wove his fingers in mine. "No, but we can make the world ours."

At that moment I wished only to shut out the rest of the world, to make this place with Alonso the whole of my world. "Then let's stay through Christmas. Pretend this paradise will never end."

He stood and pulled me into his embrace, tightening his muscular arms around my waist and bringing his lips to my ear. "You are my paradise, *mi dulce*."

> <

The Saturday after Christmas Alonso called to me from the door. "Florence, a message has come for you."

"Bring it here, please." I sat before the bedroom vanity, brushing out my hair. I loved the light in Mexico, the way its warm glow brought out the chestnut and amber tones in my hair.

Alonso walked into the bedroom and handed me an envelope addressed to Florence Walker. "Were you expecting something?"

"Perhaps it's from the jeweler, though I don't know why he didn't address it to you." (Alonso was having me fitted for an aquamarine ring.) I slipped my finger under the flap and extracted the note.

Alonso picked up the brush and ran it through my hair, looking over my shoulder.

I read the note quickly, aware of Alonso's eyes on it.

*Dear Miss Walker,*

*May I see you for a private conversation? I have an important and confidential business matter to discuss with you. Meet me at Morelos Café this morning at 11.*

*Most sincerely yours,*
*Reed Dougherty*

I folded the note. The muscles of my extremities twinged with panic. I never should have assumed I'd be safe from Dougherty, even in Mexico.

Alonso stopped mid-brush, holding a shock of my hair in his hand. "Is there a problem?"

"It's an old business acquaintance," I said, not wishing to alarm Alonso. "He wants to see me."

"How did he find you here?"

"I wish I knew." I looked at Alonso in the mirror. His expression looked askew—perplexed and perturbed. Or was it merely a distortion of the mirror?

"Should I go with you?"

"No," I said, fingering my collarbone. "It's best if I see him myself."

He released my hair and dropped a hand to my shoulder. "You are upset."

"I didn't expect to hear from him. Especially not here."

"I will not have anyone making trouble for you."

"You needn't worry about that. I can handle him."

Commanding myself to pluck up, I dressed and took a carriage to the Morelos Café. Reed Dougherty, as lanky as ever, stood beside the front door, leaning against the building as if he owned it. It appeared he'd already spent a week or two under Mexico's clear skies: A roseate tan flushed his gaunt face. And he wore the regional apparel—a casual beige suit rumpled from wear. Then again, he never had shown any interest in tidiness. He still sported his signature down-turned mustache, and had added a beard, perhaps in an attempt to dignify his odd looks and underhanded ways.

Descending from the carriage, I composed my shawl over my shoulders and ambled toward him.

He pushed himself away from the building with his shoulder, as if sloughing off a bothersome hand, and approached, a mischievous gleam overtaking his narrowed eyes. "Miss Walker, is it?"

"Mr. Dougherty," I said, not offering my hand. "You never change."

He chuckled. "No, I've kept the same name."

"Well, shall we get this over with?"

"I've asked for a quiet table for us." He motioned to an outdoor table set apart from the others under an awning. "Will this do?"

"As well as any," I said, leading the way and taking a seat.

Dougherty raised a hand, calling for a waiter. We ordered coffee.

He slung his arm around the back of his chair. "Thanks to you, I'm becoming the most traveled detective in the world."

"Why do you insist on intervening in my personal affairs?"

"You think I manufacture these affairs just to make your life miserable?"

"It certainly seems that way." I could see his face all too clearly across our platter-sized table—those penetrating dark-brown eyes, and the long nose that plunged down from his high brow and lent his expression a homely dolor.

"Well, it is rare in my line of work to enjoy such a . . . shall we say . . . involved relationship as you and I share."

"It sounds as if you've missed me, you fool."

"A fool for missing a woman of your many charms? On the contrary, my dear Miss Walker."

I had no stomach for this ludicrous banter. "Who has sent you this time?"

"The Mexican government."

"Why ever would they care about me?"

"You know very well. For starters, there's no Florence Walker in the employ of Iron Mountain Mining."

"I can't imagine the Mexican government cares about such a trifle."

"Perhaps not, but they do care about the mining contract."

"All that was quite straightforward," I said with a toss of my hand. "The highest bid won."

"And it was a relative of yours," he said, smirking.

"Of what consequence is that?"

"Don't you think other parties would be interested in how that contract was won?"

"They were obviously outbid."

Dougherty whipped out a paper and spread it on the table—my notes about the bidding. "You spied," he said. "And competitors do not consider that a legitimate way to do business."

Nausea ripped through my belly. But I forced calm into my manner. "We're in Mexico, Mr. Dougherty, where they do business just as they please."

He folded the paper and tucked it inside his suit jacket. "And where Mexican interests expect to win domestic contracts."

"The deal is closed. I can't see why the government cares in the least about me."

Dougherty reared his head back, like a horse pulled to an abrupt halt. "Because you've been gadding about with the son of the Secretary of Resources, and Secretary Elvira Pérez cannot risk any exposure."

"I will leave Mexico when I please."

"You will not only leave Mexico, you will never again see Alonso Elvira Alamo."

"You can't have me jailed for spending time with a man. That would only expose the matter."

Dougherty pressed a finger over his mouth, as if deep in thought. "Hmm, jailing you could be an option."

"You wouldn't dare have an American citizen jailed. People know where I am. And my husband wouldn't stand for it."

"Neither would your husband be pleased to hear about your Mexican lover."

I stiffened my spine and raised my chin. "You, sir, pretend to be on the side of righteousness. But your actions were directly responsible for the suicide of Johnny Graham. Have you no conscience?"

"I sleep quite well, thank you."

"Because you're a heartless reptile."

"What happened to John Graham was tragic. It's unfortunate you exploited the young man."

Without a word, the waiter placed our coffees before us and breezed away.

"Exploited? How dare you. I loved him."

Dougherty eased the cup toward his mouth and sipped the steaming brew. "I don't believe it."

"I don't care what you believe." I shoved my cup aside. "We planned to marry. Because of you and his father, I never had the chance to meet his family, to show them how much in love we were."

"Instead, you showed it by draining his bank account."

How this man curdled my blood. "What do you know, you self-righteous cockalorum? Johnny spent as he wished. I did not rob him."

"You robbed him of his future."

I sprang up and swung my open hand at him, slapping his cheek with all my might.

His head careened from the blow. He righted himself and drew a hand to his reddened cheek, then looked up at me, the oddest expression of delight twisting his features. My God, I thought, the man fancies me.

Over Dougherty's shoulder, I spotted Alonso crossing the street and hurrying toward us. I flashed a hand at him, hoping to stop him, but he continued, his jaw set with outrage.

I grabbed my purse and stepped around the table. "I've heard enough. Good day, Mr. Dougherty."

Dougherty jerked around to see whom I had signaled. He shot to his feet and spread his arms, blocking my departure. "And besides letting the Baron know about your lover, I will inform Alonso of your marriage. Unless you are out of Mexico by January 6. I must inform you the Mexican government will not abide your presence after that."

*I* had nine days to leave Mexico. And Alonso. Nine days tortured by the agony of knowing I must leave him, fears about how much his father knew, and incessant worrying about what to tell him. In the end, only one viable solution presented itself—a sudden and stealthy departure. Alonso and I had returned to Mexico City, he to his work and I to the Gran Hotel. Before he could call on me the afternoon of January 5 I checked out and left a note for him at the desk.

> *My dear Alonso,*
>   *I have tasted wonders with you. But I have built a life elsewhere and cannot turn my back on it. I will forever treasure the memories of my time with you. Please understand: It is best for you to seek happiness here without me.*
>
> *Your once in Mexico love,*
> *Florence*

Then I took a carriage to the train station and stole away. My first impulse was to travel to Michigan, to see Maman. What comfort it would be to yield to her loving embrace, hear her chatter about the goings-on in Menominee, and smell the meat-and-potatoes broth of her beef stew wafting through the hallways. But it was such a long train ride, and in the middle of winter a snowstorm might well strand me in some backwoods town. Arkansas was not far off the track, however. I could stop off there on my way to New York and pass some time with Gene. He didn't offer the kind of solace Maman did, but I could count on him for entertaining diversion and, at the same time, check on the hotel sale.

I arrived in Hot Springs without having wired ahead, more because I lacked the initiative to do so than out of any design to surprise Gene. I hired an automobile in Hot Springs—an open 1902 Rambler that bounced me mercilessly over the country roads—and arrived, depressed and irritable, at the Potash Sulphur Hotel mid-afternoon. At the check-in clerk's request, the bell-hopper slipped down the hall to summon Gene for me.

"Well, my goodness, look who's here," said Gene, rushing up to me and wrapping his long arms around me.

I held him tight, clinging hard long after he'd relaxed his grip, taking comfort in the familiar scent of cigar smoke on him. Gene, perhaps sensing my need for comfort, swayed me in his arms.

Letting go and stepping back, I looked up at him. "How about a drink?"

"By all means, Baroness. First allow me to help with your bags."

I'd asked for my favorite room, a quiet suite on the second floor that overlooked the river behind the property. We paused there long enough for me to survey the décor. "I like what you've done here—the peacock wallpaper, the ivory drapes and bedspread, the modern furnishings—all very sophisticated."

Gene bowed to me. "As you commanded, m'lady."

We strolled to the wood-paneled dining room, commandeered a corner table, and ordered highballs.

Gene leaned back in his chair and said, "Tell me about your Mexican adventure."

I looked around at what had formerly been a bright room with a creaking wood floor. Now a puddle-deep Persian carpet softened the guests' footfalls and the kitchen racket. Wooden shutters on the windows let in mere slits of light. The mahogany-stained dining tables matched the darkness of the wood paneling, lending the room a cloak-and-dagger atmosphere. "You've completely changed the look of this room."

"It suits the clientele." Gene picked up his drink and swung it toward the room's guests. "You know, the gambling type."

"Yes, yes, I'm sure it does." I'd signed off on all these changes, but now I missed the homeyness of the old breakfast room, with its cheery yellow walls, morning light streaming in the wide windows, and hospitable, well-worn chairs. "Do you ever hear from the old owners?"

"Oh, they came around for the grand opening, ogling the place like a couple of bumpkins. They complimented me, but I doubt they approved of what they saw."

I nodded. "No, I don't suppose they would. It's lost that country charm."

"But you can't argue with success. The reservations are rolling in."

"Wonderful, wonderful," I said, barely managing any lilt in my delivery. In my mind's eye I saw the hotel from afar, as if it were a dollhouse, its front cut away and its cubicles stuffed with shiny toy furniture and figurines in tailcoats and flouncing dresses. It was my dollhouse—to oversee and decorate and sell—but a dollhouse I'd somehow outgrown, a nuisance to be disposed of, an investment to turn a profit on.

"It's a long trip from Mexico City," said Gene. "You must be tired."

"That's the least of it."

"What exactly were you doing there?"

"Helping Rudolph's uncle with a business deal."

"Was it a success?"

"Yes, he's quite pleased."

Gene ducked his head to study the expression on my downturned face. "Then why so glum?"

"Things got rather complicated." I pressed my hand over my heart. "I want to tell you something, Gene."

"Is something wrong?"

"I'm in love with a man I met there."

Gene jingled the ice in his drink. "My, my, that is a predicament."

"And I can't have him, because I'm a married woman."

"I'm sorry," said Gene, patting my hand.

Tears gathered in my eyes. What good was life without Alonso? If I could have frozen one moment in time, it would have been there, in Cuernavaca, under Mexico's mountain-rimmed skies, in his embrace. But once again happiness had eluded me—no, been snatched from me. Rage boiled up, mingling with sadness; my chest compressed into a rumbling geyser. No, I told myself, you can't sit here and allow your rising torment to erupt—not in the dining room of the hotel you own, not in front of your younger brother. With the last gulp of my drink I washed down the bile of my anguish. "Come," I said, standing, "let's walk the property."

I talked Gene into hiking the complete length of the old path along the river, even though a gusty wind whipped wisps of my hair loose and lashed them across my cheeks.

Gene was recounting his last visit with Frank. "And then Frank said, 'I draw the line at you gambling away my mortgage payment.'"

"It serves you right, borrowing money from her repeatedly."

"I repaid her."

"I should hope so."

"You know, she's a bit of a speculator herself. When she visited in November, we took a walk through Hot Springs and spotted this quaint house with curlicue-wood eaves and a wraparound porch. All very gingerbread. She said it would make an excellent investment. I didn't see it myself, but she said Hot Springs would soon be booming and someday a banker or doctor would move in and want a place just like it."

"I suppose she's right, but what would you do with it meantime?"

"My point precisely. I told her that poker doesn't require as much money in advance or worry over the long run."

"Do you call her Frank?"

"Usually. I tried 'Frankie' once and she nearly slugged me."

"Really?"

"Well, no, she just said, 'Don't get cute with me.' So now the riskiest I get is 'dear' or 'my sweet.'"

"Does she make you happy?"

"Mostly."

"You don't sound very enthusiastic."

"No, I am. I do want to marry her."

"You love her, then?"

Gene kicked a branch off the trail. "In my own way. As you say, an older woman probably suits me best."

"If I know you, it's the family money that suits you."

"I take my lessons from the best, my dear Baroness."

"Well, I did introduce you. But, as you once said, she's my friend, too."

"Meaning what?"

"That she'll expect to see a great deal of me, too."

⇢⇠

Gene was not the most sympathetic soul. But he had enough charm to nudge me out of the pique that overtook me whenever I recalled Dougherty orchestrating my inglorious exit from Mexico. And I, determined to make the best of my visit, put on a pleasant face and focused my attention on the business before us, the sale of the hotel. We had one viable offer on the table, from a Chicago businessman, an Anthony Fratto.

Gene and I reviewed the paperwork in his office the next day.

"The buyers that came around before him were just fishing for a deal," he said. "But this one, it's a solid offer."

I tapped my finger on the line spelling out the offer—$205,000. Counting the original price and all the renovation, I'd already invested $86,000. "It's not enough. Any rube can see this hotel will be the first choice for the racehorse crowd."

"Word has been out about the racetrack for months now. I doubt anything better will come in."

"We have plenty of time before opening. I won't accept anything less than $220,000."

"He could walk away."

"I doubt it. But if he does, there'll be others."

"You expect me to manage this place forever?"

I cocked my head at him. "You're complaining about a steady job? About being able to help Maman?"

"I'm engaged, remember?"

"You promised you'd see this through."

"I know." Gene tugged the corner of his mouth into a pout.

"It shouldn't be much longer. Then you'll be free."

"I just don't like dawdling with Frank."

"Have you set a date yet?"

"No, Frank says we need more time."

It seemed that wasn't all Frank needed. Later that day, as I sat in the lobby reading *Twenty Thousand Leagues Under the Sea*—I'd finally found a book that could transport me out of my sorrow—Gene marched up to me. "Can you come back to my office?"

I closed my book, and he offered his hand to help me rise. I asked, "Did you hear from Fratto?"

"No," he muttered, taking such long strides I could barely keep up.

We found his assistant, William, riffling through a file cabinet in his office.

"William," said Gene. "Will you excuse us?"

"I need to find the produce order."

"Well, find it later."

William grabbed a bundle of papers and rushed off.

I sat in front of Gene's empty desk. "What's going on?"

"I just received a letter from Frank."

"Yes?"

"She's got cold feet."

"Over what?"

Gene worried his palm over his clenched hand. "Something about me not being prepared to support the two of us."

"Why all the sudden worry about that?"

Gene shook his head. "I've got a job, haven't I?"

"What did you tell her you'll do when this place sells?"

"Find work in Chicago."

"Then what's the problem?"

"I don't know."

I brushed a hand over my mouth. Frank was a very logical person; she must have had cause for concern. "Have you borrowed any more money from her?"

Gene forced the breath out of his nostrils, like a child huffing over an injustice. "Last month I borrowed two hundred dollars. But I've paid her back before. She knows that."

"When were you supposed to pay this back?"

"Last week."

"And why haven't you?"

"Because I don't have it. Unless I borrow from the hotel."

"Oh, no, you won't."

Gene pressed his palms to his desk, stiffening his arms. "But I don't want to lose her."

"I'll lend you the funds and recoup it out of your pay."

Gene nibbled at his bottom lip. "Can I send it right away?"

"First you'd better write a nice long letter."

※

Unbeknownst to me, a letter of reckoning also awaited me in New York. With matters fairly well in hand at the hotel, I traveled north, resolved to leave heartache behind and journey to England. When I arrived at my New York headquarters, the Waldorf-Astoria, the clerk handed me a note from Rudolph.

*January 8, 1903*

*My dear May,*

*It is with great sadness that I inform you I have filed for divorce. I have been patient with you, but you have repeatedly broken your promises to return. I can only conclude you have chosen to live without me. I will not tolerate this any longer. You need not contact me in the future. Please inform my solicitor (address below) of where he can correspond with you.*

*Regretfully yours,*
*Rudolph*

# WHATEVER WILL I DO?

.

*I* was alone with my sorrow over losing Alonso, my dejection at being spurned by Rudolph, and my fuming anger toward Reed Dougherty. Whenever I thought of any of them, I found myself thwarted—unable to maneuver around the sturdy obstacles thrust in my path.

I opened the drapes of my hotel room and gazed out on the avenue, at heavy-coated pedestrians hustling against a steady wind. A draft rippled through the window glass; I folded my arms against its chill. Calm yourself, I thought, you can't do anything about Alonso or Reed Dougherty. You must consider your marriage, your future.

Should I write Rudolph, tell him I would return immediately? I could explain that I'd never intended to desert him, that my family and then his uncle Philip required my assistance, that all the business I'd gotten caught up in had dragged on much longer than I'd intended.

Would he welcome me home? Or would I only humiliate myself by groveling before him? He'd sounded so sure of himself in the letter, as if he was adamant about the course he'd chosen.

And even if he were to take me back, could I actually bear life with him again? He'd turned the tables on me: He would undoubtedly expect me to live on his terms now. Could I submit to his wishes to spend months at a time with his dour mother and prying sister; bump around a quiet London home with him when the city's many offerings beckoned; and give up gay opera, theater, and parties?

When morning arrived, I knew what to do. I would visit Frank, my dear friend and sister-in-law to be. While she spent an extended winter holiday in her parents' Pittsburgh house, I could relax in the comfort of her family's well-appointed mansion, with fireplaces blazing and servants to cook and clean. I would confide in Frank, and she would help me decide what to do about Rudolph.

> <

After I greeted Mr. and Mrs. Shaver, Frank walked me up to my bedroom. I pulled her into the room and closed the door. Taking a seat on the bed, I motioned her to join me. "Oh, Frank, I've got myself in an awful fix."

"Not you—not the oh-so-clever May." She plopped down beside me. The mattress cratered under her solid weight, sliding me close to her.

"Rudolph wants a divorce."

"That's a stunner." She shook her head in disbelief. "Why?"

"He thinks I've decided to start a life here without him."

"Have you?"

"I won't deny I needed a break from him. He'd become so annoying, nagging me about the silliest things."

"Doesn't sound as if you care much for him."

"It's just that he's older. He wants different things. At first he took me to the very best theater in London and out to wonderful restaurants. He bought me jewelry, he taught me about opera, he gave me my own money. Then he turned into an old grouch, only wanting to stay home and throwing fits about me spending money."

"Then to hell with him."

"But I built a secure life with him."

"What about love?"

"Love never lasts, does it? Something always gets in the way."

Frank patted my thigh and rested her hand there. "It's devotion you want. That's more important in the long run."

"I can't say I ever really loved Rudolph. And the men I did love I couldn't have."

"Why not?"

"Oh, Frank." I reached for her hand. "Am I doomed to never have love and marriage with the same man?"

Frank shook her head in sympathy. "I hate seeing you so damn miserable."

"Look at me. I'm nearly thirty-four years old. What'll I do without my youth?"

She pulled me to her bosom and rocked me in her arms. "There, there, your Frank is here for you."

✦ ✦

Frank's tending was exactly what I needed. She must have told her parents about my dismaying circumstances: They were especially polite and solicitous, and not once did they ask a prying question or even mention Rudolph. Frank was an absolute dear. On Saturday night, she took me to a Shakespeare play—*As You Like It*. And then, the following weekend, to *A Doll's House* at a cozy playhouse with velvety forest-green seats. We even visited Harry Davis's Avenue Theater, where I saw my first moving picture, *When the Cat's Away, the Mice Will Play*, a silly but startlingly realistic picture story. On our evenings at home, rather than partaking of the usual after-dinner parlor chat with her parents, she often excused us and insisted I relax in her bedroom before retiring to my own.

I was so grateful for her many kindnesses that I took her on a shopping trip to her favorite antiques emporium, where I purchased a mantel clock that caught her eye—a lovely French piece inlaid with mother-of-pearl. It wasn't inexpensive—seventeen hundred dollars—but the cost hardly approached the value I placed on our friendship and family bond. I even found an Egyptian Isis statue for her parents, which fit perfectly with their parlor collection.

Two weeks after my arrival in Pittsburgh, a blizzard descended, a howling, bone-chilling storm that unleashed over two feet of snow. That evening, Frank stoked the fire in her bedroom fireplace to roaring and pulled our chairs close to it. I nestled into my plush armchair, listening to the blasting wind rattle the windowpanes and swing the weathervane in erratic arcs.

Frank draped a wool blanket over my lap and eased into the chair beside mine. "Awfully good news about the hotel."

Gene had wired us earlier in the day about Fratto's new offer—$225,000, even better than the minimum I'd set. "The best," I said. "What a relief not to worry about the place anymore."

"You did damn well. An excellent return."

"If all the paperwork—and money—come through."

"Don't worry," she said. "Fratto's rolling in money. And he loves to gamble."

"He does seem anxious to wrap it up."

"Believe me, he'll want in before the track opens. So he can strut around on opening day."

"I suppose Gene'll be moving to Chicago now."

Frank held her palms out toward the fire. "Maybe. Doesn't always do what I expect."

I hadn't let on that Gene had told me about Frank's reservations, but I thought if I could draw her out perhaps I could patch things up between her and Gene. "Have you had some problems with him?"

Frank drew her hands back from the fire and curled her fingers into her palms, as if to warm her fingertips. As she faced me, her face reflected the fire's licking flames. "Let's not bother ourselves over husbands or husbands-to-be tonight."

The fire crackled. A branch of kindling tumbled onto the hearth, one end of it aflame. I picked up the other end and tossed it into the fire. With a giggle I said, "Who needs them anyway?"

Frank laughed. "This room, this night. It's a helluva good place to be."

I stretched my feet out under the blanket, unlaced my boots, and wriggled my toes before the blaze. "Pour us a Cognac, will you?"

And then I told her about my Mexican adventure—about pulling off the business deal, my love affair with the son of the Secretary of Resources, and the government pressuring me to leave. I didn't bother with the part about Reed Dougherty: It would have required too much backtracking.

Frank nestled into the corner of her chair so she could face me, and, when I'd finished my story, said, "My God, you're a plucky dame."

I lifted my Cognac glass to her. "You're no poltroon yourself. Taking men on in the courtroom."

"We ought to travel together," said Frank. "We'd have a rip-roaring time."

After we'd laughed ourselves out over a few too many drinks, I made my way down the hall to my bedroom, toting my boots. The cold of the wooden floor leached the heat from the soles of my feet and set me to shivering. Although the home's Franklin stove had been well stoked with coal, its warmth failed to reach my out-of-the-way upstairs bedroom.

Quickly, I stripped off my dress, my chemise, my corset. Dancing up and down to keep warm, I wriggled into my nightgown and flipped back the blankets on my bed. I slid my hands under the top sheet, preparing to plunge under it. Its icy, slick surface chilled my hands; I yanked them away. Cupping my hands together, I stepped out into the hall and looked toward Frank's room. An orange glow flickered through her cracked door. I pranced back into her room, closed the door behind me, and ran toward her bed.

Frank flung the bedcovers aside, and I dived in. As I slithered under the blankets, she scooped me up in her arms. We rocked away in our mutual embrace, soaking up each other's body heat and giggling like schoolgirls. When Frank's touch turned amorous, I figured, if a few kisses and caresses were enough to keep her happily ensconced in the family fold, who was I to rebuff her? In the morning, I woke to her nakedness spooned against my bare back and her arm draped over my waist, enveloped in the afterglow of the guileless affection only women can share.

→←

Come the last week in February, Frank and I packed up. Frank's work beckoned her back to Chicago, and I'd decided to meet up with Daisy in New York before sailing across the great pond. Since Frank's train was slated to leave only two hours before mine, we said our good-byes to her parents and rode to the station together in the family carriage.

Frank tucked the warming blanket over our laps and sighed. "Sure wish I could spend more time with you. But this wretched trial's been delayed too many times already."

I snuggled my chilled hands under the blanket, though the day's bright sun had actually warmed the compartment to a balmy thirty degrees or so. "It's done me a world of good. Just relaxing with you."

"What'll you do now?"

"I'll wire Rudolph from New York. Tell him what ship I'm leaving on so he knows I mean it."

"You sure you want to go back to him?"

"I honestly don't know."

"Will you let me know how it comes out?"

"Yes. And you, what about you and Gene?"

Frank stared at her hands. "Didn't like what I heard in his last letter."

"But all he said is he'll see you in Chicago after visiting Maman and Paul."

Frank swung her gaze back to me. "Uh-huh, that's all he said."

Confused, I shot her a quizzical look. "What did you expect?"

"He was supposed to go to Chicago and look for work."

"You can't blame him for visiting his family. You know Maman missed him."

"He promised me he'd head straight for Chicago."

"You aren't going to hold that little thing against him, are you?"

"I've already written him. The engagement's off."

My mouth dropped open. I couldn't believe what I was hearing. "And you're only now telling me?"

"Thought he should know first. I mailed the letter last week."

"You're not going to marry him because he's visiting his mother instead of looking for a job?"

"It's not such a little thing—a man constantly borrowing money from a woman and turning lax about repaying it."

"Does he owe you anything right now?"

"No. I decided after the last go-round that he wouldn't get another penny from my pocketbook."

"Don't you love him? I know he cares for you."

"Love's not everything, is it?"

"No," I said, twisting my fingers together under the blanket. "But it's the most important thing."

"Then why are you going to London instead of Mexico?"

"I told you—it's complicated. There could be problems with Philip's business deal."

"You don't fool me. You're sly enough to work around things like that."

"Oh, no, I can't go up against the Mexican government and a business deal worth tens of thousands. Not little old me."

"Fine, just don't expect me to take on a husband that's good for nothing."

"Good for nothing?"

"You heard right."

"Frank, you're talking about my brother."

"Maybe that's why you can't see him for what he is."

"Gene's the most fun-loving young man I know. You could do worse."

Frank set her jaw and narrowed her eyes. "I don't need a husband. Can't you see that?"

"I don't know what you're talking about."

"Then you're more blind than I thought—or were you just keeping me warm for your brother?"

"That? That was nothing."

"You say that now."

I threw the blanket off my heated-up hands. "And I would have said it then. I love you as a friend."

"I refuse to be taken in by your worthless brother."

"You want to remain friends with me and cast my brother aside?"

"Are you asking me to marry him for your sake?"

"No, for his sake."

Frank placed her hand atop mine. "It's not your brother I want."

I pulled my hand away and turned, staring blankly at the passing scenery. To respond to her thinly veiled suggestion would only have encouraged a conversation I refused to broach. Frank had made it altogether clear that the engagement was over. I'd looked forward to having her as a dear sister-in-law, but apparently that wasn't enough for her. Our farewell at the train station was decidedly cool and stiff. Neither of us mentioned writing or seeing each other. And I considered it best left at that.

# ANOTHER LETTER FROM FRANK

·

*O*n Saturday evening, after the first week of the trial, I received another letter from Frank.

*Dear May,*

*Damn, you're a stubborn one. All I wanted was to meet you for a drink. The least you could have done was give the message boy a time that would've worked for you. Are you afraid to talk to your Frank? What do you have to fear from me? You sure as hell aren't following lawyer's orders! That line won't work on me. Remember the story you told me about besting the Mexican government back in '03? That's the real May.*

*You've got a birthday coming up in May, don't you? Number 48. Face it, May, you're no spring chicken anymore. You've been living off your looks and charms for an awful lot of years. Charm may never desert you, but 48 isn't so young, is it? When you were 20, 30, even 40, you could reel them in one right after another. But how many men are going to fall all over themselves for a woman pushing 50? It's about time you looked in the mirror. Men want delicate little flowers, and the bloom's off your rose, my dear.*

*When we women reach our mature years we can't just think about the next adventure. We need to consider our security, how we're going to live our years out comfortably. And an awful lot of women end up living those years without a man. They die off on us, or they hang around in a wheelchair and expect us to wipe their drool and warm up the bed for them.*

*Have you known anybody who stuck with you as many years as your Frank? We both know you go through people like whiskey*

*through a sieve. But I've always been there for you, whenever you
needed someone to keep you company between your barons and
tycoons.*

*This trial does more damage to you every day. It's not just the
Menominee papers carrying the story. People all the way to New York
City are reading about you. If you let this trial play out to its ugly
end, you're going to end up a ruined woman. Think about all those
prospective catches out there. How many New York businessmen are
going to line up to be seduced by May de Vries after she's found liable
for swindling a friend out of $100,000?*

*Let's call it off right now. I know you can come up with the money.
And once you do, I'll invest it so that it'll last us a long time. Then we
can get back to living again, and you can trust that your Frank will
always be there for you.*

*Your faithful friend,
Frank*

# THE WAX AND WANE OF HOPE

·

*W*hat had I to show for my life? Enough money from Rudolph's last allotment and the Arkansas hotel sale to see me through a good many years. But no one to enjoy it with.

More than anything, I wished to return to Alonso. But I dared not. Dougherty would certainly follow through on his threat to expose my marital status, as well as the ploy I'd used to win the mining contract—if Alonso's father hadn't already done so. And if Alonso learned all this, he might assume I never really loved him. Even if I returned to convince him otherwise, Secretary Elvira Pérez and Dougherty would no doubt do everything in their power to force my departure. And with a divorce looming, I could not depend on the Baron's protection, which might embolden them to jail me. No, that path was foreclosed.

I was inclined to determine whether Rudolph would take me back. But first I needed to settle the battle raging in me over our marriage. I'd been of mixed feelings for years, but I couldn't deny the appeal of the life I'd built with him: a respectable life in which I'd mingled with the landed and royal classes in Holland and England; attended the finest theater and opera London had to offer; and, as a baroness, commanded respect and admiration everywhere I traveled.

If I simply accepted the divorce, I'd never know whether I might reclaim some measure of happiness with Rudolph. At the least, I could try to reconcile with him and give us a second chance. Once I'd finally decided on this course, my hopes soared. I sent him a cablegram from New York: PLEASE HALT DIVORCE PROCEEDINGS STOP

BOARDING SS CEDRIC FOR LIVERPOOL IN TWO DAYS AND TRAVEL-
ING TO LONDON TO SEE YOU STOP.

Within hours I received his reply: NO NEED TO TRAVEL HERE
STOP DIVORCE TERMS CAN BE MANAGED THROUGH CORRESPON-
DENCE STOP.

Was he serious? Could he be dissuaded? Although he sounded
determined, perhaps I could devise some strategy that would instill
doubt or reawaken his love for me. I could forgo groveling and let
him think I was willing to proceed with the divorce, albeit throwing
up plenty of hurdles, and see if that gave him pause. At this point it
behooved me to seek legal counsel. I refused to turn to Frank. As far
as I was concerned, she had no place in my life.

I invited my friend Hanna Harrington in from Southampton
to luncheon at the Waldorf-Astoria. She recommended a Mr. Oli-
ver Biltwell, who happened to specialize in divorce cases for New
York's wealthiest. And she invited me to the annual Easter dinner
she hosted for her closest friends. Under the circumstances it was
especially gratifying to be welcomed back into my own circle of New
York acquaintances.

Once Rudolph's solicitor made his terms known, I secured the
services of Mr. Biltwell and countered Rudolph's ungenerous offer
with my own proposal: a financial settlement four times the size of
his offer, about $380,000, the London home, and the right to my
baroness title in perpetuity.

‹ ›

I decided to settle in New York for the time being: What other place,
outside of London, offered so much entertainment, high society,
and cachet? I checked out of the Waldorf-Astoria and moved to the
Gilsey House, which offered more amenities for a long-term stay.
As I went about renewing my New York acquaintances, I called on
Daisy to come stay with me there (just like old times) and serve as
my assistant.

She arrived at my room as arranged, at noon on March 28. When
I opened the door, she swept in and embraced me. "May, it's been far
too long."

I hugged her and grasped her hands. "My dear Daisy, I can't tell
you how many times I've wished you were at my side."

"Your letters were a delight." She raised her eyebrows in a show of mischievous camaraderie. "I've missed some high adventure."

"Ah, yes," I said, chuckling, and led her to the couch in my suite. Then I noticed: "But you've not brought a suitcase."

That dampened her—and my—spirits. She perched beside me on the couch and clasped her hands primly on her lap. "I must speak with you about Mother. I thought it best to talk in person."

"Is something wrong?"

"She's got the rheumatism. Quite bad. I've taken to doing all the cooking and cleaning and chores."

"I'm so sorry to hear that. And Dicky, how is he?"

"He drives his own coach now. We don't see much of him."

"He doesn't help with your mother at all?"

"Every now and then he brings around a tin of cookies."

"Ah, off on his own, then."

"Like father, like son."

I figured I might as well come out and ask, since Daisy seemed to be pussyfooting around. "So you'll not be able to stay with me?"

"Not without some kind of arrangement."

"Oh, I'm sure we can work something out." The truth is, she was the best assistant I could have asked for. And I needed her now more than ever.

"I'd be pleased to come back into your service if I can be sure Mother will be taken care of."

"Heavens, I won't need you twenty-four hours a day. We'll work out a schedule."

"And might you be able to pay a housemaid to attend to Mother when I'm not there?"

What could I say? I wasn't so heartless as to leave an old woman alone in her hovel. I patted her hands. "Of course, Daisy. That's no problem at all."

⇥⇤

Two weeks after I'd submitted my counteroffer, Rudolph's solicitor fired back: REQUESTED FUNDS ARE OUT OF THE QUESTION STOP THEY ARE NOT IN LINE WITH WHAT IS CUSTOMARY IN SUCH CASES STOP THE LONDON HOME HAS BEEN PUT ON THE MARKET STOP CANNOT BE CONSIDERED IN THE DIVORCE STOP.

I responded: WILL RELINQUISH ANY REQUEST FOR PROPERTY STOP REQUEST THE EQUIVALENT OF $440,000 AND THE BARON-ESS TITLE STOP. I imagined that would keep them quiet for a spell.

Rudolph and I were obviously locked in a game of offers and counteroffers. If only I had some insight into Rudolph's state of mind, I might better know how to proceed. And that made me think of Saskia and Philip, whom I missed terribly. I would have loved to dine and go to the opera with them. But circumstances precluded continuation of our friendship. I'm sure Saskia missed me as much as I missed her. And no doubt Philip still appreciated the assistance I'd provided in Mexico. But I understand family ties and loyalty as well as the next person. Our friendship, alas, had fallen casualty to my husband's impatience and intransigence.

# MY YEARS OF WANDERING

·

NEW YORK AND MENOMINEE—1903–1905

*T*hus began my years of wandering. Cut off from Alonso, thwarted by Reed Dougherty, and refused by Rudolph, I was adrift, with only a title to link me to the respectable life I'd once known. I rejected all the Baron's settlement offers, even as he inched up the financial terms. Eventually, he resorted to an arrangement that did not require my consent: a legal separation in the Dutch courts, on the grounds of abandonment, which absolved him of any financial responsibility for me and forced me to subsist on the proceeds of the hotel sale.

The world of 1903 seemed to race by without me, and newspapers touted the many amazing inventions of our "magical era of mechanical progress." Henry Ford founded an automobile company, the Wright brothers took to the air in Kitty Hawk, Harley and Davidson motorized a bicycle, and Marconi and King Edward exchanged two-way wireless messages. But I could finding nothing magical in my life, nor could I imagine a way to reinvent myself.

New York soon became tiresome, with its insufferably humid summers, blustery autumns, and snowstorms that brought the city to a mind-numbing standstill. The dreadful society pages reported on my and my acquaintances' every society appearance and related the particulars of my marital predicament to the whole of New York. Men I might enjoy passing the time with looked on me as a mere toy to be fancied, a titled woman somewhere between a husband and a divorce. I was neither fish nor fowl, neither married nor marriageable. In short, my status precluded the kind of companionship any woman in my circumstances would wish for—the attentions of a well-to-do gentleman who could offer a gallant arm and spirited company.

I struggled through winter's hardships in New York and decided that, if I must submit to the vagaries of a northern climate, I might as well do so in Menominee, where I could at least savor the comforts of hearth and kin. I released Daisy to attend to her mother's caretaking and journeyed to Michigan in the spring of 1904.

Much as I enjoyed helping Maman around the house and joshing with my brothers, I soon became bored—with the sameness of the rooms; the tedium of tired, predictable greetings with the butcher and grocer; and the utter lack of any theater, opera, or musical entertainment of at least middling quality. The best Menominee's brand-new Opera House could offer, a much-vaunted visit by John Philip Sousa, did little to endear me to its fare. I had obviously overrated the comforts of hearth and kin.

→ ←

By November of 1904, I was back in New York, though I was none too content there, either.

"New York is getting too small for me," I told Daisy.

She stood at my dresser, removing spruce-scented laundry from a canvas bag. Speaking with her back to me, she nestled my clothes into the drawers. "Where would you go?"

"London. Where there are plenty of people who knew me before I even met Rudolph."

She looked over her shoulder at me. "And would I join you?"

"I'd like nothing more. Could you?"

"It would be a hardship for Mother. Unless I could move Mildred in with her."

"If you're asking me if I can afford to do that, I certainly can. And will."

She straightened up and faced me. "When shall we go?"

"As soon as the air warms. So we can enjoy a springtime crossing."

In April 1905, Daisy and I boarded the *Carmania* for Liverpool.

# DR. ERNEST WHIDBEY

·

ON THE ATLANTIC—APRIL 1905

*A*s the ship cut through choppy gray-green seas, Daisy and I buttoned up our coats and explored the promenade deck. On the starboard side we approached a gentleman who cut a sturdy figure in a white waistcoat, sleek black lounge coat, and cuffed trousers. Each of his long steps lifted with a slight bounce, lending a hint of daring to his measured strut. He'd tucked a packet of newspapers under his arm and, judging by their roughly folded sheets, had made meticulous study of them. As we converged, he tipped his pewter-gray homburg to us and I noticed how his thick, mahogany-brown mustache accentuated broad cheekbones and bushy eyebrows.

"What an interesting-looking man," I said to Daisy.

"Shall I see what I can learn about him?"

"No, he's probably a dull face-in-a-newspaper sort."

We managed only a few strides before Daisy said, "You should be considering your finances."

"My finances are quite healthy at the moment."

"You never plan ahead."

"At least let me enjoy the crossing." I looped my arm in Daisy's. "There's something quite adventurous about being at sea, betwixt places, completely free to do as one pleases."

Daisy sighed, "If you say so."

"I do. And I enjoy the intrigue of all these strangers mingling, the thrill of letting events unfold as they may." As we rounded the bow, a nippy mist buffeted my face. I inhaled deeply. "Even the chilly air is invigorating."

I retired to my stateroom for the rest of the afternoon to read *Tom Jones* and luxuriate in the room's plush carpet, satinwood paneling, and velvet curtains. When thirst and hunger got the better of me, I called on Daisy to help me dress for dinner.

"I believe I'll go for a grand entrance this evening," I said, pointing to my dulcet-orange gown with its fashionable pigeon breast and broad sash.

Daisy had absented herself the whole afternoon, determined to hobnob on deck. Removing my gown from its hanger, she said. "I exchanged a few words with that gentleman we passed earlier."

I slipped out of my day dress. "Let me guess. . . . He's in banking or finances."

She chuckled. "No, no. Merely a doctor."

"Ah, well. Life wouldn't be nearly as exciting if I were always right."

Upon entering the lounge, I spotted this same gentleman standing near the bar, but I paid him no mind. I breezed by a few full tables and selected a small one against the wall. No sooner had I seated myself than the gentleman approached.

"Allow me to introduce myself," he said, bowing. "Dr. Ernest Whidbey."

"Dr. Whidbey," I said, reaching out my hand. "I am Baroness May de Vries."

He clapped both his hands around mine. "Honored to meet you, Baroness. May I buy you a cocktail, or perhaps a glass of champagne?"

"Champagne would be lovely."

He intercepted a waiter and placed our order.

"I had a delightful time chatting with your companion earlier," he said, seating himself.

"She's a delight to me as well. And what are the chances we would meet again after such a fleeting encounter today?"

"Not all that bad. First-class capacity is six hundred, though I'm told all the staterooms are occupied."

"The very reason I chose this ship. The rooms are luxurious, aren't they?" I studied the broad structure of his handsome face. There was something both civilized and quizzical in the uneven slant of his brow and the way one eye closed to a near squint while the other remained open and alert.

"And roomy, too. They've made good use of the boat's six-hundred-twenty-two-foot length." He tugged his shirtsleeves down from under his jacket sleeves, revealing immaculately starched white cuffs. "This happens to be the first ship outfitted with a permanent radio connection to shore stations."

"You have quite a mind for numbers and facts, Dr. Whidbey. I assume you are a physician?"

"I'm a professor of ophthalmology and otology—an eyes-and-ears man."

"A professor," I said, taking up my glass of champagne. "Then your capacity for retention must serve you well."

He cocked his head in reluctant assent. "I suppose it does. In the classroom, at least."

"Are you on holiday or business?"

"A bit of both. I'm on leave from the University of Minnesota."

How quaint, I thought—a lowly professor—though I did wonder how he managed to dress so regally. This evening he sported a midnight-blue tailcoat, bronze-colored waistcoat, white silk bow tie, and wing-collared shirt. Maybe he had inherited or married well and, with monetary matters conveniently settled, found himself free to pursue his medical interests. He might well be a learned man of integrity who also chose to enjoy what was possibly a modest fortune. Daisy would probably urge me to seek a more promising match, but I found myself falling easily into the company of this educated and unassuming man of approximately my own years. With him I felt no need to posture or worry about business machinations. So when he asked, "May I escort you to the dining saloon?" I readily assented.

→←

We made a compatible threesome—Ernest, Daisy, and I. Once or twice Daisy sought him out for her afternoon stroll; the three of us regularly lunched together; and Ernest and I took to dining in the ship's impressive Italian-style dining saloon, relaxing under its three-story-high skylight dome in the midst of Spanish-mahogany walls carved with pilasters and inlaid with ivory. Ah, such luxury.

There is nothing quite like a transatlantic crossing to help one forget the worries of the world.

Meantime, unbeknownst to me, Daisy had been gathering intelligence. Over breakfast two days from port, she informed me, "Ernest told Mr. Simon that he has an antenuptial agreement with his former wife. As long as he doesn't remarry, he collects ten thousand dollars a year. What do you think of that?"

Daisy had yet to take up her coffee cup. "I'd say you're quite excited about it."

"Don't you see? He's not free to marry, either."

"My word, Daisy. Who's thinking of marriage?"

"That's the beauty of it. No one."

Of course I understood the ramifications of Ernest's circumstances, which fortunately resembled mine, at least insofar as remarriage was concerned. But I wasn't as quick as Daisy to make the leap to any liaison. After all, his steady attentions and efficient command of daily arrangements afforded me the leisure of merely drifting along and reveling in his generosity, free from any complications. If only it had stayed that way.

# THE TRIAL

*M*onday morning found us back for week two of the trial, with me in my heather-green tweed suit—the very thing a reputable businesswoman might wear to court—and poor Judge Flanagan drumming his fingers on the table. He'd hoped to conclude the trial in a week, but as Frank's days on the stand multiplied, he should have surmised that was out of the question.

My attorney launched the day by calling Frank back to the stand, intent on demonstrating that she had prevaricated on the matter of accepting loans from me. Mr. Powers approached the witness box, brandishing a folded paper. "Miss Shaver, earlier you explained that you gave the Baroness shares of Westinghouse stock valued at about thirty-six thousand dollars, expecting to be reimbursed."

"That's correct."

"And this occurred in London, in early 1913."

"Yes."

Powers unfolded the paper and handed it to Frank. "Would you please review this memorandum?"

Frank's eyes darted over the paper with the ever-increasing speed of a runaway car. She jerked her head upright and glared at me.

Powers said, "Is that your handwriting?"

"It appears to be."

"Would you please read the document?"

"It reads, 'As security for a loan of two thousand eight hundred pounds provided to me by May de Vries, I hereby submit two hundred shares of Westinghouse stock, to be held until such time as the loan is repaid.'"

"And it is signed by you, is it not?"

"Yes, but I've never seen this document."

"Did you borrow two thousand eight hundred pounds from the Baroness in London?"

"No, I did not."

"Then how do you explain this document?"

"I have no idea where it came from."

"You did not provide two hundred shares of Westinghouse stock as loan security?"

"No, the suggestion that I borrowed money from May is absurd."

"So you deny borrowing two thousand eight hundred pounds from the Baroness?"

"Objection, argumentative," came the predictable complaint from Frank's attorney, and "Sustained," the routine refrain from Judge Flanagan.

With that, my attorney concluded his cross-examination. Frank's attorney, Sawyer, then sought to undo the damage to her reliability via his redirect, during which time Frank parroted various versions of her contention that she had neither borrowed money from me nor signed any document naming stock as surety.

At the conclusion of the morning's testimony, Judge Flanagan ordered a shortening of the luncheon recess, requesting everyone's prompt return at one-fifteen: "This isn't the only case on the docket, nor should it be taking so much of the court's time."

Upon my return, I found Frank and her attorney seated side by side at the plaintiff's bench, their heads bent together in somber exchange. I detected the aura of desperation about their manner, which surprised me not at all after my attorney had chipped away at Frank's credibility on the matter of borrowing from me.

Once the judge had called the court to order, Sawyer rose. "Your Honor, may I approach the bench?"

Judge Flanagan, no doubt sensing another obstruction to his design of moving the trial forward, intoned, "If you insist."

A whispering campaign ensued. I only caught a tiny snippet— something about a fake document—before the judge invited my attorney to join the conference. The whispers increased to hushed barks, until the judge finally splayed his hands to quiet the rival attorneys and announced, "Gentlemen, this is not a conversation to be had in hearing of the jury. I will have the jury leave."

Out they marched, a few of them visibly huffing with impatience, or perhaps frustration. They no doubt shared my sentiment: It was high time to put an end to this ridiculous trial. Behind me, I discerned an abrupt buzzing among the onlookers, who no doubt hoped for some saucy surprise.

"Very well, Mr. Sawyer," said Judge Flanagan. "You may argue your request."

"Thank you, Your Honor." Sawyer kept his back to me and addressed the judge, but I could hear the pleading in his voice. "When Dr. Whidbey brought suit against the Baroness in London, she used tactics just like the ones she's using here. That's why it's relevant."

Judge Flanagan folded his hands, obviously trying to bring patience to bear. "What tactics are you referring to?"

"Deceitful ones. Such as twisting claims and producing papers no one had seen before."

"And how is that material to this case?"

"It shows that the Baroness was willing to use deceit to fight charges against her. Just as she's doing here."

"And do any of the documents in that case bear directly on the specifics of this case?"

"Not directly. But the defendant's unscrupulous actions are much the same."

Powers stepped in. "This is prejudicial, Your Honor."

"Just a minute here." Flanagan waved Powers off. "Mr. Sawyer, have you explained the full rationale for your request?"

As Sawyer twisted around and glanced at Frank, I noticed his usually sallow complexion had tinted to an excited pink.

"To summarize," he began, "the charges in the Whidbey case are quite similar to the ones brought here. They show the Baroness has repeatedly wheedled money out of her friends and . . . ahem . . . companions. But that's not the main reason for bringing in this evidence. It'll show she stops at nothing to dodge justice. She'll lie. She'll introduce false documents. She'll produce witnesses to do her bidding. And that, Your Honor, is why I humbly request to introduce facts from the Whidbey case."

Clutching a hand over my heart, I shot Frank an open-mouthed I-can-hardly-believe-what-I'm-hearing look. I'd told her about my troubles with Whidbey, and she had obviously divulged these confidences to her attorney. I'd not, in fact, falsified any documents in that case. Rather, Whidbey's scurrilous claims required that I fight back and use any and all means to extricate myself from his vicious, unrelenting grip. It had taken years to escape him, and now my own survival strategies might be turned against me. The blood retreated from my extremities. I dropped my head and closed my eyes to still the whirring of my mind.

I heard the judge's voice. "Mr. Powers, I imagine you have something to say?"

"I most certainly do, Your Honor. But first I'd like to consult with my client. May I have some time to do that?"

"Here we go again," said Flanagan, rolling his eyes. "Yes, but please be brief."

Mr. Powers seated himself beside me. I summoned the courage to carry on with my defense. I had previously mentioned the Whidbey case to him, though I certainly hadn't anticipated its playing any role in this trial. During our ten-minute talk, Mr. Powers zeroed in on the key aspects of the case—after all, he is a fine attorney—and then he rose to approach the judge and Mr. Sawyer.

"Your Honor," he said and, after bowing to Mr. Sawyer, "my esteemed colleague, I maintain that the Whidbey case has no bearing whatsoever on the one before us. The plaintiffs do not know each other. These are quite separate matters, full continents apart. Although there are newspaper reports of this trial, the case was settled out of court, and thus no definitive ruling was made on either the merits of the case or the nature of the evidence. We have only informal information—hearsay, if you will—to discuss here. Any allegations about my client's attempts to defend herself are merely that—allegations—to which no respectable court would give serious consideration. My colleague is only trying to delay the proceedings by bringing up altogether irrelevant matters. We have plenty of evidence before us on which to decide this case. The plaintiff is attempting to impugn the reputation of my client. It is not an honorable way to conduct a civil case."

Sawyer pointed his sharp chin at Powers. "Why, you . . ."

"Mr. Powers," said the judge, "I will decide the proper way to conduct this trial."

My attorney clasped his hands over his waist and shuffled back a tiny step. "Yes, Your Honor."

"Mr. Sawyer, do you have any rebuttal?"

Sawyer's bow legs tautened as he leaned toward the judge. "I say that the pattern of behavior shown by the defendant is relevant here. The charges are strikingly similar. The defense's flimflamming tactics as well. And testimony on this matter can reveal the defendant's character."

"Yes, well," said the judge, scratching the back of his neck, "the character of the defendant is not on trial here, her actions are. And we cannot assume that actions of the past, which we have no definitive way of determining, reflect on current actions. I deny the request to introduce evidence from the Whidbey case."

Sawyer tossed his head with swaggering dispatch, as if to imply P. T. Barnum himself had minted some outrageous new hoax.

"Thank you, Your Honor," said Mr. Powers.

"Don't thank me; it's a matter of legal judgment."

Powers nodded deeply, then asked, "May I make my motion now?"

"Yes, do get on with it."

My attorney rolled back on his heels and fanned his hands out. "Of course, Your Honor. At this time, I move for dismissal of the case. I have introduced a release from debt, which the plaintiff admits to having signed in 1915. Although Miss Shaver claims she had insufficient knowledge of the document's contents, this is a straightforward document, readily understandable to a person without the slightest legal training.

"My admirable colleague has produced no testimony demonstrating the least reason to disbelieve this document. The plaintiff has merely said she was ill at the time of signing. But again, I submit that any person of ordinary capacities would understand full well that it is prudent to read agreements before signing them and that, once signed, such documents are binding.

"We have also produced checks written to Miss Shaver. Miss Shaver endorsed and cashed these checks. She contends the checks were not loans, but she cannot recall what they were for. All in all, the defense has clearly demonstrated that Miss Shaver herself received payments and gifts from the Baroness and that she absolved my client of any debts she may have incurred. This is a nuisance suit, designed to embarrass the Baroness into turning over a very large sum of money. Thus, a dismissal is not only legally defensible, but well substantiated at this point. I move for immediate dismissal of the case of Miss Frank Gray Shaver versus Baroness May de Vries."

My confidence soared. Mr. Powers had brilliantly articulated the essence of our case. I couldn't help glancing at Daisy, and there, mirrored on her alert face, was the same buoyant optimism I felt.

The judge turned his attention to Frank's attorney. "Mr. Sawyer?"

"This motion is premature, at the very least, Your Honor. The defense hasn't brought a single witness, and I've had no opportunity to cross-examine anybody about this purported release or the checks. The court would be remiss to decide the case on the basis of evidence produced but not carefully examined.

"I might add that the defense has completely ignored, in its cross-examinations, the many instances of deceit, manipulation, and downright trickery on the part of the Baroness and her underlings, ploys she used again and again over the years to part Miss Shaver from her money. This is no minor dispute—over $106,000 is at stake here—and dismissal of a case for such a large claim on the basis of a few documents of uncertain origin is nothing short of unfair. I appeal to the court to allow the trial to proceed so that the evidence as a whole may be considered by the jury."

Judge Flanagan pressed back against his chair, straightening himself to statuesque dignity. "Mr. Sawyer, Mr. Powers, I find insufficient reason to dismiss the case at this time."

My rising hopes plummeted like a balloon crashing to earth. What more did the judge require besides a document, properly signed, absolving any and all indebtedness? At the close of the day's testimony, I retreated from the courtroom knowing the case now rested on my attorney's shoulders—as well as on the witnesses he would call on my behalf. And we had yet to resolve the matter of whether I myself would take the stand.

*N*o sooner had Dr. Whidbey, Daisy, and I disembarked in Liverpool and boarded the train for London than Ernest apprised us of his intention to purchase a home not far from London—a certain Bray Lodge, on the banks of the Thames. "A stately place," he said. "Mrs. Brown-Potter lives there, but since the divorce, she's selling."

Of course I'd heard about the famous actress's marital problems. "Is the divorce final?"

"Yes. But she still goes by 'Mrs.'—I suppose because it's been her stage name so long."

Daisy picked this moment to lean across the aisle of our compartment and inform us, "I'll be in the dining car."

"Goodness," I said, knowing she'd soon request more money for her food expenses, "I swear you spend more time there than in your bed."

"At least you know where to find me."

Ernest chuckled at her jest—on occasion, Daisy had complained of difficulties locating me on ship—but I said nothing, not wanting to encourage her cheekiness.

With a spry step, she left the compartment.

I glanced at the grassy knolls of Liverpool's outskirts. I couldn't help but wonder what this purchase portended for any future Ernest might envision for us. I turned back to him. "How far along is the sale?"

"My agent says it could go through in a matter of days." He reached out and cupped his hand over mine. "Why don't I secure a room for you and Daisy at the Carlton so we can celebrate when it's settled?"

Just as I suspected—he wasn't ready to bid me good-bye anytime soon.

→ ←

I'd never before stayed at the Carlton Hotel. It was quite grand—and conveniently located at Haymarket and Pall Mall, close to the National Gallery, where I spent many a leisurely afternoon over the two weeks it took Ernest to conduct his business.

One May day, he announced he could finally lay claim to Bray Lodge. He insisted on running out and purchasing the best Laurent-Perrier he could find to mark the occasion.

A few hours later, he phoned my room. "Come, the champagne is chilled."

I changed into my lavender evening dress and joined him in his suite. He extracted the bottle from an ice bucket and removed its foil and metal capping. Whisking a napkin from the table he'd set for us, he covered the bottle and twisted its top. At the thwump of the cork, he unveiled the bottle, like a magician producing a rabbit. "Champagne, my dear?"

"How can I resist?" I casually held up my glass, hiding my surprise. Ernest had never before addressed me as "dear." Although our relations had taken a romantic turn at sea, his expressions had never been effusive. He was either only modestly taken with me or supremely sure of himself. Judging by his generosity toward me, which extended to hotel rooms for Daisy and me, fine dinners, and a set of pearl earrings, it was the latter. In any event, his manner—that of one who readily takes command and assumes without avowal that his affections are reciprocated—encouraged me to sally forth with him and enjoy the simple pleasures of drink, dinner, and desire, free from worries about entanglement.

"It's quite a lovely home," he said, pouring for both of us. "With four bedrooms, a drawing room, even a billiards room."

I delicately fingered my glass. "And of course the requisite servants."

"And a small gas stove, well-appointed kitchen, and scullery for them."

"A most complete household."

"I'm even going to have a telephone installed."

"How very modern."

We raised our glasses, and I said, "May you be quite happy there."

Lifting the glass to my mouth, I sipped. Infinitesimal bubbles burst on the fleshy underside of my upper lip. The liquid's creamy smoothness coated my tongue, as refreshing as a strained, slightly honeyed lemonade. I beamed at Ernest and raised my glass for a second quaff, as did he. The drink's effervescence permeated the roof of my mouth and shot the sensation of lightness to the very tip of my head.

"Ah, wonderful champagne." Ernest played his fingertips against the glass stem, as if it were a flute, and smiled at me. "I would love to have you come and reside at Bray Lodge. You'd have your own room. Daisy could be upper servant. I'd see to all the household expenses."

"Why, Ernest, I had no idea you entertained such an arrangement."

"Why not? We make a splendid pair. In the afternoons, when you're not shopping, you like to read or study art, and I have my newspapers to read. In the evenings, you can do as you wish, as will I, though I would insist we enjoy some of our lovely dinners together. What do you say?"

On my word, it was the most peculiar proposition ever put to me. Not that I'd never been invited to take up residence with a man before, but that the proposal should be presented so coolly, in such a business-like manner. Still, it suited me—the promise of security when my own financial resources were finite, as well as some measure of freedom near a city I loved.

I tipped my glass toward him. "I say yes. Your terms are altogether agreeable."

>‹

Bray Lodge is in the town of Maidenhead on the Thames, some twenty miles from London. Ernest and I introduced ourselves there as Dr. and Mrs. Whidbey: It simply proved more expedient than bothering with explanations that would have failed the test of salutary acceptance. Heavens, the two of us being American was challenge enough for the townspeople.

Of course, this arrangement was not without its complications.

After all, I had many friends in London, friends who knew full well that the Baron and I were not divorced. But Ernest, though happy to attend local gatherings with me, had little interest in accompanying me to London, and for once I did not mind going to the opera and playhouses without a regular male escort. The fact is, although Ernest's penchant for spouting facts and figures amused our neighbors, I did not consider it proper fodder for more cultivated conversation.

Fortunately, Ernest objected not in the least to my frequent London outings, though he unfailingly quizzed me about my companions. To squelch what appeared to be a touch of possessiveness, I led him to believe I represented myself as Mrs. Whidbey while out and about in London, which seemed to satisfy him. Besides, he managed to entertain himself quite well at a gentlemen's club in London, the Portland Club at St. James's Square, where he spent several evenings each week. After years of being cooped up with Rudolph, I found this arrangement most congenial. Another woman might have wondered what went on at a gentlemen's club, but I was pleased he had a pastime that did not place demands on me. When I asked him how he amused himself at the club, he readily explained, "At cards, my dear. That's what the club is all about."

Thus, I gladly endured the minor inconvenience of representing myself as his wife around Maidenhead. And Bray Lodge, though not extravagantly large, was sufficiently commodious for my purposes, with a closet large enough to accommodate the new gowns I had designed in London.

By the end of summer, I'd settled in nicely, though one thing perplexed me. From all appearances, Ernest lived far more comfortably on ten thousand dollars per annum than anyone but Houdini could have managed. On a late-August day, after he'd purchased an emerald pendant necklace for me and a 1905 Calthorpe automobile for himself, I invited Daisy for a stroll.

Ernest sat reading in the drawing room, in the only chair with any masculine flair, a stiff-armed leather affair with a matching ottoman. "Ernest, it's such a lovely day. I believe I'll take a walk."

He barely looked up from his newspaper. "A little warm, don't you think?"

"There's always a breeze along River Road."

"Do you mind if I don't go?"

"Not at all. I'll invite Daisy."

Once out of earshot of the house's wide-open windows, I said to Daisy, "How do you suppose he could afford a Calthorpe?"

"Maybe he's come into an inheritance."

"There's nothing to suggest that."

"All he told that Mr. Simon on the ship is that he has ten thousand dollars from his ex-wife."

I tilted my wide-brimmed hat to block the sun. "He rarely discusses money with me."

"But he has mentioned it?"

"Only in roundabout ways."

"Such as?"

"Oh, 'You don't ever need to worry about money,' or 'I intend to treat you like the Baroness you are.'"

"Do you think it has anything to do with his club?"

"I suppose he could be gambling, but that usually leads to losing large sums, not winning them."

Daisy raised her eyebrows. "I could try to find out where the money's coming from."

I stopped and gripped her arm. "Don't you dare upset the apple cart. Do you hear me?"

She studied her feet. "Yes, ma'am."

＞＜

But Daisy had a way of biding her time and springing surprises on me long after I'd forgotten such discussions. So I should have known she would snoop around sooner or later. Three days before our first Christmas in Maidenhead, Ernest and I attended an afternoon reception at the home of an elderly couple three houses away. In the late afternoon, on our way home, a downpour caught us off guard, and we scurried under the kissing gate and into the house through the servants' entryway.

As we shed our wet coats and removed our soaking shoes, Daisy greeted us. "I hope you won't mind. I gave all the servants the rest of the day off."

I merely clucked, knowing full well she'd hatched some scheme.

Ernest straightened himself up. "But we'll want dinner later."

"Oh, I'll see to that." She turned to me. "Would you like me to help you out of those wet clothes?"

She escorted me up to my boudoir, closed the door behind us, and stood with her back against it, grinning in that mischievous way of hers.

"And what exactly are you so puffed up about?" I asked, sitting at my vanity and rolling down my damp stockings.

She hushed her voice. "I had a good long look in Ernest's desk drawers."

I matched her volume. "But doesn't he keep them locked?"

"I found the key in a hidden compartment."

I heard Ernest's footfalls on the stairs and planted a finger to my lips.

Daisy came closer and asked, in her usual voice, "Should I put out the blue gown?"

"Will you brush my hair first?"

Ernest's steps reached the top of the stairs and receded down the hallway.

Daisy came up behind me and unpinned my hair.

I opened my vanity drawer so she could place the pins in their velvet box and asked, "You haven't taken anything from his drawers, have you?"

"Heavens, no."

I eyed her in the mirror. "Well?"

"He keeps a metal box in the bottom right drawer. He must carry the key, because I couldn't find it. But it's quite lightweight. Can't hold anything heavier than paper or bills."

"That's not much of a discovery."

"No, but the ledger is." She let my hair spill over her hands, arranged it behind my shoulders, and took up my brush. "It's filled with dates showing cash in and cash out. He takes out money whenever he goes to his club and puts it back in afterward. And it's nearly always more than he's taken out."

"Why, the sly devil." I rapped my fingers on the vanity. "He *is* gambling."

Daisy brushed the tips of my hair. "And winning."

"What kind of money?"

"Oh, he rarely goes out with less than a hundred pounds, and he usually comes back with two to four times that much."

"Times three or four days a week. Impressive returns."

Daisy gathered my hair in her left hand and lifted the brush to it. "Would you have ever pegged him for a card sharp?"

"Who'd suspect a professor?" I shrugged. "I suppose that's part of his ruse."

⇢⇠

Ernest must have continued his winning ways, for we lived handsomely and he never denied my requests, whether for new furnishings, a case of Burgundy, or a shipment of Russian caviar. As the fall of 1906 approached, he received inquiries from his dean at the University of Minnesota about when they might expect his return. In response, he tendered his resignation. I asked if he intended to take up an appointment here, and he laughed. "Why should I bother?"

In February of 1907, as we sat at the breakfast table gazing out on drizzly skies, he nonchalantly turned to me. "What would you say to a sailboat trip to southern France?"

"France? I love France." Rudolph had taken me to Paris only once, though I'd begged to go back.

"We could go to Nice. And Monte Carlo."

"Monte Carlo?" Now he'd piqued my interest. "Might you play some cards?"

"Certainly. I love a good game."

"You should find excellent sport there."

"A fellow from the club has invited us. An older gentleman. Victor Case."

"Will he be bringing his wife?"

"He's recently widowed. I imagine he's looking for a little diversion."

# FLIRTING WITH DANGER

·

*W*e sailed for the Mediterranean in mid-March, the three of us and two crew. Choppy waters made for an uncomfortable passage, but once we traversed the Straits of Gibraltar the weather turned mild. I rejoiced when we put in at the beautiful port of Nice, with the sparkling sea a deep azure at the horizon and, near its sun-soaked shores, milky turquoise and tepid to the touch—even this early in the spring.

After docking in the harbor, we abandoned our sailboat for the beachside Hotel Westminster. I would have liked to stay at the Excelsior Hotel Regina, where Queen Victoria herself used to vacation, but I did not press my case, since both Ernest and Victor preferred the Westminster: "It'll be easier to check on the boat from here," said Victor; and Ernest agreed, "And to sail over to Monaco whenever we wish."

After two days in Nice, we sailed for Monaco and checked in at the Hôtel Métropole. No sooner had we unpacked than Ernest dashed off to play the tables at the Casino Monte Carlo. Not wishing to languish in a hotel room, I imposed on Mr. Case to join me in exploring our new environs. He met me in the grand foyer of the casino, and we meandered among its pillars of green, brick-red, and soft yellow marble on our way to the gambling lounge.

The gambling room, as large as a dance hall, held some sixteen comfortably spaced tables. Soothing pastoral paintings inset on oval surfaces decorated its walls. A glass dome forty to fifty feet in diameter hung over the room, edged by a roof of soft greens and gold-leafed décor. Eight crystal chandeliers circled the glass dome, and candelabra sconces lined the walls, all creating a glowing, inviting light—just enough to reveal the numbers on cards and the colors of chips, but not so much as to strain the eyes. Everything conspired to keep one comfortable at the tables: the bar at the entranceway, the muted beige and turquoise of the carpet, and the tasteful though tempered décor. As Victor and I strolled the room's perimeter, I soaked up the atmosphere—the echo of chips falling on green velvet; the oh-so-serious demeanor of those gathered around the tables; the smoky haze hanging over the scene; and the dealers, all very dapper and stiff-backed.

One dealer in particular, at Ernest's table, attracted my interest. He was an olive-complexioned man who wore his midnight-black hair brushed smoothly back. His eyes were also dark, and I wondered if he might hail from southern Italy or someplace where people's complexions were naturally darker. He sported the shadow of a beard, as if he'd been unable to shave close enough to keep the whiskers at bay. I played at catching his eye, and whenever I did, he quickly looked away. It was an innocent enough game. Until Ernest, perhaps noticing the dealer's distraction, turned and discovered the cause of it—me. He frowned, and that put an end to the little flirtation.

Victor and I spent only ten minutes in the gambling room before we retreated to our rooms to rest up for dinner. That evening, Ernest, Victor, and I dined at Le Train Bleu, the restaurant adjacent to the gambling lounge. Through the dining room's glass windows, spaced at intervals along the partition wall, we could see the players yet not disrupt their concentration with the jangle of our silverware or the murmur of our voices.

"You must tell us all about your time at the tables," said Victor, clasping his hands over his belly like an apprentice awaiting instruction.

Ernest relaxed in his chair, one arm planted with authority on its arm. "They asked me to leave after two hours."

Victor pitched his head back. "They did?"

"Yes. But I spoke with the manager and returned within minutes."

I reached for Ernest's hand. "Why ever did they ask you to leave?"

"Probably because they couldn't believe I won the equivalent of thirty-five hundred pounds honestly."

"But that's incredible," said Victor. "At what?"

*"Chemin de fer."*

"They outright accused you of cheating?" I asked.

"Insinuated as much."

Victor shook his head. "But how did you do it?"

"I have a system, and I'll return tomorrow, and the next day as well."

Within one week, Ernest had amassed the equivalent of thirty-seven thousand dollars, at which point the manager of the casino begged him to accept a free week of lodging and local tours if only he would abandon the tables. After I pleaded with him to quit while he was ahead, he accepted the manager's offer—probably more to appease the manager than me—and we spent a grand week touring Èze, Antibes, Cannes, the hilltop village Mougins, the Gorges du Verdon, three excellent vineyards, and the Maison Molinard's perfume factory in Grasse (where I discovered my now signature perfume, Jasmin).

Ernest purchased my favorite "souvenir" late in the trip at a jeweler's shop in Monte Carlo.

As I leaned over the glass case, I gripped Ernest's arm. "Look at that fetching brooch."

"Hmm," he said, "a bit plain, don't you think?"

It was not the least bit plain, but I imagined Ernest was posturing because of the steep price, which the piece clearly warranted. Its platinum webs reached out from a large pearl to link an array of different-sized diamonds, like the full moon in a star-studded sky.

"Ah, madame, monsieur," said the jeweler, "I have been considering an embellishment for this piece. Come, I will show you."

He stooped to withdraw the brooch from under the glass and, with a wave of his finger, motioned us to follow him to the end of the case. He put on a pair of white gloves, buffed the brooch, and positioned it in the center of his palm. Pulling out a drawer, he curled his hand to block our view and pinched his fingers around an object. With a flourish, he unveiled the mysterious object—a black pearl. "This, you see, will make an even more, ah—how do you say it?—striking centerpiece."

"Yes," I said thoughtfully, squeezing Ernest's arm. "I like the effect."

Ernest took my hint and casually entered into a bargaining

exchange with the jeweler. When all was said and done, he'd bought it, at a cost of about sixteen thousand dollars.

"*Bien,*" said the jeweler. "The piece will be ready Friday afternoon. Will you sign, please?"

Ernest opened his palm in my direction. "You may sign, my dear."

I picked up the pen to hand to him. "No, won't you?"

He waved me off. "If you sign, you can pick it up without me."

> <

With the *Kaiser Wilhelm* and *Lusitania* steaming across the Atlantic in five days, the trip to Monte Carlo seemed a mere lark. Ernest and I made it a twice-annual holiday destination, typically traveling by boat to Le Havre and then by train to Monaco. We never again sailed with Victor Case—since Ernest had had the temerity to suggest I'd flirted with him our whole journey—nor did we bring other traveling companions, which meant I was left alone for long hours while Ernest played the gambling tables.

So I took it upon myself to make friends. On our March 1908 trip, I happened upon the fascinating Mr. Basil Zaharoff. Although we had met and conversed on only one other occasion, this time we greeted each other like old friends, as so often happens with traveling acquaintances.

"I had occasion to visit with the Duke of Norfolk in London last December," said Mr. Zaharoff. "He sends his regards, as does the Duchess."

We sat in the Hôtel Métropole lounge, near sunlit windows, in plush armchairs. "Aren't Henry and Gwendolen the most delightful couple? People talk about the age difference, but clearly they love each other."

"You know she's expecting another child?" Mr. Zaharoff stroked his chin-strip beard. His white mustache and beard set off an intelligent brow, a prominent nose, and ice-blue eyes with fleshy lids.

"Ah, the fruits of love."

Mr. Zaharoff chuckled. "Has your husband kept up his game since last . . . when was it we met, last October?"

"Yes, much to the manager's vexation."

"What's his secret?"

"If I knew, Mr. Zaharoff, I wouldn't be sitting here sipping Marguerite cocktails."

"You don't gamble yourself?"

"No, I rely on Ernest to gamble on my behalf. And you?"

"Occasionally—purely for entertainment. I prefer to conduct my business away from the tables."

"I understand you have a successful record."

"Quite. Things are rather heating up on the Continent. France has almost sixty submarines. But the Kaiser won't be outdone. He's readying the launch of a new *Unterseeboot*. U-2, it'll be called. And everyone's trying to improve on the Maxim."

"The Maxim?"

"A machine gun. Between them and the submarines, warfare is becoming very profitable business."

"Do you ever accept outside investments?"

"Occasionally, for more private dealings." He smiled and sliced his gaze from side to side. "I find women have certain advantages when it comes to business."

"We must all use whatever gifts God has given us."

"May I ask, Mrs. Whidbey, are you a patriot?"

"I would say not."

"But you're American."

"True, but it's no home to me. Before Ernest, I was a Dutch baroness, but that's in the past. And now I live in London—but only because it pleases me."

"And France?"

"France I adore, though I claim no allegiance."

Mr. Zaharoff slanted his erect torso to the side, resting his chin on a curled hand. "You strike me as one who thrills to danger."

"I admit I'm an adventurer." His unblinking eyes invited me to elaborate. "And I've never been able to determine what separates danger from adventure."

"Tell me, how would a beautiful woman such as yourself go about making herself inconspicuous?"

"Any woman is invisible in the black of mourning. Add a veil and you've as good as declared you carry the plague."

Mr. Zaharoff and I continued our friendly banter for some time, until Ernest appeared. His expression soured when he noted my company.

I did my best to displace his morose manner by making magnanimous introductions: "Mr. Zaharoff, this is my husband, the famous Dr. Ernest Whidbey," and "Ernest, let me introduce Mr. Basil Zaharoff."

After an exchange of curt pleasantries, Ernest turned to me and offered his arm. "Shall we dress for dinner, my dear?"

Ernest managed to maintain a stern silence as we navigated the corridors to our room. Once behind our closed door, however, he faced me with stiffened arms. "I do not approve of your association with that Zaharoff. Do you know anything about him?"

"Of course I do."

"Then you will understand why I prefer you not pass time with him."

"Ernest, you're being unreasonable. What am I to do all those hours you're at the table?"

"You can read. Or find some ladies to shop with."

"I have. But I refuse to turn down good conversation because of your unfounded suspicions."

"Unfounded? You think I don't see the way men look at you? The way you humor them?"

"Ernest, this is ridiculous. I was only sitting in the lounge. There was nothing untoward about it."

"That's where these things begin. I know—I was once one of those men."

"Honestly, everyone knows you and I are attached. And who hasn't seen Mr. Zaharoff with the Duchess of Villa Franca?"

"That's beside the point."

"You're being foolish," I said, reaching out in hopes of reassuring him.

He swiped my arm away, circled his hands around my neck, and squeezed.

My hands flew to his wrists, trying futilely to pull him away.

His face reddened. He shook me by the throat. "I will say once more, and only once more: Stay away from that man."

My airway collapsed under his firm grip.

He glared at me through narrow eyes. "Do you understand?"

Throaty gasps burst from the back of my mouth. I nodded as best I could, bulging my unbelieving eyes.

He released his grip. "Do you hear me?"

I clutched my throat and stepped back, words escaping me.

"Do you understand how strongly I feel about this?"

There is only one thing a woman can say under such circumstances, and I straightaway gazed meekly upon him and said it: "Yes, my dear."

But I vowed that very instant to plot a way to extricate myself from his increasingly bellicose and dangerous grip. To be anything but cautious would have been foolhardy.

# THE TRIAL

·

*W*hen, I asked myself, would Frank and her attorney wrap up their case? Sawyer opened the seventh day of the trial by calling another witness to the stand, a neighbor of Frank's parents, who, I might add, was quite far removed from the matters under consideration.

"Mrs. Schultz, I hope you're comfortable," he began, after giving the seventy-plus-year-old plenty of time to hoist her stubby frame onto the witness-box chair.

"Goodness, yes." Mrs. Schultz nodded, jiggling the wattles on her throat.

"Did you know that the friendship between the Baroness and Miss Shaver broke off in 1903?"

"I should say so. Frank told me all about it." The old woman's gaze followed Sawyer's every move, like an underling all too happy to do her master's bidding.

"What was your understanding of the reason for the break?"

"Oh, that brother of May's, Gene. He kept borrowing money from her. Frank didn't think it was at all proper. And neither did I."

"Yes, thank you," said Sawyer. He paused, perhaps groping for some strategy to blunt the gossipy edge of Mrs. Schultz's delivery. "In the years before the Baroness and Miss Shaver reconciled, did you ever see the Baroness?"

"I'd invited her to visit, and she did call on me a few times. Oh, yes, we had some cozy chats, the Baroness and me."

"And what did you talk about?"

"My dog. She loved Snookie, my now departed Boston terrier. He ran crazy circles whenever she visited."

Sawyer nodded to urge her on.

"And the weather, how I was doing, if I'd seen Frank, my prize flowers, and such and so."

My God, did she imagine the court really cared about all this drivel? Poor Mrs. Schultz had clearly reached her prattling years. I glanced at the judge, who stared vacantly at Sawyer. No doubt he shared my impatience.

Sawyer rushed in to keep her on track. "Please tell us about conversations regarding Miss Shaver. Did the Baroness ever ask about her financial circumstances?"

"Yes, the last time she visited, after Frank's father died in 1912, she asked how much money Frank had inherited. And when she'd get it."

That seemed to be the nugget Sawyer had been digging for. He explored this a bit further before relinquishing his witness to my attorney for cross-examination. And cross-examine he did.

Mr. Powers stood no more than three feet from the witness box, brushing his palms together. "Do you recall the exact words, Mrs. Schultz, that the Baroness used when she asked about the inheritance?"

"Not exactly, just that she asked."

"Was it you who brought up the passing of Mr. Shaver?"

"I don't think so. The best I remember, the Baroness brought it up. Of course, it was all over the newspapers, too."

Mr. Powers tapped a finger to his lips, pausing for a moment of contemplation. "Are you absolutely positive the Baroness brought it up?"

"Fairly positive."

"But not absolutely positive?"

"Well, not absolutely."

"Did you talk to any other people about Mr. Shaver's passing?"

"Oh, yes. Everybody in the neighborhood was upset. He was a wonderful neighbor. Always kept his grounds tidy as could be."

"Did any of them mention the matter of inheritance?"

"Yes, well, we were all curious. It was such a fancy home they had."

"Exactly which neighbors talked about the inheritance?"

"I don't know that I could say which ones did and which ones didn't. But we all talked about his passing for days and days."

"And did the newspapers mention anything about inheritance?"

"It's been so many years now. I can't say for sure."

"So you don't recall if the newspapers mentioned an inheritance; you don't remember which neighbors you discussed it with; and you can't say for certain that the Baroness brought up the matter? Is this all correct?"

"Yes, but I know she asked. I'm almost positive of that."

"That's all I have, Your Honor."

But the charade was not over. Sawyer next called Mabel Owens to the stand. Mabel, a cousin of Frank's, was about as drab as Frank was blustery, much older than Frank, and altogether refined in appearance, if not decorum. Having been widowed at the age of thirty-seven, she had taken to traveling from one relation to another, settling in their homes for months on end. In fact, I first met her while she stopped for a summer at Frank's Chicago-area home.

Sawyer swaggered to the witness box. "Mrs. Owens, when did you first meet the Baroness May de Vries?"

"In August 1913, at Frank's home in Highland Park."

"Did you talk with her about an invitation she had put to Miss Shaver?"

"Yes, May wanted Frank to go on a trip to London, but Frank hadn't accepted."

"Was Miss Shaver there when you talked about this?"

"No, it was just me and May."

"Can you tell us the gist of the discussion?"

"Yes, I told May that Frank didn't feel she could afford such an expensive trip, but May explained that she'd invited Frank as her guest and Frank wouldn't need to spend any money at all. May said she'd treat her to a first-class cabin on the *Lusitania*. I was surprised, because a trip like that would cost plenty. But May said, 'Well, I *am* very wealthy. Can't you tell?' "

"And did the Baroness attempt to demonstrate her wealth?"

"She showed me a yellow-diamond necklace and said that yellow diamonds were especially rare. And she went on and on about her first string of pearls, which were given to her in Japan in 1891. She said they hadn't even started cultivating pearls at that time and these were perfect, all balanced in size, with smooth, shimmering surfaces. She told me everything anyone would ever want to know about pearls. I believe she wished to impress me with her wealth."

Powers shot to his feet. "Objection, the witness is conjecturing about motive."

"Sustained," said the judge. "The jury will disregard the last remark."

Sawyer continued nevertheless. "Mrs. Owens, did you think that the Baroness was a wealthy woman?"

"Heavens, yes. Very wealthy."

"Did Miss Shaver take this trip with her?"

"She did, in early 1914."

"And did she tell you about it afterward?"

"She said she'd had a grand time, but she'd spent altogether too much money."

"Did this surprise you?"

"It most certainly did."

"Did you talk to Miss Shaver about this?"

"I told her I'd been given to understand that she'd be May's guest, and she just laughed it off. She said, 'When you're in May's entourage, you don't quibble about money. You just live the high life.' Afterward, I warned her to watch out for that woman."

"And did she?"

"No, she was completely in her clutches, and nothing I said deterred her. Until she finally realized May had taken her for all her money."

"And did she talk to you about this?"

"She told me she'd been tricked. She was terribly upset."

And with that, Mr. Sawyer finally announced that he had called all his witnesses, though he reserved the right to reintroduce them should the defense's testimony warrant it. My attorney opted for a brief cross-examination of Mrs. Owens, craftily pointing out how very much she herself had benefited from Frank's beneficence.

Then he called as our first witness my brother Gene, who proved quite adept at corroborating how Frank had, while sipping tea in her bedroom at the Menominee home in 1915, signed a document releasing me from all debt. Not even Sawyer's cross-examination could budge him from his clear testimony on the matter.

I felt well satisfied with how the testimony ended that day. And Sawyer hadn't yet met his match—Daisy, our prize witness.

# WHAT ARE THE RISKS?

.

When Ernest and I returned to London, I resolved to prove myself an agreeable companion, which required me to please him unerringly and avoid sparking his ire over even the smallest matter. I only occasionally ventured into London to visit friends, and I always invited Ernest to join me. He typically declined to do so, often discouraging me from going on my own. When I did find a lady friend to accompany me, I made a point of returning at a reasonable hour and informing him of the play or opera I'd attended, placing a great deal of emphasis on conversations with my lady friends.

By the winter of 1908–1909, our relations had calmed, so I ventured a proposal: "Mrs. Baker has invited me to stay at her home after the opera Saturday, should the weather turn to freezing."

Ernest and I were on our way back from London, where we had shopped for a new bedroom set. As Ernest drove the Calthorpe over the somewhat bumpy roads approaching Maidenhead, he replied, without turning his head, "I'd rather you not. We have our Sunday routine, you know."

"Yes, of course. I wouldn't want to disrupt that."

I tried a few similar ploys to see if I might ease my way out of the house by degrees, but they did not meet with success. It became clear to me that I would have to make a clean and clandestine break, but before I could do so, Ernest once again whisked us off to Monte Carlo.

I did not object to the trip, even though Ernest's suspicious watchfulness greatly reduced my leeway and enjoyment of our exotic getaway. I had taken stock of my finances and determined it would be prudent to enhance my holdings in anticipation of life after Bray Lodge. Thus, I heaped praise on him for his gambling prowess and begged him to humor me by wagering some of my money—with me as his lucky charm at the table (which had the dual benefits of reducing my boredom and assuring him I was not spending time with other men). And I always had him sign for the amount ventured. His skill at *chemin de fer* was extraordinary, though he seemed reluctant to pad my pocketbook too much, perhaps sensing that a full purse might bestow on me a dangerous degree of freedom.

So, when I learned Mr. Zaharoff had checked into the Hôtel Métropole, I found a private moment to phone him.

"Basil, how nice to hear your voice."

"How are you?" he asked.

"Unfortunately, a little under the weather." I cleared my throat. "The doctor has ordered me to stay in my room for the next few days."

"I'm so sorry. Is there anything I can do for you?"

"No, that's very kind of you."

"What a shame. I must leave Friday. I'm afraid I won't see you this visit."

"I fear not. But I did want to discuss something with you. Do you have any investment opportunities at present?"

"Quite possibly. For a cash investment of fifteen thousand pounds."

I quickly calculated. That amounted to roughly fifty-eight thousand dollars. "And what is the return on it?"

"If the deal goes through, it would be eighteen percent."

"The deal is not set?"

"It's being negotiated. But I have worked with these parties before."

"And would you require me to contribute the whole of the fifteen thousand pounds?"

"Yes, though you could find other investors. That would be between you and them. Of course, my name should never be mentioned."

"Very well. I will get the funds in London. Can we make the transfer there?"

And that is how I came to figure in a private munitions deal,

which I presumed would not benefit the Kaiser or his collabora-
tors in any way. I found two other investors in my circle of London
friends, and in March 1909, I withdrew forty-four thousand dollars,
nearly all the money I had in the world. But that is how desperate I
was. Women may have been gaining power all around the world—on
March 12, they had voted for the first time in Denmark—but that
mattered little to me, since I lived each day with a man who had
threatened to throttle me. It made me mourn my dear, sweet Johnny
all over again: Life with him would have been carefree and passion-
ate, precisely the opposite of my present lot.

Mr. Zaharoff had informed me it could take months for our
investment to materialize, and I waited anxiously through the summer, then the fall and winter, all the time worrying that I might lose
the money—and the means to escape Ernest's jealous and menacing
grip—if the deal failed.

Finally, in December of 1909, Mr. Zaharoff contacted me through
the agent at his London bank. He informed me that Britain's discovery of vast oil supplies in Persia had delayed the deal, which was
now back on track, and he desired my services to complete it. This
did not please me. I immediately wrote back, requesting a meeting
in London, as well as a schedule of repayment on my sizable investment. To my great relief, he agreed to the meeting.

Mr. Zaharoff instructed me to wear plain clothes, take a train
to the London Cannon Street Station, and meet him at the nearby
Anchor Bankside Pub on Monday, December 20. In order to escape
the house, I left while Ernest was out and told Daisy to inform him
I'd been called to the bedside of a friend's dying mother. (I also
alerted my friend to this necessary subterfuge—just in case Ernest
made inquiries.)

Dressed in modest attire, I boarded the train to London. I emerged
from the Cannon Street Station and made my way through cloudy
veils of fog, the streetlights appearing and disappearing like a sleepy
cat's eyes, the street signs elusive in the rolling brume. I doubted
anyone could have followed me, for I myself lost the way meander-
ing the streets, and finally resorted to asking a local for directions.
At the pub I found Mr. Zaharoff waiting inside the door, wearing a
worn black coat, scuffed work boots, and a floppy deerstalker.

He had secured a corner table for us, and as soon as we ordered—he suggested a simple fare of fish and chips with ale—informed me, "I do not wish you to think me dishonorable in my dealings. I have deposited half the original investment in your bank account."

"I don't consider you dishonorable, but quite tardy."

"It's best I not tell you too much. It's a three-way deal, and each transaction requires many steps. With Germany turning more bellicose each day, relations in Europe are delicate and complicated."

"You said you require my services. I have no idea what you mean by this."

"I need someone to travel to Alsace with an important document. I prefer a woman who can travel unobtrusively and with ease."

"This was not part of the original understanding."

"I do not require *you* to play this role. I can find someone else, but it will take more time. And I believe you could manage it quite well."

"What are the risks?"

"There are none—unless the lady traveler unnecessarily attracts the attention of a spy or soldier and bungles the delivery. My agent in Alsace is completely trustworthy."

"And if I were to undertake this, could I expect to be compensated?"

"Most certainly. I am prepared to deposit another five hundred pounds for the trip preparations, and, upon your return, the originally agreed-upon sum plus an additional twelve hundred pounds."

I straightened the folds of my dress. "It will be two weeks before I can travel. Christmas is approaching, and I am in the midst of a move to London."

⇥ ⇤

Mr. Zaharoff's payment provided just the funds and incentive I needed to enact my plan. Christmas celebrations at Bray Lodge went off splendidly, and I purchased an especially nice gift for Ernest: a Norfolk jacket well suited for his automobile outings. Three days after Christmas, on one of Ernest's regular Tuesday evenings at his club, I hired two men to bring a coach around. Daisy and I hurriedly packed our clothes and personal effects, and the coach transported us to London's Shaftesbury Hotel, where we had stayed on our very first visit to London. We took a suite overlooking the avenue, so that we could keep an eye on goings-on. The next day, I visited the hotel manager's office to inform him I might require the assistance of the security staff should a certain Ernest Whidbey attempt to disturb me.

The second week of January 1910, I donned a mourner's garb, complete with veil, and made my lonely pilgrimage to the village of Nancy in Alsace. The wheres and hows of my meeting with the Alsatian agent are not terribly interesting; suffice it to say that I concluded my business with Mr. Zaharoff to the satisfaction of all parties. However, I later learned that someone had taken note of my journey.

# AN IMMORAL CONSIDERATION

*S*hortly after nine on the morning of February 14, 1910, a sharp knock sounded at our hotel door. I sprang from my bed, reached for my house robe, and rushed out of the suite's bedroom. Daisy, who had already risen, looked up at me from the couch, her expression etched with concern. My God, I wondered, could it be Ernest? I whispered to her, "Ask who's calling."

She nodded and approached the door. "Who is it, please?"

"Constable Barrett. With some papers for May de Vries."

I shook my head.

Daisy spoke through the door. "My lady is not available to receive visitors."

"I'll wait. I'm instructed to hand some papers to her."

Daisy and I bustled to the bedroom and closed the door behind us.

I plopped down on the bed. "What in the world could this be about?"

"Maybe Ernest is with the constable."

"I doubt it. He couldn't very well strangle me in front of an officer."

I took my leisure dressing, for I doubted the "papers" brought good news and I wanted time to consider the possibilities. "I suppose, once Ernest got past his ranting," I said to Daisy, "he hatched some elaborate plot to corner me."

In fact, I almost hoped the matter did involve Ernest—and not my recent trip to Alsace. Or some sinister trap set by Reed Dougherty. An hour later, I opened the door to find Constable Barrett reposed against the wall.

He snapped to attention and turned to face me. "May de Vries, please."

"I am she."

"Oh . . . in that case"—he fumbled through a leather bag and extracted an oversized envelope—"this is for you, ma'am. You must sign for it."

I did the officer's bidding and joined Daisy on the couch. Opening the envelope, I pulled out a two-page document and skimmed it: "Dr. Ernest Whidbey . . . sues for repayment."

"My God," I said, snapping my head up. "He's suing me."

I clapped my eyes to the document again: ". . . black pearl brooch . . . valued at £4,217 . . . by order of court . . . appear before King's Bench Division . . . March 24, 1910."

Gaping at the page, I exclaimed, "For over twenty thousand dollars."

"What gall," said Daisy.

I threw the papers on the coffee table. "He'll not get the brooch back, or the money."

> <

I strode into court on the designated date, with Daisy at my side. We navigated the maze of wooden compartments in the windowless chamber, Daisy to the adjacent witnesses' room and me to a seat beside my solicitor, Henry Brewster. Mr. Brewster was reputed to be a tough-minded counsel; he certainly looked the part, with his severe, overhanging brow and stern demeanor. During our preparatory meetings, I found his manner diligent and no-nonsense. He'd been thorough in gathering background and subsequently suggested we levy a counterclaim—for the roughly fourteen thousand dollars I had lent Ernest to gamble in Monte Carlo, as well as fifteen thousand dollars for damages to my reputation. As Mr. Brewster explained, a civil suit is like a chess game: Strategy and cunning are everything. And, after all, I had been ill-used by Ernest, kept under his roof against my wishes after he'd promised marriage. (If my marriage to Rudolph came up, I could easily explain that Rudolph had drawn up the divorce papers and stood ready to sign.)

The jurors trudged in and seated themselves in the box to the side of the courtroom, and the judge entered and stepped up to his pedestal seat. I felt Ernest glaring at me, but I held myself still and trained my eyes on the judge.

After a flurry of preliminaries and jury instructions, Judge Darling invited Ernest's solicitor, Mr. Ainsworth, to present his case.

Mr. Ainsworth eased off his chair and arranged the flows of his black robe. The judge and solicitors looked quite ridiculous in their long robes, silly bobbed wigs, and white Pilgrim-style ties. And Ainsworth, a short elderly man with a head too large for his narrow-shouldered frame, looked especially so, preening and strutting in the manner of a child who'd finally discovered a way to fend off his bully tormentors.

He began, "M'lord and members of the jury, Dr. Ernest Whidbey's claim is very simple. He seeks to recover the loan he extended to the Baroness May de Vries, a loan she requested for the purchase of an expensive brooch. You see, Dr. Whidbey and the defendant resided together for roughly five years. During that time, the kind doctor paid all household as well as traveling expenses. After these years of support, the defendant suddenly and inexplicably fled the household, taking this brooch with her, leaving no address, and failing to repay the loan. As for her counterclaim, the requests are ludicrous, a mere attempt to skirt the issue before us. While the Baroness did loan Dr. Whidbey funds to gamble, she did so of her own initiative, requesting that he gamble on her behalf. Nor does the damages claim make any sense under the circumstances. Dr. Whidbey invited her to reside at Bray Lodge, she willingly agreed, and, furthermore, she was free to leave at any time.

"I now call Dr. Ernest Whidbey to the witness stand."

For the next few hours, I suffered through Ernest's laments: "I purchased the black-pearl brooch expressly at the Baroness's request." . . . "Why, yes, she even picked it up from the jeweler." . . . "She told me on several occasions that she found our living arrangement very agreeable." . . . "I was completely shocked by her sudden departure."

My solicitor, however, nicely countered these pronouncements by calling me to testify about Ernest's assurances of marriage.

"Yes," I explained. "It was my understanding we were to wed. Although he claimed that his former wife made that difficult."

After establishing that Ernest had, all along, showered me with his favors, including some very fine pieces of jewelry, my attorney asked, "Do you believe an immoral consideration entered into his reason for these purchases?"

I lowered my eyes to my lap. "Yes."

"And how would you characterize that expectation?"

"That I reside with him as if we were married."

"Which you did for almost five years?"

"Yes."

"Did you ever wish to quit this immoral arrangement?"

"Yes, the last few years."

"What prevented you?"

"He physically threatened me. I feared for my safety."

But of course Mr. Ainsworth insisted on cross-examining me.

I held up quite well until he launched a surprise attack.

"Baroness, do you know a man by the name of Basil Zaharoff?"

"Yes."

"What is the nature of your relationship with him?"

"I consider him an acquaintance."

"Do you, my lady, entertain all acquaintances through the night?"

Stunned, I clapped a hand to my breast.

My solicitor shot to his feet. "Objection, m'lord. Mr. Ainsworth is damning by insinuation."

Judge Darling gazed down upon Ainsworth. "Sustained. Please reframe the question, Mr. Ainsworth."

"Yes, m'lord," he said. Turning to me, he asked, "Did you travel to the Continent from the seventh to the thirteenth of January?"

"Yes."

"Did you meet Mr. Zaharoff there?"

"No, I did not."

"Why did you leave London that week?"

"To visit the church my father was baptized in."

"Where is this?"

"In Nancy, Alsace."

Ainsworth scratched his forehead. "What prompted you to do this in the middle of the winter?"

"Christmas always makes me sentimental. And it was the first time I felt free to travel there."

"This trip had nothing to do with Mr. Zaharoff?"

I huffed with impatience. "I have said I did not meet Mr. Zaharoff on this trip."

"Do you deny a romantic involvement with Mr. Zaharoff?"

I squared my shoulders. "Yes, I do."

Ainsworth further inquired into dates that I had purportedly spent in Mr. Zaharoff's company in Monte Carlo and London, but I held my own and fended off his charges. And when Daisy ascended to the witness box, she corroborated my report. Still, at the close of the session, Daisy and I immediately retired to the lounge at the Shaftesbury, where I drank three sherries to calm my rattled nerves.

# CHECKMATE

·

FROM LONDON TO EGYPT AND NEW YORK—
1910–1912

*T*he next day, Friday, Mr. Ainsworth commenced by recall-
ing Ernest to the witness box, perhaps in an attempt to
counter my testimony. My solicitor had promised a lively
questioning of Ernest, but first I had to tolerate Ainsworth's continuing examination of him, which more closely resembled a fire-
side chat than a witness-box grilling. The first two hours brought
no surprises, as Ainsworth merely afforded Ernest the opportunity
to hammer home his suspicions about my "dalliances" and to swear
before God, England, and all the specks of sand in the universe that
I had borrowed the funds for the brooch and that he had never, ever
threatened me.

Suddenly, as the luncheon break approached, Ainsworth's questioning took a startling turn.

"Dr. Whidbey, did you, after the Baroness's departure, retain any
private detectives?"

"Yes, two. First I hired a Mr. Holliday here in London. It was he
who discovered that the Baroness had traveled to the Continent. But
he did some checking around and found this American detective
who knew May—I mean, the Baroness."

"And this detective's name is . . ."

"Reed Dougherty of the Pinkerton Agency."

Oh, Lord, I thought, not Dougherty again. Not here in London.

"And what did Mr. Dougherty say about the Baroness?"

"That he'd had multiple contacts with her."

"Did he report on a criminal incident in the California city of San
Francisco?"

"Yes."

"Will you recount this?"

"She and another woman were charged with larceny after they drugged and robbed a man. But they broke out of jail before they could be prosecuted."

I turned wide-eyed to Mr. Brewster.

"Can Mr. Dougherty vouch for the fact that May de Vries was the woman in question?"

"Yes. Her photo was taken by the police."

My solicitor, taking my cue and no doubt desiring to break off this line of inquiry, rose from his seat. "Objection, my lord, this is all hearsay."

The judge pinched his brow. "Yes, I'm inclined to agree."

He looked to Ainsworth and then Ernest. "Mr. Ainsworth, Dr. Whidbey, have you any documents from this detective?"

"His correspondence to Mr. Holliday."

"Any official documents?"

"No, not official," answered Ainsworth. "But he's in transit, and we can put him on the stand next week, Your Lordship."

Judge Darling frowned. "I suggest we take our midday break now and consider how to proceed with this witness afterward."

Mr. Brewster requested that we meet over the luncheon recess, and I suggested Daisy join us. The three of us retreated to his office, where he ordered his assistant to run out for some food.

Mr. Brewster got right down to business. "Who is this Reed Dougherty?"

"A Pinkerton detective who trapped me in some compromising positions."

"And the San Francisco incident?"

"It's a frame-up."

"What about the photograph?"

"I've never seen any such photograph."

"Can you stand your own against his testimony?"

"Yes, I believe I can." But I doubted my own words. The prospect of being examined about Dougherty's testimony panicked me. I knew the scoundrel would gladly empty both barrels on me.

Mr. Brewster requested an account of any and all events that Dougherty might dredge up. I provided him, as best as I could, with the outlines of Dougherty's other potentially damaging claims—that I'd agreed to sell false stocks, tried to procure Johnny Graham's money, and spied to win a mining deal with the Mexican government—and my denials or defenses in each instance.

Still, Mr. Brewster fretted. "This considerably complicates matters."

Mr. Brewster's assistant brought us piping-hot shepherd's pies for lunch. But I hardly managed five forkfuls, so agitated was I with worries about confronting that cur Dougherty again and allowing his wild stories to ruin my reputation in London, the city where I hoped to continue to reside. I simply couldn't permit Dougherty to take the stand.

Mr. Brewster secured a taxi after our meeting in his office, and we returned to court for the afternoon session. Upon arriving in the corridors of the court building, I excused myself and visited the ladies' room. I took a stall at the far end, seated myself on the toilet, and removed a pin from my purse. Pulling my bottom lip away from the gums, I pierced myself four times with the pin, each time drawing blood.

I returned to the courtroom to find Brewster and Ainsworth in conference with the judge. I stood in the courtroom doorway beside Daisy and coughed. One cough led to another, until I buckled over, extracted my handkerchief, and coughed into it. I pulled the cloth away from my mouth. Crimson splotches of blood blotted it.

"My God, you're bleeding," said Daisy.

I swooned at the sight of my own blood.

→←

When I came to, Daisy insisted we go straightaway to my doctor's office, and she and Mr. Brewster helped me out to the curb, where they secured a taxi.

After examining me, the doctor evinced puzzlement. "I can't explain the blood. There're no other signs of tuberculosis."

"She's been laboring under a great deal of strain," Daisy volunteered.

"Well," he said, "you might want to get away if you can, perhaps to a warmer climate."

"Yes, thank you, Doctor," I said. "I believe I'll do that."

I ordered Daisy to look into travel opportunities, preferably something departing in the next several days. Once she'd returned with a report, she phoned my solicitor's office.

"Mr. Brewster," she said, "we've just returned from the doctor's office. He has ordered the Baroness to travel to Egypt. We leave in two days."

I heard Mr. Brewster's baritone resounding over the phone line, but I couldn't discern his words. Daisy nodded, scrunching her brow in concentration. She recited the name and address of my physician.

"Yes, a postponement . . . Three months? . . . That would be appreciated."

More booming bursts came from Brewster, until Daisy concluded with, "Yes, thank you very much, Mr. Brewster."

＞＜

I should have loved Egypt in springtime—the cruise to Alexandria, the train to Cairo, the excursion to the Pyramids of Giza—but the knowledge that I could neither stay forever nor escape the threat looming in London cast a pall over it all.

On May 8, Daisy and I stood before the mighty Pyramids of Giza. Just before departing London I'd received word that a Menominee family of five had been killed in a house fire, and a gloomy wariness still gripped me: The mother of the family had been a dear acquaintance of mine. And only two days earlier, King Edward VII had died while Halley's comet streaked the sky. Something in the world seemed to have tipped, as if all the universe's mighty forces had gathered to declare: We and we alone control the fates.

I said to Daisy, "What incredible monuments. Built by men long gone."

"Thousands and thousands of them."

I squinted against the bright sun reflecting off the expansive sands. "What makes one a Cleopatra while all the others are buried by the march of time?"

Daisy, her mood as glum as mine, merely shook her head.

For several minutes I gazed quietly on the pyramids while gusts of wind buffeted my dress about my legs. When our guide called out to us, we turned away from the looming monuments, into the sandy wind, and traipsed toward him.

I took Daisy's arm. "Ernest has won. I underestimated him."

"What will you do?"

"I see no alternative but to crawl back to him and beg him to dismiss the suit."

><

Once we landed in England, I sent a telegram to Ernest: RETURNING TO LONDON MAY 21 STOP MISS YOU STOP PLEASE DINE WITH ME ON MAY 23 STOP. I was quite certain he would accept the invitation; he had always enjoyed celebrating my birthday.

We met at Wiltons on Jermyn Street, a place with fond memories for me—Rudolph and I had twice dined there and on the second occasion he'd proposed to me. I chose it so that I might at least enjoy the glow of reminiscence while I subjugated myself to Ernest's wishes.

Not surprisingly, after the wicked accusations hurled about the courtroom a mere two months ago, we greeted each other tentatively.

"How was your trip?" he asked when we took our seats.

"Not particularly enjoyable. But I needed it." In the dining room's muted candlelight, I noted a darkness around his eyes, as if he'd been ill or had slept poorly.

He tapped his fingers on the table. "And your health?"

"Much better, thank you. My physician has pronounced me cured of my mysterious ailment."

"Well, that's a relief."

"How are things at your club?"

"The same." He shifted in his chair. "A bit boring, actually."

"Sometimes routine is good for us—soothing, even." I held his gaze and summoned the memory of happier times at Bray Lodge. "I have missed ours."

He smiled shyly. "May I order some champagne?"

I let the evening unfold: I gave the champagne time to lift my spirits—and quell Ernest's suspicious nature; I demurely accepted his birthday wishes. Finally, I proclaimed, lacing my words with hesitancy and humility, "Ernest . . . I don't want to go on any longer without you. . . . I wonder . . . might we take up where we left off at Christmas?"

He closed his eyes a moment and dropped his head. Looking up at me with watery eyes, he said, "Are you sure?"

"Yes, my darling, I am." I swallowed and moistened my lips. "May we?"

He reached across the table. I opened my hand and he clasped it. "Yes," he said. "How soon can you return?"

"Once we get out from under these ugly legal matters?"

"Of course, that would be best."

"If you were to sign a paper absolving me of any indebtedness, we could start fresh."

"Yes, we wouldn't want any of that hanging over us."

I immediately offered to dismiss my countersuit. He said he would withdraw his claim. We would both tell our solicitors we had reached a satisfactory agreement on our own.

It took only three days to conclude these matters. I checked with Mr. Brewster to be sure that Ernest had in fact closed the suit and then phoned him. "Darling, I'm so pleased those awful lawsuits are behind us. Can you hire a carriage to pick Daisy and me up Monday morning? We'll have everything packed and ready to go."

"Of course," he said. "I'll ask that the carriage arrive by ten in the morning."

"Lovely, I'll be home for dinner. Until then, my darling, I send you a kiss." I smacked the air by the phone's mouthpiece.

On Sunday morning, Daisy and I packed up our belongings and caught the train to Liverpool. A few days later we set sail for New York. And never again did I see Dr. Ernest Whidbey.

&gt;&lt;

Such jarring events as I had lived through with Ernest are apt to force one to re-evaluate what matters most in life. Never before had I so misjudged a man; I even feared my powers of perception might be diminishing. And now, eyes open wide to the miscalculations I had committed about the "lowly professor," I determined to retreat to the sanctuary of those I could hold close and confide in. I settled in an apartment on the Upper East Side of New York, with Daisy as my companion, and entertained old friends there. In 1912, when I received word that Frank Shaver had suffered the loss of her father, I extended my sympathies, full of hope that I might renew my friendship with the companionable and trustworthy Frank.

# THE TRIAL

*A* snowstorm had swept in overnight, bringing with it a wicked wind that swirled the snow every which way. Come morning, the city's workers endeavored to clear the main streets of snowdrifts, but the blizzard bested them. Thus, all of us who needed—or wished—to attend the trial were forced to trudge through two-foot-high drifts while snow needles blasted our cheeks.

Not surprisingly, only about thirty-five spectators, including the usual reporters and townspeople, braved the horrid storm. The judge announced we would carry on as long as the heat and lights held out. To the satisfaction of all, the radiators pinged bravely. Still, the blizzard's cold seeped through the windows, and we all sat tugging our coats about us, occasionally glancing at the eddies of snow buffeting the courtroom's narrow windows.

But I had Daisy to warm the cockles of my heart.

Mr. Powers eased into his friendly examination of Daisy. "Miss Emmett, how long have you known the Baroness?"

"Longer than she's been a baroness," said Daisy, her charming glance skittering over the jurors' onlooking faces. "We met in New York in 1891."

"And how did this meeting come about?"

"I responded to an advertisement for an assistant and companion. May hired me, and I've worked with her ever since, with only a few breaks here and there when she didn't need my services."

"And have you been pleased with your employment?"

"Oh, yes. May has been very generous with me. She even hired my brother for a while. And gave me money for my crippled mother."

"Are you acquainted with Miss Frank Shaver?"

"Very well. I accompanied May and Frank on several trips and handled many of their mutual affairs."

"What do you mean by mutual affairs?"

"They worked together on some projects. Like the remodeling of the Menominee home."

"Were you present on the *Lusitania* crossing in early 1914?"

At the mention of this journey, I invariably recalled the shock I'd experienced upon hearing that Germany had sunk the *Lusitania*. Daisy, Frank, and I had enjoyed a memorable crossing in 1914, and, one short year later, these other innocents met with unspeakable horror. How fickle destiny can be.

"Yes," Daisy replied. "We all shared a royal suite."

"And did you manage the expenses for that?"

"Yes, I did. That was one of the things May left to me."

"Can you explain how the expenses were paid?"

"The suite cost $1,010, and I secured an extra bathroom for us for $140. I paid the total costs of $1,150 out of May's funds. Frank later insisted that she make some contribution. I told her it wasn't necessary, but she wouldn't hear anything of it and gave me $500."

"You did not ask her for this money?"

"No, I only accepted it at her insistence."

"Now, you mentioned that Miss Shaver and the Baroness worked together on the remodeling of the Dugas house here in town."

"Yes, they did."

"Can you explain how this collaboration worked?"

"It wasn't very harmonious. May and Frank both wanted to remodel, but they couldn't agree on details. May was worried the remodeling would cost a fortune and asked me to restrain Frank's spending ways. But when I tried, Frank said, 'Leave it to me. This must be a palace.'"

"Was the remodeling of the bathroom one such area of differing opinions?"

"Yes. Frank wanted to splurge on a fancy bathtub that cost a thousand dollars. When I told her that was outside the budget, she told me to mind my own business."

"And did she proceed with the purchase of this costly bathtub?"

"It sits now, fancy as can be, in the upstairs bathroom."

How I loved my dear friend Daisy. She never failed to cheer me under the most dire of circumstances.

"I believe," said Powers, coasting along with his examination, "that you and Miss Shaver had occasion to work together on the funeral plans for Mrs. Dugas in October of 1913?"

"Yes, we bought the funeral flowers, and May didn't know anything about it. We didn't want to bother her while she was so broken up. The bill came to a hundred twenty-five dollars, which Frank paid."

"And did you reimburse this expense?"

"Yes, I sent Frank a check for the flowers and she sent me a note saying, 'Your check received. Thank you.'"

Mr. Powers retreated to the defendant's table, swept up a piece of paper, and brought it to the witness box. "Is this the note you're referring to?"

Daisy accepted the slip of paper. "Yes."

"And it's in Frank's handwriting?"

"Yes."

"Thank you." Powers retrieved the paper from Daisy and slipped it into the empty space in his row of papers. He ambled back to the witness box. "Now, are you aware of any occasions on which the Baroness gifted funds to Miss Shaver?"

"Yes, when we returned from London in early 1914, I remember May handing Frank a thousand dollars."

"And how do you know this money was a gift?"

"I recall May saying, 'Here, Frank, spend this however you want.'"

"Did Miss Shaver protest this gift?"

"Oh, no. She took it and stuffed it in her bag. She was even a little huffy about it. Afterward, May told me she felt unappreciated."

"Are you personally aware of any other gifts the Baroness made to Miss Shaver?"

"Oh, there were many. On the 1914 trip—I remember it well, because May kept checking the papers for news about the Mexican revolution—May took her shopping. I went along, too. May bought two new dresses and a pair of shoes for Frank. She wore one of her dresses and the new shoes to the opera the next night. May told her she looked splendid, and Frank thanked her for the gifts."

"Would it be fair to say that the Baroness was generous with Miss Shaver?"

"Very much so."

"And did Miss Shaver appreciate her generosity?"

"Mostly. Sometimes I think she felt competitive and tried to outdo May with the gifts."

"Competitive, you say?"

"Yes, I think it was a game to her. She wanted to prove to May that she had money, too."

Sawyer, undoubtedly worried about Daisy's continuing along these lines, pounded a fist on the table. "Objection. Motive is imputed."

"Sustained," said Judge Flanagan. "The jury will ignore this remark."

Powers placed a hand on the witness box and turned to Daisy. "To your knowledge, was Miss Shaver in the habit of bestowing gifts on ladies she favored?"

"Oh, yes, Frank often boasted about girls she'd been involved with."

"Objection," hollered Sawyer. "This is immaterial, as well as sweeping and unsubstantiated."

"Mr. Powers," said the judge, "I'll advise you to avoid such broad questioning."

"Yes, Your Honor," Powers said, then turned back to Daisy. "Did you have occasion to conduct some business on behalf of Miss Shaver with a Miss Nell McDaniel?"

"Yes, I did. Miss Shaver told me they'd been friends for six years, that Nell was a beautiful girl, and that she'd taken her to Alaska. But then the friendship turned sour, and Frank asked me to go to her office and get some things back from her."

"Did you do so?"

"Yes, I picked up a real-estate deed and some stock certificates from Miss McDaniel, and she told me to tell Frank she was the biggest Indian-giver she ever knew."

"Thank you, Miss Emmett." Powers turned from the witness box. "Your witness, Mr. Sawyer."

Sawyer attempted varied methods to upend Daisy: implying her financial circumstances depended on my own "assets and largesse"; insinuating that she and I were partners in schemes to extricate money; and even referring to her and my brothers as my "henchmen." (Such an ugly word; Sawyer was certainly crossing the line of civil discourse.) But Daisy handily outmaneuvered him. She smiled through her testimony, kept her hands planted on her lap, and exuded her usual calm aplomb.

Powers responded not by redirecting Daisy's testimony but, rather, by calling Frank to answer Daisy's charges. The flowers for my mother's funeral? Never reimbursed, she said, though she couldn't explain the note Daisy referred to. What about the thousand dollars I had handed over to her? She claimed it was not a gift but return of a loan, though she had no document to prove this. And the costly home remodeling? She wanted to please me and, besides, she was part owner in the house and expected the remodeling to enhance its value. She even went so far as to contend the bathtub had cost only $140. What about the gifts I had made to her? Those, she exclaimed, were mere trifles compared with the thousands of dollars' worth of gifts she had showered on me. And in reference to the Nell McDaniel matter, Frank claimed that Nell had reneged on their understanding and that she'd never intended these items to be gifts.

Poor, poor Frank—she was on the run now.

# A DESPERATE LETTER FROM FRANK

MENOMINEE—JANUARY 31, 1917

*Dear May,*

*You damn fool. Don't you see where this is headed? The jury will rule for me, and you'll be in water as hot as Hades. I don't believe for one minute you don't have the money. That claim of poverty stinks to high heaven. Next you'll be telling me Mr. Rockefeller begs on street corners.*

*You've got two choices: You can settle right now and agree to pay the money. We can keep the arrangement confidential and nobody but us and our attorneys will know the terms. That'd keep your reputation intact.*

*Or you can let this thing play out and have your loss splattered all over the Chicago, New York, and who knows what other newspapers. And if that happens, I've got a surprise waiting for you—a special visitor that you'll recognize in the courtroom tomorrow. That should be enough to make you think twice about ducking your responsibility!*

*I hope you understand what's going to happen if you refuse to come up with the money. All your assets will be claimed by the court. Think about it. Do you really want your precious jewelry auctioned off?*

*You're a fool, May, a damn fool. I gave you a way out, but no, you're dead set on your stubborn ways. If you let the jury decide this, it'll be good-bye between us forever.*

*Your old friend,*
*Frank*

If Frank thought threats of this nature were sufficient to force my hand, she guessed wrong. Only I did wonder who the "special visitor" might be. Surely she couldn't have tracked Ernest down. After all, the judge had ruled that the London lawsuit was immaterial. I hoped to God it wasn't that blackguard Reed Dougherty.

# THE TRIAL

*T*he blizzard passed in the night, and the town awakened to clear skies and temperatures hovering near zero. A stillness hung over the streets, as if everybody had paused to contemplate the sparkling white expanses coating rooftops, yards, and woods.

Except me. I was as jumpy as a racehorse at the starting line. With the trial's judgment fast approaching, I could think of little other than flight. Yet here I sat in the courtroom, contemplating sunshine slanting through the windows.

"Mr. Powers," intoned Judge Flanagan, "you may call your next witness."

My attorney stood and walked around the defendant's table. A streak of sunshine rippled over his head and shoulders as he advanced to the front of the courtroom. "Your Honor, I have a short statement on that matter. May I?"

"As long as it is relevant."

"Your Honor," he said, and, turning to face the jury, "gentlemen of the jury. The Baroness May de Vries has decided not to testify before you."

Gasps coursed through the courtroom. The jury members gaped at each other, their jaws flopping open.

Powers forged ahead. "She loves this town too much to be subjected to scrutiny before the dear people she has known all her life. She considers Menominee her home town, her sanctuary."

The judge frowned in that threatening way of his, and I feared he might cut off Mr. Powers's statement.

If Powers discerned the judge's intent, he disregarded it, sweeping a hand toward the windows. "For not far from this very place, beside St. Ann's Church, rests her dear mother."

"Mr. Powers," said Flanagan, "the court has heard your announcement."

This was too much for me—the mention of my mother, whom I grieved still, and Flanagan belittling the matter of my testimony. With tears blurring my vision, I scooped up my coat and rushed down the aisle. As I neared the door, a man rose and placed his hand on the knob.

My God—it *was* Reed Dougherty. He opened the door for me; I avoided his eye and rushed down the stairs to the first-floor foyer, nearly losing my footing. Steps beat down the stairs after me. No, I thought, I won't speak to Dougherty. Not now, not ever again if I can help it. Why was he here—other than to persist in his torment of me? I'd never once mentioned him to Frank. How did she manage to find him? And what could he have to do with this trial? My stomach curdled. I dashed toward the ladies' restroom at the rear of the corridor, determined to dodge him.

"Are you all right?" It had been Gene, my dear brother, bounding down the stairs after me.

I turned and ran to him. He rushed up and wrapped his arms around me.

"I can't stay here," I managed to say, the tears coming fast now. "Please, take me home."

⇥ ⇤

When Gene and Paul returned for lunch, they informed me I'd missed Mr. Sawyer's closing statement. Paul asked if I wanted a report on it.

"Not really." I stood over the stove warming up two-day-old venison stew. "But did you see that tall, lanky man at the back of the courtroom?"

"Never saw him before," said Gene. "Must be some new reporter."

"Did he talk to Frank? Or her lawyer? Or anybody else?"

"Not that I saw," Gene said, fetching some bowls from the cupboard.

Paul eyed me. "You know him?"

"Just wondering who he might be." I leaned over the kettle and stirred from the bottom, releasing the stew's sweet meaty scent. I'd added a few spoons of Maman's secret ingredient—molasses.

"Stew's plenty hot," I said.

"Sit down," said Paul. "We'll serve."

As I turned toward the kitchen table, I caught Gene and Paul exchanging looks. "All right, you two. I know a conspiracy when I see it. What's on your minds?"

"Good God," said Gene, "you're starting to sound like a lawyer."

Tokyo's toenails clicked on the kitchen floor as he followed me to the table. "Do you blame me? I bet *you* can't think of anything but this beastly trial, either."

At that they both hung their heads, guilty as charged. Paul opened the bread box, grabbed the half loaf left over from Wednesday's baking, and sliced it. Gene set the table and served up the stew.

"Well?" I asked as they sat and scraped their chairs up to the table.

Paul lifted his spoon and held it poised over his bowl. "We've been thinking we ought to ask you a few things."

"Mm-hmm." I spooned up a mouthful of the steaming stew and chewed around a gristly hunk of meat. Although the stew wanted something to balance out the meat's toughness, I had oversweetened the broth.

Paul shifted on his haunches. "If we lose, the judge might slap an order on the business. Use the inventory to pay off the judgment."

I plucked the gristle from my mouth and held it down for Tokyo. He daintily nibbled at my fingers, extracting the treat. "We're not going to lose," I said. "We've got a signed release."

Gene sprang upright in his chair. "But Sawyer claims it's not legitimate."

I calmly met his eyes. "He can't very well explain away Frank's signature."

"He says it was obtained under duress."

I sighed. This hardly warranted a response.

Paul rested a hand on Gene's arm, as if signaling him to restrain himself. "We just want to put our minds at ease. We wouldn't lose the business, would we?"

"No," I said. "You'll still have your business."

Paul ignored the wisps of steam rising from his bowl. "Frank holds half interest in the house. Even if she loses, we figure she'll want to be bought out."

"Sure she will. She's shown her colors, hasn't she?"

Gene glanced at Paul, then turned to me. "We don't have that kind of money."

"I know that."

Paul leaned toward me, resting his forearms on the table. "Do you?"

"Not handy," I said.

"But you can get it, right?"

"Sure I can."

"Where?"

I hated how Paul always questioned me. "It's better if I don't say. Do you think I was fool enough to declare everything in my list of assets? Now, don't ask again. I've already said too much."

Paul studied me, as if contemplating his next move.

I reached my hands out, resting one on Gene's forearm and the other on Paul's. "You're my brothers. I won't let you down."

Gene raised his bowed head, as if ashamed of asking me about money in the first place, and nodded, regarding me with a feeble smile.

Paul swiped a hand over his mouth, shaking his head like the cynic he is.

I slapped their arms. "Now, eat your stew. There's a trial to wrap up this afternoon."

→ ←

I knew my attorney well enough to understand he was at his best when granted free rein to spin out his case, uninterrupted by objections. His closing statement afforded just that opportunity, though my pleasure in it was dimmed by the presence of Reed Dougherty in the back row. I had, however, devised a plan to avoid him: My attorney had promised to stand by my side and fend off any questioners whenever I entered or exited the courtroom.

"Gentlemen, you have heard Mr. Sawyer's case. It is based on the word of the plaintiff, on claims she's made against the Baroness after their many years of friendship. At any point she could have withdrawn from the friendship, refused to take expensive trips with her, turned down invitations to parties. But she knowingly continued this association for over five years, from 1901 to 1903 and again from 1912 until just last year. She has freely admitted she enjoyed her association with the Baroness; even after they quarreled in 1903, she was overjoyed at the resumption of the friendship.

"This raises significant questions about the timing of her lawsuit. If she truly felt that she was being taken advantage of, she could have demanded to set matters straight at any juncture. But she didn't. Until now. Why now? Because she has spent all her inheritance and sees the chance to replenish her funds by going after the Baroness's money.

"The plaintiff claims that she was tricked into turning over her whole inheritance, that my client schemed all these years to part her from her money. But let us consider the beginnings of their friendship. When they met in 1901, my client bore the title of baroness, bought and sold property in Arkansas, and was welcomed at royal courts all over Europe. She and the Baron owned homes in Holland and London. And the plaintiff? She had recently embarked on her new law practice outside Chicago. Her parents provided her with an annual allowance of three thousand dollars to help her launch this practice.

"I ask you, gentlemen, how was my client to look upon this budding friendship? She, a world-traveled baroness and owner of land on two continents, befriending a young woman beginning what is an improbable career for a lady? What kind of an attraction would three thousand dollars per annum have been to a baroness? It is preposterous to assume she had any designs on Miss Shaver's money. Quite the contrary, it was the plaintiff who stood to benefit from this new friendship."

How I wished I could have cheered Mr. Powers on—so brilliant was his oratory. He recounted the early years of our friendship, further hammering home his point that money could not have motivated my decision to befriend Frank.

"The defense has introduced a release bearing the signature of Miss Shaver, a release that absolves the Baroness of any and all purported debt. You have been told by the plaintiff that she didn't carefully read this release because she was ill at the time. I hope you will pardon my skepticism, but I simply cannot reconcile this claim with the plaintiff's learned status and profession. You have seen her on the stand for many hours over these last two weeks. She is a woman with a keen intellect and a quick mind. She graduated from the University of Pennsylvania with a bachelor's degree. The University of Michigan—a most prestigious university—admitted her to its law school. She studied there, obtained her law degree, and passed the requisite exam to practice law in the state of Illinois. Her well-to-do parents raised her to understand the workings of the world well enough that she was able to travel independently between their home in Pittsburgh and her adopted city of Chicago. She ventured all over Europe and even to Algiers with the Baroness, exotic places most Americans never get a chance to see.

"Miss Frank Shaver is no fool, nor is she ignorant of the worth of a dollar. In truth, she is a highly intelligent, well-educated woman who knows how to conduct herself in the world's capital cities. Her claim not to know the value of a dollar is ludicrous, her defense of not comprehending a release from debt insulting to this court. She is a lawyer, a lawyer with the best possible training and standing. No lawyer of such stature can pretend to misunderstand a contract of a mere sentence or two."

Mr. Powers next confronted the insinuations by Sawyer that the release was obtained under duress or falsified. Powers handily concluded there was no way to prove this shaky assertion, pointing out that Miss Shaver herself admitted the document bore her signature, that she remembered the occasion on which it was signed, and that Mr. Gene Dugas had witnessed the signing.

"As for the Baroness's family and friends, I sat quietly by while Mr. Sawyer referred to these parties as 'henchmen of the Baroness.' Every defense witness who took the stand was insulted by this lawyer. The plaintiff's side made every attempt to disgrace them, not with solid charges, but with insinuation and innuendo—for that is all they had.

"But I will have my say now. Paul and Gene Dugas are upstanding citizens of this community. They have no criminal record. They have never engaged in any untoward financial deals. They are honest men who work side by side at this town's automobile business. Many of the citizens of Menominee, Marinette, and the surrounding farms and towns have purchased automobiles from them. They are known to all who have had dealings with them as reputable businessmen. They shop at the same stores as you, they hunt the same woods, they attend the same church. These are honorable men.

"And as for Daisy Emmett, here is a woman who has served as a loyal assistant to the Baroness for over twenty years. And how is her fine and loyal character painted? As a henchman? This is the lady who took charge of the funeral for the Baroness's mother at a time when the Baroness and her brothers were weighed down with grief. That is the sort of person Miss Daisy Emmett is, gentlemen, a faithful lady who has served her employer and cared for her own poor and crippled mother for many years.

"Let us look at the central charge here. The plaintiff and her attorney would have you believe that my client set her sights on a pot of gold, systematically mined it, and then cast Miss Shaver aside. I ask you to consider all aspects of this allegation. Was the plaintiff passive during the whole of this friendship? Of course not—she freely entered into it and gladly accompanied the Baroness on many pleasure trips. Was she made of gold? I have already explained that Miss Shaver was no paragon of wealth when she and the Baroness first became acquainted. To assert that the Baroness considered her a 'pot of gold' simply does not square with reality.

"Did my client cast Miss Shaver aside, as she claims, like a hot penny? Recall for yourselves how this friendship met its recent demise. It was Miss Shaver who pressed the issue of money upon the Baroness. After telling her own cousin, Mrs. Owens, that one didn't worry about money with the Baroness, Miss Shaver suddenly decided to worry about her own, just when she depleted the money she freely spent accompanying the Baroness on trips. She was no unwilling guest on these cross-Atlantic adventures. Nobody kidnapped her and forced her to take the train to New York City to celebrate New Year's Eve. No one handcuffed her and spirited her off to Montreal for a birthday party. Oh, no, Miss Shaver came to enjoy this life of luxury; she only cried foul when she realized she had spent all her inheritance.

"As for the Baroness, you may wonder why she refused to take the stand herself. But consider how the attorney for the plaintiff badgered her brothers and Miss Emmett, called them henchmen, insinuated they were liars. No, Baroness May de Vries loves this town too dearly to be insulted with lies and insinuations that are beneath her. This community is dearer to her than any place on earth. Her lovely mother lived out her last years here, and she is buried in this community of her friends and family. The Baroness will not allow the plaintiff's attorney to tarnish her mother's memory.

"I submit, gentlemen, that this lawsuit is intended to harass the Baroness into turning over a very large sum of money to Miss Shaver—money that is not hers to claim. The only just conclusion to this case is to find for the defendant, Baroness May de Vries.

"Dear gentlemen, my client and I thank you for your patience and your service in the name of justice."

# THE VERDICT

*I* tiptoed into Gene's bedroom. Laying my hand on his blanketed shoulder, I nudged him. "Gene, wake up."

He moaned and turned toward me. "What time is it?"

"Nearly seven. You have to take me to the train station."

He blinked his eyes open. "What? You're leaving?"

"Yes."

"You can't do that."

"I have to get the money."

I was dumbfounded—there can be no other word for it. To think those jurors sat in the jury room for six-plus hours poring over my purported debts. To think they ignored the release Frank had signed. To think they ordered me to pay her fifty-seven thousand dollars. Unbelievable.

Gene raised himself up on his elbows. "Does Paul know?"

"No, he wouldn't understand. Now, get up."

"Paul told me to make sure you don't sneak off."

"Sneak off?" It was just like Paul to obstruct me. "I have to get the money."

"Where?"

"I can't tell you that."

"We might lose the house and the business and you can't tell me?"

Paul had obviously involved Gene in his plot to foil me. Well, he wasn't the only one who could cook up a plan. "Just get up. I have something to show you."

Tokyo nosed his way through the cracked door and whimpered at my feet.

Gene flopped back on his pillow. "I'm not taking Tokyo out. You do it."

"Fine. Now, hurry."

I'd dressed in my warmest attire—my black gown with fluted collar. After easing my fur hat over my coiffed hair and donning my moleskin coat and leather gloves, I led Tokyo out the front door, down our shoveled walkway, and onto the sidewalk. A short distance behind me I discerned the idling of an automobile, but strolled along as if I cared not a jot. Over the course of the trial, I'd granted a few interviews to newspapermen who had staked me out, but I was in no mood to talk to them this morning, let alone allow them—or Dougherty—to sniff out my imminent departure.

I ambled to the end of the block, the snow on the walkway creaking and crunching underfoot. Turning back, I could see, three doors down from the house, the auto's gray fumes billowing against dawn's eerie pink; it was one of the ubiquitous black Model T's driven by Menominee's few taxi drivers. I pretended indifference, not wishing to attract attention or raise suspicions. When I turned up the walk to our front door, the driver made no move. Still, I didn't like the looks of it—a taxi parked in clear view of the house the morning after the trial's conclusion.

I found Gene in the kitchen in a red flannel shirt and baggy wool pants, his hair pillow-flattened in back and sticking out on top. As Tokyo scampered up to him, I asked, "Everybody still sleeping?"

"I guess," he said, standing at the stove and warming the kettle and his spread-out hands over the flames.

I extracted the baby announcement letter from Helen and David O'Neill from my purse and showed the envelope to Gene, pointing to its Chicago postmark. "Some friends are keeping my money for me. But you mustn't tell anyone where I'm going."

He kept his hands open to the blaze. "What about Daisy?"

"I left her a note. Can you bring the car up to the back door?"

He swung around to face me. "And what do I tell Paul?"

"That I've gone to get the money."

"He won't believe that."

"You have to trust me, Gene. It's our only chance."

"Let me wake Paul up and see what he says."

"No, if I miss this train my plan won't work. I'm the only one who can retrieve the money."

"You promise you're telling the truth?"

I gripped his shirtsleeve and looked up into his eyes. "Yes. Now, hurry."

We loaded up my three suitcases. As our car turned onto the street, I ducked down in the front seat.

"What in the world?" Gene asked.

"I thought a reporter might be lurking about."

"No, no cars around."

I righted myself. "Oh, I thought I saw one earlier."

We reached the train station near the tail end of boarding time. After I purchased my ticket and the attendant loaded my suitcases onto the wagon, Gene accompanied me to the platform.

I knew I might never see him again, but I couldn't pour my heart out to him. I dropped my travel bag down and, gripping Tokyo's leash, reached my arms around him. "Love you, little brother."

He leaned over to hug me, but his grip was limp. "Will you send the money or come back with it?"

"I can't say yet."

Gene released his hold. "When will we hear from you?"

"Give me two weeks."

The stationmaster hollered, "All aboard."

"You better get going," said Gene.

I grabbed my case and stepped up into the car. As I coaxed Tokyo up the stairs, I turned toward the platform. Gene stood just as I'd left him, groggy and slump-shouldered. I waved to him. He lifted his hand to elbow level and opened it to a lackluster wave. Poor Gene. What did he have to look forward to now but dreary Menominee?

To conserve funds, I'd taken a second-class seat, which I straightaway found and settled into, removing my hat and coat and turning to the window. I was in no mood for conversation. All the money I had to my name was a meager $1,863. I had left Daisy word to await my instructions. Soon I'd no longer be able to afford her services, and she'd eventually make her way back to New York, but I'd not go there. In fact, I'd get as far away from here as I could. Look at this countryside—nothing but snow-covered fields and logged-out woods as far as the eye can see.

Here and there, we whisked past isolated farmhouses, so similar one could be forgiven for picturing their inhabitants as paper cut-outs of men a-milking in dungarees and pink-cheeked wives bustling about their kitchens. And had someone ordained that they all paint their houses white and their barns red?

No, I thought, even Canada is too close. Nor would I get near the war in Europe, especially with the United States about to enter the fray any day. I'll cross the Pacific, find some haven to make a fresh start, and tell no one of my whereabouts. Forty-seven is not so very old. My figure is still pleasing, my hair mostly brown.

A voice startled me out of my reverie. "Why, Baroness de Vries."

I looked up. Reed Dougherty's gaunt face loomed over me. My God, might he foil my escape? What I wouldn't give to make him disappear. If only Daisy were with me, we could plot to throw him in a ditch. I summoned a cool "Good day, Mr. Dougherty."

"Would you care to accompany me to the dining car? I'll gladly buy you breakfast."

Would I never be free of this cursed man, with his bent for inserting himself in my life at the least opportune moment? He'd obviously been watching me from the taxi this morning. "You are too kind," I said. "But I really have no appetite."

"Surely you wouldn't mind a cup of coffee."

"My apologies, Mr. Dougherty, but it is the company I would mind."

"Come, now. There is a little detail we really must discuss. It'd be a shame to dine alone when we could be enjoying lively company."

There was no hiding from him now—or the latest "little detail" he intended to harass me with. I herded Tokyo into his traveling case and rose from my seat. No words passed between Dougherty and me as we shuffled through the swaying cars.

"Are you sure you won't eat anything?" Mr. Dougherty asked once the waiter visited our table.

My stomach had awakened, and I decided I might as well allow Dougherty to buy my breakfast. "Perhaps some griddle cakes to warm me up. And coffee."

Mr. Dougherty ordered eggs and potatoes and began his questioning, as I knew he would.

"Might I ask where you're bound?"

"Of course you understand I have some business to attend to."

"Ah, yes, perhaps there are some assets you must sell?"

"What business is it of yours, Mr. Dougherty?"

"It's only fair to inform you that Miss Shaver has secured my services."

"Frank did not learn of you from me. You must have contacted her."

"On the contrary, it was she who contacted me."

Our coffee arrived, and I stirred a generous helping of cream into mine. "I don't believe you."

Dougherty drank his black. Raising the cup to his narrow lips, he said, "Have I ever deceived you, madam?"

"In fact, you have. The very first time we met."

"Yes, of course." He put on a rakish sneer. "I plead guilty. In the line of duty and all that."

"So why should I believe you now?"

"If you must know, Miss Shaver learned of me through Dr. Whidbey's London detective."

"And straightaway hired you?"

"No, she only hired me yesterday, after the verdict came in."

"So you traveled all the way up here just in case she might hire you?" That seemed odd. I couldn't help but wonder if Ernest too had hired Dougherty. "Or are you also in Dr. Whidbey's employ?"

"No, but I learned some very interesting things during my London visit."

"What happened in London has no bearing on the current situation."

"I couldn't say that. But my foremost concern is the money you owe Miss Shaver."

"Why do you think I left town?"

"You mean other than to jump the judgment?"

"I'm going to secure the funds."

He took a sip of coffee and wrapped his hands around his cup. "And I'm going to make sure you do."

I sighed, to show how tiresome I found this line of conversation. "You needn't worry."

The waiter wheeled the tray to our table and slipped our breakfast plates before us.

I studied Dougherty's face. He still sported a mustache and beard, which no doubt hid some of the age lines creeping onto his long face. For the first time I noticed gray tingeing the dark hair at his temples. "Have you a family, Mr. Dougherty?"

"A wife, but no children."

"What a shame. I'm sure you would make a wonderful father."

"I hardly make a good husband, traveling as much as I do."

I extracted my napkin from under my silverware. "Perhaps one of these days you'll settle down."

"Not in the near future."

"Then I'm sorry for your wife. She must miss you terribly when you travel."

He shrugged, as if embarrassed at being found out.

"Why, look," I said, "you traveled all the way to Menominee before you'd even secured the case."

"My employer did, of course, approve the trip." Dougherty took up his knife and fork.

"And do I have him to thank for this breakfast?"

"My dear Baroness, when did you ever question who was paying your way?"

"Why, whenever I suspected their motives."

He tossed his head back in laughter. "I truly have missed our chats. Please, do enjoy your breakfast."

→←

I hadn't planned on Dougherty's watching over me like a devoted dog the whole train ride. He probably intended to hound me until I paid the fifty-seven-thousand-dollar judgment, and I simply couldn't allow him to corner me. I had purchased fare no farther than Chicago, to allow myself time to determine my next destination, but hadn't told him I intended to stop there.

After I alighted from the train and gathered my luggage for taxi transport, Dougherty approached.

"Baroness de Vries, you weren't going to leave without saying good-bye."

"How could I be so rude?"

"Are you staying long in my fair city?"

"Yes," I said, hoping to throw him off my trail. "I intend to stop a few weeks to see to some business matters."

"And might I ask where you're staying?"

"No, you may not."

"My agreement with Miss Shaver requires me to keep you in my sights."

"That won't be necessary. I understand I must abide by the court's judgment."

"You have proven yourself a most dangerous woman, a woman not to be trusted."

"Claiming I'm dangerous is merely a means to feather your nest. You, sir, are the height of perversity." I signaled to the taxi edging toward me.

"You know if you don't produce the money the house and your brothers' automobile business will be taken over by the court?"

I turned away from him and reached for the cab door.

He cut between me and the auto. "Do you really want to drag your own flesh and blood down with you?"

"You needn't interject yourself in my affairs, Mr. Dougherty." I stepped around him.

He turned on his heel and clapped a hand on the cab door. Reaching into his inside suit pocket, he extracted a folded paper and, one-handed, flapped it open. "I have here documentation of the insurance money Lloyd's paid out on your yellow-diamond necklace, a necklace you happen to be in possession of."

Blood rushed up my neck, into my cheeks, over my forehead. I felt my ears might explode from the pressure.

He cocked his head. "And Scotland Yard would certainly be interested in that little detail."

I glared into his beady eyes. The scoundrel had been toying with me, like a cat batting a mouse about, waiting until the last possible moment to pounce. As never before, I grasped the urge to murder. If I'd had a gun in my hand, I would have leveled it at him.

He opened the taxi door. "But I'm sure we can reach an agreeable arrangement. Which hotel do you wish to register at?"

In a flash it became clear to me—I would need to either bargain with or outwit him. Forcing calm into my voice, I stated, "The Congress."

He motioned for me to enter the taxi and slid in after me. After loading our luggage, the driver sped off.

Relaxing into his seat as if he were in his own private parlor, Dougherty said, "I believe you'll find my proposal quite generous. If you produce fifty-seven thousand dollars and the necklace, I'll turn the piece over to Lloyd's. I won't even mention you or your accomplices."

"Where did you ever get the idea I own such a necklace?"

His crossed one leg over the other. "Apparently, you couldn't resist showing it off to Miss Shaver."

# A GAME OF CAT AND MOUSE

•

*D*ougherty accompanied me to the hotel, where I secured a suite large enough to accommodate myself and Daisy. He agreed to allow me four days to produce the fifty-seven thousand dollars, during which time he would keep me under surveillance. If I failed to deliver the funds and my yellow-diamond necklace at 5 p.m. on Tuesday, February 6, he would seize all my belongings and alert Scotland Yard to my "crime of insurance fraud." And he warned me against trying to slip away: "After all, I've never failed to track you down."

I immediately wired Daisy: LEAVE ON MORNING TRAIN FOR CHICAGO STOP COME TO CONGRESS HOTEL STOP. That would put Daisy into Chicago the next evening, Saturday.

I spent Saturday window-shopping all around Chicago, to give myself time to think, and to keep Mr. Dougherty's colleague occupied. The pudgy fellow I roused from his lobby roost tagged after me all afternoon, likely walking off a few pounds that day, which he promptly replaced over dinner across the Congress dining room from me. Watching him chew his cud while he kept his eyes fastened on me was enough to resolve me to take all future meals in the suite.

Once Daisy arrived, I explained the dire circumstances.

She sat beside me on the sofa in our room, her still-packed suitcases piled beside the wall and her coat cast over them. "Good heavens, that devil really has boxed you in this time."

"Yes, I fear that myself."

"Can you come up with the money?"

I drummed my fingers on the sofa arm. "Even if I sold all my jewels, I couldn't get enough value on such short notice."

I hadn't told Daisy about Dougherty's mention of the yellow-diamond necklace and threat of insurance fraud. It would only have prompted her to panicked flight, and I needed her assistance. Still, perhaps because she feared detection as an accomplice, she introduced the topic.

"Shouldn't you at least get rid of the yellow-diamond necklace? So it won't be found on you?"

"I can't bear to part with it. And we shouldn't risk its falling into police hands."

"What about your brothers? And the house?"

"Everyone, including my brothers, must stand on their own two feet at some point. After all, that's what I've done all these years."

> <

I refused to allow Dougherty to defeat me, even as I despaired of finding a way to escape his clutches. I could think of only one strategy, a fairly risky one at that. If it failed, I would find myself held hostage to a fifty-seven-thousand-dollar judgment—and charged with insurance fraud in London. With so much at stake, I at least had to try.

Since Dougherty was probably having my phone calls listened in on, Daisy left the hotel—we had ascertained that they had no interest in tracking her—to walk Tokyo and telephone my dear Chicago friends Helen and David O'Neill. Would they be so kind as to come visit me at the Congress with their newborn baby? Yes, they'd be happy to. Daisy arranged for them to visit on Monday afternoon.

They arrived at one; shortly afterward, Daisy left to run errands and determine which member of the Pinkerton team was encamped in the lobby.

"Helen, dear, show me little Elizabeth," I said, after taking their coats.

"I must thank you for that lovely rattle," Helen said as she unwrapped the baby's swaddling blanket and handed her to me.

"Nothing is too good for my favorite couple and their new baby." I scooped the baby into my arms. Tokyo circled at my feet—jealous of the baby, I imagined.

Helen leaned over her baby. "Isn't she the most beautiful bundle of pinkness you've ever seen?"

David, a handsome young man of modest height, edged closer,

forming us into a triangle with the infant at its center. Baby Elizabeth jerked her freed arms at her sides.

David held out his little finger for her to grasp. "I call her bouncy Betsy."

I gazed into one-month-old Elizabeth's face, at her placid blue eyes, cherub lips, plump cheeks, and smooth forehead. She seemed to be looking right at me. Admiring the blond fuzz swirling atop her head, I said, "She's all wonderment and innocence, the little darling."

We passed an agreeable visit in the suite, the three of us, plus baby Elizabeth, catching up on the news, and then I requested their assistance with a delicate matter. Of course they had read about the lawsuit in the Chicago papers, so I gave them the inside story about its most unfair outcome and how I needed to travel out of town, unnoticed. The lovelies were only too willing to help, so, after Helen nursed the baby, she and I retired to the bedroom to enact step one of the plan.

Helen, a shapely woman two inches taller than I, removed her dress while I slipped out of mine. I tried hers on. Though a little roomy around my middle parts—Helen had let it out to accommodate her post-baby waistline—it otherwise fit well.

Helen regarded me, one hand on her hip, "Yes, I think that will do."

Helen put my dress on and smoothed her hands over it. "It's a bit snug, but I can stand it for an hour or two."

We quit the bedroom and rejoined David, the baby, and Daisy, who had just returned from her errands.

"Which one's in the lobby, Daisy?" I asked.

"It's Dougherty."

"Oh, yes, he's a sly one," I said, careful not to sound too alarmed, for I did not wish to alert Helen and David to the danger of our mission. But my heart fluttered with anxiety over the prospects for my plan; eagle-eyed Dougherty would be watching everyone who passed through the lobby.

I donned the new shoes Daisy had purchased for me, a pair of high enough elevation so I could approximate Helen's height, and examined myself in the mirror. "Well, I'm not fooling myself—or any of you, I suspect."

"But your outfit's not complete," offered Daisy.

"No, my coat and hat are the finishing touches," said Helen.

I turned to Helen. "Show me how you hold little Elizabeth. How you walk."

Helen picked the napping baby up off the couch, nestled her against her shoulder, and wrapped both arms lovingly around her. Baby Elizabeth did not wake. As Helen strolled from one end of the room to the other, I studied the evenness of her short steps.

She stopped before me and gently passed Elizabeth to me. "Now you try."

I carefully snuggled Elizabeth against me and adjusted my two-armed hold so that the baby and I fit comfortably into each other. Imitating Helen's gait, I walked from one end of the room to the other.

Helen watched me cross in front of her. "Relax. Hold your shoulders level."

I realized I had slanted my frame, as if to compensate for the baby's weight. Correcting the balance of my shoulders, I took up my walk again.

"Much better," Helen said.

"Slip your hips back a bit," said David. "Helen's caboose is more pronounced than yours."

Everyone chuckled at that, and I tried the walk again, this time pushing my hips back a bit, but it felt awkward and off balance.

"No, that's not enough," said David.

"I've got it. Hold on a minute," Daisy said. She fetched one of my cotton dresses and tied the arms around my middle, tucking its folds across my buttocks to give them more heft. "Now put on Helen's coat."

I eased the sleeping baby down onto the couch, and Helen helped me into her coat. I buttoned it up and walked, turning around in front of David.

He watched me closely. "Yes, that's more like Helen."

I stepped across the room and back a few times, pretending I held the baby in my arms as I practiced my posture and gait.

I glanced at each of them. "Am I ready, do you think?"

Helen nodded.

"I believe you've got it now," David said.

"Yes," said Daisy, "that walk doesn't resemble yours too much."

"Then let's be off," I said to David, knowing I needed to act quickly and with confidence to ward off the anxiety rising in me.

He stood and took up his coat.

I embraced Daisy. "I don't know when I can be in touch again."

"I understand." She gripped me in a smothering hug. "Take care of yourself."

I leaned over and patted Tokyo on the head. "Be good for Daisy." I hated to leave my dear Tokyo behind, but Daisy loved him equally well, and I couldn't exactly melt into the masses with him. Still, I kept my voice nonchalant so as not to alarm him. Unfortunately, his whimper suggested he already discerned something was afoot.

"Are you ready, David?" I asked, accepting Helen's broad-brimmed hat from her.

"Yes, my dear," he said, pretending to be my husband.

I placed Helen's hat on my head, dropping the front to obscure my face, and clasped her purse.

Helen bundled Elizabeth's blanket tight around her and handed her to me. "She's waking up. If she starts crying, just bounce her a bit. She's a good baby."

David opened the door for me, and we headed for the elevator. On the way down, I felt Elizabeth squirming in my arms. I looked at David. "She's uncomfortable, I think."

"I imagine she's doing what babies do best."

"Oh," I said.

The elevator dinged and I stepped out, concentrating on my walk. David took my arm, and we marched forward. Elizabeth wriggled. As we reached the middle of the lobby, she unleashed a streak of screaming "waah"s. I bounced her, not daring to raise my head for fear of being identified by Dougherty. Surely he was watching us.

David put his arm around me and leaned in, bringing his face close to Elizabeth's. He cooed, "Sweet baby Betsy, sweet little girl."

Still she wailed. I seethed with worry over the spectacle we were making. It took all my concentration to strike the right gait and keep my eyes trained on Elizabeth.

The doorman stepped up as we approached and opened the door for us. A gust of wind hit us, upending my hat. David grabbed it in midair and clamped it back on my head. I reached out and pulled the blanket forward to shield Elizabeth's head. I dared not look around. I kept all my attention focused on baby Elizabeth.

David stepped forward and hailed a cab.

"Here we are," he said, opening the car door for us.

I eased in, bottom first, and swiveled around, scooting over to accommodate David and keeping my head bent down toward the baby.

David slammed the door shut behind him and ordered the cab driver, "One twenty West Delaware."

I maintained my silence, even pressing a finger to my lips to warn David not to speak, fully aware that Dougherty might decide to interview cabdrivers once he discovered my absence.

Together we fussed over the baby, with me muttering sweet words and David cooing to her, all the way up the steps to their red-brick home.

"Were we followed?" I asked David as we stepped inside. Baby Elizabeth had calmed herself during the taxi ride, but now she started wailing again.

"No, I don't believe so." He closed the door and looked out on the street. "Not a vehicle in sight."

"Thank heavens. Now, what can Elizabeth want?"

"I wonder—would you mind changing her?"

"Not at all." Could it be? Had I eluded Dougherty for the first time in my life?

"Come, I'll show you her room."

Once David had situated me upstairs at Elizabeth's changing table, I asked, "Would you mind keeping watch? And hollering if anybody approaches the house?"

If changing a baby's diaper was the price to pay for occupying my nervous hands, I gladly applied myself to the task, though I couldn't stop wondering what to do should David issue a warning. I'd have to leave Elizabeth kicking in the middle of her bassinet and run for the back door—without any of my belongings.

The minutes spent cleaning up baby Elizabeth, pinning her in a fresh diaper, and slipping her into a long flannel gown ticked by without alarm. I carried Elizabeth down the stairs and rejoined David in the front parlor. Helen showed up in a taxi less than an hour later, with my belongings packed away in Daisy's suitcases. David carried my luggage out the back door, arranged it in his car, and drove me to the train station in Aurora, west of Chicago and far from the Pinkerton's watchful eyes.

I thanked him profusely for his and Helen's assistance and boarded the Burlington line for points west. Relaxing in my seat, I watched the Illinois scenery slip by—the quaint homes on the edge of Aurora, the corn-stubbled fields covered with sparkling snow, the silos standing tall. I'd take trains across the whole country, to the end of the line. Once I reached the West Coast, I'd set sail for fresh terrain. Wouldn't Reed Dougherty be surprised when he rapped on my hotel door twenty-four hours hence only to learn from Daisy that I had—here Daisy would, according to rehearsal, throw up her hands and say "poof"—completely vanished?

# DISPATCH

·

## 1918

*W*orry not, dear reader, for in the contest of wits and wiles, I have bested the Pinkertons. Dougherty will never find me here, comfortably tucked away in the hilltop home of a British expatriate in Hong Kong. My new patron, Mr. Templeton, has shown the utmost respect for my tender state of widowhood. He does not press me on the matter of marriage, nor will he allow me to exhaust my limited assets while I battle my stepson over my husband's estate. He doesn't even mind that I sometimes moon over the photograph of my late husband as a young man—the picture I've saved all these years of Johnny.

Hong Kong is an agreeable and befitting place for a woman of my circumstances to settle. I pass my days reading and managing the house servants, and my evenings strolling Hong Kong's corridors with Mr. Templeton. In fact, there's not a reason in the world it would ever occur to anyone here that Mrs. Maude Jackson, a demure widow seeking a peaceful place to mourn her departed, loving husband, was once considered the most dangerous woman in the world.

# ACKNOWLEDGMENTS

.

This novel is inspired by the true story of May Dugas, whose exploits were reported in a pamphlet authored by Lloyd Wendt, *Life of May Dugas of Menominee*. Little documentation of May's life exists outside of Wendt's (not always accurate) account and newspaper stories about her.

Although this is a work of fiction, numerous key events and the many travels recounted in this book did take place—for instance, May's encounters with a Pinkerton detective and her marriage to a Dutch baron, though the timeline is sometimes altered for narrative flow. Many other events and some of the settings are fabrications, albeit invented with the intent of capturing the spirit and adventures of this fascinating woman. Also, the names of some whom she encountered, including the Baron, have been changed for the sake of discretion.

I would like to thank some of the many people who assisted and supported me on this project: for her wisdom and sure guiding hand, Jessica Morrell; Bill Brooks for believing in me all these years; for her spot-on and inspiring critiques, Cynthia Whitcomb; the wonderful women in my writing group for teaching me so much about writing—Kimberly Gadette, Joyce Lekas, Darlene Pagan, Kathlene Postma, and Naseem Rakha; for assistance obtaining newspaper accounts of the 1917 trial, Amber Allard of Spies County Library; Elsa Ramo, for her legal advice; and Menominee-area resident Janet Callow, eminent expert on the life of May Dugas, for sharing her research. Special thanks go out to my dynamite agent, Stephanie Cabot, her terrific assistant, Anna Worrall, and my most amiable and excellent editor at Doubleday, Melissa Danaczko. I must recognize my life partner, Deborah Zita, researcher extraordinaire, who unearthed innumerable details for this novel. I am grateful to her for gracefully enduring my own writing adventures and misadventures over the years.

# BIBLIOGRAPHY AND RESOURCES

·

Abbott, Karen. *Sin in the Second City: Madams, Ministers, Playboys, and the Battle for American's Soul.* New York: Random House, 2007.

"Amazing Romance, An," *Otautau Standard and Wallace County Chronicle,* March 24, 1914: 2.

"American's Suit Against Baroness," *New York Times,* January 21, 1914.

Asbury, Herbert. *The Barbary Coast: An Informal History of the San Francisco Under-world.* New York: Thunder's Mouth Press, 1933.

———. *The Gangs of Chicago.* New York: Thunder's Mouth Press, 1940/1986.

"Baroness Accused of $125,000 Swindle," *New York Times,* January 10, 1917.

"Baroness Answers Charges of Fraud," *New York Times,* January 13, 1917.

"Baroness Collapses," *New York Times,* January 22, 1914.

"Baroness Sued. Is Ill Here," *New York Times,* June 11, 1913.

"Black Pearl Case Settled," *New York Times,* February 2, 1912.

Callow, Janet. "Baroness May de Pallandt van Eerde." Presentation for the Upper Peninsula Michigan History Conference, Menonimee, Mich., June 2010.

Dreiser, Theodore. *Sister Carrie.* New York: Barnes & Noble Classics, 1900/2005.

Fielding, Henry. *Tom Jones.* New York: Fine Creative Media, Inc., 1749/2004.

"J. D. Kilpatrick's Suicide," *New York Times,* September 22, 1903: 14.

Kendall, Todd D. "Carrie Watson—Come In, Gentlemen." Chicago Crime Scenes Project. Retrieved September 9, 2009, from http://chicagocrimescenes .blogspot.com/2009/01/carrie-watson-come-in-gentlemen.html.

"Kilpatrick Death Mystery," *New York Times,* September 23, 1903: 14.

McCormick, Donald. *Peddler of Death: The Life and Times of Sir Basil Zaharoff.* New York: Holt, Rinehart & Winston, 1965.

McLaren, Angus. *Sexual Blackmail: A Modern History.* Cambridge, Mass.: Harvard University Library, 2002.

*Menominee Herald-Leader.* Numerous articles from issues dated October, 3, 1903; September 16, 1916; January 20–February 3, 1917; May 8–12, 1917; June 11, 1917; July 25, 1917; August 1–8, 1917.

Nelson, Donald R. "Former Bordello Steeped in Local Lore," *Portland Tribune,* September 28, 2001.

"Pallandt Suit Settled," *New York Times,* April 23, 1914.

Sawyer, Alvah L. *A History of the Northern Peninsula of Michigan and Its People.* Chicago: Lewis Publishing Company, 1911.

Seagraves, Anne. *Soiled Doves: Prostitution in the Early West.* Hayden, Idaho: Wesanne Publications, 1994.

"Sues on Gift to Baroness," *New York Times,* January 14, 1914.

"Suit over $15,000 Brooch," *New York Times,* February 1, 1912.

"Value of Black Pearls," *New York Times,* February 18, 1912.

Wendt, Lloyd. *Life of May Dugas of Menominee.* Menominee, Mich.: Menominee County Research Center, n.d.

Maryka Biaggio is a former psychology professor turned novelist with a passion for historical fiction.